Dang, there was that smile again—

the one that made Chance want to haul her off that horse and kiss her until they both felt like whooping and hollering.

Yeah, he knew what Gabriella was playing at. He was only too happy to play along.

The moment that thought crossed his mind, it dragged a different thought along for the ride. What if this—the sob story about her mom, the smiles, especially the kiss—all of it was just playing? What if she was playing him?

He'd thought her brother had been one of his best friends—a man he could trust with his life. Where had that gotten him?

What if she was just trying to muck up the works with her bright smiles and warm looks and sweet, hot kisses? What if she was trying to get him distracted or off balance?

What if she was using him?

But why? That was the question he couldn't answer.

He wanted to protect her, by God.

But who would protect him from her?

* * *

What a Rancher Wants

Texas Cattleman's Club: The Missing Mogul novel —Love and scandal meet in Royal, Texas!

WHAT A RANCHER WANTS

BY
SARAH M. ANDERSON

MILLS & BOON®

Published in Great Britain 2014
by Mills & Boon, an imprint of Harlequin (UK) Limited,
Eton House, 18-24 Paradise Road, Richmond, Surrey, TW9 1SR

Special thanks and acknowledgement to Sarah M. Anderson for her contribution to the Texas Cattleman's Club: The Missing Mogul series.

ISBN: 978 0 263 91456 6

51-0214

Harlequin (UK) Limited's policy is to use papers that are natural, renewable and recyclable products and made from wood grown in sustainable forests. The logging and manufacturing processes conform to the legal environmental regulations of the country of origin.

Printed and bound in Spain
by Blackprint CPI, Barcelona

Award-winning author **Sarah M. Anderson** may live east of the Mississippi River, but her heart lies out West on the Great Plains. With a lifelong love of horses and two history teachers for parents, she had plenty of encouragement to learn everything she could about the tribes of the Great Plains.

When she started writing, it wasn't long before her characters found themselves out in South Dakota among the Lakota Sioux. She loves to put people from two different worlds into new situations and to see how their backgrounds and cultures take them someplace they never thought they'd go.

When not helping out at her son's school or walking her rescue dogs, Sarah spends her days having conversations with imaginary cowboys and American Indians, all of which is surprisingly well-tolerated by her wonderful husband. Readers can find out more about Sarah's love of cowboys and Indians at www.sarahmanderson.com.

To Amy, who always appreciates a good Texasism—
and a good Texan! The best kinds of friends are the
ones where it doesn't matter how long it's been
or where you are—you're always able
to pick up right where you left off.

One

"*¡Dios mío!*" Gabriella del Toro hissed under her breath. Blood welled up from the cut she'd inflicted upon herself with the can opener. She sighed. As if anything else could have gone wrong.

From his seat at the breakfast table, Joaquin, her bodyguard, looked up from his tablet. "I'm fine," she said, answering his unspoken question. "Just a cut."

She looked down at the injury. She had not anticipated that fixing some broth and toast for her brother, Alejandro, would be so difficult. But then, everything was difficult right now. While she had spent time in the kitchen back at Las Cruces, the ancestral del Toro estate west of Mexico City, she'd never actually prepared anything more than tea and coffee. Their cook had thought that preparing meals was beneath the lady of the house, even if the lady had been only twelve. No one had thought to teach Gabriella the first thing about cooking since…her *tía* had tried to show her how to make tortillas from scratch.

Gabriella had been seven the last time Papa had taken her and Alejandro to see their mother's sister. A full twenty years had passed since then.

As Gabriella rinsed the cut under the faucet and wrapped her wounded finger in a towel, she mentally bemoaned how this must look. She was the daughter of Rodrigo del Toro, one of the most powerful legitimate businessmen in all of Mexico. She was one of the most sought-after jewelry designers in Mexico City. She regularly transformed hunks of metal and pieces of rock into wearable art with a Mayan influence.

But at this moment, she was every heiress stereotype rolled into one. She couldn't even open a can of soup.

The bleeding staunched, she went looking for a bandage. She heard Joaquin stand and trail her out of the kitchen, although he kept a polite distance. She'd rarely been apart from the large, mostly silent man since her father had hired him to protect her when she had been thirteen. She was now twenty-seven. Joaquin Baptiste was nearing forty, but he had showed no signs of slowing down. Secretly, Gabriella hoped he never would. He was far more concerned with her happiness than her father—or even her brother—had ever been. That, and he had never let any harm befall her. Even if it did make dating…challenging.

She walked to the bathroom and found a box of bandages in a cabinet, mentally cursing her clumsiness the whole time. The cut was on the edge of her index finger. It would make holding pliers while she shaped wire almost impossible.

Gabriella caught herself. Her pliers were not here, nor were any of her other jewelry-making supplies. It had not been possible to pack up all her tools. Besides, she had been under the impression that they would only be in America long enough to collect Alejandro.

Her poor brother. Her poor father, for that matter. The del Toro family was forever haunted by the specter of abductions, but they'd all thought Alejandro would be safe in Texas. Kidnappings for profit weren't nearly as common in America as they were in Mexico, Alejandro had argued when Rodrigo had hatched this scheme to send him north to America to "investigate" an energy company he wanted to acquire. Alejandro had refused to bring Carlos, his personal guard. He had told Rodrigo he would not go if he weren't allowed to do things the American way.

The thing that Gabriella still could not believe was that their father had relented and Alejandro had been allowed to live alone, as an American would. Alejandro had assumed the identity of Alex Santiago and come north alone a little more than two years ago.

Gabriella had suffered a bout of jealousy at that. She longed to be free to come and go as she pleased, but her father would not hear of it. She had stayed at Las Cruces, under constant watch of Joaquin—and Rodrigo.

At least, she had been jealous—until Alejandro had been kidnapped. However, the kidnappers had not demanded an exorbitant ransom, as was the usual custom. Instead, there had been no word from them—or Alejandro, until he had been found in the back of a coyote's truck. Coyotes smuggled immigrants. Alejandro, the son of Rodrigo del Toro, had been thrown in with the poor things desperate to start a new life in America.

The kidnappers had not treated Alejandro well. Although his wounds were healing, he had no memory of the attack, which meant he had no information to give the law-enforcement officers who occasionally checked on him. The case had stalled. Alejandro had returned, mostly whole, to his home in Royal, Texas. Now that his life was no longer in immediate danger, Gabriella had gotten the sense that the police weren't as dedicated to finding the criminals who had abducted him in the first place. Still, they were "requesting" that Alejandro remain in the country. Truthfully, Alejandro had showed no signs of wanting to go. He stayed in his room, resting or watching football—what the Americans called soccer.

Alejandro showed almost no signs of memory, except

his love of football. He didn't seem to remember her, or Papa. In fact, the only reaction they'd gotten out of him beyond a mumbled thank-you when she brought him his meals was when Papa had announced they would be returning to Las Cruces within the week. Only then had Alejandro sparked to life, insisting that he was not going anywhere. Then he had locked himself in his room.

So Rodrigo had set up temporary headquarters in a set of rooms in Alejandro's home in Royal that had recently been home to Mia Hughes, the former housekeeper. Papa was simultaneously running Del Toro Energy and utilizing his vast resources to identify the culprits that had taken Alejandro. Rodrigo was not about to let anyone get away with assaulting any member of his family. Gabriella could only hope that, when he caught the perpetrators, he wouldn't do something that would land him in an American prison.

Which meant that Gabriella had no idea how long the del Toro family would be trapped in this house together.

This was also why Joaquin was standing outside the bathroom as Gabriella tended her injury. If she had ever hoped of having the kind of freedom that Alejandro had tasted for two years, those hopes were now dashed. Her father would not allow her to go unguarded. Not after nearly losing his son.

Still, she was in America instead of in Las Cruces, and that was something. True, she had not seen much of America beyond the small private airport where the family jet had landed, or the dark night sky that had made it almost impossible to see this country where she suspected her brother had been his happiest. No, she'd mostly seen the Royal Hospital and then, the inside of Alejandro's house.

Thus far, she was underwhelmed by America.

She longed to do something besides tend to a frustratingly silent Alejandro or to defuse her father's angry outbursts. As much as she never thought she would say it, she missed Las Cruces. True, she had not been allowed to leave the estate's grounds, but within its securely patrolled borders, she'd had far more freedom than she'd had in Royal, Texas. She'd been able to chat with the maids and the cook. She'd been able to go to her workshop and work on her jewelry designs. She'd been able to saddle up Ixchel, her Azteca horse and, with Joaquin, ride wherever she pleased on Las Cruces' extensive grounds. It hadn't been true freedom. More like a reasonable facsimile of freedom.

But it was still more than what she had at the moment. Here, she was trapped with an invalid, an irate father and Joaquin, who, bless him, had never been much for conversation. The only break in the monotony had been the brief appearances of Maria, Alejandro's maid, as well as Nathan Battle, the local sheriff, and Bailey Collins, the state investigator who had been assigned to Alejandro's case.

Honestly, she wasn't sure how much longer she could stand it.

Gabriella wrapped the bandage around her finger, wishing she could wrap her head around the situation. For as long as she could remember, her world had been a safe, if constrained place. Now, with Alejandro's kidnapping, discovery and subsequent memory loss, everything was turned upside down.

In the midst of feeling sorry for herself, the doorbell chimed.

Perhaps Maria had returned. Gabriella liked talking to her. It was a relief to have a normal conversation with another woman, even if it was mere small talk about the weather and groceries. Anything to break up the monotony of the days in Alejandro's house.

She hurried out of the bathroom. Joaquin followed her to the door. They'd already reached an understanding that, in lieu of hiring more help—something her father was not interested in—Gabriella would answer the door and Joaquin would stand guard, ready to spring into action.

The bell chimed again, causing Gabriella to hurry. It couldn't be Maria—she wasn't that impatient. Which meant it was either the sheriff or the state investigator. Which meant her father would spend the better part of his afternoon raging at American injustices.

Resigned to her fate, Gabriella paused to catch her breath at the front door before opening it. She was, for the foreseeable future, the lady of the house. It was best to present the del Toro family in a positive light—all the more so because Maria had indicated that some members of the community were suspicious of the family of Alex Santiago. She checked her reflection in the hall mirror, thankful that the only thing out of place was the bandage on her finger, and affixed a warm smile to her face. She'd played the hostess for her father's business dinners before. She knew her role well.

Neither Sheriff Battle nor Agent Collins stood on the front stoop. Instead it was a cowboy—a tall, broad cowboy wearing a heathered sports jacket, a dark gray shirt and a dark pair of jeans over his gray ostrich cowboy boots. The moment he saw her, he whipped his brown felt hat off of his head and held it to his chest.

Oh. Green eyes. *¡Dios mío!* she had never seen eyes so green in her entire life. They were beautiful—the color of the spring grass at Las Cruces. For a moment looking into his eyes felt… It felt like coming home. His gaze affected her in a way she'd never before experienced.

"Howdy, ma'am." His voice was rough around the edges, as if he'd been outdoors in the February wind for some time. As he looked at her, one corner of his mouth crooked up, as if he were not surprised to see her, just pleased. "I'd like to talk to Alex, if he's up to it."

She was staring, she realized too late. Perhaps that was

because she hadn't seen too many outsiders recently. But the way this cowboy—for there could be no doubt that was what he was—was looking at her had rooted her to the spot.

His smile deepened as he held out one hand. "I'm Chance McDaniel. I don't believe I've had the pleasure, Miss…?"

Any homecoming died in the air between them. Chance McDaniel? What she knew of this man was limited, but it did nothing to endear him to her—or her father. According to Sheriff Battle and Agent Collins, Mr. McDaniel had been close friends with Alejandro—or rather, with Alex Santiago. However, he was also one of the leading suspects in Alejandro's disappearance—a crime of which he had not been cleared.

What was he doing here? More to the point, what was she going to do about it?

Behind her, Joaquin moved, his hand slipping up under his jacket. Gabriella quickly remembered herself. She could not imagine what would have led a leading suspect to ask to speak to the victim of a crime, but she also couldn't have Joaquin pulling a weapon on him. This wasn't Mexico, after all.

With a quick look that had Joaquin stopping in his tracks, Gabriella remembered her warm smile. "Hello, Mr. McDaniel. Won't you please enter?" Instead of shaking his outstretched hand, she stepped back, narrowly missing Joaquin, and motioned for Chance to enter.

He stood there for a beat too long before letting his hand fall to his side as he took long strides into the foyer. He moved with a confident ease, projecting strength with each step. Of course he was confident. Otherwise he wouldn't have dared ask to see Alejandro.

Upon seeing Joaquin glowering off to one side, Mr. McDaniel offered up a, "Howdy, *señor*."

Behind his back, where he could not see it, a small smile danced across Gabriella's lips. She had not believed that real cowboys would actually speak in such colloquial language. It should have sounded ridiculous, but with Mr. McDaniel's rough-edged voice, it sent shivers down her spine.

Joaquin did not respond, of course. He stood like a statue at the edge of the room, his gaze trained on Mr. McDaniel.

Mr. McDaniel obviously knew his way around the house. He headed straight for the living room before seeming to remember himself. He paused and turned back to her. "I'm sorry, I didn't catch your name, Miss…?" As he said it, his gaze worked its way up and down Gabriella.

She could see him taking in her crisp white shirt—thankfully unstained with the failed efforts at lunch—and her slim black pants underneath the knee-length, coral-colored sweater-coat that contrasted perfectly with the heavy rope of turquoise and silver she wore around her neck, with earrings to match. He was trying to determine if she was the new housekeeper or not, Gabriella decided, as if every woman of Hispanic origins came to America to be a maid. However, she knew that very few maids dressed as she did. Which assumption would he go with?

If this man had been anyone other than the prime suspect in Alejandro's disappearance, she would have hurried to put him at ease. She decided to let him wait. After all, she'd had to wait to learn if her brother was even alive. Someone else should feel as anxious as she had, even for a solitary minute.

She said, "May I get you some tea?" in her nicest tone.

Instead of looking irritated or even uncomfortable, Mr. McDaniel gave her the kind of grin that he probably used to get the average woman to fall all over him. Well, he was about to learn that Gabriella was not the average woman, even if she did suddenly feel a bit unsettled at the warmth in his eyes. "Much obliged, ma'am."

Gabriella motioned him to the living room and then walked slowly and deliberately into the kitchen. Thankfully, making tea was her specialty and she already had a pitcher of iced tea steeping. It only took a minute to assemble a tray of two glasses and some biscuits. The whole time, she strained to hear any other noise coming from the house. If Alejandro had heard the door, he gave no indication of venturing downstairs to see who it was. But it also appeared that Papa had not heard the visitor arrive, which was probably for the best.

If Mr. McDaniel had had something to do with Alejandro's disappearance, there was a chance that Gabriella could "sweet talk" it out of him, as the Americans would say. If Papa stormed into the room and began making accusations, who knew what would happen?

She knew Papa would be furious that she had not let him handle the visitor personally. She was well-versed in the art of gentle conversation, after all, and had been told she was a beautiful woman on numerous occasions. She could handle a man like Chance McDaniel. Besides, it wasn't as if she was in actual danger. Joaquin was with her.

Mr. McDaniel had been sitting in the chair that faced Joaquin, apparently engaging in a staring match. But when Gabriella entered with the tray, he quickly stood. "Thank you for the tea."

Gabriella set the tray on the table, but neither of them made a move to pick up a glass. Instead she found herself staring at Chance McDaniel again, wondering what kind of man he was—the kind who would befriend a foreigner or the kind who would attack an unarmed man?

She sat in the leather armchair opposite the one he'd claimed. Joaquin moved forward to stand behind the back of her chair, an unmistakable warning in his presence. If this Mr. McDaniel tried anything, he wouldn't live to regret it.

A fact that he seemed to understand. Without another word, he sat, his gaze never leaving her face.

As she let the moment stretch, she again noted the way his presence left her feeling…unsettled. He'd dropped his hat on a side table. She could see his dark blond hair. He wore it quite short, but that apparently did nothing to stop the way it laid in waves on his head. He was freshly shaved but, aside from the boots and the hat, wore no other adornment.

He does not need any, she thought. The thought warmed her.

Finally he began to shift in his seat. She should not delay anymore, lest Papa burst into the room, ready to avenge his son.

"It is a pleasure to make your acquaintance, Mr. McDaniel. Alejandro had spoken of you to me." A touch of color deepened on Mr. McDaniel's cheeks. *¡Dios mío!* he was more than attractive. "I am Gabriella del Toro, Alejandro's sister."

This pronouncement hung in the air like a cloud ready to burst with rain. "I was not aware that Alex had a sister," he finally said. There was no mistaking the hurt undertone in his voice. "But then, I guess that there's plenty I didn't know about Alex. Like that his name is Alejandro." He looked to Joaquin over her shoulder. "Are you his brother, then?"

Gabriella laughed lightly. "Joaquin? No. He is my personal bodyguard. As I'm sure you can understand, Mr. McDaniel, the del Toro family must take every precaution."

Mr. McDaniel nodded. "How is he? Alex, I mean." He ran a hand over his hair. "I was hoping to talk to him, if he was feeling up to it."

Gabriella detected nothing deceptive in his voice or his

posture. "Alejandro is still recovering from his ordeal." Then, to Joaquin, she said, *"Devrions-nous dire à Papa première ou Alejandro qu'il est ici?"* in French. *Should we tell Papa first or Alejandro that he's here?*

She'd chosen French because she assumed that an American cowboy living in Texas probably spoke enough Spanish to catch what she said. Therefore, she was completely unprepared when Mr. McDaniel said, with great effort, *"Je peux dit moi"* in an accent that was so bad he was almost unintelligible. However, she was fairly certain he'd meant to say, *I can tell them myself.* What he'd actually said was, *I can tell me.*

Again, a smile crossed her lips. "You speak French."

More color came to his cheeks. She felt herself leaning forward to get a better look at him. "Not as beautifully as you do, but yeah, I took a couple of years in high school." His eyes twinkled. "My Spanish is better. I'm assuming that was the point?"

He had her. "Indeed," she admitted, impressed. A man who spoke in "howdys" and "ma'ams" who also conversed in Spanish and attempted French—with a sense of humor? With a compliment—she spoke French beautifully?

Gabriella could see how her brother would have befriended this man. Alejandro was drawn to people who had an easy way. She wasn't different, except that instead of making friends at work or on the social scene, that meant that she'd become fast friends with the hired help at Las Cruces.

What kind of cowboy was Chance McDaniel? Did he know how to ride? She glanced at his hands. They were clean, but rough with calluses. He was a man who was not afraid of hard work.

A shiver ran through her body. She thought she'd done a fine job of hiding it from Mr. McDaniel, but then his eyes widened and what had twinkled in them…changed. Deepened.

In that instant it became clear that Chance McDaniel was indeed a threat. To her, though—not necessarily her brother. Because the way that this man was looking at her—as though he was coming home, too—was something she had not expected.

Two

So Alex had a sister. Just another lie. Add it to the pile.

As mad as Chance wanted to be at the man he'd called friend, he couldn't quite get a grip on anger. Instead he was lost in the depths of chocolate-brown eyes.

Gabriella del Toro. He wanted to say her name out loud, to feel the way the syllables rolled over his tongue like single-malt whiskey. He didn't. Not now, anyway. The guy standing over her looked as though he might shoot Chance if he dared sully her name.

He needed to get back on track here. He knew the del Toro family had been in Alex's house for several weeks now—Nathan Battle had shared that over a drink at the Texas Cattleman's Club. But no other gossip had trickled down. Nathan was being tight-lipped about the whole damn thing, except to say that, as far as the local law was concerned, Chance was in the clear.

That meant the state investigator still considered him a suspect.

As did the del Toro family, apparently. Chance had to admit he was impressed. Gabriella del Toro may look like a polished socialite, but she'd made him sweat like a seasoned pro. He could only hope she hadn't realized how uncomfortable he'd been, what with that "personal bodyguard" trying to kill him with looks alone.

This whole situation was still something he couldn't get his head around. Alex was back, safe and sound, but without much of an idea of who he was—hell, who anyone in Royal, Texas, was. The whole town was still on high alert, suspicious of anyone who might have ever had a bone to pick with Alex Santiago. This apparently included him.

"So, your bodyguard speaks French?" He honestly didn't know what else to say. He wanted to talk to Alex again; find out if he remembered anything else. As much as he hated to admit it, the odds were decent that someone in Royal had done this to his friend. The only other option was that Mexican drug violence was bleeding its way far north of the border.

"Of course," Gabriella said, as if every meathead in the world spoke several languages. "Since he joined me for my lessons, it was only natural that he learn with me and the other children at home."

"More brothers and sisters?" How could he have ever felt that he knew Alex? The man had done nothing but lie to him from the moment he'd arrived in Royal. Chance had thought he'd been friends with the man. Hell, he'd even done the honorable thing and stepped aside when Alex had showed an interest in Chance's lady friend, Cara Windsor. Or had that been part of the setup, too? Because if Alex had wanted to destroy Chance's life, he was doing a damn fine job of it.

"Oh, no, Mr. McDaniel." Gabriella had a soft laugh, delicate. Made him think of a butterfly landing quickly on a flower before moving on. "My tutors taught the children of our staff. We almost had enough students for a regular school." Her features softened. "My mother believed it was our duty to educate those who serve us."

Alex had never mentioned his mother. But then, he

hadn't mentioned a sister, either. "It must have been hard on your mother when Alex went missing."

A shadow crossed Gabriella's face, blocking out the light of her smile. "She has been dead for twenty-three years, Mr. McDaniel."

Okay, so maybe Alex had a good reason for not talking about his mother. "My apologies. I didn't know."

She tilted her head in appreciation, and then the shadow was gone. Her behavior was refined, her manners impeccable—even when she'd let him sweat, she'd been perfectly polite about it.

Chance was suddenly possessed—there wasn't another word for it—to ask if Gabriella rode horses. Alex had come out to McDaniel's Acres, Chance's homestead, to ride on numerous occasions. Alex had talked about his stables back home; how he'd always loved the freedom of riding.

Cara Windsor had never enjoyed riding with Chance. She didn't like the smell of the barn, had no particular talent for riding and was too terrified of being stepped on to consider brushing down a horse.

Chance had finished sowing his wild oats years ago. Since then, he'd worked on making McDaniel's Acres a profitable piece of land. He'd like to have someone to ride with him, someone to take his meals with—and share his bed with. But the land had taken all his time and there weren't too many women left in Royal who'd cotton to his way of life. Ranching the land—even if it was a dude ranch and the bunkhouse was now a five-star hotel where city folks paid a hefty price to be pretend cowboys for the week—was still a hard life, full of early summer mornings and cold winter nights.

"Do you ride horses?" Chance wouldn't have thought it possible, but the bodyguard's glare got meaner. "Alex would come out to the ranch and we'd ride."

He thought he saw a small smile ghost its way across Gabriella's very full lips. "I ride."

Two simple little words that had the immediate effect of cranking his temperature up a notch or two. "You should come out to the ranch sometime—McDaniel's Acres. This part of Texas is beautiful—the best way to see it is from horseback."

He wanted to think that he was asking only because he was concerned with clearing his name. If he couldn't talk with Alex and see what he remembered, the next best thing he could hope for was to talk with his beautiful sister. Maybe he could find out if anything about Alex had been on the level or if their entire friendship had been nothing but lies.

But he'd be lying if he didn't admit that spending some time out on the range with Gabriella had the potential to be fun.

"That would be out of the question, I'm afraid." She was back to blushing again, which made her look innocent. Which gave him some not-so-innocent thoughts. "I never go anywhere without Joaquin."

The big man grunted in agreement. Hey, what did Chance know—the bodyguard was capable of something besides glaring.

Chance made a snap decision. "He can come along. I've got a mule that can handle him. The more, the merrier." Which was a bold-faced lie, but he knew damn good and well that he wasn't going to find out anything today. "If you want," he added.

"How big is your ranch?" She leaned forward, causing the white shirt she was wearing to gape at the neck.

If Alex were here, he'd punch Chance in the arm for ogling his sister. As it was, Chance half expected to be shot. "About 400 acres. We've got cattle as well as some chickens, a few sheep and goats, and a few alpacas—the kids love them. And horses, of course. I run a dude ranch and hotel on the property," he added, hoping that made him sound more like a businessman making a pitch and less like a love-struck teenager angling for a date. "We give trail rides all the time. I'd be happy to show you around."

This was mostly true. He did lead trail rides—when it wasn't the middle of February. The winter hadn't held a great deal of snow to this point, but the wind could be vicious. He had no idea why he thought a ride with a refined woman such as Gabriella del Toro would be a good idea in this weather.

Oh, right—because he was hoping to find out something more about Alex.

He hoped she'd say yes. He hoped she could handle herself on a horse. Hell, he just hoped he wasn't about to be shot. Chance looked down at Gabriella's hands. Despite her polished appearance, he saw that her nails weren't long and manicured, but short and bare. Her hands were delicate, with long, thin fingers that showed signs of heavy use—and a bandage on her index finger. "Did you hurt yourself?"

That pink blush graced her cheeks. She dropped her gaze, but then looked up at him through thick lashes. "Just a cut. I was attempting to prepare some soup for Alejandro."

Attempting? He grinned at her. "When you come out for a ride, we'll have dinner. Franny Peterson is the best cook in Royal—she makes dinner for my guests. She'd be delighted to meet Alex's family. They always got along famously."

Her smile tightened. "Alejandro often visited your home?"

"Yup."

"Was he…?" She looked down at her bandaged hand, unable to finish the sentence.

This must be so hard on her, he realized. Then he remembered—he hadn't come here to flirt with Alex's sister, no matter how fun it might become. He had a purpose here. "How is he? Any better?"

Everything that had been warm and light about Gabriella shut down on him. She didn't so much as move, but he felt the walls that went up between them.

Gabriella said, "He is much the same," in a voice that was probably supposed to sound as though she wasn't giving anything away. But he heard the sadness in her tone.

Gabriella appeared to care for her brother. For some reason, that made Chance happy. He didn't know why.

"Can I see him?"

Joaquin stiffened behind her as Gabriella said, "I do not think that would be wise, Mr. McDaniel. He is still healing. The doctors have said he needs quiet and darkness for his brain to recover from the trauma he's suffered."

"Mr. McDaniel is my father. Call me Chance. Everyone does. Even Alex."

Then she looked up at him, the full force of her brown eyes boring into him. "I do not think that would be wise, Mr. McDaniel."

Hell, he'd overstepped, but he couldn't figure out which thing had been too far. He couldn't tell which part had pushed her over the edge. Was it the familiarity of using his given name—or of calling Alex by his American name? Whatever it had been, he was losing her. "I just thought that if he, you know, saw me, it might jog his memory. He might remember who I was."

Lots of women had cried on Chance's shoulder in his time—he was the kind of guy that women felt comfortable enough with that they could occasionally pour their hearts out to him. But when Gabriella del Toro lifted her gaze to his face, he was sure he'd never seen a sadder woman in his life.

"I had hoped that, as well."

It shouldn't have bothered him this much—he had known Gabriella for all of twenty minutes. But the pain in her voice cut right through him and, just like that, he felt the same way he'd felt when he'd first heard that Alex had gone missing—as though a part of him had been hacked off with a rusty saw.

He wanted to go to her, offer her a sympathetic shoulder to lean on. He wanted her to know that, despite what she might have heard, he'd had nothing to do with Alex's disappearance—that he only wanted what was best for his friend. And his friend's family.

But he also didn't want to bleed today. So instead of risking the wrath of Joaquin the bodyguard, he pulled his wallet out of his back pocket and fished out one of his seldom-used business cards. It was a little worn around the edges because he needed them so rarely. Everyone in Royal knew him and how to get ahold of him.

But if Alex couldn't remember Chance—couldn't remember his own sister—then there was zero point in expecting him to tell Gabriella what Chance's phone number was. He held the card out to her. "If anything changes—if you need my help in any way, here's my number. I can be here in twenty minutes if Alex needs me." He swallowed, hoping he wasn't about to find himself thrown out of the house. "If you need me."

She stood. For a moment he thought she would once again tell him that she didn't think that a wise idea, but then she took the offered card. Her fingertips grazed the edge of his—a small touch, but one that made him want to smile again. "Thank you."

"Who are you?" a voice thundered from behind him. Then he asked the same thing in Spanish. *"¿Quién es?"*

Chance barely caught the look of alarm on Gabriella's face before he spun around to see the man who could only be Alex's father filling the kitchen doorway. The older man stood with his feet spread, his hands on his hips and his chest puffed up. He was nearly as tall as Chance was—maybe a few inches shorter than Alex. He could have been Alex's twin, if it weren't for the lines etched into his forehead. Same black hair, same build—but the face was all different. Alex had an easy smile and warm eyes—the kind of guy a man could knock back a beer or two with on a Friday night.

This was not a man who probably ever knocked back a couple of beers. No doubt about it, this was the senior del Toro. Rodrigo. Nathan had said the old man was a force to be reckoned with. He hadn't been lying.

"Papa," Gabriella said in a soft—but not weak—voice. "This is Chance McDaniel, Alejandro's friend."

He sure did appreciate her putting it in those terms, as opposed to mentioning that he was also the lead suspect in Alex's disappearance.

Not that she needed to. Rodrigo's eyes blazed with an undisguised hatred at Chance's name. *"¿Qué está haciendo aquí?"* he snarled as Gabriella went to stand next to her father. Chance felt Joaquin come up behind him; probably just close enough to grab Chance if he made a funny move.

What was Chance doing here? Rodrigo must not be as perceptive as his daughter. Gabriella had assumed that Chance spoke Spanish, but Rodrigo had incorrectly assumed Chance did not. So he said, *"Hola, Señor del Toro. Alex hablaba bien de usted." Alex spoke well of you.*

Or at least, that's what he hoped he'd said. Alex had always spoken in crisp English, much the way Gabriella did. Chance had never had private tutors, unless one counted the hired hands on the ranch—and they'd spent more time teaching him to cuss in Spanish than to make polite greetings.

When this didn't get him shot, he added in his most polite business voice that he had come to see Alex. And he made damn sure not to flinch in Joaquin's direction when the big man huffed. This would be a bad time to show any sign of nerves or fear. So Chance kept his face calm and his gaze steady. He may be a cowboy, by God, but he was a McDaniel and no one—not even Rodrigo del Toro—was going to stare him down.

Then he saw the corners of Gabriella's mouth curve into a small smile. Even if Rodrigo hated his guts, at the very least, Chance had said what she'd wanted to hear.

"You are not welcome in this house," Rodrigo said, switching back to English. His accent was thicker, less crisp—but his words flowed easily.

"Papa," Gabriella said as she put a hand on his arm.

"Gabriella," he shot back. She pulled her hand away and cast her gaze to the ground. "You are not welcome in this house," he repeated, his voice a notch louder.

That did it. Chance could handle a man trying to bullshit him, but to speak to his daughter in such a callous manner? Nope. Not happening. "Last I heard, this was still Alex's house and I'd bet dollars to doughnuts that I've spent more time here than you have. I'm welcome here until Alex says otherwise." He saw the look of alarm on Gabriella's face. *"Señor,"* he said in his most dismissive voice.

Still, he wasn't stupid. He'd worn out his welcome in a big way. Before Joaquin could grab him by the scruff of his neck, he snatched his hat off the side table. "Ms. del Toro, it was a pleasure to meet you." He then turned to Joaquin and was unsurprised to see the man's fists swinging by his sides. "Keep up the good work, Joaquin."

He heard footsteps behind him and tensed, expecting a blow of some kind. He was surprised, however, when Gabriella slipped past him to reach the door before him. She opened it and stood to the side with a confused look on her face. "I will tell Alejandro you stopped by," she said.

Chance glanced back over his shoulder. Joaquin was fewer than five feet away—for a big man, he could move like a cat when he wanted to, apparently. Rodrigo del Toro had not moved from the doorway, though. He stood there with his arms crossed, glaring as if he possessed laser vision or something. Chance couldn't help himself. He tipped his hat to the older man, knowing it'd piss him off.

Then he turned back to Gabriella. "I hope he won't be too mad." That got him a worried smile telling him exactly how bad Rodrigo would be after he left. "Call me for anything. The offer to ride stands."

She did not meet his gaze, but he saw the delicate pink that rushed to her cheeks.

"Gabriella," Rodrigo roared.

"Goodbye, Mr. McDaniel." She shut the door behind him.

Chance walked out to his truck and then turned to look at Alex's house. He didn't see Alex's face in any of the upper windows.

He had a feeling he'd be hearing from Gabriella. Maybe not today, maybe not tomorrow—but soon. The way her eyes had lit up when he'd talked about riding the range? Yeah, she was going to call—especially if she was stuck in that house with a silent shadow of a bodyguard and a raging father. Not to mention a brother who didn't remember her.

He hoped Gabriella was as good as her word and told Alex that Chance had come by.

That would make her better than her brother.

Because as of now, his word meant nothing to Chance.

Three

It took four days before Chance's cell phone rang. He'd just gotten back to the barn from checking on the ponds for the cattle. When his phone rang, it played Alex's ringtone. For a moment Chance thought it was Alex; that he had his memory back, that he wanted to tell Chance about everything—which may or may not include his sister.

He handed Ranger, his horse, to Marty and grabbed his phone out of its holster. "Hello?"

"Ah, yes—Mr. McDaniel?"

Gabriella's soft voice flowed around him. Chance was simultaneously disappointed that it wasn't Alex and thrilled that she'd called. "I told you to call me Chance, Gabriella."

There was something of an awkward pause. He could almost see her trying to decide if she was going to call him what he wanted her to. Because he sure as hell wanted to hear what her accent would do with his name.

But it didn't look as if it was going to happen right now, so he redirected the conversation. "Any change in Alex?"

"No. He is still…resting." She sounded not awesome, frankly. Tired and worried, but underneath that, he could hear frustration. She was doing a damn fine job hiding it, but he could still tell.

"Is your father still mad at me?"

"Papa is only concerned with Alejandro's well-being." Her answer came without hesitation. In fact, it almost sounded as though she'd rehearsed it.

He grinned. That was a *yes,* loud and clear. "So, you need to get out of the house for a while? I've got a beauty of a quarter horse named Nightingale that'd love to ride you around."

She didn't say anything at first, but he heard her sigh—a sound of relief. Oh, yeah—he had her.

His mind hurried to put images with the sounds coming across his phone. He could see her full, red lips slightly parted as she exhaled, see her thick lashes fluttering at the thought of going for a ride with him.

Then, because apparently he enjoyed torturing himself, his mind turned those images in a different direction—her smooth hair all mussed up against a pillow as he coaxed little noises out of her. As she rode *him.*

He went hard in his jeans at the thought.

"You said you had a mule for Joaquin?"

"Yup." Chance walked down the aisle of his barn and stopped in front of Beast's stall. The animal was a giant mule that came from a donkey crossed with a draft horse. Beast's mother had been a Belgian, which meant he was a solid seventeen hands high and built like a tank.

Chance had found that having a larger animal around meant more guests could take a trail ride—something that they'd appreciated. Most trail rides capped rider weight around two hundred fifty pounds, maybe a bit more. Beast let some folks who'd never been allowed on a horse to take their first ride—which was good for business. "This fellow can handle up to three fifty. Shouldn't be a problem—if Joaquin eats a small breakfast, that is."

She laughed at this and again Chance was reminded of

butterflies fluttering among the spring flowers. "I'll be sure to tell him that."

"When do you want to come out?" It was Thursday. The weekend was suddenly looking up. By a lot. "The forecast is calling for clear skies for the next few days."

"When are you available?"

Hell, he was available anytime she wanted him to be. But then Marty walked over and said, in a quiet voice, "Don't forget the wedding Saturday."

Damn. It was February, after all. The dude ranch business may have slowed down, but the destination wedding business was still moving along at a decent clip. "We're hosting a wedding on Saturday night for a party from Houston." Double damn it. Saturday would have been a great time to get to know Gabriella a little better—or at least to figure out if all the del Toros lied as much as Alex did. "How about…?" His mind spun. Saturday was out. "Sunday afternoon?"

"That would not be possible." He couldn't help but notice that she hadn't said, "Mr. McDaniel." Of course, she also hadn't said, "Chance." Still, it was progress. "It is Sunday, after all."

Ah. He hadn't considered that. Alex had gone to the local Catholic church on occasion, but the way Gabriella said it made it clear that she was more than just an occasional churchgoer. Did that make her more honest than her brother? Or just more guilty when she lied?

He could feel this opportunity slipping through his fingers. There was no way in hell Rodrigo del Toro would let him back in the house, which meant this was the only way possible to find out what the hell was going on.

That only left him with one choice. "How about tomorrow morning? We'll be setting up for a wedding, but I've got a good crew. We can head out around…say, ten, then have lunch?"

Say yes, he thought. *Please say yes.* God, how he wanted to know if she rode or if she was the kind of "rider" who just thought horses were pretty.

She was silent, but that didn't mean everything was quiet on her end. Although it was faint, he was pretty sure he heard Rodrigo shout, "Gabriella!" followed by a string of Spanish that Chance couldn't make out.

"Ten tomorrow," she said simply before the call ended.

Chance grinned down at his phone. He knew he needed to keep his eyes peeled and his defenses up. Alex had screwed him over pretty damn badly and while McDaniel's Acres was still operating in the black, he hadn't had as much local business because of all the rumors.

He needed to find out what Alex remembered. That had to be his first goal tomorrow. It should be his only goal, too. Tomorrow should have nothing to do with wanting to hear Gabriella's tongue roll over his name, *nothing* to do with wanting to roll his own tongue over a few other things. This was about clearing his name, damn it.

Still. She'd called. They were going to ride.

Yup. The weekend was looking much better.

Gabriella was up early the next morning. She was usually up by six-thirty, but today she was out of bed at a quarter to six.

She would have liked to have had a cup of coffee without waking Joaquin, but as he slept in the living room—the better to hear anyone breaking in—she had no choice but to get him up early.

"*Buenos días,* Joaquin," she said the moment she entered the living room. Joaquin did not appreciate people trying to sneak past him. The first time she'd tried that—she'd been fifteen and dying to get out of the house—he'd grabbed her by the calf so hard that she'd had bruises for weeks. He'd apologized profusely, of course—he had been dead asleep and had not realized it was his charge sneaking around instead of a villain.

Without hesitation, Joaquin sat up from the couch, his eyes already alert as he scanned the room.

"I awoke early," she explained as he removed his gun from underneath the pillow he'd been sleeping on and slid it back into its holster. "Nothing is wrong. Coffee?"

Joaquin nodded and scrubbed a hand over his face. Then he stood and began his morning perimeter check, prowling around the house as silent as a breeze, checking the locks and windows. Of course Alejandro had had a security system installed, but security systems could always be bypassed. Gabriella knew he wouldn't attend to any of his needs until he was confident the del Toro family was safe.

Gabriella made the coffee extra strong. She was excited about the day in a way that she had not felt since she'd convinced Papa to allow her to accompany him north to America.

Finally she was going to see something of Texas—something more than the lovely vista visible through Alejandro's windows. From horseback, no less! Back home at Las Cruces, she'd ridden every day. In the few weeks she'd been here, she hadn't seen a horse. Stir-crazy, she thought was the American phrase for it. Because that's what she was. And that's why she was up before the sun.

Joaquin appeared in the kitchen. He accepted his mug of coffee and sat at the table, his tablet in front of him. Joaquin was forever scanning news sites, looking for any information that might pose a threat to the del Toro family.

But he didn't power the device up. Instead, as he sipped his coffee, he looked at Gabriella.

She knew that look. True, Joaquin was not much of a talker, but he'd been with her long enough that he rarely had to say anything to communicate with her. Right now, he was wondering if he should let her go for a ride with Chance McDaniel.

"Maria will be by today to straighten up," Gabriella said defensively. "She'll be preparing a week's worth of dinners. If Alejandro needs me, she knows how to get ahold of me. And Papa will be here. Alejandro will not be alone."

Joaquin raised an eyebrow. It wasn't enough to convince him, so she went on. "You heard what Mr. McDaniel said—he has over 400 acres of land. We're merely seeing if there's anywhere he could have hidden Alejandro away for a few weeks. An outbuilding or an abandoned cabin, perhaps."

That got her an even more skeptical look. Joaquin was clearly thinking that the local law enforcement had probably already scoured the land and had turned up nothing.

Gabriella sighed in frustration. If she couldn't convince Joaquin, there was no hope in convincing her father. "We'll be having lunch," she went on, hoping to sound like a dispassionate investigator instead of a younger version of herself, chafing at the restrictions that kept her safe. "I'll have the chance to talk with his staff, see if they have anything to say about him or Alejandro."

Joaquin shook his head, a motion of pity.

Fine. Have it your way, she thought. "If I don't get out of this house—even for a morning—I will make your day a living hell, Joaquin. I will make you help organize my closet and debate a new hairstyle and do some online shopping and I will ask you if you think those pants make my bottom look large. And then I will experiment with new ingredients in the kitchen and ask you to try the new soup or the new dessert. Is that what you want?"

She did not often throw a fit. She was no longer the headstrong thirteen-year-old who had rebelled whenever she could. She had accepted her lot, wrapped in a cocoon of safety, at her father's command. His only concern was her well-being, after all.

Her well-being depended on a few hours away from her family. That was that.

She leaned back on the counter and waited. She knew that her attempts at cooking usually resulted in a smoke alarm going off. Plus, like any self-respecting male, forcing Joaquin to give his opinion on clothing and hairstyles ranked just below being shot. If she tried hard—and started trying on shoes—she could make him wish someone would kill him just to put him out of his misery.

She got out the bowls and the cereal before she set the milk on the table. "Perhaps I shall try pancakes again," she mused. "They weren't *that* bad last time, were they?"

They had, of course, been horrid—not even the dogs would eat them. They'd been less "cake" and more "biscuit" in texture—and of course she'd burned them. Papa and Alejandro had gamely tried them, as had Joaquin, who had suffered from indigestion for the next two days.

Joaquin shot her a surprisingly dirty look as he rubbed his chest. Clearly he was remembering the indigestion, as well. "I will kill him if he touches you," he said, his voice creaky from lack of use.

Gabriella smiled. She'd broken him, which was no mean feat in and of itself. Joaquin was trained to resist torture, but no technique could defend against her attempts at cooking. "Of course," she agreed, trying to contain her excitement. "Papa would expect nothing less."

She finished her cold breakfast and went up to shower. Her heart was racing as she dressed and braided her hair back into a long, secure rope.

She wanted to get to McDaniel's Acres as soon as possible, but she had one thing to do first.

Gabriella assembled a tray with not-too-burned toast, cold cereal, orange juice and a thermos of coffee and headed upstairs. She juggled the tray and knocked on the door. "Alejandro? It's me. Gabriella."

The door cracked open and Alejandro stood in front of her. He gave her a look that made her wonder if her knew who she was. He wore a rumpled white tee and plaid pajama bottoms.

Nothing had changed. Oh, how she wished that one day he'd wake up and be her brother again. She lifted his breakfast. "I brought you food. Are you hungry?"

Alejandro stared at her a moment longer, as if he wasn't seeing her but through her. "Thank you," he mumbled, stepping to the side so she could enter.

The room was a disaster. The sheets were in a heap on the floor, socks were everywhere and the television was on the blue screen. It looked as though Alejandro hadn't left this room in weeks—because he hadn't. "Your housekeeper, Maria, will be here today. She'll prepare you lunch and tidy up this room. She will also do any laundry you require."

This announcement was met with Alejandro slumping back onto his bed, staring at the blue screen.

Gabriella set his tray down and gathered up the remains of last night's dinner. It hurt her to see her brother like this. At first, she'd been so relieved that he'd been found, but without his memory, it was almost as if he were still lost. Right in front of her, but still lost.

"I'm going to be visiting your old friend, Chance McDaniel, today," she said, more to keep the tears at bay than anything else.

Then something unusual happened. Alejandro's head snapped up and his eyes focused on her. For the first time in weeks, she felt as if he knew who she was. Or, at the very least, who Mr. McDaniel was.

Was that it? Did he remember something about Chance McDaniel—something connected with his abduction?

Just as her hopes began to rise, he said, "Everyone keeps talking about him, but..." He shrugged his shoulders and looked away.

This time, however, she wasn't so sure that he didn't know. His gaze had been too direct, too knowing. "He invited me out to ride at his ranch," she continued, busying herself with gathering up his dirty clothes—and keeping a close eye on him. "Joaquin will be joining me, of course."

Her brother was stroking his chin now, looking thoughtful—and very aware.

"Papa agreed," Gabriella went on, fluffing his pillows. "He thought it would give me the chance to see if Mr. McDaniel has any place where he could hide a person."

Out of the corner of her eye, she saw him shake his head. It was a small gesture, but it seemed as if Alejandro thought this little mission was foolish.

Gabriella couldn't contain herself any longer. She fell on her knees in front of Alejandro, taking his hands in hers. "If you could tell me anything—something you remember, some sound, *something*—I will help you." That unfocused blankness stole back over his face. "Don't you trust me, *hermano?*"

At first she did not think he was going to respond. But then he disentangled his hands from hers and patted her on the cheek. "You are..."

Gabriella's throat closed up. Did he remember her?

"You are a nice lady," he finished. "Have fun riding."

Then he was gone, flopping back onto his bed and grabbing the remote. Within seconds, the sounds of football filled the room.

Gabriella stood, blinking hard against the tears in her eyes. If he was in there—and, for the first time in days, she had hope that he was—then one thing was painfully clear.

He didn't trust her.

Gabriella pulled the door shut behind her and paused to

collect herself. Alejandro had managed to say something to her, after all. If he suspected Mr. McDaniel had had a part in his kidnapping, surely he would not have told her to have fun riding with the man.

But he had. She was a nice lady, whatever that meant, and she should have fun.

So that was exactly what she was going to do.

Four

With Joaquin in the driver's seat, Gabriella arrived at McDaniel's Acres at 9:55 a.m. They drove under the rustic gate that welcomed visitors before they continued up a long, winding drive of blacktop.

Gabriella leaned close to the tinted windows in the backseat, trying to take in the magnitude of the land they were crossing.

Hills rolled in all directions. Clusters of trees followed what was probably an arroyo or creek, but there weren't the old-growth forests that ringed Las Cruces. Instead low shrubs and those famous tumbleweeds dotted the landscape.

What would the hills look like in a few months? Would Texas bluebells cover the ground, color exploding everywhere? Or would grass grow in, deep and green—like Chance McDaniel's eyes?

She straightened in her seat and glanced at Joaquin's silent form in the front seat. She was not here to think about Mr. McDaniel's eyes and she would not be here in a few months to see the spring bloom. She would be back at Las Cruces, riding her own horses and making jewelry and not attempting more pancakes under any circumstances. Alejandro would be safe and things could go back to normal. That was what she wanted, wasn't it? Everything to return to normal?

She thought back to her conversation with Alejandro. This was the most animated she'd seen him since…since Papa had told him they would all be returning to Las Cruces as soon as the hospital had released Alejandro. Alejandro had snapped to life for a brief moment to say that under no circumstances was he leaving his home or Royal, Texas. Then he had lapsed back into his blank silence.

What if Alejandro did not want things to return to normal? What if, despite his abduction, he wished to stay in America?

That may very well be the case. But why? That was the question that Gabriella had little hope of answering on her own.

She smiled. Today, she was not on her own. She was going riding—with her brother's stilted blessing—with Chance McDaniel. She would find out as much as she could about her brother's life in Texas—and about Mr. McDaniel himself.

Joaquin slowed as they approached a sign. Its four arms pointed in two directions. The Bunk House, Swimming Pool and Deliveries pointed west; Trail Rides pointed north. Joaquin kept heading straight north.

Off to the west, she could see a large building that appeared to be made out of rough-hewed logs. It stood three stories tall, with a wide porch that looked as though it probably saw a great deal of activity during the summer. Even from this distance, she could see workers hanging garlands from the beams. *Those must be for the wedding,* she thought. It looked lovely, but if she were to get married here, she'd make sure to wait for the spring bloom.

Then the road took them farther away from the house and deeper into the ranch. A series of buildings appeared. Within moments, they were parked in front of a massive barn, its bright red color a beacon in the otherwise gray surroundings. Several smaller buildings were arranged behind the red barn. Some horses were loose in paddocks around the barns, some were scratching against posts. They all had that fuzzy look of animals in late winter.

Joaquin pulled up next to a deep blue pickup, got out and came around to open Gabriella's door for her. Upon exiting the vehicle, she walked over to where one horse was rubbing its head on a post. "Itchy?" she asked, and was rewarded by the horse—a palomino—leaning his head into her hands.

Gabriella smiled as some of the weight seemed to lift itself off of her shoulders. The breeze, while cool, felt fresh on her face—hinting at the spring that was coming. The horse groaned in appreciation as she rubbed his ears. A great deal of fur was coming off in her hands, but she didn't mind. Oh, how she had missed her horses—the smell was enough to lift her spirits.

"Lucky horse," a deep, slightly raspy voice said from behind her.

Gabriella spun to see Chance McDaniel tying a horse to a hitching post. His fingers moved smoothly, but his eyes were trained on her.

Oh, she thought with a small gasp. The man who had come to the door a few days ago had looked like a cowboy, yes—but almost a formal one. But the man who stood in front of her today? Pure cowboy. He wore a denim shirt under a light brown barn jacket. She was sure he was wearing jeans, but they were obscured by the worn black leather chaps that hugged his legs. Those weren't show chaps—no, the leather had that broken-in look that said he'd worn them often. Daily. The hat was the only thing that was the same—brown felt.

That and his eyes. The green was more vivid than she remembered. And the way he looked at her? Not as if he was a wolf and she the lamb. Too many men had looked at her that way—as though she was to be sacrificed on the altar of her father's business, a merger to be made between bottom lines and not between hearts.

No, Chance McDaniel looked at her without a single dollar sign in his eyes. Instead there was something else. Something that was almost… Well, certainly *not* joy at seeing her. That would not be possible. Nonetheless, it was something that made her body warm, despite the breeze.

Gabriella could not help the wide smile that broke over her face. "Mr. McDaniel."

He notched an eyebrow in clear challenge. "What's it going to take to get you to call me Chance, Gabriella?"

Her name sounded differently when he said it—gone were the smoothly flowing vowel sounds. Instead he stretched the *ah* into a harder *a*. It should have sounded grating, but she liked the rougher sound. No one else spoke her name like that. Just him.

Joaquin stepped in front of Gabriella before she could formulate a proper response to Chance McDaniel's familiarities.

"Howdy, Joaquin." Again, Chance was not seemingly put out by the bodyguard's presence. "Let me go get Beast." Then he patted the beautiful roan quarter horse he'd hitched to the post. "This here is Nightingale—although we call her Gale for short. I hope you like her."

Then, with a little nod of his head, he turned and headed back to the barn.

Joaquin gave her a look that said, *Is he for real?*

Gabriella responded by shrugging. It would be lovely if Chance McDaniel was "real." She reached into her pocket and pulled out the bag of carrot bits she'd mutilated in the kitchen last night. She walked up to Gale and held out a carrot. Gale sniffed, then snatched the treat.

"Ah, hello," she said as Gale sniffed her hair. "Would

you like another?" She palmed another carrot, which Gale all but inhaled. "That's a good girl."

She heard the sound of hooves—large hooves—clomping on the ground. Gabriella looked up to find Chance staring at her. That warmth coursed through her body again, but she wasn't about to let anyone know that. Not even the horse. "Yes?"

"Making friends?"

"But of course." Gabriella's cheeks flushed hot as he continued to stare at her. "It worked," she added as Gale nudged her with her nose.

Then she noticed the animal he was leading. Gale was perhaps sixteen hands high, but the mule—Beast, Chance had said—made the quarter horse look like a child's pony. It wasn't that the animal was that much taller than Gale, for he wasn't, perhaps another hand—no more than four more inches. But Beast clearly outweighed the quarter horse—perhaps by as much as half a ton.

She gasped, more than a little afraid of an animal that large.

Chance grinned at her. "Nothing to be scared of. Beast is as gentle as a kitten." He patted the big animal's neck before giving Gabriella a look that had nothing to do with horses. "You should make friends with him, too."

Far more than her cheeks flushed as Gabriella took a few hesitant steps toward Beast. His long ears—almost twice as long as Gale's—swiveled toward her. "*Hola,* Beast," she said, holding out a carrot on the flat of her palm. She'd long ago learned it was best to keep her hand as flat as possible. Holding a carrot or a sugar cube by her fingertips had gotten her nipped quite badly on the finger when she'd been six.

Beast's enormous lips scraped the carrot off of her hand, causing her to giggle. "You're a good boy, aren't you?"

"One of the best," Chance agreed. He was almost shoulder to shoulder with her, his voice far smoother than she'd heard it yet.

One of Beast's plate-size feet stamped at the earth, which caused Gabriella to jump. If she hadn't known any better, she would have thought she'd felt the shock waves from the impact. Chance laughed. "He likes you," he said, that twinkle in his eye.

"How can you tell?" She'd been stepped on by horses before, but Beast looked as if he would break every bone in her foot. She was in no mood to find out.

"If he didn't, he'd back up. He's predictable like that." Chance handed the reins to Joaquin. "There's a mounting block over there." Then he turned to Gabriella, that same twinkle shining brightly. "Let me help you up."

He crouched next to Gale's side and laced his fingers together. Gabriella hesitated—she could swing into the saddle by herself—but if she wanted to make friends with Chance, she needed to be friendly. So she placed her foot in his hand and let him boost her up onto the horse's back. Once she was in the saddle, he put his hand on her calf, right above her riding boot, and guided her foot into the stirrup.

Her breath caught at the too-familiar touch. She hardly knew this man and still had not ascertained if he was a danger to Alejandro or to her—but the way his hand had felt strong and sure against her leg had not felt like a risk. Instead it had felt…safe. Which was ridiculous. She did not need his help getting settled into the saddle. He started around to the other side of the horse, but Gabriella quickly put her foot in the stirrup.

Then he untied the reins and handed them to her. "Be right back," he said, leaving her in a state of unfamiliar confusion.

People, as a rule, did not touch her. To do so was to invite Joaquin to beat them senseless. And yet, Chance

McDaniel had put his hands on her as if it were the most natural thing in the world.

She turned the horse until she could see Joaquin, who had indeed used the mounting block and was now sitting astride Beast. He gave her a look that said, "Are you okay?"

"I am fine," she replied, although she wasn't sure how true that was. "You?"

Joaquin looked down at the ground and managed to nod his head.

"You okay up there, big guy?" Chance came trotting out of the barn on a dappled gelding. When Joaquin nodded again, Chance asked, "What do you ride at home?"

"Joaquin rides an Andalusian and I prefer my Azteca, Ixchel."

"I know what an Andalusian is, but what's an Azteca?" As he asked, he pointed his horse away from the barn. Gabriella fell in stride next to him, with Joaquin bringing up the rear.

"A mix of Andalusian, quarter horse and Mexican crillo," she explained. "Ixchel is a paint. She is a well-trained animal. I always wanted to show her, but..." That had been another source of rebellion when she'd been fourteen and fifteen. Other girls in her social circle were making weekend trips to competitions and talking of Olympic dreams—all activities that were forbidden to Gabriella.

"Why didn't you?" Chance kept his gaze forward. His posture was relaxed, but she could hear something in his voice that was far more than casual curiosity.

"Papa said that the competitions were not secure enough and he could not guarantee my safety if I went."

That got a reaction out of him. "Beg pardon?"

"Joaquin is an excellent bodyguard, but in a crowded space filled with horses and people, he cannot control the situation the way he can at Las Cruces. That's our family estate," she hurried to add.

"Wait, so—are you telling me that you don't have a bodyguard because of what happened to Alex?"

She could not decide if she liked the confusion in his voice. On the one hand, it was quite clear that Chance McDaniel had not known that—which was good because it meant that he had not done any surveillance or research into the del Toro family's comings and goings.

However, on the other hand, the way Chance said it made it clear that the idea of constant security sounded like more than a little overkill.

"Joaquin has been with me for fourteen years," she said, knowing that would only add fuel to Chance's curiosity.

"Are you serious?"

"Of course. Mexico is not a safe place for the wealthy. People are kidnapped for exorbitant ransoms. It's a business."

He appeared to mull over this information as the trail lead them farther and farther away from the buildings. "Is that normal, then? To have a bodyguard for a decade and a half?"

"Oh, I have had a guard my entire life. Papa hired Joaquin after he bested my former guard, Raul."

She felt as if she might be giving too much away—this was the sort of information that could be used to help formulate an abduction—but it didn't feel as though she was feeding him the things he wanted to know. Instead he seemed genuinely shocked.

"What do you mean, 'bested'?" His voice was level, but there was no mistaking the concern.

She warmed at his tone. Perhaps she shouldn't find it comforting that he was worried about her. Perhaps this was him on a fact-finding mission about how the del Toro family operated.

But she didn't think so. "All of the guards in our family

have to withstand tests, if you will, of their ability to keep us safe. If they fail in their mission, they are replaced."

Chance pulled his horse to an abrupt stop, which caused her horse to stop, as well. "What?" His tone was not pleased.

"It is not as bad as it sounds." But this defense didn't strike her as being particularly truthful.

"Doesn't that scare the hell out of you?"

She couldn't meet his gaze. "Usually the attempts are not very serious."

"But not always."

"No," she replied softly. "Not always."

The last time, the "pretend" kidnappers had taken their assignment a bit too seriously. Gabriella had been driving into Mexico City to meet with a gallery owner about showing her latest collection of jewelry when… Of course, their car was completely bulletproof, so Gabriella had not been in real danger. Or so she told herself time and time again.

"How bad was it?"

The sound of Chance's voice—low and with a slight rasp to it—called her back from her fear. She looked into his eyes and again was struck with that odd sense of coming home. "Joaquin defended me with honor—as he always does."

"How many times has this happened?"

The look on Chance's face wouldn't let her go. He was serious but underneath that was a different emotion—fury. "Usually once a year."

Chance let loose with a string of curse words quite unlike anything Gabriella had ever heard—at least, not all at once. The sudden explosion of sound should have been alarming but instead Gabriella found herself grinning and then giggling. She cast a glance back at Joaquin, who was as impassive as ever.

"—lower than a rattler's belly in a wagon rut!" Chance

finished with a flourish. "Can you tell me why, on God's green earth, a man would do that to his own daughter?"

"He had Alejandro's guards tested, as well," she told him, wondering when she had become the focus of his attention—and wondering if that was necessarily a warning sign. If it was, surely Joaquin would have rounded on Chance by now.

That statement did not seem to appease Chance's temper. "You've got to be pulling my chain. *Why?*"

He didn't know. She found a measure of relief in that—the more time she spent with Chance, the less she suspected him in Alejandro's disappearance. Or, at the very least, the less she suspected him of targeting the del Toro family for its fortune. He may have still had a hand in Alejandro's disappearance, but she could not believe that he had known that Alex Santiago was Alejandro del Toro.

Gabriella opened her mouth to tell him, but the words wouldn't come. The memories were too hard to deal with, even after twenty-three years. But he sat there, still, those beautiful eyes of his staring at her, expecting an answer.

When she could not give him one, she turned her horse back up the trail and urged her to a fast walk.

Apparently, Chance was in no mood to let her walk away from him—even if it was on horseback. He came level with her in moments, his mount easily keeping pace with Gale. "Who?" he asked, his tone more gentle than before.

"Our mother," she replied, trying to keep her own voice level. She couldn't risk a glance at him, though, so she kept her eyes focused on the land around them. "According to the police, she was killed when she tried to escape." Very few kidnappings ended that way—dead people were worth nothing, while living people were worth money. And wasn't money the whole point?

But Elena del Toro had not been a docile victim. "She

had fought them." That point made Gabriella proud of her mother but, at the same time, it infuriated her. Elena had not gone as meek as a church mouse—but if she had, would she still be here? Would everything have been different?

Would Gabriella have more than a few hazy memories of her own mother?

"When?"

"I was four. Alejandro was eight." She'd always been jealous of Alejandro. He had memories that Gabriella never would, after all. He remembered birthdays and Christmases, trips to visit Tía Manuela and church. All Gabriella had was a random collection of images, the strongest of which had always been of helping her mother choose the beads for the rosaries she made for the staff's Christmas presents.

That had been what she had been doing the day of the abduction—journeying to a market to buy beads and supplies for the rosaries that she and Gabriella were going to make that day.

An act of kindness that had gotten her killed.

"He never told me." There was a touch of hurt in Chance's words.

"He..." She took in another breath of fresh air. At least she wasn't trapped in the house, she told herself. At least she was on a horse. "He remembers more than I do. It is painful for us."

"Of course."

They fell into silence after that. Soon, she could see nothing but wilderness around her. The ribbon of trees she'd seen earlier was winding its way closer to the path they were on. The trees were trying to bud out. She could see the tips of the bare branches turning red with new growth.

Gabriella put thoughts of her mother out of her mind. It was not difficult—she'd had a great deal of practice. "We don't have winter in Mexico City. This is all so different here. Even the horses are different."

"Wait until they start shedding," Chance said with a chuckle. "The mess is something." They rode on in silence, then he said, "That hill over there? Nothing but bluebells in the spring."

"I would love to see them." Would they still be here in the spring, barricaded in Alejandro's house and hoping that *today* would be the day he remembered?

"If you're still here, you'll have to come back." He cleared his throat. "Do you know if you'll still be here?"

She shook her head. Was he asking because he was trying to pinpoint the best time to make another attempt—or was there something more genuine in his tone? "Alejandro does not want to return with us."

That still confused her, but now that she'd gotten out of the house and was riding across Texas, perhaps she could see why Alejandro wanted to stay.

"How is he today?"

"The same." Chance did not need to know that his name had caused a flash of recognition in Alejandro. Not yet, anyway.

They rode on, with Chance pointing out the features of the land and Gabriella trying to imagine how it would wear its spring coat. "Is it different than your ranch?" Chance asked.

They were still riding side by side, with Joaquin several feet behind them. For the first time in a great long while, Gabriella had the illusion of freedom. She was riding across land that was not surrounded by fences and patrolled by armed guards. No other signs of civilization crowded the view.

"Yes," she answered as the breeze played over her face. "We have far more trees. We do not have winter as a season—it does not get below freezing, except in very rare cases. Right now is a dry time." The ranch would be wearing its shades of brown. "I had hoped to see snow."

"We don't get a heckuva lot of snow," Chance replied. "Although when we do, it's real pretty. Makes the world look all new."

She looked at him as he rode. He sat tall in the saddle, one hand casually resting on his muscled thigh. He seemed perfectly at ease riding next to her. A true cowboy, she thought with a small smile.

He turned his head and caught the smile. "What?"

She could feel her cheeks flushing, so she quickly came up with a response to hide her embarrassment. "You said Alejandro would ride here with you?"

"Yup." Chance's gaze darkened. "He liked to race. Franny, my cook, would pack us a lunch and then we'd see who could make it to this shady spot down by the creek first."

It was obvious from his tone that the memory hurt him—not the pain of what had happened, though, but the pain of what he had lost.

Without thinking about it, she reached across the distance that separated them and touched his arm. "He will come back to us."

Chance met her gaze with nothing but challenge. "Which *he* is that? Your brother or my friend? Because I don't think that's the same man."

Then he looked back over his shoulder. Gabriella did the same. Joaquin was only a few feet behind them.

She sighed in frustration. Just the illusion of freedom. Not the real thing.

Five

Was she pulling his leg? Or was Gabriella del Toro being honest with him? And, more importantly, would Chance be able to tell the difference?

After all, he'd thought that Alex Santiago had always been an up-front kind of guy, and see where that had gotten him? The main suspect in Alex's kidnapping.

But Gabriella… She was something different. He didn't want to think that she'd been lying to him, not about her mother. The pain in her eyes had been all too real to be an act.

He was pretty sure. Recently he hadn't been the best judge of character.

He still couldn't get his head around what she'd said. He'd sort of understood the need for a bodyguard—after all, Alex had been kidnapped by someone, and if his family was as wealthy as they said they were, Chance could see why the del Toros would need twenty-four-hour protection.

But her mother being kidnapped when Gabriella was four—and killed? Her father keeping her under constant surveillance ever since—and occasionally scaring the hell out of her?

Chance had not particularly liked the man at their first meeting. Now? He had no idea how he was supposed to not punch the living daylights out of Rodrigo del Toro without getting shot. To put his daughter through attempted kidnappings—some of which had obviously terrified her—was right smack-dab between cruel and unusual.

He snuck a glance at Gabriella out of the corner of his eye as they rode down the path. She didn't look as though she was about to start sobbing, which was a small comfort. Chance prided himself on his honest dealings with the fairer sex, but crying women always made him nervous.

Her shoulders were back, her head up. Instead of jeans and cowboy boots, she was wearing a pair of buck-colored riding pants that fit her better than any glove ever could and English-style riding boots. She wore what appeared to be a sweater underneath a long jacket—not quite the barn-coat style he wore, but much more tailored to her shape.

Not that he was noticing her shape, but in that outfit, how could he not? She'd been stunning when he'd first seen her, but the long sweater-coat she'd had on had hidden some of the curves that were now highlighted. The woman had a hell of a body—the kind that made him want to slide his hands down her hips and hold on tight.

She was something different—not like women here. If a local woman had a body like that, she'd either be forever dieting to lose that elusive last ten pounds or dressed to maximize her assets—to use her body as a weapon.

Gabriella appeared to be neither of those things. Instead she looked stunningly regal, not cowered or afraid. Maybe that was because of the man behind them who probably had Chance in his sights. But maybe it was because she wasn't that bothered by the little story she'd told.

That thought depressed the hell out of him, but he wasn't exactly sure why.

Then she spoke. "Can I... Can I see the picnic spot?" Her voice quivered a bit, as if she was trying to master her feelings.

"You wanna race?" He didn't know what else to say. There was something bothering him about her little story—well, there was a hell of a lot that bothered him about it. But there was something that didn't add up.

She gave him a knowing smile. "I would love to, but I doubt that Beast would be able to keep up with your quarter horses and Joaquin will not appreciate being left behind."

Then he realized what it was—the bodyguard.

"Hey, if you're father's such a hard-ass—" She shot him a scolding look. "Pardon my French," he quickly added. "But if your father is so *concerned* with his family's safety, how come Alex didn't have a bodyguard up here? Aside from Mia, he lived alone. No armed thugs anywhere."

If anything, Gabriella blushed harder, which had the unfortunate side effect of making Chance forget what he'd asked. Truthfully, he couldn't remember a woman looking nearly as beautiful up on horseback as she did right now. Although she'd been a little skittish around Beast, she was perfectly at ease. Her long, lean legs gripped the saddle as if it was second nature to her.

Cara had never been as comfortable in the saddle as Gabriella was—and that was something that couldn't be faked. It would almost be worth getting plugged in the back just to watch her ride, hell-for-leather.

"As I'm sure you can appreciate, Mr. McDaniel—"

"Chance."

She turned to look at him, a warm smile on her face. "Chance."

The way she said his name—as though she was savoring a fine wine—made something clench low in his gut. In that moment he honestly didn't care if her brother was a habitual liar or her father was a sadistic control freak. He didn't much care if she was making up heart-wrenching stories to jerk him around. All he wanted to do was to see if she'd kiss him back, because he sure as hell wanted to kiss her.

"As I'm sure you can appreciate," she went on, a coy smile curving her full lips upward, "neither Alejandro nor I has always *enjoyed,* shall we say, the full protection our guards provide."

"Teenage rebellion?"

She nodded as the horses continued toward the picnic spot. "When Alejandro took a job at Del Toro Energy upon completing his studies, he moved to an apartment in Mexico City. He still had a guard, but he was allowed to come and go as he pleased. He went to clubs and events all over the city. He was very popular."

He heard a faint note of pain in her voice, one that said, loud and clear, that she had not been allowed to do any of those things. And just like that, Chance wanted to deck Rodrigo for keeping his daughter under what sounded like house arrest for her entire life. "He was popular here, too. A great guy." Or he had been, anyway.

She nodded in appreciation of that. "I am glad to hear it. When Papa wanted him to come north, Alejandro said he would not do it if he had to bring Carlos with him—that was his guard. He said Americans did not live like that."

He wanted to be known as an American, not a Mexican, Chance thought. Just part of the act.

"Of course," she mused, "he was still abducted, so I am not sure how sound his theory was."

"We're here," he said as a smaller trail branched off from the main path. Chance urged his horse forward to lead the way through the trees.

For every question Gabriella answered, he had another three. She had a good enough reason that Alex hadn't had a bodyguard in Texas—but why the hell had his father wanted him to come here in the first place? And why under an assumed name?

Had anything—the drinks at the club, the picnics by the creek—about Alex Santiago been real? Or had it all been part of some grand plan? Ruining his good name couldn't be it, although it sure felt personal on a bunch of different levels. But he'd never heard of Rodrigo del Toro before the man had showed up in Royal, causing a ruckus and bossing around the locals, so Chance didn't think that was it.

If it had all been fake, how much of what Gabriella said was trustworthy? Everything about her said genteel and proper—a noblewoman in the twenty-first century. She blushed easily but didn't lose her cool. She spoke of her life with a measure of reserve, without blatantly angling for sympathy.

Hell, he didn't know what to make of her.

So he stopped and dismounted near the creek. It was so low as to be nonexistent—not enough rain or snow this winter to balance out the last few years of drought that had savaged Texas. Chance sighed heavily. Trucking in water for his cattle wasn't cheap or easy, but if he didn't, he wouldn't have any animals for his dude ranch. People might still come for the rustic bunkhouse hotel or the trail rides—when the temperatures weren't over a hundred degrees, that was—but it wouldn't be as many.

Damn, but they needed rain.

"Need help?" he asked her, but before the words were out of his mouth, she was on the ground, loosening Gale's cinch and patting the horse on the neck. She grinned at him over Gale's neck. Right. She could handle herself.

So, feeling obligated, he turned to Joaquin. "How about you?" The big man on the big horse shook his head.

"He is fine," Gabriella translated. "He is better able to monitor the situation from horseback."

"Plus, no mounting block," Chance said, half to her and half to the guard.

"True." She said it, but Joaquin nodded in agreement.

He had to hand it to her—he could easily believe that Joaquin had been shadowing her for more than a decade. They had the kind of unspoken understanding that only came with years of constant contact. He found himself wondering how old Joaquin was. He had to be too old for Gabriella, didn't he? Surely Rodrigo del Toro wouldn't have tolerated his daughter being attracted to someone who was basically hired help?

The picnic spot was a small clearing on the edge of what used to be his creek. There was enough space for the horses to graze, but the trees stood tall here, blocking out the worst of the Texas heat in the summer.

"Have you lived here your whole life?" she asked as she walked around.

He wished he'd had Franny pack a lunch for them. He didn't want to take her back to the bunkhouse, to know that other ears were listening.

"Yup." He pointed to the low branch that reached across the creek bed. "See that rope burn? I used to swing into the water here. Over where that shallow puddle is? When the creek was full, that was my swimming hole—almost seven feet deep."

He picked up a rock and tossed it into the puddle. It made a depressingly small *plunk.* The creek hadn't been full in years. Man, he wished it would rain.

"Did you and Alejandro swim?"

Chance chuckled. "Nope. I think he waded in once." Then, because he couldn't help the vision that floated up in front of his eyes of Gabriella in some sort of swimsuit, he asked, "Do you swim?"

She didn't answer right away, instead, bending over and picking up a rock of her own. "We have a pool on our estate." She threw the rock, hitting the dead center of his swimming puddle.

"I put a pool in up at the bunkhouse when I opened

the hotel," he said, wondering if she'd have a one piece or a bikini—and how little that bikini might cover. Didn't matter—she'd fill it out. All of it. "We'll open it up in a few months."

The *if you're still here* hung out there, but now he wasn't sure that Gabriella—or Alex—would still be here. The more he learned about Rodrigo del Toro, the more he believed the older man would do anything to make sure his family was "secure."

She could easily be playing the poor-little-rich-girl card right now—held virtual prisoner by her mean father, never allowed to roam outside, never allowed to live a normal life. She could be trying to pluck at his heartstrings; make him feel as though he was her only possible savior from a life of house arrest.

She would be—if she was trying to manipulate him. He felt sure about that.

She turned to him, a sunny smile brightening her face. "When did you open the hotel?"

"A couple of years ago. I host theme weddings and week-long vacation packages. Hell—"

She shot him a look. "Heck," he corrected himself, "I even hosted a *Dallas*-themed murder mystery dinner when they launched the reboot on TV."

Nothing in her face changed—not on the surface, anyway, but it was like watching a shadow pass over her face. Everything about her got…colder. "The land is valuable to you?"

What the hell? He'd lost her—and he had no idea why. "It's been in my family for almost a hundred years—I'm the fourth generation of McDaniels to ranch here. There was no way I was going to let it go without a fight. Running a hotel and dude ranch may not be the same kind of hard work my grandpa did, but I do all right." Far better than his parents had done, that was for sure.

She gave him a measured look for another beat or two, then the shadow moved on and she was walking back over to Gale, tightening the cinch and swinging up into the saddle as though she'd been doing it all her life. She sure hadn't needed his help mounting up earlier and he felt a little stupid for having done so.

But he'd wanted to touch her, to see what she'd do. Would she have taken it as the come-on it sort of was—and would she have tried to use the attraction he obviously felt to her advantage?

She hadn't. She'd just looked down at him with that confused, almost innocent air about her. Which had done things to him.

Things that might get him shot by the end of the day.

He mounted up and they headed back down the trail toward the bunkhouse. "Franny will have lunch waiting on us," he said into the silence, although she had not questioned them returning the way they came.

"Tell me more about Alejandro here." The way she said it, it was less a conversation, more a cross-examination.

Yeah, this wasn't datelike activity. This was riding with the enemy—a woman who had access to the one man who could clear Chance's name in this whole mess. A man who apparently didn't remember a damn thing. A man who might be vulnerable to suggestion.

It didn't matter how attracted he was to Gabriella del Toro, how touching her stories were. Hell, it didn't matter a damn bit how well she rode. The only thing that mattered was clearing his name. A distant second to that was figuring out what had happened to his friend.

"What do you want to know?"

"You said he was popular here?"

"Yup. He rolled in and started throwing money around like it was confetti. A lot of people were suspicious, but money talks." Hell, he'd been one of the doubters—what had Alex Santiago known about Royal, Texas?

"Indeed." She didn't seem surprised by these statements. Then she turned her face toward his and broke out an absolutely stunning smile. "What is the phrase? All hat, no cows?"

The laugh burst out of him before he could think better of it. She giggled along with him, even as she looked mildly embarrassed. "Close, really close," he said, wiping an honest-to-God tear from his eye. Man, he hadn't laughed that hard since… Well, since before Alex had gone missing. "All hat, no cattle. But you've got the drift."

She gave him a funny look—funny confused, not funny amused. Although she still looked amused. "The what?"

"The drift. You understand the basic idea of all hat, no cattle." He looked at her. "Say, where'd you learn to speak English?"

Color rushed to her cheeks, which had him staring. "Am I not making myself clear?"

"No—it's not that at all." Jeez, he was sticking his foot in his mouth. "You've got a different accent. Not quite Mexican, but not American, either. It's real pretty," he added, although he didn't know why.

Well, he knew why. It was the same reason he shouldn't be complimenting her. Any attraction he felt for Gabriella del Toro was irrelevant. He had to remember that.

This was going to prove hard, what with her fluttering her thick black eyelashes at him and looking all pleased with his compliments. "Papa did not like the American accent. All of my tutors were British."

Chance was getting the feeling that dear ol' Papa didn't like anything American—which led to the inevitable question of why he had sent his son up here. "Alex's tutors—were they British, too?" Because Alex hadn't talked quite the way Gabriella had. He'd gotten the drift of all hat, no cattle from the get-go, no explanation needed.

At that, her cheeks flushed and she dropped her gaze away from his. *That'd be a no,* he thought. Then she answered the question. "Papa saw more value for Alejandro to be familiar with American slang."

Okay, so Rodrigo had raised his son to be a— What? A mole? Trained him to infiltrate the bustling urban hub of Royal, Texas?

And he held his daughter to a different set of standards—like a bird in a gilded cage.

Chance detested men like Rodrigo del Toro—men who used their family as pawns and, worse, who hid their manipulations behind the façade of concern and care. His own parents might not have had much of a go at running a successful ranch, but by God they'd loved him—and each other—and done everything they could to raise him up right.

This meant not saying the things that were running loose in his head right now, because it was clear that, no matter what he thought about the man, his daughter somehow managed to still love him. Instead he damn near bit his tongue trying to keep his mouth shut. It wasn't his place to judge what went on in other people's families. He wasn't about to start casting stones. Lord knew he had enough sin.

So he took the easy way out. "Well, if you need anything explained, you let me know."

"I will."

Funny, he thought as the barn came into view.

She sounded as if she meant it.

Six

They rode up to the barn and dismounted. "Where do the saddles go?" she asked as Marty came out to meet them.

Chance looked over and saw that she already had the saddle off the horse and was standing there as if he expected her to rub ol' Gale down herself. "Marty'll get it."

"I don't mind. I curry my horse at home."

Behind her, Joaquin nodded. He'd managed to stick the dismount and was also undoing Beast's cinch.

Gabriella may be coddled, but she wasn't spoiled. "Marty will get it," he repeated. A flash of defiance crossed her face, so he added, "Fran's got lunch waiting on us."

She looked as if she wanted to argue, but at the mention of lunch, everything changed. "Of course—I forgot. I groom Ixchel." She handed the saddle over to Marty, who looked bemused by a guest insisting on working.

They began the short walk up to the bunkhouse. "What does So-cheel mean?"

"Ixchel," she repeated, her lips smoothing out all the rough edges of the word. "She is the Mayan goddess of midwifery and, to a lesser extent, medicine."

"Sure." He'd never heard of her, but that didn't mean it was a weird name. But he wasn't going to say that.

Not that he needed to. She gave him a sly look and said, “Is it so much different than naming a horse after the founder of modern nursing—Florence Nightingale?”

He was probably gaping at her, but he couldn’t help himself.

She laughed. That light, easy sound. “Although I am sure you had the songbird in mind, yes?”

“Yeah, that was what I was going for. Seem to have missed it by a country mile, though.”

“Is that different than a city mile, then?”

“Sort of. Fewer sidewalks, more twists and turns. Have to go slower.”

They reached the front doors of the Bunk House. He held the door for her, but Joaquin—who had trailed them the entire time—insisted that Chance go in second.

“Oh,” Gabriella breathed in that slightly surprised voice as she looked around.

“It’s not a real bunkhouse,” he explained as she gaped at the three-story lobby, finished in rough-hewed logs and decorated with plush leather furniture and thick Navajo rugs. The decorator he’d hired had wanted to use deer antlers as accessories—for lamps and chandeliers and whatnot—as well as cowhides for rugs, but Chance had put his foot down. He didn’t live *in* the bunkhouse, but it was still his home and he wasn’t about to have the McDaniel name associated with clichés like that.

“The old bunkhouse was falling apart—Marty liked it, but he was the only one. So I had it leveled and I built this one.”

She did a slow turn as she stared up at a three-tiered wrought-iron chandelier with mica shades before turning to face the massive stone hearth, the chimney running up the length of the wall. “I used Texas red sandstone—rough-cut—for the chimney and had the chandeliers custom-made by a guy I know.”

"Amazing," she said as she did another slow turn. "You live here?"

"Nope. My house is a little farther out on the range. I grew up in that house."

"Oh, you live with your parents, as well?"

He wanted to be amused. If an American woman had asked that question, it would have been loaded with disgust that a grown man still lived with his momma. But for Gabriella, no such disgust existed. If anything, she sounded happy to have found a bit of common ground with him.

"They passed on. Back when I was in college. I'm the only McDaniel left."

Maybe he shouldn't have put it in exactly those terms, because Gabriella looked at him with her big, beautiful eyes—eyes that pooled with unshed tears. She reached out and laid her hand on his arm for the second time today. "Oh—my apologies. I didn't know."

More than anything, he wanted to touch her back—to put his hand on top of hers, to feel her skin underneath his.

Light flashed off of her neck and, for the first time, he noticed the jewelry she was wearing today. Whereas she'd had on ropes of turquoise in Alex's house, today she had on simple silver crosses.

He leaned in closer. Maybe not so simple. The surface of the cross at her neck was hammered, but the texture was so finely done that it looked solid from a distance. In the center was a green stone—small, but exquisitely cut. A perfect emerald.

She noticed him looking and tilted her head back, giving him full view of her smooth collarbone. He forgot about the necklace until she said, "The earrings match."

He dragged his gaze away from her chest and up to her ears. The crosses did indeed match—hammered silver with a small but perfectly cut emerald in the center. "They're stunning."

"Thank you." A soft pink blush flooded her cheeks—and edged down her collarbone.

Innocent, he thought. Sweet and innocent, with a hint of pride in her tone.

Unless it was all an act.

"Did you make them?"

"Yes. That is my business."

He knew he was probably staring at her with his mouth open like a catfish, but he couldn't help it. The work was amazing—not some mass-produced, made-in-China crap that any teenager could buy at a mall. "You make jewelry?"

"Yes." She removed one earring, then the other. Finally, moving at a speed that made something deep inside Chance hurt, she lifted her hair away from her neck and unfastened the necklace. She was still fully dressed, of course, but watching her remove her jewelry was one of the more erotic moments of Chance's life. Something about it felt intimate—forbidden, almost.

If he wasn't staring at her before, he sure as hell was now.

"There is a trick," she explained, taking a few steps over to the table in the center of the lobby. "The pieces are interlocking."

As he watched, her fingers nimbly arranged the three crosses. The interior arms of the two earring crosses slipped behind the top of the cross pendant, then she snapped the arms of the pendant behind the center of the smaller crosses. "It took me months to figure out how to balance the needed thickness to make them lock into place with the flexibility to bend but retain their shape." She demonstrated by picking the trio of crosses up and giving it a light shake. It didn't fall apart.

"You made that?"

"The three crosses," she said, a pleased smile on her face. "Tres Cruces—that is the name of my business." She put the assembled piece into his hand and then turned it over. "This is my mark."

She pointed to a small indent on the back of each separate piece—and damned if it wasn't three crosses lined up exactly as she'd arranged them on his table. Tres Cruces—tTt.

"I didn't realize you were so accomplished." Too late, he did realize that was a backhanded sort of compliment. "I mean, I didn't realize you did metalwork. Obviously, I realized you were quite accomplished—figured that out when you spoke such pretty French." She giggled at him and he felt foolish—but also pleased. "Yeah, I'll stop talking now. First rule of holes and all that."

Her eyes still brimming with good humor, she said, "The first rule of holes? What is that?"

"The first rule of holes—when you're in one, stop digging."

"Ah. An Americanism." She still looked a little confused. "What hole are you in that you must stop digging?"

Chance ran a hand through his hair. "Yeah—I'm embarrassing myself." But he had to admit it was sort of worth it to hear the lightness of her laughter. "Do me a favor and save me from myself—tell me about your business."

Just then, Carlotta, a receptionist at the front desk, hurried past him. "*Buenos días,* Señor McDaniel."

"*Buenos días,* Carlotta," he replied, handing Gabriella's three crosses back to her and forcing himself to take a step away. Not only was he running the risk of Joaquin plugging him in the back, but if Chance's staff saw him making googly eyes at a woman—well, word would get around.

He wasn't interested in one-night—or one-afternoon—stands. He didn't want to be the last McDaniel, but so far he hadn't done a bang-up job of finding a woman who'd cotton to his way of life. Cara Windsor sure hadn't, although he'd thought for a while she might be willing to give it a go. Before Alex Santiago had come and turned his whole life upside down.

"Carlotta, can you tell Fran we're here?"

Carlotta snuck a curious glance in at Gabriella before she said, *"Sí, señor."*

Chance watched her go, wondering how fast news of Gabriella's arrival would spread through his staff—and whether anyone would believe that he wasn't making the moves on Gabriella.

He sighed heavily. Just another sordid tale in the life of a fictional character named Chance McDaniel—first he kidnapped his best friend and dumped him south of the border, then he wined and dined his best friend's sister, no doubt corrupting her innocence. What next—he'd been plotting to overthrow the mayor? Conducting satanic rituals on his land? He was getting damn tired of people choosing to believe what they wanted about his life instead of what was true. He'd hoped things would get better now that Alex had been found, but with his memory gone, he hadn't exactly been able to prove that Chance had had nothing to do with his disappearance.

He forced himself back to the present, but it was tough. Gabriella spun his head around way too easily. "The restaurant is this way."

He led Gabriella and Joaquin off to the north side of the lobby, where an open doorway was framed with huge rough-cut logs. The restaurant wasn't a big thing—twenty tables—but it did a brisk business thanks to Franny's cooking.

Chance guided Gabriella—with Joaquin close behind them—to two tables in the corner of the restaurant. It was quiet today—they had a few people already here for the wedding tomorrow, but most of them were out doing wedding-related preparations for tomorrow.

Basically, they had the place to themselves.

"The tables are rather small," Gabriella noted, one of her delicately curved eyebrows lifting in what he hoped was amusement and not irritation.

"We like to promote a quiet atmosphere here, so, yeah—Joaquin, you'll be at this table here." Chance saw the look that the two exchanged, but he didn't care. Sure, Joaquin was probably a great guy, but Chance would like to get through a conversation with Gabriella without having the big man staring daggers at him. Besides, Gabriella seemed to be smiling. "You've got your back to a wall and full view of the room. Try not to shoot anyone, okay?"

Joaquin glared at him.

Franny came bustling out of the kitchen, wiping her hands on her apron. A big woman, Franny was in her mid-fifties, her children grown and living in Houston. She'd taken it upon herself to look after Chance. Some days, he could do without being henpecked, but most of the time, he appreciated that there was always someone on his side.

Franny not only didn't believe the rumors but would take a wooden spoon to anyone who dared repeat them in her presence. "It took you long enough," she began, wagging a finger at Chance as she scolded him. "'Bout thought I was going to have to eat the chicken all by myself." Then she rounded on Gabriella and all of her mother-hen attitude melted into a warm, broad smile that matched her warm, broad body. "Well, now—is this our Alex's sister?"

Gabriella glanced at Chance. He could tell this announcement made her uncomfortable, but he doubted that Franny had noticed the same thing. Instead, Gabriella said, "Hello. Yes, I'm, um, Alex's sister. Gabriella del Toro." She held out her hand.

But instead of shaking, Franny swallowed her up in a big old hug. Gabriella let out a little squeak.

"It's such a pleasure to meet you. We were so worried about Alex—why, that boy's practically family out here."

Fran finally released her grip on Gabriella to wipe a tear from her eye. "I was so afraid some drug cartel had gotten him or something—that violence slips a little farther north every year. And then, everyone tried to pin it on our Chance—all because of a woman! Well, I never." She clucked.

"Ah, yes," Gabriella said in a soft voice. "We do not believe it was a cartel."

Something in Chance hardened at her tone—and not the fun way, either. He'd never believed it'd been a cartel out for revenge—but then, he'd always believed that Alex had been a stand-up guy.

What did Gabriella believe? She had to have heard the rumors—maybe the law officers still investigating the case had mentioned him as a suspect. Did she believe them?

Damn that Alex Santiago—or Alejandro del Toro. Damn both of them. If he'd been up front from the get-go, none of this would have happened. If he could remember something—anything—Chance could get on with his life.

"And who is this fine specimen?" Franny had finally noticed Joaquin. "My, my!" She walked over to him and squeezed his bicep. "Hello there. I'm Fran."

Gabriella giggled as Joaquin blushed and blushed hard. It was, hands down, the biggest reaction Chance had seen anyone get out of the man. "It is a pleasure to meet you," he offered in a tentative voice.

"Now, you all sit yourselves down and let Franny get you some lunch." She winked at Chance as she ushered Gabriella over to the table with him. "Best fried chicken in the state!"

When she was gone, Gabriella turned to look at him. She kept on looking at him as he held out her chair for her and when he'd taken his seat across from her. Her gaze wasn't distrustful, not entirely—but it was clear that Franny had said something that she hadn't liked.

Here it comes, he thought.

But Gabriella waited until Franny had delivered salads and iced tea to both tables before speaking. "What did Franny mean, all because of a woman?"

He considered his position carefully before continuing. "Alex had a lady friend."

This was not the answer she was looking for. "Do you mean Cara Windsor, whose father owns Windsor Energy?"

Was that it? He'd been hearing the rumors—that Windsor Energy was the reason Alex had come to Royal in the first place. That would make sense, Chance figured. Maybe Rodrigo del Toro had wanted to check out his north-of-the-border competition. Industrial espionage.

Had industrial espionage been why Alex had taken Cara? The thought burned at the back of Chance's throat and Franny's sweet iced tea did nothing to cool him down. Cara had taken quite a shine to Alex—so much so that Chance had felt the only honorable thing to do was to step aside and let nature take its course. Had that all been a lie, too?

"I didn't have a damn thing to do with Alex's disappearance," he heard himself say.

"But you had been seeing this Cara Windsor." Gabriella's statement was quiet, as if she didn't want Joaquin to overhear her.

"We dated, but she was crazy for your brother. So I stepped aside. I cared for them both. Thought they'd be happy together." How stupid had he been? Had they all been?

Alejandro del Toro had been a mole from the very start. Chance had welcomed him into his life, onto his land—hell, into the Texas Cattleman's Club as a friend. He'd given up his girl in the name of honor and friendship. Not only had he been burned, but Cara had, too.

"You are angry." There wasn't much comfort in Gabriella's voice. Just an observation.

"You're damn straight I'm angry. I thought I had a friend, but it was an imaginary character named Alex Santiago. Then when he up and disappeared, everyone pointed their fingers at me, claiming I'd done it, maybe killed him because I was upset about Cara. Well, I am upset about Cara. I cared for her—enough to let her go—and it got us both burned. Maybe if I'd fought a little harder for her, he wouldn't have had the chance to screw her over like he screwed me over."

He immediately felt like a jerk—but hell, yeah, he was mad. He'd been watching his temper for far too long. Something had to give.

He waited. Gabriella would have something to say—but what? Denials? Defending her poor, injured brother? Accusing Chance of being as guilty as everyone said he was?

He wanted her to do just that—give him a good reason to hate her, to hate the entire del Toro family. Hell, he was worked up enough he wouldn't mind going a round or two with Joaquin—fists only, not guns. He was so damn tired of defending himself when he'd done nothing wrong. Not a single damn thing.

Franny came back out with plates of her fried chicken and Chance took the opportunity to dig in. Few things in this world were as good as Franny's fried chicken. Some people had encouraged her to open her own restaurant, but so far Chance had managed to hang on to her by taking care of the details—he provided the space and the staff and did the books, as well. All she had to do here was cook, which was fine by him.

"How you all doing?" she asked as she cleared the mostly uneaten salad plates. Her voice was light, but Chance could see that she was concerned.

He needed to stop grousing before he sent Gabriella

scurrying home with horror stories about how short-tempered he was. "Better now that your fried chicken's here."

"Go on, now," she said, gently swatting his arm before bustling back to flirt—yes, *flirt*—with Joaquin.

Gabriella watched her with amusement. "I do not think I have seen Joaquin blush that much in all our years together," she said in that quiet voice of hers.

He liked that quiet voice. He liked that she had things she wanted to say to him and only him. "Is that a bad thing?" Chance would never forgive himself if something bad happened to Franny.

"No, I do not believe it is," she said with a knowing wink.

Chance felt his mood improve. "So," he said, remembering where they'd left off before he'd lost his temper. "Tell me about Tres Cruces. Did you make that turquoise set you were wearing on Monday?"

She nodded. He could tell she was pleased that he remembered. "I was so very young when my mother died, you understand."

For a second Chance was afraid he'd asked the wrong question, but she went on without missing a beat. "I have so few memories of her, but one thing that has always stuck with me was that Mama liked to make rosaries for the staff for Christmas. She would let me pick out the beads and help me string them on the wire. When I dropped them—and I *always* dropped them—she would laugh and we would make a game out of who could collect the most beads the fastest." Her voice was softer, lighter—like a small girl lost in a happy thought. "I remember that clearly."

She smiled at the thought and he realized this was probably her most precious memory—and she'd shared it with him. It made him want to pull her into his arms and buy her more beads and take her on more rides—all so she could have a few more good memories. "So you learned from her?"

"In a way. It made me feel closer to her. I strung beads for a while, but soon I ran out of ideas and I wanted to try something new. Papa encouraged me, so there I was, this gap-toothed girl of ten, learning how to solder from one of the gardeners."

Chance whistled. "You were soldering at ten? I'm impressed."

"Alejandro used to tease me so," she said, her eyes lighting up. "My fingertips were always stained and I had little burns in much of my clothing. I was quite a sight in church on Sundays!"

They laughed, the tension of earlier gone. Maybe Chance would have to revise his opinion of Rodrigo del Toro—a little, anyway. Not too many fathers would let their daughters take up metalwork at an age when most girls were playing with dolls and painting their nails. "So you've been making jewelry for years?"

She shot him a sly look that made his blood pump faster. "Not all of it was a success, you understand."

"You should have seen the first fence I put up by myself. Not a straight line for a mile."

Something in her eyes…deepened. "A country mile?"

He grinned at her. She was a quick study—intelligent, beautiful *and* talented. Man, if things were different, he'd do a hell of a lot more than just take her out for a morning ride and then feed her fried chicken. Dinner with candles, a nice wine—maybe a long drive home on a slow country road? Too damn bad things weren't different. "Sure seemed longer when I was digging those post holes."

Behind him, he thought he heard Joaquin snort. Yeah, he forgot—they weren't exactly alone. What a pain in the backside. "So you make everything by hand?"

She nodded as she ate. "I have gallery shows in Mexico City. Most of my pieces are one-of-a-kind creations and I do a great deal of custom work. More than enough to keep me busy."

"Are you working here?"

"No," and the way she said it made it pretty clear that she missed it. "I was operating under the impression that we would not be in America long enough to pack up my tools and supplies." The more she talked, the sadder she looked. "I appear to have been mistaken."

Boy, no wonder she looked depressed. As far as he could tell, she spent her time riding her horse and making amazing jewelry. But at Alex's house? She had access to neither of those things.

"Any time you want to come out and ride," he offered, "you let me know. I'm hosting a wedding tomorrow, but I'll make time to hit the trail with you."

Her big eyes looked up at him with undisguised gratitude. "Thank you." Then she leaned forward. "I must admit, I was jealous of Alejandro coming to America, but this is the first time I've been able to get away from the house and see anything."

"I can show you around. For a town this size, there's a lot to do. We've got some good restaurants." He kept his voice level.

She didn't reply for a moment. Instead she looked at him through her thick lashes, her lips curved into the kind of smile that practically begged a man to come on over and kiss them. "Are you asking me out to dinner?"

The question felt like a trap because, yeah, he was asking her out to dinner. "I'm sure Alex would want to know that his little sister is enjoying herself in Texas—seeing the sights, that sort of thing. Not much point in coming to America if you're going to be stuck in a house."

He must not have done such a good job of covering his

tracks, because she shot him a look that was all kinds of hot and not a whole lot of innocent. “Joaquin will have to come along, of course.”

“Of course.” He tried to make it sound as if it was no big deal—just an armed chaperone. But if that was what it took to get her out of the house, then so be it.

Gabriella del Toro wasn’t exactly a woman he could trust and, beyond that, she wasn’t exactly in play, what with being a beautiful Mexican heiress with a domineering father and a lying, cheating dirtbag for a brother. She would only be here for as long as Alex couldn’t remember who’d kidnapped him, then she’d be back south of the border again, locked up in her little castle and he’d never see her again.

But she’d unsaddled her horse. She soldered for fun. She spoke three languages.

And—this was the important part—she was sitting over there looking as if dinner was exactly what she had in mind.

“I think,” she said, and he heard something new in her voice—soft, yes, but now it was mixed with what sounded like desire, “that dinner would be lovely.”

Yeah, lovely.

Just like her.

Seven

When was the last time she'd had a date?

Gabriella mulled this question over on the drive back to Alejandro's house. Dating had been, by and large, a phase of life that she had skipped. She'd kissed a few grooms in the stable, but that had usually been retaliation against her father and his many rules. And they had never progressed past a few kisses—the grooms had been far more worried about being caught than Gabriella had been.

Then there had been her *quinceañera,* which had been a two-day-long festival her father had hired a party planner to orchestrate. Everything about her fifteenth birthday had been planned, including who her *chambelanes,* or dance partners, would be. Her father had chosen the son of one of his business partners, Raoul Viega, to be her first dance.

Ah, Raoul. That was probably as close as she could come to having dated. He was the same age as Alejandro and had attended the same university, although the two men had never been close friends. Raoul had been her escort at various points throughout the years, accompanying her to formal parties for Del Toro Energy and dinners at Los Pinos, the presidential estate.

She had kissed Raoul, of course. Occasionally because she had wanted to, often because he had kissed her first—

but mostly because she'd felt that each kiss was a small act of rebellion. A dare to Joaquin to report her activities back to her father, as he had always done about everything else.

To his credit, Joaquin had never related her "dates" to her father in the exact way that they happened. But Raoul had grown bored with simple kisses and Joaquin's presence had not allowed anything more…exciting to occur. Soon, Raoul had only taken her out when polite society dictated it, and those events had grown further and further apart. She had last seen him at her most recent gallery opening, eight months ago—and he'd accompanied a beautiful blond woman to the event.

Gabriella had gone with her father.

She'd been so miserable. Alejandro was in Texas—with no guards, no surveillance—and she had been stuck at Las Cruces, going places with Joaquin and her father. She knew she had no right to complain—she had never been cold or hungry, never been treated as chattel—but she'd still fallen into a deep depression after that. She didn't want to retreat further into herself—further away from the rest of the world. She'd wanted more than that.

She didn't want it on her father's terms, no matter how well-meaning those terms were.

Which is how she'd wound up in Texas, having lunch with Chance McDaniel. On her terms.

Raoul had always resented Joaquin's necessary presence, making rude comments about her guard when he could clearly hear them. Perhaps that was why Joaquin had never allowed Raoul and Gabriella to be alone long enough for anything else to happen besides those quick kisses.

But Chance? Well, that was different. It was quite clear that Chance was not exactly enamored with Joaquin accompanying her on the ride, but he had done an admirable job of including Joaquin.

Gabriella looked at Joaquin. He was tapping his fingertips on the steering wheel as he navigated the vehicle back to Alejandro's house. She leaned forward and caught the sound of humming—faint, but unmistakable.

She smiled with joy. He may never say it out loud—and certainly not in so many words—but Joaquin had enjoyed himself today, as well. What had been his favorite part—the ride or the meal? Or had it been the cook, Franny?

Excellent. If Joaquin had had a nice time and Gabriella's safety had never been in question—which, despite a rather strong set of hugs from Franny, it hadn't—then there could be no good reason not to return to McDaniel's Acres for another ride.

For the first time since she'd arrived in Texas, happiness flooded Gabriella. This was why she'd come, after all—to get off the estate, to see something new. To taste the freedom that Alejandro had enjoyed for two years.

Lost in this pleased state, they arrived back at the house and Joaquin escorted her inside. At first she didn't notice anything amiss, but then she heard it—a deep male voice that sounded as if the speaker hadn't talked for years, coming from the kitchen.

She rushed past Joaquin to find Alejandro sitting at the kitchen table. He'd showered and shaved since the morning, and had dressed in a white button-up shirt and clean jeans. He was drinking a cup of coffee and talking to Maria, the housekeeper, as if this were a normal Friday. When she entered the room, he looked up and smiled at her.

As though he knew who she was.

"Alejandro!" But that was all she could say as she threw herself at him. Her throat closed up and she was suddenly crying. He was back, the brother she remembered—not the stranger who'd come home from the hospital.

Wasn't he? As she clung to his neck, she waited for some sign from him that he did, in fact, remember her beyond the nice lady who brought him breakfast. For a moment nothing happened and she lost all hope. Nothing had changed, except he'd left his room. That was it.

But then he said, "Hi, sis," and hugged her back. "I've missed you."

"You know me?" she demanded, trying to keep herself composed. But then he leaned back and looked her in the eyes and she saw him. Her brother.

"I couldn't forget my little sister."

She almost cried. Alejandro was *here*. "I have been so worried about you," she said as she hugged him again. "You must tell me what you remember." Then, before she could stop herself, she added, "You must tell me if Chance McDaniel had anything to do with it."

A shade crossed over his face and she felt him slipping away from her. As if he was pretending.

She recalled that morning, when Chance's name had sparked some recognition in Alejandro's eyes. She'd thought he didn't trust her with whatever the truth was—but now?

What if it wasn't that he didn't trust her, but that he didn't trust Chance? Was Alejandro still afraid of his former friend?

But then he said, "Did you go for a ride?"

"Yes." The wash of confusion she felt right now did nothing to help her nerves. She disentangled herself from him and took a seat across the table.

"Oh, did you ride with Chance? He leads trail ride groups all the time," Maria said as she set a cup of strong coffee down in front of Gabriella.

"Thank you so much," Gabriella replied. Up until now, Maria had practically been her best friend here in Texas, the one woman she could talk to.

But right now, she had a great deal to discuss with her

brother and she'd like that conversation to be as far from prying ears as possible.

"I was filling Alex in on some stuff," Maria went on, wiping down the countertop as she spoke. Then, in the distance, the dryer buzzed. "Laundry!"

And they were alone. Well, Joaquin was still there, but it was essentially the same thing. Gabriella had so many things she wanted to ask Alejandro, but she didn't want to overload him and she also didn't want him to shut down on her again. So she sipped her coffee before asking, "Have you talked to Papa yet?"

"No," he said, not meeting her gaze. "He is in a meeting, I think."

She heard the disappointment in his voice. He'd finally decided to come down—and no matter what he said, she believed it was a conscious decision—and Papa hadn't taken the time to greet him.

"He has been very worried about you," she explained. It felt hollow. "We all have."

"I…didn't want you to worry." Again, he sounded as though he was measuring his words, testing the waters on how much information he could reveal. "I'm glad you are here."

Perhaps he was not comfortable with Joaquin? Of course Alejandro knew Joaquin was a trusted part of the security detail, but then, it had been years since the two men had spent a great deal of time in each other's company. Joaquin had become her guard when Alejandro was preparing to go to university.

"Joaquin, please tell Papa that Alejandro is feeling better."

No one moved for what felt like a very long time. If anything, Alejandro looked pleased with her directive, but he was careful not to actually smile. For his part, Joaquin seemed torn on what he should actually do. He was her guard, but his first duty had always been to Rodrigo del Toro. No doubt he was weighing fetching his boss versus listening to Gabriella and Alejandro's conversation.

"Please," Gabriella said with more insistence. "Papa will want to know that Alejandro is up."

Finally, Joaquin acknowledged her with a nod of his head and left the room. Gabriella and Alejandro sat for a moment longer, but she wasn't about to waste this precious time with him. "Tell me what you remember."

"Not much," he admitted, scrubbing a hand over his chin again.

"You know who I am?"

"My sister. Gabriella."

"Do you know who Joaquin is? Do you remember Papa?"

"Yes." He answered without hesitation, his gaze never leaving hers.

"Do you know our business?"

"Del Toro Energy."

He had to have been faking it this morning. Heavens, he had to have been faking it for some time. But how long? Had he had his memory back the whole time?

"Do you remember Chance McDaniel?"

At this, Alejandro blinked. He clasped his hands in front of him and stared at his thumbs. "Not really," he mumbled. But she could hear the untruth in his voice.

"What about Cara Windsor? Of Windsor Energy?"

Everything about him froze, answering the question in a way that words never could.

"Because I have heard rumors," Gabriella went on, pressing her advantage, "that you stole this Cara Windsor from Chance and that is why he took you and dumped you back in Mexico—it was revenge. Is that what happened?"

But before he could answer, Papa burst into the kitchen, followed closely by Joaquin. "Alejandro!" Papa bellowed.

Then he swept his son into his arms and patted him on the back with such force that Alejandro turned red in the face. "We must call the doctors and the police," Papa said. "We will find the people who did this to you and I will make them pay."

Alejandro shot a worried look at Gabriella. Yes, he had answered her questions. But he clearly did not want to answer more questions—questions with a bigger audience.

"Papa," she said, putting a hand on his arm. "Alejandro has just started to feel like himself. Perhaps it would be best to let him rest up for a few more days before we allow the authorities to question him. We do not want to risk making things worse."

Alejandro shot her a grateful look as Papa restrained himself. "Yes, yes, of course. Come, son, sit down. Have some coffee."

Then Maria bustled back in and the kitchen was filled with the sounds of talking and cooking as Papa and Maria both tried to encourage Alejandro to share more of what he remembered. But, for the most part, he said little more than "No, not really" or "I'm not sure" while he stared at his hands.

It was only after Maria had left—with enough dinners in the refrigerator so that Gabriella would not have to attempt cooking for another week—and Papa had taken another call from his office that she had the chance to ask the question that had burned in her mind the entire afternoon.

"Alejandro," she said, careful to keep her voice light. Joaquin was still in the room, after all. True, he was scrolling on his tablet, but they both knew he was listening. "I know you do not recall very much, but I had a nice ride today with Chance McDaniel. He showed me a place where you would picnic."

He made a face that reminded her of the one time Alejandro had caught her kissing one of the grooms. She had been fourteen.

Was that what this was now? Obviously, Alejandro had his secrets and would go so far to protect them as to lock himself in his room for weeks on end. As of yet, she did not have any secrets to speak of—except for the fact that she was sure her trip to McDaniel Acres had been less about proving Chance's guilt and more about Chance.

Yes, it was quite clear that Alejandro remembered the picnic spot—and did not necessarily approve of Chance taking her there. Just as he had not approved of her lowering herself to the level of kissing the hired help. "Chance has asked to escort me on other rides and to dinner. With Joaquin accompanying us, of course."

"Is that so," he said in that thoughtful voice, the one he'd used that morning. At least this time he hadn't said, "Who?"

He hadn't forbidden her to do those things—not a hint of worry at her being in the company of Chance McDaniel. Just…thoughtfulness. "Yes. So until you can remember anything about Chance McDaniel in connection with your abduction, I shall continue to do so. This is a good opportunity to investigate if he had any true motivations for wanting to harm you, after all."

Alejandro was shaking his head again—a small gesture, but one that made it clear that he didn't agree with this particular part of the plan.

She could hear Papa shouting in the distance. It sounded as if his business call had not gone according to plan and Gabriella doubted if she would get another quiet moment to speak with her brother for the rest of the day.

She stood and, under the pretense of gathering up Alejandro's cup to refill it, whispered, "Your secrets are safe with me."

He gave a curt nod with his head and then Papa was

back in the room, shouting about a deal that was on the verge of collapse.

Gabriella would keep her promise. If she kept the secret that Alejandro had been feeling better for some time… Well, then he would be in her debt. And that was not a bad place to have one's older brother.

But that didn't mean she wouldn't find out a little bit more.

Including whether or not Chance McDaniel would resort to violence to win Cara Windsor back.

Eight

Chance watched as the big black SUV pulled up along the paddock. The wedding was over and, being a Monday afternoon, his hotel was remarkably empty. This was as close to free time as he got.

And he was spending it with Gabriella del Toro.

He was *not* excited about her coming back out to the ranch. As far as he knew, she was being sent out here by that overbearing father of hers to look for "evidence" of his guilt or something ridiculous.

That didn't explain why he was looking forward to another ride. Maybe today, they'd get to race a little. Then they'd have dinner. He hadn't wanted to push his luck, so they'd still be eating Franny's home cooking. She'd saved him a couple of nice steaks with nothing more than, "Sure seems like a sweetheart," as an editorial comment.

Then Joaquin opened the back door and Gabriella's long legs slid out of the car. He saw today that instead of her riding jodhpurs and British-style boots, she had on a pair of sleek gray cowboy boots, a pair of dark jeans that fit her better than any pair of gloves ever could with a black belt at the waist and a light-colored denim shirt. God help him, she pulled a straw hat out of the backseat and settled it onto her black hair, once again pulled into a low braid. She was wearing her three crosses again, but that was it.

She'd been more of a princess the last time he'd seen her—both times, actually. But today? She was a cowgirl. She stepped around her guard and spotted him inside the barn door. Even at fifty feet, give or take, the sunlight shone off of her wide smile.

Oh, man—he was in trouble. What had been beautiful and refined before was now a little rougher looking, a little more ready to race.

A lot more ready to ride.

"Couldn't stay away, huh?" He couldn't help himself.

"I know Gale missed me—and my carrots," she replied as she headed toward him, her long legs closing the distance between them faster than he would have liked. The woman moved with a grace that he wanted to be sure to appreciate properly and he figured he was less likely to get blindsided by Joaquin if he was staring from a safe distance.

"I don't have her saddled yet." This had been on purpose. Part of her story hinged on being this great horsewoman. He wanted to see exactly how well she did with old Gale. "Beast is ready to go," he added to Joaquin. No need to push his luck with the big man.

She arched a manicured eyebrow at him, accepting his challenge. "Come on," he said, nodding his head in Gale's direction.

Gabriella walked beside him, her hand close enough to touch. Maybe he was imagining things, but he swore he could feel the warmth of her fingers as they swung past his hand. But Joaquin was about five feet behind them, so Chance kept his hands to himself.

He led her into the barn to where Gale was tethered in the middle of the aisle, her saddle waiting on the stall door. A bucket with a curry comb inside it was on the floor.

Maybe this wasn't a fair test—maybe she only rode in English saddles back home. But before he could tell her he'd do it, she had the comb in hand and was brushing down Gale's back, murmuring in Spanish the whole time.

Her English accent may be British, but damned if her Spanish wasn't pure poetry. Grooming a horse had never sounded so…sultry.

She settled the saddle blanket onto Gale's back. Then, exactly like a woman who knew what she was doing, she looped the stirrup over the horn of the saddle and set—not plopped—the saddle onto Gale's back.

A novice would have thrown the saddle up there, which made even the mellowest animal skitter around. But Gabriella had done everything perfectly.

As he watched, her fingers nimbly tightened the cinch strap and then she unhooked Gale from the tethers. When she turned to face Chance, the smile on her face was nothing short of victorious. She'd known exactly what he was about and more than exceeded his expectations.

What could he expect from her in bed? Her fingers moving with ease over his skin, her body responding to his every challenge?

Behind him, Joaquin cleared his throat.

Man, this was getting to be a problem.

Gabriella didn't seem concerned by the big man with the gun. Instead she only had eyes for him. "What would you like to show me today, Chance?"

Yes! a primitive part of his brain crowed in victory. His name on her lips had an immediate—and slightly awkward—effect on him. He went hard. Fast.

Luckily, between the jeans, the chaps and his buckle, there was little chance that anyone would notice his discomfort. Because that's what it was about to be, as she led Gale past him and he followed, eyeing his horse. Discomfort was mounting up with an erection. It bordered on hazardous to his health.

"I have a surprise for you," he replied, watching her hips sway as she walked out into the sunshine.

She paused and he felt Joaquin bristle. Oh, hell. Yeah, she probably didn't consider surprises a good thing. So he added, "A different part of the ranch—the part that tourists don't see. I want you to meet Slim."

Her cautious smile came back. "Slim? Is that a man or an animal?"

"He's a man," Chance replied, taking hold of her reins so she could mount up. "He's what we here in Texas call 'a crusty ol' fart.'"

She swung up into the saddle without a problem and he was forced to watch her bottom—full and round and barely contained by the jeans she wore—settle into the saddle. All he wanted to do was to run his fingers over that bottom and feel the fullness fill his hands.

This line of thinking did nothing to relieve his current condition.

Gabriella laughed again, her soft voice filling his ears. Man, he was in *so* much trouble. "I'm not entirely sure I understood that. Perhaps you should show me?"

Oh, he had things he wanted to show her, all right. But there were a few problems with that—problems that were bigger than Joaquin, who'd managed to heave his mass up onto Beast.

Problems such as Alex's missing memory. And half the town still thinking Chance had tried to do Alex in over a woman. And their father hating his ever-loving guts.

Beyond that, he had bigger problems. Maybe Alex would miraculously recover and Chance's name would be cleared and he could go back to being Chance McDaniel instead of the fictional character that looked just like him.

He had a terrible feeling that Alex might not be too

thrilled to know that Chance was having less-than-pure thoughts about his little sister.

Gabriella spun Gale in a neat circle so that she could look at him. Her eyes glowed with a warmth he hadn't seen in a woman's gaze in a long time. "Shall we?"

Was there any way to win here?

Nope.

"By all means, we shall."

He knew one thing. This whole mess might blow up in his face at any second.

But he wasn't going to quit trying.

Gabriella rode next to Chance. She couldn't keep the smile off her face, and she knew it. The breeze today held a hint of spring that made everything look greener.

Including his eyes. She couldn't help but meet Chance's gaze as he pointed things out. They took a different path this time, one that lead far away from the well-worn trail they'd taken to the picnic spot last time. But instead of growing more narrow or showing other signs of disuse, the path widened, tire treads clearly visible in the hardened dirt.

So wherever he was taking her wasn't some secret hidden away from the rest of the world. That was good.

Because when he'd said their destination was a surprise today, she'd been more than a little shocked that Joaquin hadn't hustled her back into the car at once. Taking her someplace where no one would think to look for them—or hear a struggle, much less gunshots—would be unacceptable.

But unless they changed course soon, it was clear that they were going someplace that was easily accessible and widely traveled.

"How is Alex today?"

The question seemed innocent—and sincere—but Gabriella hesitated. Papa had insisted that no one outside of the family know about Alejandro's recovery. He was afraid that if people knew Alejandro was starting to remember, his attackers would make another attempt. "Not much has changed," she lied, feeling horrid about doing so.

Chance seemed to take her at her word. Instead of pressing her further, he continued to point out features of his ranch.

"And over there," he said, pointing at a neat two-story house with a wide porch, "is my place."

"Lovely," she said. It was a bright yellow with green shutters. Empty flower planters hung under the windows. What did it look like on the inside? Back at Las Cruces, they had public rooms in the front where Papa took visitors. Those parlors were kept in a state of high shine in anticipation of impressing visitors.

But the rest of the house was far more comfortable. These had been the rooms that Gabriella had grown up in—the kitchen where she'd eaten her meals, the library where she'd taken her lessons with the other children on the estate—and her room. Those were the rooms she missed now.

Was Chance the same? Was the bunkhouse, as he called his motel, his public parlor? What did his private rooms look like? "Do I get a tour?"

Chance shot her a look she couldn't quite read. Was he pleased she'd showed an interest? Or was there something more to it? "Not today. I usually have one of the hotel maids come down every other week. It's kind of a mess right now." Then he leaned toward her. "Besides, not sure your man there would think that was a good idea."

Gabriella felt herself sigh. Chance was correct. No matter how she tried to dress it up as part of her investigation into Alejandro's abduction, seeing where Chance McDaniel lived had nothing to do with her brother and everything to do with the man riding next to her.

At least he hadn't said no. Just not today. That implied that he might very well show her his home at a later time.

Because he anticipated more rides.

They rode past the sunny house and on to a series of sheds and buildings, all made of corrugated metal. "What's this?"

"The shop area." He rode up to the first building and dismounted, tying his horse to a post. "Here, let me help you."

She tensed, almost expecting him to lift her out of the saddle and definitely wishing he would. She would love to feel his callused hands settle around her waist—would love to feel them on her skin.

But he didn't. Perhaps ever-mindful of Joaquin, he took the reins and held Gale still while Gabriella dismounted. Then he kept a respectable distance between them as he led her into the first building. "Here's where we keep the mowers and ATVs—we use this stuff every day around here," he said, his voice echoing off the metal walls.

"How…nice," she replied, not knowing what else she was supposed to say.

They walked to the next building. "The bigger tractors and implements are in here. We rotate planting cover crops and alfalfa in the fields. Over there's my baler," he said, pointing to a large, square machine.

"Lovely." As lovely as one could consider a baler. Whatever that was.

They walked past the baler and through a door at the back of the building. Joaquin kept close, no doubt worried about an ambush.

They entered what was clearly a workroom, the sounds of grinding metal filling the air. "Hey, Slim!" Chance yelled loudly, but the grinding didn't let up. "Be right back," he said to them as he headed toward the noise.

Gabriella looked around. *What a workroom,* she thought in awe. Pegboards lined the walls with such a variety of tools as she had never seen—and that was saying something. She had a well-appointed workroom back on the estate in an outbuilding, but this was something on an entirely different scale. Clamps, pliers, screwdrivers and so much more hung from the pegboards in descending order. She had smaller tools, but some of those clamps were designed to hold posts together, it appeared.

And those were just the tools on the walls. In her shop, she had a kiln and a small, portable furnace to melt her metal, grinders and other tools to shape the stones. Here, there were planers, lathes, saws and all manner of woodworking tools. Then, in the back, she spied a furnace—an honest-to-goodness furnace, the kind used to fire iron.

Suddenly the grinding stopped and she heard an older male voice say, "Eh? Oh, Chance, my boy!"

Then an older man that matched the voice came into view, a visor pushed back on his head, a dirty kerchief tied at his neck and a worn apron covering up his clothes. His steel-toed boots were so old that the steel was no longer covered by leather. He was patting Chance on the shoulder with a massive gloved hand.

"Brought someone to meet you," Chance was saying. He turned to Gabriella. "Gabriella, this is Daryl Slocum—also known as Slim."

Although he was probably well into his sixties—it was difficult to tell with the gear he had on—Slim rolled his eyes. "Never did cotton to the name Daryl."

What did "cotton" mean? Besides a plant they made fabric from.

"Slim," Chance went on before she could figure it out, "over there is Joaquin and this is Gabriella del Toro." Slim gave her a sideways glance, which made Chance add, "Alex's sister."

As realization dawned in Slim's eyes, Gabriella felt uncharacteristically frustrated. Of course she was "Alex's" sister—but she hated that being the thing everyone knew her by. She was always Alejandro's sister or Rodrigo's daughter. It was only when it came to her jewelry—her art—that she was Gabriella. That was how she preferred it.

Slim nodded—actually, it was almost a bow. "Well, howdy do, ma'am. A pleasure." But Slim made no move to shake her hand or—thankfully—hug her as Franny had done. "We sure were glad when they found Alex. I've been praying for him."

The sentiment caught her off guard. "Why, thank you. He is a little better."

At this, Chance gave her a quizzical look—one so brief she wasn't sure she'd actually seen it. Then he was talking again. "Slim made the chandeliers in the bunkhouse."

"You did? Those were beautiful!"

Slim blushed a deep maroon. "Shucks, it weren't nothin'. Just testing out a few designs. And I bought the shades." He said this last bit as if it made the ironwork little better than a pile of metal.

"They were perfect for the space. Simply amazing." She was being honest, too.

"Gabriella here is an artist." Chance motioned her closer. "Show him your stuff."

She frowned at Chance for the "stuff," but she removed her jewelry and pieced it together for Slim.

"I'll be dipped—you made that?" Slim whistled long and low when she nodded, pleased with the compliment.

At least, she assumed it was a compliment. She wasn't sure what "dipped" meant in this context.

"Gabriella's going to be staying on in Royal for a bit longer," Chance explained as Slim tried his hand at assembling the three crosses. "I thought she might need to borrow some tools."

What? Had he said—borrow *tools?*

Slim grinned. "Sure. Lemme show you what I got—no gold or silver, but I got a little bit of everything."

Even though Gabriella followed Slim, she couldn't absorb what he was showing her. All she could do was stare at Chance.

He was providing her with tools—the very things she hadn't taken the time to pack. Working on her jewelry and riding were the two things she'd missed most about Las Cruces—and Chance McDaniel was single-handedly giving her both. Without her having to ask. He just did it.

She thought Slim was showing her industrial-size spools of wire, but all she saw was Chance. Then his gaze met hers and she was filled with that unexpected sense of coming home. The emotion was so strong that her legs felt a little weak.

Of course Papa and Alejandro took care of her, but their definition of "taking care of her" was usually more limited to what was too unsafe for her to do—show her horses, attend university, date. To do anything outside of the patrolled walls of Las Cruces. Taking care of her was locking her up tight and giving her just enough to do to make her forget about being a prisoner in her own home.

Chance? He showed her around. He introduced her to people who obviously cared for him. He didn't keep himself separate from the staff the way Papa did. Instead he acted as if they were his family, and they the same.

Perhaps she was being foolish. This was probably nothing more than Chance had done for Alejandro, after all—welcomed him onto his land and into his life. Perhaps this was the sort of man Chance McDaniel was—friend to one and all.

But when Slim led them back through a row, Chance

put his hand on her. It was a light touch—one that started at her shoulder, one that probably signaled nothing more than a polite "you go first." But when she did, his hand did not leave her.

Instead his fingertips floated over her shoulder and down her back, ending above her bottom before they moved sideways. Then, briefly, he rested his hand on her waist.

The touch was unlike anything she'd ever felt before. Luiz, the stable boy, had touched her with fumbling, unsure hands. Raoul, her frequent escort to public events, had always taken hold of her arm as if he already owned her. There had never been a moment in which he'd asked for permission—not from her. Her father had given Raoul permission to accompany her and that was all the permission he needed.

But Chance's touch? It was something soft and gentle—confident but unassuming. His hand lingered at her waist for a moment longer, then they were through the narrow row and, with a final gentle squeeze, he withdrew.

"I do a lot of wrought iron," Slim was saying, but Gabriella found herself turning back to look at Chance.

"You okay?" he asked in a tone of voice that felt every bit as confident as his hand had.

"I…" She cleared her throat, thankful that Slim was now demonstrating his bellows. "I am surprised, that is all."

One of his eyebrows moved up, making him look playful. "A good surprise?"

"One of the best I have ever had." She wanted to do something completely rash, like throw her arms around his neck and show him exactly what she thought of his surprise—but then a blast of heat from Slim's furnace hit her.

"Any time you want to come out, you just give me a call. Slim here has been working on the ranch for close to fifty years. He's got every tool known to mankind. Never throws anything away."

Then—in full view of both Slim and Joaquin—he reached over and ran his hand down the length of her arm, lightly squeezing before he withdrew and took a step away from her.

Not a touch of ownership. A question. Asking permission.

Suddenly she wanted to say *yes* in a way she'd never wanted to before.

She glanced at Joaquin. The scowl on his face was more than enough to remind her that saying *yes* to Chance—heavens, just saying *thank you* in the way she wanted to—would be a challenge. How would she convince him to join her here on a regular basis? Working in the shop had nothing to do with investigating the ranch in regard to Alejandro's disappearance.

"So," Slim said, seemingly unaware of the unspoken battle she was waging with herself. "Whaddya think?"

"I have never worked in iron." She did not want to refuse Chance's gifts and it had nothing to do with not wanting to insult his honor. It had everything to do with the gratitude that filled her as she looked around the shop.

She could ride. She could work—not as she normally did, but it would be a new skill all the same. And—most importantly—she could be free of the confines of Alejandro's house.

She could be here. With Chance.

"Heck fire, I'll teach you! We'll start with the basics and then you can try your hand at some smaller pieces. I got some extra aprons—not sure if I've got one big enough for your husband there," he added as an afterthought.

"Joaquin is not my husband. He is my guard."

"Oh—right, my bad. I bet you all are a little jumpy

after what happened to our Alex. Sure, bring him along. Franny'll feed him if he helps out!"

At this, Joaquin's face turned a brighter shade of red, although nothing else about him changed. The others might not have noticed his blush, but Gabriella did.

Maybe, Gabriella thought with a new hopefulness rising up in her, it would not be so very difficult to convince Joaquin to return to the ranch on a more regular basis after all.

She looked at Chance and smiled. "My door is always open," he said, and she knew he was trying to sound as if this open invitation was the sort he would make to any visitor to his ranch.

But that's not what she heard. Instead she heard an unspoken *to you* in there—"My door is always open to you."

Then he added, "All you have to do is ask, Gabriella. The answer will be yes."

Yes.

The answer would be *yes.*

Nine

The look on Gabriella's face was something to behold.

As they said their goodbyes to Slim and headed back to where the horses were tethered, she kept those big beautiful eyes latched on to him with the kind of look that made him wish he was in a honky-tonk and it was Friday night.

When they made it back to the horses, she turned to him. "You did this for me?"

"Yup." Out of the corner of his eye, he saw Joaquin take hold of Beast's reins. He wasn't making any sudden moves toward his weapon.

Gabriella didn't seem concerned about whatever Joaquin may or may not be doing. She only had eyes for him.

Which had been the point.

She took a step closer to him. The space between them was only a couple of feet, but it sure felt a lot less than that. He could almost reach out and touch her again.

He did no such thing.

But God help him, he wanted to—and not as if he was afraid of who might be watching. He wanted to pull her into his arms and take the kiss that she sure looked as though she wanted to give him.

"This is the most thoughtful thing anyone has ever done for me." Her voice was soft. Warm.

Inviting.

He stood rooted to the spot because if he moved, he knew he'd take what she was offering and he also knew that he'd get shot and he really wished he didn't know both of those things at the same time. "Welcome," he managed to say without pulling her into his chest.

She shot him a look that took everything soft and sweet about her and turned it hard and needy in a heartbeat. "I would like for you to put your hands in your pockets."

If anyone else had asked him to do that, Chance would have known they were planning on punching him and he'd have had none of it. But Gabriella wasn't going to crack him across the cheek because of Slim, was she?

The light in her eyes said no. Hell, everything about her said no.

So he did.

Her gaze flicked back to where Chance was pretty sure Joaquin was still watching them. He could only hope the barrel of a gun wasn't pointed at the back of his skull. "As you can see, he is not touching me," she said in an all-too-businesslike voice.

Then, before he could make any sense of that, she stepped toward him, flung her arms around his neck and kissed the holy hell out of him. Her teeth clipped his lower lip and he desperately wanted to tilt his head to the side so that he could taste her better—taste all of her—but he couldn't move. He didn't dare.

When it ended—and damn it, it did end—she pulled away so quickly she almost stumbled. And he almost got his hands jerked out of his pockets to grab her.

She regained her footing and took that all-important step away from him. "You see? He did not touch me."

She wasn't talking to him. She was talking to Joaquin. It was almost as if she had something to prove and he was it.

"I want to race back to the barn," she announced, her color high and her eyes bright. "Straight back."

He knew she was asking her guard—not him—but he answered anyway. He barely managed to avoid saying *darlin'* but somehow he kept that part in his head only. "All you had to do was ask. You knew the answer would be yes."

Man, that smile—her wanting to race—that *kiss*.

They mounted up and took off, hell-for-leather. He could hear Gabriella's laughter over the pounding of the horses' hooves—even over the sound of Joaquin cussing in an interesting mixture of English and Spanish.

Was he a greedy bastard? Maybe. Maybe that's exactly why he reined Ranger in a bit, why he let Gale pull ahead. He couldn't touch her—even she admitted as much with her request to put his hands in his pockets.

But he sure as hell was going to watch her ride.

Her backside fit into that saddle as though he'd had it custom-made for her. She rode low against Gale's neck, no doubt urging the horse on faster. He had a hell of a view.

She liked to ride. Hell, she *loved* to ride. She was interested in stuff like wrought iron. She saddled her horse. He'd be willing to bet a steak dinner she'd muck the barn. For a sheltered, refined woman, she wasn't afraid of the hard work that made up most of his days.

He'd never met another woman like her. Cara hadn't been willing to get a little dusty, a little dirty. Cara had never wanted to ride so hard the horses worked themselves into a lather.

Gabriella let out a whoop as Gale charged over a small hill. They were close to the barn, but if he could, he'd watch her ride with this wild abandon all damn day.

And all night. His mind took the view of Gabriella riding hard in the saddle and put it right into his big king bed. Oh, she'd ride him, all right. After that kiss, there wasn't any doubt in his mind about it. He could only hope he could make her whoop and holler as much as racing did.

Far too soon, the barn came into view. He had no idea if Joaquin was behind them—he hadn't hung around to see if the big man had been able to keep up—but he couldn't bring himself to care. His blood was pounding and he couldn't remember feeling this damned happy.

Gabriella slowed Gale to a trot, which meant he had to stop focusing on the way she filled out a saddle and start thinking with his brain again.

"That was so much fun!" she said. "Can we do that tomorrow?"

"You already know what I'm gonna say to that, don't you?"

She gave him the kind of look out of the corner of her eye that made him want to say to hell with Joaquin and guards and what her father might say if he knew she'd kissed him. All he wanted to do was to change course and lead her back to his home—the one that stood silent and empty out on the range, except for when the maid came to clean—and lead her up to his bed.

She was a bright, shining star in the middle of his dark Texas winter and all he wanted to do was to bask in her light. Bask in *her*.

But he also didn't want to die today. So he went a different direction. "Have you managed to get out of the house? I mean, besides to come here."

Some of the light died in her eyes. It hurt him to watch. "I got a haircut, but otherwise, no."

"Tell you what. After we ride tomorrow, I'll take you out. Royal's a nice town. You should see it."

"Really?" Her eyes brightened, but it was short-lived. "Do you think Papa will allow it?"

He was willing to bet the answer was going to be no to that one, but he wasn't about to let something ridiculous like a grown woman asking for parental permission to muck up his date. "Do you want to go out?"

He hadn't asked that particular question in, well, probably close to twenty years. Dates as an adult were more "Can I escort you to an event" than "Going out."

But what was he supposed to do? Part of Gabriella—the social part—still seemed very much the sheltered young girl. No matter how much energy she'd put into kissing him or how good she looked on a horse, he had the feeling he couldn't rush it.

She tilted her head, as if she were debating the question. "Yes," she said, and it did sound like her final answer. "I would like to go out."

Just then, Joaquin came riding up. Beast's sides were heaving and the man on his back looked mad enough to kill Chance the slow, painful way—and, what's more, he looked as though he was going to enjoy doing it.

But before Joaquin could do anything else, Gabriella announced, "Chance will be escorting me out to dinner in Royal tomorrow night, Joaquin," in that same all-business voice.

Joaquin opened his mouth to say something, but she held up a hand and cut him off. "I came here to see America. Chance is merely showing me around."

There was no *merely* about it, not after that kiss. But if that's what it took, then that's what it took. "Yup. You're coming, right?" Because he also had a feeling that trying to cut the big man out was the surest way to not get a date with Gabriella del Toro.

Joaquin towered over them from Beast's big back, clearly displeased with this situation. Would he sign off on Gabriella coming back out to the ranch tomorrow to spend the day hammering iron?

"Or," Gabriella said, and Chance heard a new note in her voice—hard. Stubborn. Suddenly, Gabriella was a woman who could be cruel when she wanted to be—and right now, she wanted to be. "Or I could spend tomorrow cooking. Perhaps I could try lasagna again. I only burned the noodles that one time."

Burned the noodles? Hoo, boy—that sounded like something the hogs wouldn't even eat.

At the look on Joaquin's face, Chance had to bite his tongue to keep from laughing. It was obvious from the way the big guy's lips curled in disgust and he rubbed his chest right where heartburn probably hit him that, despite Gabriella's many talents, cooking was not something she did well.

"The Texas Cattleman's Club has a great restaurant." He said it to Gabriella, but he pitched his voice so that Joaquin would get the message loud and clear. "Some of the best steaks in Texas."

Dang, there was that smile again—the one that made him want to haul her off that horse and kiss her until they both felt like whooping and hollering.

Yeah, he knew what she was playing at. He was only too happy to play along.

The moment that thought crossed his mind, it dragged a different thought along for the ride. What if this—the sob story about her mom, the smiles, especially the kiss—all of it, was just playing? What if she was playing him?

He'd thought Alex Santiago had been one of his best friends—a man he could trust with his life. Where had that gotten him?

Dumped by his lady friend, Cara. The prime suspect in the kidnapping and assault of Alejandro del Toro. A veritable pariah in his hometown.

Alex Santiago—Alejandro del Toro—whoever the hell was locked up in that house—had done his damnedest to screw up Chance's whole life.

How quick had Gabriella del Toro turned on Joaquin to

get what she wanted? He wouldn't have thought a woman could make cooking dinner sound so mean-spirited, but she did.

What if she didn't like him? What if she was trying to muck up the works with her bright smiles and warm looks and sweet, hot kisses? What if she was trying to get him distracted or off balance?

What if she was using him?

But why? That was the question he couldn't answer. Of course, he didn't exactly have a handle as to why Alex had screwed him over, either. All he knew was that he had been screwed over. Royally.

Then Joaquin sighed so heavily that it almost blew Chance's hat off his head.

"Excellent." She did sound awfully damn pleased. But then she added, "I am sure Papa will be so busy with his work he will not notice I am out," in the hurt kind of voice that did its best to rip his heart out of his chest.

He wanted to protect her, by God.

But who would protect him from her?

Gabriella prepared for her date with the greatest of care. She took extra time with her hair and makeup and chose her outfit with Chance in mind.

The day had been something special. She'd met Chance at his barn at nine that morning. They'd taken a slow ride out to Slim's workshop, where Chance had left her and Joaquin for several hours. Then he'd arrived at a quarter to twelve with a basket.

They'd had lunch at the picnic spot. The sun had been just warm enough. Plus, Joaquin had taken his meal leaning back against a tree, which had provided them with enough privacy to have a real conversation as they ate Franny's cold fried chicken and potato salad and drank sweet iced tea.

It had been one of the more romantic events in her life. Just a quiet meal in a secluded, wooded location. She'd almost been able to pretend that Joaquin hadn't been there.

But not so much that she'd done the rash thing and kissed Chance again.

Even though she had wanted to.

After they'd packed up the saddlebags, they'd ridden back to the workshop. Gabriella had made some good progress in hammering. She'd only been able to produce a slightly flat, lumpy piece of wrought iron, but she'd managed to do so with Slim's approval.

Chance had returned for her at three. He'd admired her lump of iron and then offered to race her back to the barn. However, her arms had felt like lead after the work she'd done, so they'd rode at an easy pace.

"I'll pick you up tonight…say, around six-thirty?" is what he'd said from the safety of the saddle.

"Yes. Dinner at your club, correct?"

And he'd flashed her that grin that always made her feel as though she'd returned home after a long, arduous journey. "You betcha."

So now, after one of the best days in her memory, she was trying to gauge what people wore to dine at private clubs in Texas. Was her black pencil skirt and green silk top too much? But they were in Texas. Perhaps it would not be enough. This was the nicest outfit that wasn't a gown and wasn't pants she'd packed. If she threw the matching jacket on over it, she could attend a business meeting with Papa or go to court, if that was what was required.

She was a mess of confusion. She couldn't believe she'd kissed Chance yesterday—and so boldly, in front of Joaquin. That was out of character for her. What was worse, she couldn't believe she *hadn't* kissed him today.

What was she thinking? Chance hadn't been cleared in Alejandro's abduction. Her brother could have been concealed in any one of those buildings—and those were the ones that Chance had chosen to show her. He probably had any number of other buildings across his property.

He'd taken her riding. He'd introduced her to those people who seemed closest to him. Heavens, she was learning to work in wrought iron because he had realized how much she missed her work.

Never before had she felt a man pay such attention to her—her, not her security detail, not to everyone around her.

Just her. When she was with Chance, she felt as if she was the only woman in the world.

As she tried to decide if she would stick with her emerald Tres Cruces set or if she wanted to go with the bold gold necklace that was comprised of a rectangular plate inlaid with emeralds and rubies, someone knocked on her door. "Yes?"

It was Alejandro. He looked better today than he had yesterday and three times better than he had the day before. He seemed to be remembering how to exist in his own skin again after a long holiday somewhere else.

"Alejandro! How are you? Is everything all right?"

He flinched. "Fine," he said, coming in to sit on the end of her bed.

"Are you sure? Do you feel well?"

"No. I just..."

"What? Do you remember something? Something about Chance?"

"No—why?" He looked her over—her tight skirt and the close-cut emerald-green silk top. For her, the outfit displayed a surprising amount of cleavage.

They stared at each other. Gabriella was trying to gauge what her brother might do if he correctly guessed that her interest in Chance McDaniel had nothing to do with the kidnapping. Would he forbid her from seeing Chance? Or tell Papa—who would then forbid her from seeing Chance again and also subject her to another lecture about her safety being the most important thing?

She could *not* bear another lecture about how her safety was his only priority. What of her happiness? Did that mean nothing to him?

Did that mean anything to Alejandro?

"I want you to call me Alex from now on," Alejandro announced into the tense silence.

"What?"

"Alex. That's my name."

She opened her mouth to ask if he was feeling well or perhaps if he had bumped his head again. But she quickly shut it. The look on her brother's face was not confused or unsure. He was quite serious.

What was she to make of this? He'd said it in that American accent of his. Now that she thought about it, she wasn't sure she'd heard him say a thing in Spanish since she'd arrived in Texas. And now he was choosing his American name.

"I'm going out with Chance tonight." She couldn't imagine another situation where she would be so honest about her feelings, except for this one. "He has also extended an open invitation to ride whenever I so choose and also to join Slim in the workshop, should I wish to learn how to work wrought iron."

Alejandro—Alex—nodded. "Which horse does he have you riding?"

"Nightingale."

Alex gave her a surprised look. "She's one of his prize mares. He doesn't normally let anyone ride her."

"Who did you ride?" It seemed as if a great deal of his memory had "suddenly" returned.

"Quarter horse named Spike. He gave me that horse because he knew his Ranger could always beat Spike."

She grinned at him. "Joaquin rides this massive animal called Beast. I think he may be afraid of the…mule? Yes, mule."

"Beast?" Alex laughed and slapped his knee. It seemed very much the sort of thing Chance would do, but it was not something she could remember her brother doing. How much better was he feeling? "I'd like to see Joaquin afraid of anything!"

"Joaquin does not trust Chance. He does not want me to see him."

Now was the time for honesty. If Alejandro—Alex—oh, heavens, that was going to take some getting used to—objected to her being in Chance's company, he would have to speak his piece or hold it forever.

He did no such thing. Instead he said, "Now that I'm better, Papa expects me to spend more time working with him. He has some deals that are taking up his time."

Although she did not think he meant the words to hurt her, they did anyway. All Papa cared about was that she was safe. After that basic requirement had been met, he cared very little at all.

Alex stood. "I can keep him distracted. There's no need for you to stare at the walls." Gabriella was struck dumb as he walked over to her and placed a brotherly kiss on her forehead. "Go. Have fun."

"I shall," she managed to reply.

Alex turned to leave, but paused with his hand on the doorknob. "I have one request."

"Name it." For the gift he was giving her, she would do anything he asked.

"Take Joaquin, to be safe—and don't tell Chance I'm better. Not yet."

Before she could ask him what he meant by that, he was gone.

The doorbell rang. Chance was here for her.

She knew that Alex would not answer it.

Ten

Chance was feeling good about tonight. Mostly because Gabriella had given him a little peck on the cheek when she'd come to the door, but also because she'd been up in the front seat of his extended cab F-250 and Joaquin had sat in the back.

Chance held the door for Gabriella at the entrance to the Texas Cattleman's Club. He hadn't been here in a long while. Things had gotten to the point where he hadn't been comfortable coming into his favorite hangout. The TCC had become less a place to have a beer than an exercise in navigating shark-infested waters. Better to stay home and eat Franny's cooking or shoot the breeze with Marty and Slim. There, at least, no one treated him like a convicted criminal who hadn't managed to get arrested yet.

Coming here tonight was a risk. But Alex was back. Maybe not all back in the head, but he was no longer missing. People had to have realized that Chance hadn't had a damn thing to do with the whole mess. Right?

He sure as hell hoped so as Joaquin brought up the rear of their little party. Three was starting to be very crowded. But he put on a happy face and guided Gabriella into the TCC.

"They just added the day care," he said, showing Gabriella the new center.

She gave him an odd look as she said, "Very nice," and he realized what he'd said.

They. Not *we.*

"I voted for it," he hurried to add. When had the TCC become a *they?* Probably about the time he'd become a suspect.

Maybe this wasn't such a good idea.

Before he could do anything—point toward the dining room, announce that he'd remembered the restaurant was closed tonight and they should try Claire's instead, a voice called out, "Chance! Where have you been, man?"

Chance whipped around to see Sam Gordon bearing down on them, a huge grin on his face. Someone here was glad to see him. Thank God for small favors. "Sam, you old dog—what's this I hear about Lila?"

"Twins! Girls! Twin girls! Brook was six pounds, six ounces and Eve—she was seven minutes after Brook—was six pounds, four ounces." Sam giggled—a sound that Chance was positive he'd never heard the man make.

"That Lila of yours is quite a woman!" He meant it. Even though there wasn't a lot of love lost between Chance and Beau Hacket, Lila had always gone to great lengths to distance herself from her father and brother. Chance had admired her for striking out on her own and making her own way. A way that now included Sam Gordon.

"I'm so amazed by her." Sam's voice drifted off into sheer awe. But then he snapped back to himself. "Here—cigars for everyone!" And he thrust two cigars at Chance.

Then, a moment later, he offered one to Joaquin. "Here you go, *amigo.*" This time he didn't sound quite so overjoyed.

Sam's gaze darted from Chance to Gabriella to Joaquin—who, after a moment's hesitation, took the proffered cigar with a mumbled, *"Gracias. Felicitaciónes."*

Was this about to go south on him? Only one way to find out. Chance bit the bullet. "Sam Gordon, this is Gabriella del Toro and Joaquin. They're my guests for dinner tonight."

Sam's eyebrows shot so far up at this announcement that they darn near cleared his forehead. "Well, a pleasure to meet you, Ms. del Toro." But he didn't offer his hand. Instead he sort of bowed—without taking his eyes off Joaquin *or* the slight bulge in his jacket where his gun was. "Uh, how is Alex? Or is it Alejandro?"

Chance felt Gabriella stiffen beside him, but her face betrayed no other emotion than pleasantness. It was the exact same expression she'd had on her face when he'd walked into Alex's house and found her the first time.

Then, he hadn't noticed anything was wrong. Now? Now that he'd spent his afternoons riding with her and had meals with her and seen the real her? Now he could tell that she was nervous. Unsure of what to do next.

He could sympathize.

"Thank you for your concern," she finally said in her soft voice. "He is doing better. And he prefers to be called Alex."

"Okay, great—good to hear." Sam and Gabriella made a little more small talk about babies, but Chance wasn't paying attention.

Instead he was staring at Gabriella. They'd spent a better part of the past week together and she'd said nothing about Alex wanting to be called Alex. She'd called him Alejandro when they were together. Always.

Whenever he asked about Alex, she said he was the same. When had he decided he wanted to be called Alex? And why hadn't she told Chance that?

Was she lying to Sam? Or had she been lying to him?

Damn.

"Well, see you around, old dog," Sam said as he clapped Chance on the back.

"And congratulations again on the girls," Chance said as Sam left them.

The three of them stood there for a second. Across the room, Chance noticed Paul Windsor talking to some of his buddies. He'd spent time with Paul when he and Cara had been dating. Paul was a nice enough fellow, but Chance hadn't liked the man's attitude toward his daughter—as if she were merely a pawn to be used as he saw fit for the family business, Windsor Energy. Chance had always had the feeling that he didn't bring enough to the table for Cara and that, if the relationship had gotten that far, Paul wouldn't have given him permission to ask for Cara's hand in marriage.

Since Chance had become a suspect in Alex Santiago's disappearance, Paul Windsor had acted plenty justified in feeling that Chance had never been good enough for Cara. Paul had been one of the first to question Chance's possible motives. Hell, it was almost as if the man wanted Chance to take the blame.

Paul glanced across the space and met Chance's eyes before he turned a mercenary look to Gabriella. Something cold flittered over his face and, with a smile that bordered on cruel, turned back to his conversation. The whole thing had taken ten seconds, tops, but a worried pit in Chance's stomach made him think there'd been something else going on—something beyond Paul Windsor feeling justified that Chance as a kidnapping suspect proved that he'd never been good enough for Cara.

Chance didn't like this. He didn't like always feeling guilty until proved innocent and he sure as hell didn't like feeling the same way about Gabriella. He didn't want to think she was anything like her brother. He wanted to believe that she'd been nothing but up front with him—that everything she'd said was the truth, the whole truth and nothing but the truth.

Except that every time he started to believe that, she'd do something that threw her whole character into question. Such as tell Sam Gordon instead of Chance that her brother was Alex and not Alejandro.

Damn it all.

He skipped the rest of the tour and ushered them toward the restaurant. For a Monday, the place was hopping. Over half the tables were full, and warm laughter filled the room. As the server lead them to a table—for three, double damn it—the laughter died off as people watched him walk with the traitor Alex's sister and her armed thug.

It made a part of him ache. Would he ever get to feel as though he was part of this again? Or would he always be tainted by someone else's guilt?

Yeah, this had been an epic mistake. But it was too late now. Everyone knew he was here and, between Sam Gordon and Paul Windsor, they probably all knew who Gabriella was, to boot. He had no choice but to brazen this out. McDaniels did not tuck tail and run.

He let Joaquin have the seat with his back to the wall and held the chair for Gabriella so that she could have a nice view of the room. He put his back to the room as a sign to Joaquin that he wasn't worried.

They placed their orders and waited. Long gone was the easy conversation from the picnic lunch today. Instead Gabriella sat with her hands primly folded in her lap, her shoulders back and that blankly pleasant look on her face. To a stranger—to most of the people in this room—she would look perfectly normal.

But he could tell she wasn't. Her lips were pressed together extra hard, without a trace of the easy smile that she favored him with.

At least Joaquin pretty much looked and acted the same as always—grumpy, borderline violent and put out to be here.

Every so often, Chance would hear his name. He'd crane around in his seat only to realize that no one was talking *to* him—they were talking *about* him. All of Paul Windsor's cronies appeared to be working overtime to spread God only knew what kind of rumors about him. Or Gabriella. Or, worse yet, him *and* Gabriella. He didn't want to guess what they were saying about Joaquin.

No one came over to talk. Sam Gordon had been a fluke, that much was obvious. Instead people waved at him and went back to whatever gossip they were intent on spreading like manure on a field.

The waitress brought their food. After several minutes of silent eating, Gabriella set her knife and fork aside and folded her hands in her lap again. "What's the matter?" Had this evening gone so wrong that even the food had not lived up to expectations?

She sighed, but her shoulders didn't slump down in defeat. Just a lone little weary sigh. "Is it that they are afraid of me? Or you?"

"I don't think they're afraid of either of us. Maybe Joaquin." At this, the big man managed to actually look guilty. "Sorry. It's just…this is a small town. Word gets around fast."

"Ah." She dropped her gaze, the barest hint of color in her cheeks. "We are the evening's entertainment?"

"It's my fault. I thought…" Well, he'd thought people might be decent, or at least give him the benefit of the doubt.

He decided to change the subject. "He wants to be called Alex now, does he?"

The color in her cheeks deepened. Why did she have to be so beautiful? Why did he have to be so attracted to her? Why couldn't things be simpler, as they'd been long before Alex Santiago had mucked up his world?

"He seems to respond better to that name. I'm..." She swallowed. She was about to lie to him, he realized. He could see it coming and couldn't do a damn thing about it. "I'm hoping it will help his recovery to stick to the name that draws a more positive reaction from him."

"Is that a fact." It wasn't a question.

"Yes." She cleared her throat. By now her cheeks were redder than a tomato in August. But she lifted her head, that blank pleasantness almost a challenge to him. "I do not wish to speak of him tonight."

That meant she wasn't going to try to backtrack out of her lie. But it also meant she wasn't going to tell him another one. "Well, you just let me know when you do wish to speak of him, okay?"

The look of pain that bled the beautiful right out of her blush made him feel like a jerk. But he wasn't the one who was being jerky here, was he? She'd told the lie. She expected him to go along with it? He was an honest fellow. He was not the bad guy here.

Yeah, dinner had been a mistake.

"It's not like that." Her voice was so soft he almost didn't hear her.

"You tell me what it's like, then. You know why we're the evening's entertainment? It's because your brother—him of which we do not speak—rolled into town and decided I was an easy mark. He set me up, stole my girl and disappeared, leaving me to deal with the wreckage."

Joaquin shot him a look and Chance realized that his voice might have gotten a little louder. Okay, a lot louder. But damn it, he was tired of being the one everyone gossiped about. He wanted his name cleared so things could go back to normal.

Back to being lonely.

No. He pushed back against that thought, against the thought of Gabriella astride Gale. Against the quiet of the picnic lunch today. So what if he'd had more fun in the past week than he'd had in months? So what if Franny adored her and Slim thought she was "somethin'"? So what if Gabriella had kissed him as though her life depended on it—and if he'd thought of nothing but ever since?

None of that mattered. She'd go back to Mexico and he'd still be here in Royal, dealing with the wreckage.

Too late, he realized the restaurant was silent. Everyone was listening to them now.

"Let's just go," he said. It came out as a snarl, but what the hell.

"Yes." She stood, as composed as ever. Only the slightest downturn at the corner of her mouth gave her away. "Let's."

The drive home was painful. He pulled up in front of Alex's house. In the dark, the place had a malicious look to it, as if it had already eaten Alex and was waiting to swallow Gabriella, too.

He put the truck in park but didn't shut it off. Which made him feel even worse. He *was* being a jerk now, not even offering to walk her to the door. That's why she had an armed guard, right?

"Joaquin," she said in her all-business voice. "Please go check on Alex."

The big man huffed behind Chance and made no move to exit the vehicle.

"Now, please. I wish to speak to Chance alone." It was the most polite order he'd ever heard anyone give.

Yeah, Chance said silently to himself. He had a few things he wanted to say without risking a near-death experience. *Get out of the truck, man.*

Joaquin didn't.

Gabriella turned to glare at her guard. "I am twenty-seven years of age, Joaquin. I have the right to have a private conversation without having it reported back to my father. Stop treating me like a child or I will have you reassigned." She leaned back, her voice dropping a dangerous octave. "And I *will* have you reassigned."

Man, if he'd thought the silence had been heavy before, it was downright crushing now. But he didn't want to say anything. This was clearly between the two of them and it sure looked as though Gabriella could defend herself.

Then, unexpectedly, Joaquin yielded. The truck door opened and shut, and he was gone. He crossed in front of the truck and shot Chance a mean look before he walked up the path to the front door. But the door didn't open. So they weren't truly alone.

Before Chance could determine how much Joaquin could see from his perch on the porch a good fifty feet away, Gabriella grabbed him and hauled his face down to hers. The kiss this time was different—instead of the happy-to-the-point-of-ecstatic kiss that she'd given him yesterday, this one had an edge to it. As though she was trying to prove something.

He couldn't tell who she was trying to prove it to—him or herself.

Well, she could keep on trying. He wasn't playing this game. He kept his hands on the wheel.

When her tongue traced his lips, his resolve started to waver. It wavered a whole hell of a lot more when she slid her fingers up into his hair. The feeling of her hands on him did some mighty funny things to him. In fact, the things that were happening below his belt were freaking *hilarious.*

He couldn't think. Well, he could, but that wasn't thinking in a right sense. Instead of thinking about whether or not he could trust her, he was thinking about the way her teeth felt as she nipped at his lower lip.

She pulled away. He couldn't believe how much it hurt to let her do it, but he kept his white-knuckled grip on the steering wheel. Hell, he was lucky he hadn't snapped the whole thing off the steering column at this rate.

"Do you want me?" she breathed as she ran her fingers over his cheeks. Her chest was heaving and, in that top, that was saying something. She sounded seductive—hell, she *was* seductive—but there was something else in her eyes. It almost looked as though she was afraid of what he might say.

Was it a trick question? Because the answer was *yes.* She may be setting him up but he wasn't sure he gave a damn.

Don't be an idiot. He hadn't asked enough questions when he'd let Cara go. He needed answers almost as much as he needed to pull her into his arms.

"I want the woman who likes to ride and work metal and laughs like butterflies in the breeze. I don't want the woman who hides lies behind a blank smile."

He felt her pull away, even though her hands stayed on him. "I am the woman who rides and works metal." Then she let go of him—but only long enough to duck under his arm that was still holding on to the steering wheel for dear life. She straddled him. Her slim black skirt—the one that made her backside look even better than a pair of jeans ever could—bunched up at her hips. "That's who I am."

His arms were shaking from the effort of *not* touching her. Because he wasn't. No way in hell. She was doing this. She was doing *all* of this.

She leaned her forehead against him. Her thighs—strong from years of riding—gripped his and he felt the tantalizing heat of her center through his jeans. How strong did one man have to be? Because a lesser man would wrap his arms around her and take what she was offering.

But taking a woman with an audience—if Joaquin was

still watching from the stoop or if he'd gone inside and alerted Alex or her father of what was happening—was too stupid of a risk to take. So, even though it was the most painful thing he could remember doing—way more painful than getting kicked by that calf in the shin when he was ten—he kept his hands on the steering wheel.

It only got worse when she kissed him again—a kiss that started out soft and gentle and maybe even a little hesitant—just like her. Then it got hot, fast. Her hips ground down on his and she pressed those beautiful breasts against his chest. Only some lousy clothes separated them. That was not a whole lot and way, *way* too much.

He pulled his head back, but the rest of him had no place to go. She had him pinned. "Don't lie to me, Gabriella. I won't stand for it."

She nodded, looking sad and sensual at the same time. That, almost more than her sweet body or sweeter face, made him want to wrap her up and hold her tight. "This is the truth, Chance. I ride. I work metal. And you make me laugh. That's who I am. That's who I get to be with you." Her fingers traced a path from his cheeks to his jaw, as though she was exploring him when what she was really doing was burning him with her touch. "No one else. Just you."

He shouldn't believe her. She was setting him up and sooner or later, he was going to fall—hard.

Hell, he was already falling for the woman who'd had smudges of soot on her forehead the whole time they'd sat by the bank of his dry creek. He was already falling for the woman who was perfectly comfortable chatting with Franny or working with Slim, for the woman who saddled her own horse and rode hell-for-leather.

He wanted that woman to be the one in his arms. God, he'd never wanted anything so bad.

Then she said in a breathy whisper, "That's who I am, because of you," and he felt lost to her.

This time, he was the one doing the kissing. He managed to keep his hands on the wheel because if he didn't, he'd be pulling her shirt over her head and trying to get his buckle undone and filling his hands with her soft skin.

Yeah, it was probably going to get him beat to a pulp, but he didn't give a damn. It was worth it to feel her passion surging against him, to feel the heat of her body setting his on fire. He wanted to bury himself in her and make her cry out with pleasure. He wanted to surrender himself to her in a way that he had never wanted to before. Anything was worth this moment with her.

Anything she asked of him was hers.

So when she said, "Can I come back to the ranch tomorrow?" all he could do was kiss her again, feel the way her body fit over his.

"You already knew the answer. All you had to do was ask."

Her face lit up into a wide smile, the kind that couldn't be faked. "Thank you." She said it in words and with another kiss.

He needed to say good-night to her and walk her to the door. But he couldn't help taking another kiss from her. And another. And just one more. He couldn't quite get enough of her. Everything about her overrode his better judgment. Even if things were as normal as possible—Gabriella was still Alex's little sister. And a man had to tread lightly when it came to making out in a truck with his best friend's sister.

Then, unexpectedly, a light came on in the house. It wasn't a spotlight that hit them in the truck or anything, but it meant someone was moving around in the front of the house. Someone who might see them.

Both Chance and Gabriella reacted at the same time,

jolting against each other. Which made him groan in frustration. Another day with Gabriella, another night in unsatisfied agony.

"I should go," she said in a near whisper.

"Yeah." *No.*

She slid off his lap and lifted her bottom off the seat so she could pull her skirt back down.

How far gone was he? So far that he almost slid his hand up her exposed leg, almost cupped that curvy bottom in his hands and *almost* pulled her right back onto his lap.

"I'll walk you up." It was the least he could do. Plus, it'd give him another few minutes of being close to her.

They got out of the car. She adjusted her skirt one final time, then held out her hand to him. They walked up to the front step, where Joaquin stood, waiting. He glared at Chance extra hard, but Chance ignored the big man. "You want to do some more work in the shop tomorrow?"

One of her fingers traced over his knuckle. It sent a jolt of heat through him that not even Joaquin could temper. "But of course."

"What time can I expect you?" The more important question was, what time would she leave? She'd come home today to change for the date disaster. He had no desire to repeat dinner at the club. But that didn't mean he was out of options.

When she didn't answer immediately, he jumped into the gap. "Franny would be happy to make us dinner, or we could try Claire's." Even in the dim light, he could see the look of terror cross her face. "Claire's is different. Quieter." More dimly lit, more private. People went to the TCC to see and be seen. People went to Claire's when they didn't want to look at anyone but the other person at their table. And he didn't want to look at anyone but Gabriella.

He hadn't been to Claire's since…well, since he'd given Cara his blessing to start seeing Alex. They'd had their first date at the restaurant, and it had seemed fitting to bring the relationship full circle. Since then, he hadn't had anyone he wanted to take.

Plus, at Claire's it wouldn't be a big deal if Joaquin sat at a different table. No more of this three's-a-crowd crap.

"If you say Claire's will be fine, I trust you." He could see that the prospect of another outing into greater Royal still made her nervous, but at least she wasn't hiding behind that blankness again.

"I've got meetings all morning with people about a wedding—including a tasting for lunch. If you came out after lunch, we could go straight to dinner."

She frowned, her lips twisted into a displeased grimace. "In case you didn't notice, by the time I get done at the furnace, I'm in no shape to be seen."

"I don't know about that." Before he could stop himself, he reached up and touched her forehead, where she'd had the smudge earlier this afternoon. Her lips twisted even more, but he could see that she was trying hard not to smile at him—and failing. "But don't forget, I live right there. You could use my shower to get cleaned up." He swallowed, knowing full well Joaquin was memorizing every word.

The look on her face made it real clear that she didn't want to come all the way back here. He understood—he'd gone out with a girl in high school who'd had a rough dad. Their dates had always started the minute the final school bell rang. Coming home had meant another chance to be stopped by her father. Obviously it was the same for Gabriella.

Chance didn't know if Rodrigo del Toro was a violent man. But he sure as hell wasn't pleasant to be around.

"I would like that." She leaned up and brushed her lips across his. It took more than effort than he liked to keep from sweeping her into his arms and kissing the hell out of her. But he managed to keep the brakes on. "Tomorrow, then."

"Tomorrow," he called to her as she strode past Joaquin and into the house.

The big man favored Chance with another murderous glare before he turned and slammed the door in Chance's face.

Yeah.

Man, he couldn't remember the last time he'd looked this forward to a Tuesday.

Eleven

The moment the door shut, Gabriella spun on her guard. “You are out of line, Joaquin. *Out of line.*”

Joaquin glared at her, but he did not respond.

Gabriella could not remember being madder than she was at this precise moment. There were many times she had been upset. When her brother had been granted permission to get his own apartment in Mexico City, she’d been beyond furious. And not because he was moving out for good.

Because the announcement had been book-ended by her father’s decision that she not be allowed to go to university. For her safety, of course.

Gabriella had rebelled long and hard. She’d cut her hair off with a pair of shears, leaving her beautiful tresses on the ground and what was left on her head an uneven mess. She’d gotten tattoos all over her arms and neck. True, they’d been drawn on with pen instead of with a needle, but it had been worth it for the look of horror on her father’s face.

It had taken weeks for the drawings to wash away, years for her hair to grow back.

She’d wanted to go to university for the sake of going—for being anywhere but home. It hadn’t been that different than any other teenage girl wanting to spread her wings and fly.

Normally, when she was upset, she threatened Joaquin with small things—her cooking, shoe shopping. It was a little game they played with each other. She had long since stopped asking for things she knew she would not get and fought only the small things she could.

This was different. This was not for the sake of going. No man—with the possible exception of Joaquin himself—had ever paid this kind of attention to her. Treated her as anything more than a fine china doll to be locked in a case and gazed at on occasion.

Chance treated her like the flesh-and-blood woman she was.

She had not lied to Chance. When she was on his ranch, riding his horse, working in his shop, she felt like the woman she always wanted to be. It wasn't that different than what she did at home. But a picnic lunch? Dinners out?

A man who made her blood sing? Who saw her first and her family name last?

She would fight for that.

"I want to be with him. Are you going to stop me?"

Joaquin flinched, his jaw set. But still he did not speak.

She heard noises overhead. She had only a matter of moments before her father or brother came down. If it was Papa, he might start questioning where she'd been, who she'd been with. She did not want to lie to him. He may have kept her wrapped up like a china doll he was afraid of dropping but she still loved him.

"Are you going to tell on me as if I'm a little girl?"

Joaquin dropped his gaze to his shoes and she knew he would. The white-hot rage that coursed through her was only tempered by a wave of sadness. She might get to see

Chance for a while, but sooner or later it would come to an end.

Sooner or later, she'd be put back in her glass case, a fragile thing to be protected above all else.

"After all this time—all the years you've stood by my side—I thought you might want me to be happy. I thought... I thought you might work for me. Not for Papa."

He did not correct her. In fact, he did nothing but continue to stare at the tips of his shoes.

Ah.

Her time with Chance was limited. Her path and his would not cross again once she returned to Mexico. But she would have even less time now than she'd hoped.

She might only get one more day. One more evening to feel as special, as *free,* as he made her feel.

She had best make the most of it.

Chance sat in his living room across from Joaquin. Upstairs, he could hear the running water in his shower.

The shower that currently contained one very nude Gabriella del Toro.

If this were any other situation, Chance wouldn't be in the middle of a staring match with a man. He'd have shucked his own clothes and offered his services in washing her back. And her front. And all the parts in between.

To hell with dinner. They'd never make it past the top step.

And yet, here he sat. With Joaquin.

If it were any other woman, this wouldn't be worth it.

But Gabriella was.

At least the place was clean. His home wasn't the Ritz, but the old place suited him just fine. Three bedrooms upstairs, with a kitchen, dining room and parlor downstairs. And he'd had Lupe come in today and give it a thorough once-over. He hoped Gabriella thought it was okay.

He heard the water shut off. God, she was probably rubbing a towel all over her wet body. Then sliding into a pair of little lacy panties. Settling her full breasts into an equally lacy bra. Would she be zipping up another body-hugging skirt or maybe a pair of tight slacks?

Although he didn't move, Chance was pretty sure Joaquin made a noise of displeasure in the back of his throat. Great.

"You know I'm not going to hurt her, right?"

Joaquin raised an eyebrow in what looked a hell of a lot like disbelief.

"And that I didn't do a thing to her brother?"

The other eyebrow went up. Yeah, Joaquin didn't believe a word he said.

Chance sighed. He'd have a more successful conversation with his horse. "I just want her to be happy. That's all. That doesn't make me the bad guy here."

At this, Joaquin's face—well, it didn't crumble. Chance wasn't sure he even moved a muscle. But he went from looking dangerous to looking…sheepish? Was that possible?

"Ready," Gabriella called from the top of the stairs.

Chance and Joaquin stood at the same time as Gabriella made her way downstairs. She had on a cream-colored skirt with a purple top and a pair of purple shoes. The skirt cupped her bottom and flared out, while the top didn't have sleeves. Everything clung to her like a second skin.

Yeah, if it wasn't for the bodyguard, they wouldn't make it out of the house tonight.

"What do you think?" Gabriella spun in a slow circle for Chance. That's when he saw that her top also didn't have a whole lot of fabric in the back. It was one of those halter tops that tied at the neck and left most of her back bare and begging to be touched.

Man, did he want to touch.

"Well?" She'd turned back to face him again, her smile both knowing and somehow coy.

He managed to drag his eyes away from where he could now clearly see her nipples outlined in the thin fabric. "I don't want you to get cold." There. That was a reasonable thing to say that didn't sound as if he was a slobbering horn-dog teenager who couldn't get past the fact that she wasn't wearing a bra.

"Oh! The jacket! I'll be right back."

Chance was treated to the view of Gabriella's legs and backside climbing the stairs. Wow. *Wow.* He wanted to get to dinner. The sooner they ate, the sooner they could come back.

At least, he hoped they were coming back. When Gabriella reappeared in a matching cream-colored jacket, he was relieved to see that she didn't have the bag of toiletries she'd packed. Good. She was coming back here tonight to get her things. The question was, how long would she stay?

More importantly, what would he do when she left?

Yeah, that was the question of the day. Of the month.

"Shall we?" He managed to get the door opened.

"Is it all right if Joaquin drives?" Gabriella's voice was light as she said this, but Chance heard an undercurrent of tension.

Was she nervous about dinner? He'd called ahead and reserved two tables, including the most private table in the restaurant, one tucked back in a little nook. He was lucky that Valentine's Day had passed. There was no way he would have gotten that table on such short notice before that.

If Joaquin drove, they'd have to bring him home, right? He could only hope the big man wouldn't make him walk the fifteen miles. "That's fine." He held the back door of the big SUV open for her as Joaquin clomped around to the driver's side door. Then, once Gabriella had slid in, he climbed in after her.

And was thrilled to find that she hadn't scooted all the way over to the other side. Instead she sat right in the middle—close enough to touch.

So he shut the door, buckled up and touched. He draped his arm around her shoulder and pulled her tighter against him.

She sighed, her body molding itself to him. She rested her head on his shoulder and then placed her left hand on his thigh. It wasn't an overt come-on, but the feeling of her curled into him was more than enough to drive him to distraction.

Even though he was not, in fact, driving, he still had to make sure they got to where they were going. So, with Gabriella holding on to him as tightly as he was holding on to her, he gave Joaquin directions to Claire's.

The whole time, he kept wondering how much longer he'd have. How much longer until Alex started feeling better? Until they caught the bastards that had kidnapped him in the first place? Until the entire del Toro family packed up and went south of the border?

How much longer would he have to look forward to saddling up with Gabriella and riding the range? To finding her all smudged and happy from another day spent at the furnace in Slim's shop? To seeing her get all dressed up for a night out on the town?

He laced his fingers with hers. Her hands weren't the babied softness of a woman who was afraid of work, afraid of messing up her manicure. They were clean but she had calluses on the sides of her fingers and a few small scars on the back where she'd probably caught a piece of hot metal at some point.

God, he hoped he wasn't making the biggest mistake of his life.

They arrived at Claire's right at six-thirty. Chance didn't wait to see if Joaquin would open the door for them. He didn't think it'd go over real well if he started treating the big man like a chauffeur. So he hopped out and held out a hand for Gabriella.

He didn't let go of her once she'd gotten her feet under her, either. He was tired of pretending he wasn't interested in her. The little "conversation" in the front seat of his truck last night made pretending pointless.

"Hello, Mr. McDaniel." The hostess gave them a polite smile and added, "This way, please," before anyone could say anything else.

Gabriella's hand tightened around his as they walked into the restaurant. "You called ahead?"

"I'm not leaving anything to chance tonight." That included condoms. Hell, he didn't know if they'd get to that point—or how—but after the way she'd straddled him last night?

She shot him a red-hot smile. "Good thinking."

Oh, yeah.

The place wasn't packed but it wasn't empty, either. Chance saw Ryan Grant sitting with a beautiful redhead. It wasn't until he waved and Ryan waved back that the woman turned—and he recognized Piper Kindred.

"Friends?" Gabriella asked, her grip tightening on his.

"Yup." Obviously, Ryan and Piper were here on a date. Just like Chance and Gabriella.

So Chance tipped his hat to Ryan and Piper and led Gabriella away and back to the secluded table.

"Enjoy," their hostess said.

She motioned Joaquin to a small table on the other side of the aisle. The big man could keep an eye on them—and the rest of the restaurant—but he wasn't at their table. That's all Chance wanted.

Well, it wasn't all he wanted.

But it was what he would take for at the moment.

Gabriella settled into the chair that Chance held for her and focused on breathing. She couldn't even see the couple that Chance had recognized earlier. She had no way of knowing if they were talking about him—or her. But the greetings had seemed friendly and neither the man nor the woman had given her the kind of look that she'd gotten last night at the club—the vicious, gleeful kind of look that went with gossip.

"Wine?" Chance asked, looking over the list.

"Yes, please." He seemed more relaxed here than he had at the club last night. She needed to be the same.

She wanted to be the same. Alex had managed to keep Papa busy this morning. She had come up with every single menial errand and task that Joaquin could do for her to keep him too busy to have a private word with Papa. But she knew she couldn't do that all day, every day. Sooner or later, Joaquin would provide a status update to Papa and her time with Chance would end.

So she had to make the most of tonight. She *would* make the most of it.

But first, wine.

They ordered—he got the prime rib, she ordered the black and blue steak salad with a bottle of Shiraz to share. She was trying not to look at Joaquin. She wanted this illusion of freedom, didn't she? She wanted this taste of a life outside of her father's control.

She wanted Chance.

Judging from the way his jaw had dropped when she'd first walked down the stairs in her slinkiest top, he wanted her, too.

That was what she needed to focus on. Not the roiling nerves that had her stomach in a state of distress and not whatever anyone else in the restaurant may or may not be saying about her and Chance.

Just the way he'd looked at her, as if she was the only woman in the world. As if he'd wanted to sweep her into his arms and carry her right back up to that big bed in his room—because of course she'd peeked in and looked at how big his bed was. More than big enough for two people. The coverlet was a quilt done in blues and whites—old-fashioned, yes, but well loved and well taken care of. It had seemed perfectly in place in his home.

She wanted to get back to that bed tonight.

She glanced up at Chance and found him staring at her. "Yes?"

"You look amazing tonight."

She felt the heat of the blush rush to her cheeks, but she didn't try to distract from it with a soft platitude. Instead she let the smile take hold of her lips. "Thank you."

He leaned forward. "Do you know how much longer you're going to be in Royal?"

"Until Alex has been cleared by his doctors and the police to return." Of course, Alex would have to actually meet with the doctors and officers to be cleared for travel—something he seemed in no great hurry to do.

"So you don't know when you're going to leave." It didn't quite sound like a question—more like a rumination.

"No."

"And you'll go back to your estate near Mexico City?"

"Yes." Why was he asking about her travel plans?

"Do you ever leave the estate? Do you travel?"

She regarded him for a moment. "I go into the city for gallery openings. That occurs once or twice a year."

"How about visitors? Do you ever have visitors at the estate?"

Gabriella couldn't help herself. She glanced at Joaquin,

who was staring at both of them, as was expected. "Why do you ask?"

Chance looked down at his hands. He'd started rubbing his knuckles, as if he were looking for a fight.

Or as if he were nervous.

"It's just that..." He cleared his throat and reached his hand halfway across the table, waiting for her to place her hand in his. "Please, Gabriella."

He *was* nervous. That had the direct effect of making her nervous.

But she couldn't resist the pull of his hand. She let the tips of her fingers skim over his palm before they locked hands together.

"I haven't had a serious relationship in a while. I mean, yeah, I was dating Cara Windsor, but that was more because we were friends who got on well. I couldn't see her making a place for herself out on the ranch. She didn't like riding and was more than a little afraid of Slim."

"Why are you telling me this?" She did not wish to speak of old girlfriends. She may not have a great deal of dating experience, but she was reasonably sure that this was the wrong way to seduce someone.

"Because after Cara left me for Alex, I told myself I was done. There weren't too many women left in Royal who'd cotton to my way of living. I get up before dawn in the summer and don't sit back down until the sun sets. I smell like horse and cow and dirt for most of the day."

He was pouring his heart out, of that much she was certain. But... "What does 'cotton' mean?" She felt dumb for asking, but she recalled Slim saying that about his given name and she hadn't yet figured out what it meant.

The grin that he gave her put her at ease. He didn't think she was dumb for asking. "Take to. Like. No one else in this town cares to live the kind of life I live. Cara is a wonderful woman, but that's not the kind of life she wanted and we both knew it. She was happier with your brother. That was the life she wanted and I accepted that."

She flinched. She couldn't help it. Talking about Alex would mean that she would either have to lie to Chance or betray her brother's confidences, and she did not want to do either of those things. "I do not wish to speak of him. Not now."

He nodded in agreement. "I don't, either. I want you to understand. After Cara and I were done, I'd…I'd given up hoping that there was a woman in this world who would fit in mine."

He tightened his grip on her as he lifted his gaze to meet her. His eyes—those beautiful bright green eyes that always made her feel as though she'd come home—made her want to do far more than hold hands.

His mouth crooked in a smile. "Then I met you. And everything changed."

The air rushed out of her lungs as she gripped his hand with all her might. She felt as if she might fall out of her chair otherwise.

This…this was being seduced. His words took all of her worries and pushed them right out of her head. Who cared about old girlfriends or injured brothers? She didn't. She cared for Chance.

"I know we can't keep doing this forever," he went on, dropping his gaze back to where their hands were connected. He turned her hand over and started rubbing his thumb over her wrist, sending delicious shivers up her back. "I know it'll come to an end and you'll be in Mexico and I'll be in Texas. But that doesn't mean we have to let this die on the vine."

She wasn't sure what "die on the vine" meant, but she was very sure she didn't care. "What are you saying?"

"My life is here. That land has been in my family for over a hundred years and I can't walk away from that. But

I don't want to let you go, Gabriella. If you want me to, I'll come see you. We have slow times where I can get away for a week or two. And you're always welcome at the ranch."

She opened her mouth to say something—but the problem was she didn't know what to say. Not with him speaking words such as these.

Words no man had ever said to her. No man had ever *tried* to say to her. No man had ever gone out of his way to accommodate her structured lifestyle. That Chance would make the effort was, in and of itself, an impressive act.

Then he swallowed. "What I'm saying is, I'm falling in love with you and I don't want to let that go when you leave Texas."

"¡Dios mío!" she heard herself breathe. Did he just say he was in love? With *her?*

His crooked grin got a little more worried. "Did you mean that in a good way?"

When she still couldn't come up with a reasonable response, he leaned away from her. But he didn't let her go. "If you don't feel the same, I understand. You've got a lot to deal with as it is and it's not my place to make your life more complicated than it already is. No harm, no foul."

He started to pull his hand away from hers, but she refused to let him. So she was having trouble finding the words. There were other ways to express herself.

That was how she came to be half out of her chair, reaching across the table until she had grabbed Chance's shirt in her hands and hauled him to her. She crushed her lips to his.

Yes, this—this was exactly what she wanted. The words of love—not words she read in a book or watched two characters say to each other in a telenovela, but words spoken directly to her. About her.

At this precise moment, nothing else mattered. Not Joaquin sitting ten feet away, not the other people dining in the restaurant. She did not care what her brother or her father might say about such a bold action on her behalf.

All she cared about—all she wanted to care about—was Chance falling in love with her.

She was falling in love with Chance.

But the kiss was awkward over the table and only became more so when the waitress arrived with their meals.

Gabriella let go of Chance and sat with a thud in her chair. The two of them stared at each other for a moment as the waitress tried to act as if she hadn't seen anything unusual at all.

Then Chance turned his attention to the server. "Can we get the food wrapped up to go? Quickly?"

The waitress smirked but said, "Of course," as she picked up the tray and disappeared into the kitchen.

"You wanna get out of here?"

Gabriella didn't bother to look at Joaquin. She already knew he would not be happy with this turn of events. For all she knew, she was only hastening the day when Papa would not let her see Chance again with her brazen behavior.

But she would have this night with him, one way or the other.

"Yes," she said.

And that was final.

Twelve

Somehow they got out of the restaurant and into her SUV. It seemed as though Joaquin was in no hurry to drive them anywhere, but Chance didn't give a flying damn. They left the big man in the restaurant and hustled to the car. Chance was in the backseat with Gabriella and the windows were tinted. Close enough.

He managed to get the door shut behind them and to set the boxed-up meals down behind the seat before his hands were all over Gabriella.

And, boy, her hands were all over him as she fell back against the seat and pulled him on top of her. She grabbed his backside and pulled him into her, pushing her skirt up. Despite the clothing, he could feel the warm heat of her core. Her hands worked their way up from his butt to his back as she felt his muscles.

Her touch alone was enough to push him right up to the edge of his control. Combine that with the way her legs slid around him? Damn. "I want you so much," he whispered as he propped himself up on his arms. This had the nice effect of pushing his erection harder against her warmth. "*So* much."

"Yes. Me, too. Oh, yes," she moaned as he pivoted his hips, tested the limits of his pants. "Oh, Chance."

Hearing her mouth say his name that way—as though he meant everything to her—was all he wanted. Yeah, the sex would be amazing, he didn't doubt that. But he wanted so much more than that.

Her. That was all.

His tongue swept into her mouth as he managed to balance himself so that he could touch her generous breasts. Nope, no bra—and he'd never been happier. He stroked her through the thin fabric and was rewarded when her nipple went rock-hard.

"Yeah," he said as her hips bucked against his. "Just like that. God, you're beautiful, Gabriella. Tell me what you like. Everything you want."

Her hands stilled against him. Something seemed off as she said, "Chance…" but before she could finish her thought, the driver's side door opened.

Crap on toast. Joaquin. Chance had been so wrapped up in Gabriella—literally and figuratively—that he'd actually forgotten about the big man. And the fact that they were still in a car.

He sat up so Gabriella could get herself put back together. Joaquin seemed to be doing the same thing—he hadn't gotten into the vehicle yet.

Shuddering, Gabriella managed to get her skirt rearranged. Then she said, "Joaquin, please take us back to Chance's house," in a voice that didn't sound embarrassed. A little happy, but not embarrassed.

Maybe sneaking around the hired help was something she was used to. If she wasn't going to act guilty about this, then he wasn't, either.

He wasn't sure Joaquin was on board, though. Now that Chance had himself under control—okay, *more* under control—he could see the big man glaring at him from where he stood outside the door.

"Please," Gabriella repeated. This time Chance heard a note of desperation in her voice.

"I'm not going to hurt her," Chance added, unsure if he should be saying anything.

But he didn't want to sit here in the back of this vehicle in what was, essentially, a Mexican standoff with an actual Mexican. He wanted to get someplace that had a locking door and pillows, and he wanted to get there sooner rather than later.

That wasn't Joaquin's idea of a good evening, apparently. The next thing Chance knew, Gabriella had jolted forward and was half draped over the front passenger seat. "This is my choice. I choose to go home with him and I choose to go to bed with him. There is nothing you can do tonight that will stop me. You can either guard me as you have sworn to do or leave me alone and go back to Papa."

Boy, he loved it when she was fiery—except for that one word: *tonight*. He didn't like that word. It begged the question—what could Joaquin do tomorrow to keep Gabriella from him?

"Fine." She turned to Chance, her eyes flashing with righteous fury. "Get out."

"What?"

"Your friends in the restaurant—would they give us a ride home?"

Chance's mouth flopped open. "Uh…"

"Or taxis? Do you have taxis in this town?"

"Sure." Boy, remind him not to get on Gabriella's bad side. He wasn't surprised that Rodrigo lived up to the family name—del Toro was "of the bull"—but for the first time, he truly grasped how bullheaded Gabriella could be.

He was sure she was bluffing—maybe. Either way, he wasn't about to leave her side. He opened the door and got one leg out before Joaquin spoke.

"I will drive you." He sounded as if he had a gun jammed in his back. Maybe that's how he felt.

"To Chance's home?" Maybe Gabriella was less a bull and more a pit bull, because she wasn't about to let this go.

"Sí," the big man sighed wearily, as if the fifteen-mile-drive was a death march.

"Thank you." Gabriella pulled Chance back into the vehicle and slid her hand down his inner thigh.

And just like that, he didn't give a damn for what Joaquin might do tomorrow.

The pain of keeping his hands to himself was a new kind of hell, but soon enough the vehicle lurched to a sudden halt. Both of them startled. Chance saw they were at his house. Thank God for that.

He got out of the car, finally. Walking wasn't going to be the easiest thing he'd ever done, but he'd manage somehow.

Gabriella started to get out with him, but then she stopped. "My shoes..."

"You don't need them." He pulled her out and into his arms. "I'll carry you."

"Oh," she breathed, her eyes glazed over with desire. Then she tucked her head against his neck and kissed him there. His knees shook. "If you insist."

"I do." He turned toward the door and saw Joaquin standing next to it, looking as pissed as he possibly could. Chance didn't think issuing orders would go over real well, but he was sick to death of tiptoeing around the big man. "Will you keep an eye on the house? I don't want anyone to try to barge in on us." Including Joaquin.

"Please," Gabriella added.

Joaquin nodded—a swift, curt movement of his head. But he stepped aside.

Finally. Chance took the steps as fast as he could; took the hallway back to his room faster. He couldn't wait to pick up right where he'd left off in the car—with Gabriella holding on to her composure by the thinnest of threads.

He sat her on the bed, where she peeled off her jacket as he kicked off his shoes. Maybe later there'd be time for nice and slow. But the backseat tonight—hell, the front seat last night—had him primed. And, given the way she grabbed at his belt, she was rarin' to go, too.

But he didn't want to go *that* fast. Yeah, he was hard up—very hard up—but he wasn't the kind of man who took without giving anything back. So he grabbed her hands and held them away from his groin. "Slow down, woman."

"I don't want to slow down." She tested his grip on her. "I've waited for this for so long… I don't want to wait a moment longer."

He grinned as he pushed her back on the bed. Then he took the kiss on her lips she had waiting for him as he let his body settle over hers. "I want to do this right, Gabriella. Slow can be just as good as fast." To emphasize his point, he ground his hips into hers and was rewarded with a low moan of pleasure. "Slow can be better."

"All right. But I still want to see you." She pulled her hands free and began working at the buttons on his shirt. "Please."

"All you had to do was ask." He sat back and let her get the shirt undone, but then he stood and shucked both the shirt and jacket together before taking care of his pants himself. He couldn't have her touching him right now, not until he got himself a little more under control.

"Your turn." He knelt on the bed and lifted her hair away from her neck. Then he undid the tie of her top and let it fall forward.

He expected her to touch him while he did this, but she didn't. She sat there. Was she trembling? "If you want me to stop…" he offered, trying to sound as sincere as possible. If she'd changed her mind, he'd respect that. Even if it killed him.

"No! I want this. You." Then she swallowed.

She was nervous, he realized—but he wasn't sure why. Maybe she'd never had someone as big as him? And if not, should he take that as a compliment?

He leaned back, taking the time to admire her breasts. Even then, he couldn't help but notice that her gaze was locked onto his erection. "You are *so* beautiful," he told her as he cupped her chin in his hand and lifted her face up to his.

Then he stepped back and pulled her to her feet. He unzipped the skirt and let it fall with a swish to the ground. He filled his hands with the creamy skin of her hips—not the stick-thin hips of a woman who starved herself to fit some crazy notion of beauty, but the full, glorious hips of a woman. "So beautiful," he repeated as he slid his hands underneath her silky panties and slid them off.

Then there was nothing left between them. He pressed his lips against the base of her neck and felt the crazy-fast speed of her pulse. "You okay?" But he asked this as he ran his tongue over her the edge of her earlobe.

"I… It's…too slow. I want to go faster."

This pulled him up short. "Why?" Maybe she liked it fast? After all, she'd gone from zero to sixty in about 1.3 seconds last night in his truck.

She looked down at his straining erection and then, with a hesitant hand, reached out and touched him. Just the tip of her finger brushing the tip of his penis. As if she was afraid of it.

As if she'd never done this.

It hit him like a bolt out of the blue. "Gabriella, have you ever been with a man before?"

Before he could process this—she was a *virgin?*—she took him firmly in hand and stroked. It wasn't a particularly skilled stroke, but he was already so worked up that it temporarily short-circuited his brain.

"That…that does not matter, does it? You have, haven't you?"

Hell *yes,* it mattered. It mattered a lot. He hadn't been with a virgin since back when *he'd* been a virgin. Even at seventeen, the sex had been so awkward, so mind-bogglingly *bad* that his girlfriend had pretty much dumped him and he hadn't been all that sad to see her go. It was one of his least favorite memories involving the opposite sex. Hell, it *was* his least favorite one.

He'd gotten better, of course. Practice made perfect and he had a couple of lady friends who'd taught him the finer points of pleasing a female. At thirty-two, he'd gotten quite good.

But still…she was a virgin. At twenty-seven. It boggled his mind.

"Maybe we shouldn't do this." Being the first was a big responsibility. Bigger, given how long she'd waited.

"No!" Her head shot up, nearly clipping him in the chin. "No. I want this."

She gracefully fell to her knees. He knew what she was about to do—push him past the point of reason—and he tried to stop it, but the woman was hell-bent on changing his mind for him.

Her hands still trembling, she knelt in front of him. "I understand the process," she said, her voice flashing between confident and nervous. "I…have been told that it will not hurt because I spend so much time riding." Then she leaned forward and pressed those beautiful lips to his tip. "Do not deny me this, Chance. Please."

Then she took him in her mouth and it was all he could do to keep steady. Yeah, he'd say she had a pretty good grasp on "the process," as she'd put it. She swirled her tongue around him, one hand on his base, one hand wrapped around his leg for balance.

Had she ever done this—go down on someone? No, he didn't think so. She was too hesitant and, yes, too awkward to send him over the edge, but he didn't care. A twenty-seven-year-old virgin.

Anyone but him.

He looked down at Gabriella, doing her level best to seduce him. This was going to be tricky. How could he make it worth it for her—while also making sure she didn't feel like a failure of a woman for being inexperienced?

"Please," she said, pausing to catch her breath. She leaned her head against his thigh and traced his length with her fingertips. "*Please,* Chance. Do not treat me like a china doll that must be locked away. Treat me like a woman. I can see how much you want me." She stroked him again, making him twitch. "Can't you see how much I want you?" Then she took him in her mouth again.

Treat her like a woman who raced horses and looked as beautiful in a welder's apron as she did in a backless top and skirt.

He stroked her hair as she tried to time her hand movements to her mouth at a rate of speed that wasn't going to do anything but lead to inappropriate chafing. "Slow." He managed to get the word out through gritted teeth. "Go slow. Let me watch you."

Then she looked up at him, her eyes wide as her lips encircled him. The look in her eyes—*damn.* So innocent, so sexual at the same time. Desperate for him, for his approval. It was like a punch to the gut.

And she slowed way, *way* down. She was licking him like he was an ice cream cone and she was going to devour him one bite at a time.

Oh, yeah—she'd managed to push him past the point

of reason. "Yeah," he groaned as she licked him up and down again. "Just like that—*yeah.*"

She pulled away and kissed his thigh again. "That was good?"

"That was *great.*"

She looked up at him, her face beaming with satisfaction. Thank heavens that had been the right thing to say. But when she made a move to go down on him again, he pulled her up. "My turn, beautiful."

Before he laid her out on the bed and took what she wanted him to have, he wrapped his arms around her and held her. "If something doesn't work, you tell me. Okay?"

She felt so damn good against his chest, her head resting almost on his shoulder. She fit against him. With him. Then she said, "I can do that?"

It broke his heart a little bit, that she would even question her right to have a say in her own pleasure.

Then he realized that he'd been questioning that very thing a matter of moments earlier. She knew what she wanted. She'd been brave enough to ask for it.

And he had told her all she had to do was ask—the answer would be yes.

"Yup." He backed her up to the bed and laid her out on it. "Something not working, something you want to try—just ask, babe."

She scooted farther back onto the bed, giving him plenty of room—and a hell of a view of her luscious body. "All right."

"Do you want me to do to you what you did to me?" He'd been with a few women who weren't comfortable with oral sex. As much as he wanted to taste her—*all* of her—he felt it was only right to ask.

Her sensual smile stiffened. "I think…maybe it would be better to…you know…first."

Yeah, he'd guessed right on that one. She may have convinced him, but she was still nervous. "Maybe later?"

That got him a wicked grin. "Perhaps."

He leaned over and snagged a condom from the bedside table. She watched as he rolled it on. Then he covered her body with his. She tensed, as if she expected him to plunge into the gap, but he didn't. He focused on relaxing her—he ran his tongue over her dark nipples, blowing on them to make them tighten up. And to listen to her gasp in surprise.

"Good?"

"Oh, yes."

"Good." He worked his way up her chest to her neck, where he kissed and sucked while fondling her breasts until she was right where she'd been in the backseat of the car—bucking against him, her body begging for his. The whole time, her hands moved over his back—testing the muscles, digging into his skin when he did something she particularly liked.

He reached down between her legs and skimmed his hand over the glossy hair that covered her there. Untrimmed, untamed—just her in her natural state. He stroked her sex, feeling the tremors that shook her. "Good?"

"Ah, Chance," was the response he got, low and throaty in his ear.

He slipped one finger inside her. When her muscles clamped down on him, he about lost it then and there. But he focused on her, kissing her as she moaned at his touch.

He couldn't take it anymore. He was doing his damnedest to put her first, but he needed the release that was pounding in his blood. He needed her more than he'd ever needed any other woman.

He had to do this right.

Thirteen

Gabriella was having trouble breathing. Chance was doing things to her—things that she'd read about, *dreamed* about—but nothing had prepared her for the way his touch affected her.

She'd touched herself. She was only human, after all. She'd been about fifteen when she'd discovered that rubbing herself felt good and, if she kept doing it, it then felt great. Chance was rubbing her in that manner and it did feel good.

But he was inside her, too—and that was so much *more* than she'd expected. What was she supposed to be feeling? What if she wasn't doing this right? She'd basically thrown herself at his feet in such a scandalous way that she still couldn't believe she'd taken him into her mouth.

Then he pulled back. "You're so beautiful," he said in a voice that set her shaking again. Then, leaning back on one hand, he fitted himself against her and began to push.

Again, she wasn't sure what to expect. In books, a man often sank himself into his woman, an action that was quick and decisive and always painted as being very manly, even if it did mean that the woman hurt more because of it.

Chance did not do that. He moved slowly and paused

often. All the while, he kept kissing her lips, her neck, her shoulders. Then he would push forward again.

It didn't hurt. Thank heavens. It wasn't entirely comfortable, but she'd read about the pain of the quick tearing that went with this. No pain, no tearing.

Finally, Chance was fully inside her. "Doing okay?" he asked.

None of this was what she'd thought. She didn't even know the right way to respond to that thoughtful question. "I…um…yes?" She hadn't meant for it to come out as a question. She was sure there was nothing appealing about a woman who didn't have the first clue what she was doing in bed.

But instead of laughing or mocking her, Chance took a deep breath. As he did so, his hips moved—not a big gesture, but enough that she felt it deep inside. "You feel *so* good," he said, his voice little better than a whisper.

"Do I?"

"Oh, yeah." Then he flashed the crooked grin at her that made her forget all about what she may or may not supposed to be doing. All she could think of was being here, right now, with Chance. "Now for the fun part."

Oh, thank goodness—this hadn't been the fun part. Well, some of it had been fun, but she didn't yet see what everyone always made such a fuss about.

Then he moved. He pulled back and thrust forward, and then he did it again. Not the frenzied pace or hip-slamming often seen in movies—not that. This was slow, as he'd promised. It didn't hurt. His body covered hers, her body covered his and then—

Then he shifted a little and thrust in again and her world changed.

"Oh!" she gasped as the sensation went from *more* to *not enough* in a heartbeat. His body tapped hers with exquisite precision—a craftsman hammering a fine piece of gold—and suddenly her body rang with sensation.

It was as if he was the artist and she was the medium. He lifted her arms over her head and caught one of her nipples in his mouth as he rotated his hips into hers. Then he slid his hands under her bottom and guided her to wrap her legs around his waist. She moved the way he wanted her to, trusting that he would make this everything she'd hoped for. Better than she'd hoped for.

"You feel amazing," he said in that low voice that made her want to melt.

"Yes." Her body seemed to have developed a mind of its own. Instead of him moving her legs or arms, she was moving them herself—touching him however she could. Instead of him rotating his hips against her, she was swaying against him, testing the ways he filled her.

"Yeah, like that," he grunted in approval. "Does that feel good?"

"Yes." And it did. But… "I need more."

"All you had to do was ask." Chance pushed back onto his heels and pulled her bottom against him at a new angle. Then, as he began to thrust with a renewed vigor, he licked his fingertips and pressed them against her sex.

"Oh. *Oh!*" Overwhelmed with the pleasure that was both outside and inside her, she struggled to find something to hold on to. He was sitting too far back for her to reach him, let alone kiss him. She had to content herself with grabbing his forearm. But even that wasn't enough. As the pleasure built to heights she'd never dreamed of reaching by herself, she realized she was thrashing in the bed. It didn't seem dignified. But she was powerless to stop as long as he held her captive with his touch.

"Come on, babe." He spoke through gritted teeth. "So. Beautiful. Come for me."

She wanted to—oh, how she wanted to—but instead

of pushing her over the edge, his words called her back to herself. What if she couldn't come? Would he be insulted that he hadn't succeeded?

As these thoughts swirled around her desire, he leaned forward—without taking his fingers off her sex—and pried one of her hands from his arm. "Show me what you need."

Was he serious?

Oh, yes—he was quite serious. With his gaze locked onto hers, he ran his tongue over the tips of her fingers. Then he guided her hand down. "Show me," he said, half begging and half ordering.

So she did. She pressed against her most sensitive spot—his fingertips covering hers—and rubbed in the way that had always worked before.

Heat flooded her body as he held the eye contact. "So beautiful," he groaned before his body crashed into hers. He roared, a deep sound that did something to her—something she couldn't explain. He wasn't holding back, wasn't being calm and all-knowing—none of that.

She was doing that to *him.*

She didn't know if she pressed harder or if it was him or if they both did—but her body seized up and unleashed a climax upon her unlike anything she'd ever experienced before. Her body curled up on his, her back coming all the way off the bed as she shook around him—a work of art they'd made together.

The next thing she knew, Chance's arms were wrapped around her as he lowered her back onto the bed. "Did it hurt?" he asked, his voice concerned as he pulled free—but didn't let her go.

"What? No—it was—it was—" That was when she realized she was crying.

Oh, no. She was crying. In his bed.

This was the most embarrassing thing that had ever happened to her.

She ducked her head against his shoulder, too ashamed to look him in the eye. Chance chuckled and for the life of her, she couldn't tell if he was laughing at her or not. "It was…good?"

She nodded against his chest, thankful he couldn't see her stupid tears. Why was she crying? It had been the most wonderful thing that she'd ever felt! It was exactly what she'd wanted, exactly what she'd saved herself for all these years! Chance had put her needs first—he hadn't treated her like some fragile thing he was afraid to touch, nor had he treated her as a disposable woman like some girls on staff sometimes complained about.

"Was that the first time that happened?"

She nodded, trying in vain to get her emotions under control. Oh, this was not a sexy, sophisticated response. She was a blubbering idiot.

This realization only made things worse.

Chance pulled back and lifted her chin until she had no choice but to look at him. "You were amazing, you know? I'm so glad you came. I've never seen anyone as beautiful as you were. As you are."

"But…I'm a mess."

He grinned at her, but it wasn't the cocky grin that made her blood run hot. This grin made her feel safe in his arms, as if it were okay if she was sobbing in his bed. "You're not a mess. You're a woman. The one I'm in love with."

"Oh." And just like that, she no longer felt like an idiot, blubbering or otherwise.

She felt like she'd come home.

"I wish you could stay the night."

Gabriella had climbed back into his bed after they'd both taken a moment to clean up. She was curled into him underneath the covers, her body pressed against his.

Part of him wanted her to fall asleep because if she fell asleep, she'd stay.

He knew that wasn't going to happen. This moment was just that—a moment. One that would be too short.

"I wish I could, as well." As she spoke, she traced a path on his chest. Dang if her touch—light and sweet and hot all at the same time—didn't make him want to break out in goose bumps.

"We don't have much time, do we?"

She'd been a virgin who'd given herself to him. And it'd either been really bad or... He'd made her cry. That was a first for him. He'd been terrified that he'd hurt her but he didn't think she could lie about something like that. Instead, her emotions had been laid bare for him. As she'd been.

He still couldn't wrap his head around the whole thing, so he wrapped his arms around her instead.

Gabriella sighed against his chest, holding tighter to him. "No, we do not have much time." She sounded so sad about it.

He realized she was answering a different question—one that had nothing to do with tonight and everything to do with tomorrow. Or the next day. Or—if he were lucky—next month.

Suddenly he was talking without being entirely sure of what he was saying. "Whatever you want—that's what I'll do, babe. We can find a way to make this work. My door is always open to you or I'll come see you—all you have to do is ask and I'll be there."

She didn't say anything for a long moment. Instead she pressed her hand flat against his chest, right over his heart. "I want..." She trailed off, as though she didn't know how to actually say the words.

He leaned over to kiss her forehead, but he didn't rush

into the gap. She could ask him for anything. He had to make sure she knew that.

"I want to be with you as long as I can." Her voice was barely a whisper against his skin.

Because there'd come a time when she couldn't—when her path and his would stop crossing. When she'd stop defying Joaquin and, by extension, her father.

"Let's start with tomorrow. One day at a time. What do you want to do?"

She went back to tracing his skin again. It took a heck of a lot of effort to not roll into her, to not feel her body moving beneath his again.

"It might be…suspicious if we spent another evening together."

He ran through his schedule. The time between Valentine's Day and Mother's Day was pretty slow for him. He had a meeting with an ad firm in Houston to talk about commercials, but that was next week. Not tomorrow. "Luckily, I've got all day. Can you come out to work in the shop?"

"I believe so."

That was not the confidence-inspiring answer he was looking for, but he knew it was as good as it got. "You come out to work in the shop and I'll have lunch here for us." Franny would pack him up some sandwiches. If he was lucky, she might even do it without commentary.

"Just lunch?" He didn't have to look at her to know that she was smiling in that sly way of hers.

"I've got all afternoon, babe."

"Yes." She hummed against him. "*That* is what I want."

"Good." Even as he said it, he heard the sounds of heavy footsteps pacing downstairs. Joaquin was getting impatient, no doubt. They didn't have very long at all.

So he kissed her again, praying he'd see her right back here again tomorrow. "Because that's what I want, too."

* * *

For three days—three of the best days in Chance's memory—they got what they wanted. He met Gabriella at the barn in the morning where, after some not-so-quick kissing in the tack room, they'd mount up and race out to the shop. He'd kiss her goodbye for the morning and tend to the business of the ranch before he picked up lunch. They'd ride back to his house, have the kind of sex that got better every single time and eventually get around to reheating Franny's lunch.

Eventually.

The more time they spent together, the more comfortable Gabriella seemed to get about asking for what she wanted. She may have been a virgin, but she'd *thought* about sex a great deal. True, she couldn't meet his eyes when she asked if they could make love with him behind, but she'd asked. That was the important point. That and the explosive sex.

She also asked if they could have another picnic—and do it outside. Chance's first reaction was that it wasn't warm enough—they should wait for the weather to turn—but then he remembered their time was short. So he packed a couple of blankets and they kept most of their clothes on.

The more love they made, the more Chance wanted to make love with her. Even though they had sex every day, he still went to sleep with a hard-on that led to crazy dreams—dreams where Gabriella was sometimes older, sometimes with a baby on her hip, sometimes holding a red-hot spike and wearing a welder's mask. Every time, though, she'd look up at him through those thick lashes and say, "I want..." Even in his dreams, he did whatever he could to give her what she wanted.

Man, he was so gone. So damn *gone*.

Of course, he still had to deal with Joaquin, damn him. Franny always packed a double helping of the day's special for the big man. Joaquin stayed downstairs when Chance and Gabriella were upstairs and the day they had the picnic sex, he mounted up on Beast and rode a perimeter around them—far enough away that he couldn't hear moans, but close enough that he could hear the screams of terror he seemed to be expecting constantly.

Saturday rolled around. Slim didn't work on the weekends, so there was no good reason to justify Gabriella coming out to the ranch bright and early. Plus, she'd said she'd thought Alex might be feeling a little better and she wanted to spend some time with him. How was he supposed to begrudge her that?

They were going to give Claire's another go tonight to see if they could make it through a meal before he started peeling her clothes off her. The plan was that Gabriella would come out around five.

That didn't explain why Chance was showered and shaved by three-thirty, which left him an hour and a half of staring at the clock. Great.

He emailed a couple of clients about their upcoming events at McDaniel's Acres, thought about how he wanted his commercials to go—and kept staring at the clock. The minutes refused to tick by at any normal speed, damn them.

Finally he heard a car door slam outside. *Thank God.* He hurried to get the front door open for her. They had some time before their dinner reservations. Maybe she'd tell him something else she wanted, something they could do right now. Yeah, that'd be—

"Chance?"

As he swung the door open, he pulled up short. It wasn't Gabriella rushing to throw her arms around him—it was his old flame, Cara Windsor. And she was crying.

Aw, hell.

"Cara?" he asked as she clung to him. "What's wrong,

honey?" She'd been coming to him a lot, complaining about how Alex didn't remember her. It was hard to be sympathetic. Part of him didn't want to know. Part of him—a small part, but it was still there—wanted to let her twist in the wind for choosing a lying, cheating bastard over him.

"Oh, I'm so sorry—I didn't know where else to go. I don't know who else I can trust."

At least, that's what Chance thought she said. It was sort of hard to tell, what with the sobbing.

"Slow down, honey." Yeah, that small part of him might be happy watching her twist, but he pushed it back. They'd parted as friends—and she obviously needed a friend. He patted her on the back. "Tell me what's wrong."

"It's—" She didn't get very far before she buried her head on his shoulder.

Hell, not again. Chance managed to kick the door shut and guide her over to his couch. "There, there," he said, rubbing her back as she cried her eyes out. It probably wasn't the best thing to say, but he didn't have any better ideas.

He'd known Cara for a long time. They'd been friends before they were lovers, then back to friends again and she'd been crying on his shoulder about Alex for weeks now. But this was different. He'd never seen her this upset, and that worried him.

When she finally seemed to have cried most of it out, he tried again. "What's wrong? Are you in trouble?"

She looked at him, her light blue eyes watery and red. "Yeah, you could say that."

It broke his heart, just a little. "Tell me what happened and I'll try to fix it."

"You can't." Her eyes started to leak again, but she didn't start crying. "I...I messed up, Chance. I messed up real bad."

"What happened?"

"You know how worried I was about him, when he went missing."

"I know," he said in his most patient voice.

"And you know I never thought you were behind it." She got that steely look in her eyes, which momentarily chased her sadness away. "I *know* you weren't."

"I sure do appreciate that, honey. What happened now?" Because if this was just rehashing the past—again—well, he had a date to go on.

"One of the times I went to see him and he didn't remember me..." She dropped her gaze, suddenly finding her manicure very interesting. "So I...I had sex with him. To see if that would help him. Remember me."

"O...kay." This was exactly the sort of information he did *not* need to know. Not now, not ever.

"And now..." She covered her mouth with her hand, as if the words were cutting her on their way out. "And now I'm pregnant." She started to sob again in earnest.

"Oh, honey." Chance put his arm around her shoulders. This was exactly the kind of mess he couldn't fix. Alex was barely feeling "better," according to Gabriella. Had he even remembered he'd loved Cara yet?

Damn that man all over again. Why had he come up here and thrown a monkey wrench in all of their lives? Because as god-awful as it had been being guilty until proved innocent in Alex's abduction, that was a temporary thing. Nothing like having a baby. *Nothing.*

"I don't know what to do." Cara wept, pretty much trashing his date shirt. "I didn't know who else to trust. What am I going to tell my daddy?"

Oh, hell. It's not as if there was any love lost between Chance and Paul Windsor—but even Chance could see that springing "pregnant with the amnesiac's baby" on the old man would be a bad idea.

So he tried to deal with first things first. "Have you seen a doctor?"

She shook her head against his shoulder.

"That needs to happen. You schedule an appointment and get all checked out and we'll go from there, okay?" He tilted her head up to his and stared into her watery eyes. "You take care of you and that baby first. We'll deal with the rest of it second."

She gave him a weak smile as she nodded. He'd thought he'd loved this woman once. Maybe he had, but it hadn't been the same thing he felt for Gabriella. What he and Cara had shared was closer to a relationship borne of comfort and familiarity instead of passion and love.

"You're a good man, Chance McDaniel." It came out sniffly. "I was afraid you might tell me I'd gotten exactly what I'd deserved for leaving you."

"I wouldn't do that." He meant it, too. He'd lost this woman, but maybe he'd never had her. Now that he had Gabriella—now that he had tasted true passion—he knew that it was for the best.

"I know. I knew I could trust you." She leaned up and pressed a kiss to his cheek.

A sharp gasp cut through the room, making him turn toward the now-open door—and the woman standing in it.

Oh, *hell.* Gabriella.

Her eyes cut between Chance and Cara at an alarming rate of speed. "Babe," he got out, trying to pull free of Cara's arms and stand all at the same time.

But before he could do any of that, she turned and marched right back out.

"Was that…Alex's sister?" Cara let him go, thank God.

He didn't answer. He flat-out ran to catch up with Gabriella, but he was too late. Joaquin was shutting the back door.

"It's not what it looked like," Chance said, putting his

life on the line to keep walking toward the car. "I need to talk to her."

Joaquin gave no sign that he'd heard Chance. "Joaquin! *¡Vámonos!*" came a muffled cry from the backseat.

Shit. She was already crying. "I need to talk to her," he demanded as he kept walking toward the car. "I didn't do anything."

Joaquin pulled his piece on Chance in one smooth motion, leveling the barrel at Chance's guts.

Cara appeared in the doorway. "What's going on?" Then she squeaked. "Chance! He's got a gun!"

He didn't take his eyes off the weapon. "Go inside, Cara. Joaquin, I'd never hurt her. Never. You know I wouldn't."

"Joaquin! *¡Llévame a casa ahora!*" Gabriella's voice was close to hysterical.

The weirdest thing happened. Joaquin's mouth opened and he said, "Stay away from her." He holstered his gun and walked around to the driver's side of the vehicle. With a final cutting look, the big man climbed in and peeled off, leaving Chance in a cloud of dust, wondering if he'd actually heard Joaquin talk.

He couldn't do anything but watch the vehicle disappear down the road at a high rate of speed. It felt as though his heart was being dragged along behind it, tied to the bumper. The pain almost doubled him over. He wanted to go after her—but he didn't want to die. Even if not going after her felt a little bit like dying anyway.

"Chance?" Cara came out and put a hand on his arm. "Are you okay? Did he shoot you? Do you want me to call Nathan?"

"No." Involving the local sheriff in this would only make everything a million times worse. Yeah, he could have Joaquin arrested—and yeah, he'd like to see the big man rot in jail for a couple of years—but what would that get him?

It wouldn't get him Gabriella. He knew damn good and well that he'd never see her again.

He *had* to see her again. If he could explain what had happened, this whole misunderstanding would melt into nothingness. Because that's what it was—nothing.

He'd explain that Cara was in a bit of trouble—that she'd come to him for advice, that was all. All she wanted from him was a shoulder to cry on. No one had been seducing anyone.

"That was Alex's sister, wasn't it? Oh, God, Chance. Did I mess something up?"

"No, honey. Just a misunderstanding." He patted her on the hand. "Something I've got to get cleared up."

"I didn't know that you were seeing her." Cara's eyes were watering with more vim and vigor now. "I'll go talk to her."

He couldn't see that going well, either. He'd seen Gabriella turn on Joaquin enough to know she had a lot of fight in her. What would she do to Cara? "Let me handle this. Her bodyguard is a mean sucker. I don't want you in harm's way, okay? You focus on you, Cara. You and your baby. Let me worry about this."

She gave him that weak smile. "Will you tell Alex? About me? And the baby?"

"That's not my place, honey."

They stood there in pained silence for a moment, watching the cloud of dust stirred up by Joaquin's driving settle back over the land. Before long, there wouldn't be any sign that they'd been here at all. The land had a way of doing that—taking whatever it'd seen and returning it to the dirt. The land had taken in all of his family, his hopes for a family of his own, all of his blood, sweat and tears. It would continue on long after he'd left.

No. He wouldn't let his feeling for Gabriella settle. This wasn't over. He wasn't going to let Gabriella go without a fight the way he'd let Cara go.

He had to go after her.

Fourteen

By the time Chance got Cara on her way with the promise to call her doctor first thing Monday morning, almost forty minutes had passed. Damn it all.

He didn't have much of anything that resembled a plan, beyond finding Gabriella. That was it. It would have to be enough. It had to be. He wasn't going to let it end this way. Maybe it would end, sooner or later, but to have her think he'd been cheating? To have her think he didn't love her? Nope. Not happening. She could still end it, but she was going to know the truth of the matter.

So when Alex del Toro's red Ferrari went zooming past him on a deserted road at the edge of Royal, Chance slammed on the brakes. All he could think was, *Alex?*

Alex had clearly thought the same thing—he'd turned his Ferrari around and pulled up behind Chance's truck.

Both of them got out at the same time. "Alex?" Chance said first. "Man, where have you—"

That was as far as he got before Alex reared back and punched him. Pain exploding around his eye, Chance stumbled to the side, barely managing to keep his feet under him. "What the hell, man?"

"Stand up so I can punch you again, McDaniel," Alex growled.

"Not without a damn good reason," Chance replied, blinking through the pain. He did stand, but he made sure it was out of swinging range.

Then he realized that Alex called him McDaniel—just as he's always said it after Chance had beaten him in a race out to the swimming hole. "You know who I am?"

"Of course I know who you are, you ass. You broke my sister's heart." Alex took a few quick steps, his fist balled up and ready to swing.

"Damn it, knock it off! I didn't break anyone's heart!" Chance sidestepped his *former* friend. He didn't want to hit the man with amnesia. If he still had it.

He caught Alex's arm on the swing-through and pushed, backing him into his Ferrari door. "Who was she?" Alex sneered. "A guest? Or an old girlfriend?"

He charged again. Chance had no choice. He ducked down and caught Alex around the waist. This time, it wasn't a defensive push. This time, Chance slammed Alex into the side of his car with enough force that the man groaned.

But he let go and stood back. "Shut up and listen, you idiot. It *was* an old girlfriend—Cara Windsor. Remember her? You stole her from me and she fell in love with you."

"Cara?" Oh, yeah—the way Alex hissed that? He knew exactly who Cara was. "You're screwing around on my sister with *Cara?* I'm going to kill you, McDaniel."

"The hell you are. Shut up and listen for a moment."

"To what? You explain how you made a move on my woman while I was sick?"

"Yeah, because you're so damn sick right now you can hardly throw a punch." He touched the side of his face, which was already swelling. But, miracle of miracles, Alex didn't charge him again.

"Fine. You have two minutes."

Chance took a breath, hoping that would help his now

throbbing head. It didn't. He'd promised Cara not an hour ago that he wouldn't tell Alex about her and the baby—Alex's baby. But he couldn't have the man thinking Chance would step out on Gabriella.

"Think, man—why would Cara come crying on my shoulder? Because that's what she was doing—crying to me because she's been worried sick about *you,* you lying, thieving bastard." There. That was almost the truth. Cara had been worried for weeks and she'd probably been feeling sick. Alex was the root cause of both problems. Not a lie.

Plus, it felt damn good to call Alex out. "Or do you believe the same lies about me that everyone else believes? That I kidnapped you to win her back? No, wait—I forgot. The only liar here is you, *Alejandro.*"

"Don't call me that," he replied in a low voice.

"Why not? It's your name, isn't it?"

"Not anymore."

Chance threw his hands up. "And I'm supposed to take you at your word, right? Because you've never lied to me? You've always been an up-front guy? *Wrong.* Hell, I don't know who you are or why you came to Texas. All I know is that, by being your friend, you screwed my life up pretty damn bad and that I'm in love with your sister."

He hadn't actually meant to say that last part about Gabriella, but he'd built up a head of steam and it had slipped out.

The two of them stood there for a moment, the shock of Chance's words tripping them both up.

When Alex didn't take another swing at him, Chance hung his head. "Look—I don't know who you are or why you strung me along for close to a year. And right now, I don't much care. I'm going to go talk to Gabriella. I would never hurt her and I sure as hell would never cheat on her."

He turned and started walking back to his truck.

"Wait," Alex called out behind him. "Joaquin will kill you. I'm surprised he didn't earlier."

Yeah, that made two of them. He looked back over his shoulder at Alex. "If it's all the same to you, I'll risk it."

"No," Alex said again. He moved, but instead of throwing another punch, he grabbed Chance's arm. "It would destroy her."

Chance turned to look at Alex—a hard look. The man dropped his hand from Chance's arm. "Oh, so you remember who she is now?"

Alex couldn't meet his eyes. "She is my sister. I would do anything to protect her."

Suddenly, Chance had the urge to deck Alex and it had nothing to do with the black eye he was working on. "Stop protecting her, for God's sake. She's a grown woman. Let her do whatever the hell she wants. That's *all* she wants, you know."

"Let me talk to her," Alex went on, almost as if Chance hadn't spoken. "She's upset. She said she saw another woman kiss you. She's never had her heart broken before." He looked up at Chance but instead of his earlier rage, he was more confused this time. And less violent. "Was Cara kissing you?"

"On the cheek, damn it!" He grabbed the collar of his shirt, still messed up from Cara's crying, and held it out for Alex to see. "The literal shoulder to cry on! And what the hell are you doing out here, worried about your sister? Do you have any idea how *worried* Cara is about you? How 'seducing' me is the very last damn thing she's thinking of? How, even if there was a shot in hell that she was trying to seduce me I'd never let it get that far because, unlike *some* people, I respect my friends." Alex had the freaking nerve to look wounded by this statement, which only made Chance madder. "Mind your own damn business, Alex, and for the love of everything holy, let me mind mine!"

He turned and stomped off toward his truck, wrenching the door open with more force than was technically necessary.

"Joaquin *will* kill you if you show up at my house," Alex called after him.

"I'm not letting her go. Not like this," Chance called back, one foot in the truck.

"Let me talk to her. I owe you that."

Chance glared at the man. "You owe me a crap-ton more than that, *amigo.* Or did I forget to mention that the whole town thinks I tried to kill you?"

Alex had the decency to look ashamed at this. "Let me talk to her. I'll tell her what happened. She needs to calm down—once she calms down, Joaquin will calm down."

Chance didn't move. *He* wanted to be the one to talk to Gabriella, but…Joaquin *would* kill him without blinking an eye. "And you expect me to take you at your word like the same old sucker, huh? Fool me once, shame on you. Fool me twice, shame on me."

Now it was Alex's turn to hang his head. "I do not want your blood on my hands, Chance." He looked up and Chance thought he saw something honest in the man's eyes. "You have always been and will always be my friend. That part was real."

Or was it another lie, added to a pile of lies? "I don't believe you."

"Believe this—I've never seen Gabriella as happy as she is when she comes back from her time with you. It's like… it's like she's become the woman she always wanted to be but never had the courage to try before. I know what our father's like—I've tried so hard to step out of his shadow… She never had the chance. Until she met you."

Damn it, was Chance going to fall for this line of bull?

Yeah, he was. Because he could see the truth of the words. Rodrigo del Toro was a monster of a man. Plus,

Gabriella had said as much—when she was with him, she was the woman she wanted to be. He'd believed her then.

He believed Alex now.

"You screw me over again and we won't have to worry about Joaquin. Do I make myself clear?"

Alex sighed, looking as if that was what he'd expected, but somehow it was still disappointing. "Crystal. I'll call you tomorrow. We'll have to work around my father. Hopefully, she can get out for dinner. Is that okay?"

No. But what other plan did he have? He didn't trust Alex but he believed Joaquin would shoot him and it would destroy Gabriella. Besides, he didn't particularly want to die today. Or tomorrow, for that matter.

So, against his better judgment, he put his faith in the one man who didn't deserve it—Alex del Toro.

"Yeah, call me tomorrow."

"I will," Alex promised.

"You damn well better."

"That was Cara? *Windsor?*" Gabriella couldn't get her head around it. The woman Chance was rumored to have kidnapped Alex for was the one in his arms? On his couch?

"Yes." Alex looked terrible, but it wasn't the same kind of terrible that he'd been faking for weeks. This time, Gabriella thought he looked…guilty.

"But they weren't kissing. He was just comforting her? Because she was—what? Upset about you?"

"Yes," Alex repeated, looking even more miserable.

"And this was all one giant misunderstanding, was it?" At least they were alone. Joaquin had not followed her into her room when she'd rushed into the house and thrown herself on her bed in a truly melodramatic fashion. For that she was grateful. She could only hope he had not returned to McDaniel's Acres to finish Chance off.

"Yes."

Gabriella's cheeks burned, but she couldn't tell if that was out of relief or embarrassment. When she'd seen Chance with his arms around that blond woman, she'd experienced a shock so physical that it had been all she could do not to lose her stomach's contents right then and there.

Chance had said he'd loved her. And he'd been holding another woman.

All she'd been able to think was that she'd been a fool. She'd saved herself, and for what? She was just as disposable as all the maids had complained about during her youth. Disposable and replaceable.

She'd been the same fool her brother had been; falling for the sweet words of a man who would *always* betray the del Toro family at the first available moment.

But here sat Alex, protesting that she had somehow *not* seen what she'd seen, that Chance had not been wooing another woman. She didn't know if she should be happy that Chance was as trustworthy as she believed him to be or embarrassed that she hadn't trusted him even more.

She didn't want to see Chance just yet, not until she could sort through all the conflicting feelings that were making breathing a difficult chore. And Alex, despite his earnest intentions, had not seen what she'd seen.

Which meant there was only one other person she could ask.

"Where is your phone?"

"What?" Alex gave her an odd look, but he dug it out of his pocket. "Why?"

"I do not have Cara Windsor's number. You do. Call her. I want to speak to this woman."

He paled. "I don't know if that's a good idea…"

A flash of anger pushed back against her confused relief. "You do not think *what* is a good idea? Me, talking to another woman? Me, attempting to resolve a problem on my own? Me, being responsible for my own fate? I want to talk to Cara. If you do not give me her number, I will find another way to get it. And I will not hesitate to tell everyone in this three-horse town that your mind is as solid as it was the day you came north of the border!"

Alex gaped at her in shock, as if she had never spoken to him in such a way. Perhaps she hadn't, but she was sick to death of her family smothering her. She wanted to breathe without having to account to someone for her need of oxygen.

Then his mouth quirked up into a smile as he began tapping his screen. "A *two*-horse town. Not three. Didn't Chance teach you anything?"

"He taught me *many* things," she retorted. She couldn't even blush when he shot her a surprised look. She held out her hand for the phone.

"Should have let Joaquin shoot him," he muttered as he handed the ringing phone over.

"Alex? Baby, is that you? Oh, thank God!" The woman's voice on the other end of the phone spoke so fast that Gabriella had trouble understanding her. "Baby, I've been so worried about you—when can I see you?"

This Cara did not sound particularly guilty about being caught kissing Chance. If anything, she sounded as though she was crying.

"Ah, hello? This is Gabriella del Toro. Alex's sister." She looked at Alex, who had leaned in close to listen to the conversation. She couldn't decipher the look on his face, though.

"Oh." This momentary disappointment was quickly erased by concern. "Is he all right? Is everything okay?"

"Alex is fine." Although Cara Windsor sounded somewhat hysterical, Gabriella couldn't say that was a bad thing. Her concern for Alex—and her lack of concern for Chance—was a good sign.

But emotions were easy to fake over the phone. "I think

there may have been a misunderstanding earlier today. I'd like to meet you in person so we can get it cleared up."

"Chance would never cheat on you. I mean, he'd never cheat on anyone—he's not like that. This is all my fault…" She sounded as if she were crying again.

"Is there somewhere we could go for coffee to talk?"

"Do you…? Can I see Alex? Will he come with you?"

At this, Alex shook his head. "Ah, no. Not yet. But soon, I believe."

"All right." Cara sniffed. "We can meet at the Royal Diner—in an hour? Does that work for you?"

Gabriella looked at the clock. It was seven now. By eight, the dinner crowd of a diner should have cleared. Besides, she probably needed to fix her makeup and change into more appropriate clothing. Something far less revealing. "That would be fine. I'll see you then."

She ended the call and handed the phone back to her brother. "Thank you."

"Don't tell her I remember."

"Why not? She's obviously worried about you." Her frustration bubbled over. "I'm tired of living inside your deceptions, Alex. When will it all end?"

He took her hand then, patting it as if she was a small child again. Then he stood.

"Soon. I promise."

Perhaps she shouldn't be so disappointed by this small lie, not compared to all the rest. But she was.

She wished she could believe him.

Exactly an hour later Joaquin pulled up outside the Royal Diner. He was not happy about this excursion. Gabriella could tell by the way he would not meet her gaze, but she did not care.

Not when there was a chance that Chance had been honest with her. She had to know.

She recognized Cara immediately. The slim blonde was sitting in a booth at the back, dabbing at her eyes and staring at the coffee cup in front of her.

Gabriella did not want to do this. She was in no mood to offer up her heart just to have it ripped out of her chest for the second time today.

But she needed to know that Chance wouldn't have betrayed her. She needed to *believe* it.

"Cara?" When the woman looked up and gave her a sad smile, Gabriella slid into the booth. Joaquin took a spot at the counter, but he wasn't within earshot. Not if Gabriella kept her voice low.

A waitress immediately brought over a cup of coffee. "Anything else, hon?"

"We're fine, Amanda," Cara answered. "Thanks."

"Let me know." This Amanda gave Cara a quick squeeze on the shoulder before making her rounds to the other patrons of the diner.

"I suppose there's no good way to start, is there?" Cara sat back, her chin a little higher but her eyes still quite red. "I'd heard you were in town, but I didn't realize that you and Chance…"

She did not want to know what other people were "realizing" about her and Chance. So she hurried to cut Cara off.

"And I had only recently found out about you," Gabriella admitted.

"How is Alex? Does he…does he remember me?" Her eyes began to water again.

Gabriella felt a deep level of sympathy with this woman—a woman she would have been willing to throw to the wolves earlier today. She knew how painful it was when Alex wouldn't remember her. What if Chance suddenly didn't remember her? It would break her heart over and over again.

She chose her words carefully. "He is…improving." She couldn't say more, no matter how dishonest it was.

"Oh, that's good. That's better than…than—" Cara broke off, covering her mouth with her hand. "I'm glad you called," she went on when she had herself back under control. "I feel terrible about what happened this afternoon. I went to see Chance because, well, because I needed a friend and that's what Chance is—a friend. He's a wonderful man and it's been awful that people have been spreading lies about him, about how he hurt Alex to get me back. Chance isn't like that—he never has been. He cares for his friends—even when his friend dumped him for his best friend." Her face twisted into a mask of pain and guilt.

"I see," Gabriella said, wondering if she could trust this woman or if the weeping was all part of the act.

Cara must have heard the doubt in Gabriella's voice because she looked up and said, "I went to see Chance today because I'm pregnant with Alex's baby and he doesn't remember me. I…I don't know what to do."

"¡Dios mío!" Gabriella whispered, trying to process all the information Cara Windsor had just shared. Her brain tried to filter the fact that Alex would be a father in three different languages but all that happened was a hum of noise in her head. "A *baby?* Alex's baby?"

"When Alex's number came up on my phone, I was so excited— If I could tell him what's happened, maybe I could help him remember. I just want him to remember that he loved me."

Gabriella knew those feelings—weeks of being trapped in a house with a man who wasn't entirely her brother anymore and trying everything she could to help his memory. She felt for Cara Windsor. But she had to guard her own heart first. "There is nothing between you and Chance?"

Cara shook her head vigorously. "We're friends. We've always been friends. I think we'll always be friends—but nothing more. I love Alex Santiago." Her eyes began to water again. "The man I thought Alex was."

Gabriella could not help herself. She leaned forward and placed her hand on Cara's. "He loved you, too. I am certain of it. I believe he still does, but it's buried deep inside." That was not a lie, either. The only difference was that Alex was willfully keeping those emotions buried—it had nothing to do with head trauma.

"Thank you. Thank you for meeting me and letting me explain about Chance. I want him to be happy. He's a kind, sweet man and I tried so hard to love him. But then I met your brother..." She trailed off, looking lost in thought. "I asked Chance not to tell Alex I was expecting. I know we just met and you don't owe me a thing, but can I ask the same of you? I want to tell him face-to-face. Maybe it'll help."

Another lie. Gabriella tried very hard to keep the weariness off her face. Everyone had secrets that must be kept at all costs. Was she any different? She was in Chance's bed—something she did not want her father to find out under any circumstances.

And now this. A baby complicated things in ways that she had not dreamed were possible. What would Rodrigo del Toro do when he found out that his daughter was sleeping with a rancher and his son had fathered a child? She did not even want to contemplate the scene.

"No matter what, that baby is family, which makes you family." Gabriella felt herself tearing up as she spoke the words. "I won't tell Alex, but if there is anything I can do for you, do not hesitate to ask. The del Toro family has considerable resources at our disposal."

"The only thing I want is my Alex back," Cara said.

"We all do," Gabriella agreed. "We all do."

Fifteen

Chance slept fitfully with his phone in his hand, his boots by the side of the bed and an ice pack on his face. He knew that Gabriella wasn't going to call him at five in the morning to kiss and make up, but he couldn't help himself.

He had terrible dreams about Alex kicking him while he was down and Gabriella being pulled away from him.

He shouldn't have trusted the man, he decided as he made coffee at five-fifteen, his phone within easy reach on the counter. He should have risked being gut-shot by that damn guard so that he could be the one to talk to Gabriella. None of this second-hand horseshit. He didn't exactly know how the del Toro family operated—although he had a damn good idea—but the buck always stopped with the McDaniel men. He'd been comforting Cara. It should have been his job to make things right with Gabriella.

Six o'clock passed at slower than molasses in January. Seven did the same. By the time eight crawled by, Chance had drunk way too much coffee and was officially jittery.

Maybe he should go on over to the house. Hadn't that been a romantic movie back in the 80s? *Say...Something?* No, *Say Anything*—that'd been the movie where the guy stood on his car and blasted music from a boom box to wake up his girlfriend after a fight.

Chance went so far as to dig out his iPod before he realized he probably couldn't crank the volume loud enough for her to hear it in Alex's big house. Besides, the neighbors would probably call the cops on him. Nathan Battle, the sheriff, probably wouldn't arrest him, but it'd make a hell of a scene—and not the kind that would sway Gabriella to take him back.

Damn it all. He was going to drive himself insane in record time. If patience was a virtue, Chance was up to his eyeballs in sin right about now. How on God's green earth was he supposed to hold out until dinner tonight?

So when his phone rang at eight-thirty, he physically pounced on the damn thing in his eagerness to answer it. *Please be Gabriella,* he thought as he touched the screen, even though it was Alex's number. *Please be Gabriella.* "Hello?"

"Chance?"

At any point in the past few months, Chance would have been thrilled to hear his friend call him by name. Except for right now. "Yeah?"

"Tell me Gabriella is with you," Alex said, and Chance heard the panic in the man's voice.

"What do you mean? Of course she's not with me. I'm sitting here waiting for you to call and tell me everyone's calmed down. Where is she?"

"I don't know. She's not in her room and Joaquin says he hasn't seen her this morning."

"Have you searched the house?"

"I even checked the pool and the clubhouse—she's *gone.*"

Jesus, Alex was supposed to be calming her down—she wouldn't have done anything drastic, would she?

No. He didn't believe she'd do something like that. But that didn't mean something drastic hadn't happened.

"Check the damn house again. I'm coming over. Call Nathan."

"Papa doesn't want me to. We don't even know if she's missing. Chance—"

Hell, no. Alex wasn't going to pull the same line of bull about how he should handle this. This was exactly what Chance got for letting another man fight his battles. "I'm coming over." He hung up and dialed again. Carlotta answered at the front desk of the Bunk House. "Good morning, *señor.*"

"Carlotta, Gabriella has disappeared. We may have another kidnapping on our hands. Have the maids check every single room in the hotel, no exceptions. Wake up the whole damn place if you have to." He hung up and dialed a second time. "Marty? Gabriella's gone missing. Round up as many men as you can and start combing the range. Check Slim's shop first, the swimming hole second. Call me the moment you find her."

It was possible that she'd gone to those places—someplace quiet and familiar, where she could think.

But something told him that wasn't the case. What if the people who'd taken Alex had come for Gabriella? The thought made his stomach turn and turn hard. As much as she'd tried to keep a stiff upper lip when she'd told him about her mother's kidnapping and the attempts—both real and staged—on her life, he'd been able to tell that being taken was the scariest thing in her life.

God, he prayed as he drove at top speed, *keep her safe. Even if she's not mine to hold, keep her safe. Don't let her be scared.* Gabriella was a religious woman. Hopefully someone was answering prayers up there today.

She never went anywhere without Joaquin. Sometimes, after they'd made love and were lying in bed, she'd told him more about her life on her father's estate. She'd told him about a stable boy she'd kissed more out of defiance than love, about cutting off her hair when she was forbidden to go to "university," as she put it. She even told him about Raoul, the man her father allowed to escort her to events, and how he would put his hands on her as if he owned her. Which was why she'd never slept with him.

Never once had she mentioned actually sneaking out and giving old Joaquin a run for his money.

Something about this whole thing smelled worse than a cow patty in the summer sun.

He made it to Alex's house in record time. The place was quiet, like it was another regular Saturday morning. Obviously, Alex had not called the damn cops. Yet. What was wrong with that man?

He didn't bother with such crap as ringing a doorbell or knocking. He opened that door and walked right in to find Alex on the phone and Joaquin slumped down on the couch. Something was even more wrong than he thought.

"I got the maids checking the hotel and Marty checking the ranch," he said with no other introduction. "Where the hell is your father?"

Alex shot him a frantic look. "He's 'in a meeting' if you can believe that," Alex snapped before turning back to the phone. "Yes, I know—but I'd appreciate it if you could check. Thanks." He ended the call. "I've checked the pool and clubhouse again, gone through the house top to bottom. Nathan's going to start looking." Then, looking contrite, he added, "Sorry about your face."

The black eye Alex had given him was the least of his worries. "You actually called the sheriff?"

"Papa said not to, then locked himself in his office. Something's off and I don't like it."

"Yeah," Chance said, turning to the only other person in the room—the only person who wasn't frantic. "Yeah, something sure as hell seems off. Where is she?"

Joaquin didn't respond. Not in words, anyway. But he leaned forward and put his head in his hands.

Suddenly, Chance wished to holy hell that he'd brought his shotgun. Screw that. He could do a hell of a lot of damage without one.

He walked up to Joaquin, grabbed the man by the shirt and hauled him to his feet. That the big man didn't offer any resistance only confirmed Chance's suspicions. "Where the hell is she? You never let her out of your sight. For God's sake, you sit in my living room when we're in bed to make sure that no one bothers us."

"Man," Alex whispered. "I don't want to know that about my sister."

Joaquin dropped his eyes.

"I'd have thought," Chance said, ignoring Alex and giving Joaquin a little shake, "after *all this time,* you wanted her to be happy. That was why you let her be with me—it made her happy to ride and to work metal and to fall in love. But you never cared about her, did you? She was just some girl you had to watch. Just an *assignment* you had to complete. Tell me where she is, Joaquin, or you'll rot in hell for the rest of this eternity and the next."

The big man was silent, as if Chance had already broken him but hadn't realized it yet. "You know who took her and you let them do it," he yelled in Joaquin's face, hoping to get a reaction—any reaction—out of him. "You rat bastard, you *let* them do it."

"Correction," a stern voice with a thick accent announced from behind Chance. He let go of Joaquin, who dropped like a sack of potatoes, and spun to face Rodrigo del Toro. "He did not go with Gabriella because I ordered him not to."

"Another sick little test? You disgust me. The way you treat your daughter—*both* your children—is nothing short of criminal."

Chance realized too late that he was shouting at Gabriella's father, but he didn't care. This man—this monster—had done something with her and Chance *had* to get her back.

For his part, Rodrigo looked unmoved by Chance's insults. Instead he turned to Alex. "*This* is the man you befriended?" He looked to Joaquin. "*This* is the man you allowed my daughter to spend time with?" Both times, he spoke as if Chance were a piece of crap he'd stepped in. "I held you to a higher standard, Joaquin. I entrusted you with the thing that was most precious to me and you failed. Your services are no longer required by the del Toro family."

"Gabriella is *not* a thing," Chance growled. He'd never wanted to hit a man so hard in his entire life. One well-placed punch could take the older man down for good. "She's a woman. Where the hell is she?"

Not that Rodrigo was worried about getting punched. "When Joaquin told me of her involvement with a *rancher* like you, I knew I could not allow it to continue."

"What did you do, Papa?" Alex sounded as if his world was crumbling—and he couldn't do anything but watch it go. Why the hell wasn't he madder? Chance wondered. Why the hell wasn't he freaking *furious?*

"Raoul Viega came for her," Rodrigo said in a matter-of-fact tone. "Clearly, Gabriella is no longer happy at Las Cruces and, equally clearly, she is ready to be married. Raoul is from a suitable class. His father is a valuable business partner. This will cement our ties and Raoul will keep her safe."

"You—what? You *gave* her to Raoul?" Chance could not believe the words coming out of this man's mouth. Of all the bat-shit-crazy things he'd ever heard, treating your daughter like a party favor had to rank right up there.

"She is my daughter," Rodrigo replied in the haughtiest voice Chance had ever heard. "I will do with her as I see fit."

"The hell you will." Chance spun back to where Joaquin sat collapsed on the couch, looking for all the world as if he'd been shot and was bleeding out. "I'm hiring—head of security at McDaniel's Acres. New position—just opened up. You interested?"

"Qué?"

"He fired you. I'm hiring you. The first job I have for you is finding Gabriella. You in?"

Joaquin gaped at him, so Chance turned to Alex. "You in?"

"You would not dare," Rodrigo threatened. "Alejandro, you would not *dare* go against my direct orders."

Behind him, Chance felt Joaquin get to his feet. He braced for a blow, but what came next was an even bigger surprise. "They left half an hour ago. I know his car."

Rodrigo's face contorted with unmasked rage. "You will *suffer* for this, Joaquin."

Chance kept looking at Alex. Just yesterday, he'd told Chance that he knew what his father was like. Well, Chance did now, too. "You *in?* I can't wait around all day."

"Alejandro!" Rodrigo roared.

Alex dropped his head like a small boy who'd been beaten down one too many times. But then he lifted his head, his eyes lit with new fire. "My name," he said to his father as he began walking toward the door, "is Alex."

"Let's get gone," Chance said, clapping his old friend on the back and doing his level best to ignore the threats in both Spanish and English that followed the three men out of the house. He shut the door to block the older man out.

They had to get Gabriella before she made it south of the border. Even if she decided that he'd been nothing more than a great way to spend the time while she was stuck in Texas—even if she never wanted to see him again, he couldn't stand by while some entitled business brat took her home and married her.

"We've got a lot of road to cover. Call Nathan back and tell him what we know. Maybe one of his cop buddies can get their car stopped before they hit the border."

"Done. I'll follow you in my car." Alex was dialing before Joaquin got the car door shut.

"Keep up," was all Chance said. Then they were gone.

Sixteen

"I want," Gabriella said in the most level voice she could manage, "to go home."

Raoul snorted in the way that had always reminded her of a pig snuffling in its trough. "We'll be home soon enough. You will enjoy Casa Catalina. Your father will have your things sent over. You will want for nothing."

"I want," she repeated with a little more force, "to go back to Alex's house. Right *now.*"

Raoul snorted again. Then he reached over and grabbed her thigh with more pressure than was comfortable. "You will grow to love Casa Catalina. You will grow to love *me.* We shall be married next week." And he squeezed her thigh hard enough to leave marks through the jeans she'd hurried into this morning, half-asleep when Joaquin had come into her room and told her to get dressed.

It hurt, but she refused to let a whimper of pain escape her lips. She would not let this man know that she was terrified of what he was saying. "When my papa finds out what you have done…" But even as she said it, she knew it was not the case.

"I'll have you know, *muñequita,* that he called me yesterday and told me to come get you. He said you weren't safe in America anymore."

Muñequita. Little doll. It was supposed to be a term of endearment, but it grated on her very last nerve. A little china doll to be locked behind glass, protected from everything. Protected from *life.* A doll was all she was to her father and that's all she was to Raoul.

With a final squeeze, Raoul took his hand off her leg.

Gabriella kept her mouth shut. Arguing was pointless. Obviously, Raoul would not be swayed from the path he and her father had agreed on. She was to be married within a week to this man, who would lock her up on a different estate and only touch her when he wanted to, not when she wanted him to. That, of course, would be never. The only man she wanted to touch her was Chance. Raoul may think he'd have an easy time of it now that she was no longer a virgin, but she would fight him every step of the way.

Starting now. What were her options? She could hit him with something. She had grabbed her purse on her way out to the garage, where Joaquin had said someone was waiting for her. She'd foolishly hoped it was Chance making some grand romantic gesture. Instead she'd found herself being roughly shoved into the open door of Raoul's Porsche. Joaquin had closed the door, narrowly missing her foot, and then Raoul had been backing out of the garage, locking the doors as he went.

Texas was a large state and, as far as she could tell, Raoul was obeying all traffic laws. He probably thought it prudent to avoid getting pulled over by a police officer. Soon, they would be near Midland, Texas—if she could only get out of the car, there was a chance she could find someone who would help her. She had her phone—surely a 9-1-1 call would bring the police?

If she hit Raoul, he might lose control of his car and wreck—which would kill them both.

For the first time in her life Gabriella understood how her mother must have felt when she'd been taken from the market so many years ago. Would Gabriella risk death to get back to the man she loved, as her mother had done to get back to her? Or was it better to go along quietly and wait for a better opportunity to happen?

If she did not hit Raoul, what were her other options? Midland was approximately four hours from Ciudad Juarez, the closest border crossing. Raoul probably had his family plane on the other side of the border—on this short notice, he probably hadn't been able to get clearance to land in America without arousing the suspicions of drug-enforcement officers.

Raoul might stop at a restroom before they crossed the border, especially if she threatened to relieve herself in the seat of his favorite car. She could try to slip away then. Or she could cause a scene at the border crossing. It might get her arrested and searched by the American customs officials, but it would keep her from getting on a plane with Raoul. Once he had her in Mexico, on his personal property, it would be much, *much* harder to get free of him.

What would her mother have done? She would have hit Raoul. She would not have waited for the just-right time. Mama would have been frantic to get back to her children, Gabriella realized. For so long, Gabriella had felt anger toward her mother for not going along—for not living to tell the tale. But now she understood. Fear had driven Mama to desperate measures.

Still, if she were going to hit Raoul, it would be better if he were not driving.

They were nearing the edge of Midland now. Billboards advertising fast-food restaurant were visible in the distance. But they were still far away from anything that resembled hustle or bustle, especially this early on a Saturday. She should wait until they were in a more populated area—safety in numbers and all that.

Unexpectedly a blue pickup pulled up alongside the

Porsche. *Odd,* Gabriella thought as the vehicle started honking, *that looks like Chance's truck.*

The truck shot forward and then came to a screeching halt some hundred feet in front of Raoul's car, blocking the road entirely.

"¿Qué carajo?" Raoul sputtered, swerving wildly.

Joaquin got out and began to walk toward the car, almost as if he wanted Raoul to run him down in the line of duty.

"¡Mierda!" Raoul cried, jerking the wheel so violently that Gabriella was sure the Porsche went up on two wheels. They spun in a tight circle before coming to a rest in the middle of the road.

When her head stopped spinning, she realized Raoul was trying to open the glove box. Of course—she should have realized he probably had a weapon with him. The moment he got it open, she slammed it shut on his fingers. He howled. Seconds later, the driver's door opened and Raoul was unceremoniously jerked out of the car.

Then her door opened and Chance was there. He held out a hand for her. "Are you okay, babe?"

"Take your hands off me, *idiota!*" Raoul shouted from the other side of the car.

"I got you," Chance said, his voice low and reassuring. "You can get out now. He can't touch you again."

She took his hand and was surprised to see that her arm was trembling. He helped her out of the car and pulled her into a strong embrace. Her whole body started to shake.

"I got you, babe," he said as he walked her away from the Porsche. "I got you."

"Chance," she managed to say, but her throat closed up, pushing her dangerously close to crying. And she would not let Raoul see her cry.

"She is mine!" Raoul yelled across the highway. *"¡Es mía!"*

"I'm taking her back where she belongs." Heavens, was that her brother? Had he been in the truck?

"She's coming to Mexico with me," Raoul all but snarled. "That is what Rodrigo and I agreed upon." He then made a little squeaking noise. Had Joaquin hit him? Or had Alex?

"Are you okay?" Chance asked again. His arms were still around her, his chest warm against hers. It was still early enough that there wasn't any other traffic on the road.

"Some bruises," she admitted, trying to block out the sounds of Raoul and Alex arguing about who had the right to take her to which home.

She didn't want anyone to take her. She just wanted to *go*.

Chance pushed her back so he could look at her. "I called Nathan. He'll arrest him for battery and attempted kidnapping."

She gasped as she got a good look at his face. "What happened?" she asked as she touched the massive black eye that covered half his face.

His smile was crooked, which made him wince. "Your brother punched me because I made you cry."

"¡Dios!" The tears tried to move up again, but the sounds of shouting reminded her that she couldn't fall apart, not yet.

"I want you to hear it from me," he went on, completely ignoring the argument behind him, "that there's nothing going on between me and Cara. She's got a problem and she needed a shoulder to cry on and some advice—nothing more. I would *never* step out on you."

She knew that, of course—but to hear him say it made her weak not with fear but with relief. "I know. I talked with her last night. We met at the diner. She explained her...problem to me." She grinned up at him. "What does 'step out' mean?"

His smile got wider. "Cheat, babe. I'd never cheat."

Behind them, the sound of the fight was getting louder. "What do you want to do?"

Part of her wanted him to sweep her off her feet and carry her away from all of this—Raoul, Joaquin, Alex. From her father, who'd arranged this "marriage."

"Because whatever you want," he said, his poor bruised face quite serious, "the answer is yes."

He was asking her. Not even Alex was asking what she wanted—he was still arguing with Raoul about who got to do what with her.

"If you want to go with this *cabrón,*" Chance said, pronouncing the profanity in Spanish perfectly, "then I'll step aside. If you want to go back to Alex's house and stay with your father, that's fine, too."

"I do not want to do either of those things. I never want to see Raoul again."

That time, Chance did not wince through his grin. "Done." He turned. "Joaquin! See that Raoul leaves. Alone."

"Sí," Joaquin replied, shoving Raoul toward the Porsche.

"Wait—I think Raoul has a gun in the glove box." She could see him firing at all of them as he drove away, not caring who he hit.

One of Chance's eyebrows—the one over the unbruised eye—jumped up. "Check the glove box first," he yelled over his shoulder.

Gabriella watched in amazement as Joaquin did exactly what Chance asked of him. He shoved Raoul roughly at Alex, who caught the man and held him tight. The Joaquin went through the car, starting with the glove box. He pulled out the handgun but found nothing else.

Chance kept a strong arm around her shoulder, but he didn't try to shield her from the scene in front of them. It was then that she saw Alex's red Ferrari behind Raoul's car. Raoul was completely blocked in. For some reason, it made her happy that her brother had come with Chance, even if he was arguing that Gabriella should go back with him.

Chance turned back to her, that twinkle in his eyes. "Will you get in the truck so I can move it? I don't want to be in Raoul's way as he leaves."

She nodded and climbed up. Alex went back to his car to move it, as well, but Joaquin stood on the shoulder of the road, Raoul's gun aimed at the area where Raoul's knee probably was on the other side of the car door.

Chance slid into the driver's seat and moved the truck off to the side of the road. Raoul roared past them, making a variety of offensive hand gestures as he went.

Then it was quiet. Gabriella looked in the rearview mirror. Joaquin crossed the road, his eyes trained on Raoul's rapidly disappearing car.

"What happened?" Chance asked, reaching over—but not taking her hand. Waiting for him. Asking permission.

She didn't hesitate. She entwined her fingers with his. "Joaquin woke me up and hurried me downstairs. Before I knew it, I was in the car and Raoul was driving off. He said…he said my father called him because I wasn't safe in America anymore."

"Yeah, that's pretty much what he told me, too."

"Why is Joaquin taking orders from you? *He* betrayed me. *He* put me in the car with Raoul."

"Well, now—funny story." He ran his thumb over her knuckles. "I think ol' Joaquin felt lower than a rattler's belly in a wheel rut about that—and then your father up and fired him on the spot because the big man let you spend time with me. So I hired him—head of security on McDaniel's Acres. New position."

Gabriella shook her head, unsure if she could trust her ears. "You *hired* Joaquin?"

"He took the job. Told me what Raoul was driving, which way he'd gone."

Well. There was that. Joaquin felt remorse and had tried to redeem himself. Alex cared enough to help find her.

But Chance had come for her. She knew that neither her brother nor her bodyguard would have attempted this grand rescue without Chance pulling them both along.

"So now," Chance said, raising her hand to his lips and kissing it, "I think it's time for you to tell me what you want to happen next."

She looked around. A few cars had gone past them. Joaquin was still standing opposite Chance's truck, the gun nowhere in sight. Alex was in his car behind the truck.

"I want to do what I want. I want to come and go and not have to report in or be 'protected.' I want to ride and work metal and be happy. I want to be free."

Chance looked down at where their hands were joined. It was almost as if this pronouncement worried him. Then he said, "Hang on." He let go of her hand and opened his door. "Joaquin—you want to get a ride back with Alex? Come out to the ranch later. We'll start the paperwork."

Joaquin stared at the two of them for a moment before nodding his head and walking back to Alex's car. Carefully, her brother drove over the grassy median until he was pointed back toward Royal, Texas.

She waited until Alex's car was gone. Alone. They were finally, truly alone. Up to this point, Chance had been wonderful asking her what she wanted. But the truth was she wanted him. And she wanted to be sure that he wanted her, too. So she asked, "What about you?"

"I want to keep my land in McDaniels' hands. I want to come home to a good woman in my bed. I want to have some babies that learn to ride horses and jump into swimming holes." His voice was low. She looked at him. From this side, she couldn't see his bruised face at all. "I'd like to do all those things with you."

Yes. To share her bed with him, to be a mother—the things that had always seemed out of reach. "Will you have Joaquin follow me around? I don't want to be protected anymore, Chance."

"Nope. If you want to go for a ride or to town for coffee alone, that's fine by me. If you want Joaquin to drive you, that's okay, too. But if you want me to come with you," he said, looking her in the eye, "well, all you have to do is ask. You already know the answer."

Yes. The answer would be *yes.*

"I do not want to live in sin. I will attend church every Sunday."

The corner of his mouth crooked up in the way that spoke volumes about what kind of sin he might be able to live with. "I can have a preacher at the ranch tomorrow morning."

She tilted his face. The bruise was truly spectacular—one that would take some time to fade away. "Perhaps we should wait. Just a little bit."

But did that mean she would have to go back to Alex's house? Where her father would no doubt try to bend her to his will again?

Chance must have read her mind. "You know, I got this great big hotel—real nice place. Not too crowded right now. You can have any room you want, for as long as you want."

"And Joaquin?" She *so* wanted to be free—not just the illusion of freedom, but the real thing. And yet…the idea scared her, just a little. This must be how a caged animal felt when it was finally released back into the wild—freedom could be a little overwhelming.

"I got a room for him on the ground floor where he can

keep tabs on who's coming and going. Franny'll cook him dinner. I'm not worried about him."

Yes, she thought, that would be good. She did not know if she would ever see her father again. But Joaquin—he had always been more of a father to her, anyway. "I can set up my workshop?"

"We'll get your horse shipped up—all your things. Anything you want." He leaned over, cupping her chin in his hand and lifted her mouth to his. "Gabriella del Toro, will you marry me?"

She could not help herself. "You already know the answer, don't you, Chance McDaniel?"

"Yeah," he said, brushing his lips against hers. "I do."

* * * * *

"I'm going along with your plan because you've given me no choice, but I am not sleeping with you, Nathan Reed."

His heavy brows rose in response to her declaration. "I hadn't planned on seducing you." Nate stood up and rounded the coffee table. He leaned over her, trapping her between the long length of his arms.

Annie eased back into the couch, but there wasn't anywhere else to go. She could only breathe in his cologne and remember that same scent on her pillows as she'd slept in this very suite. Back then, Nate had had the ability to play her body like a musical instrument he'd studied his whole life. She'd never been with another man who could bring her pleasure like he had. What they had had was explosive. Mind-blowing.

The closer he came to her, the more she wondered if that connection had severed during their time apart. It didn't feel like it.

His gaze raked over her body. "But if I did...what's so wrong with that? It's not a crime to sleep with your own husband, Annie."

BACK IN HER HUSBAND'S BED

BY
ANDREA LAURENCE

MILLS & BOON

Published in Great Britain 2014
by Mills & Boon, an imprint of Harlequin (UK) Limited,
Eton House, 18-24 Paradise Road, Richmond, Surrey, TW9 1SR

ISBN: 978 0 263 91456 6

51-0214

Harlequin (UK) Limited's policy is to use papers that are natural, renewable and recyclable products and made from wood grown in sustainable forests. The logging and manufacturing processes conform to the legal environmental regulations of the country of origin.

Printed and bound in Spain
by Blackprint CPI, Barcelona

Andrea Laurence is an award-winning contemporary romance author who has been a lover of books and writing stories since she learned to read. She always dreamed of seeing her work in print and is thrilled to be able to share her books with the world. A dedicated West Coast girl transplanted into the Deep South, she's working on her own "happily ever after" with her boyfriend and five fur-babies. You can contact Andrea at her website: www.andrealaurence.com.

To My Awesome Editor, Shana Smith–

Thank you for rescuing me and this book from the slush pile and seeing us for the diamonds in the (very) rough that we were. Even when this story didn't seem like it would work out, you didn't give up on it or my ability to make it shine. You may not know this, but when you found me, I was on the verge of giving up and I'm so glad I didn't. You have quite literally changed my life and I can't send enough cookies and cupcakes to thank you for it.

One

"Mr. Reed, our facial recognition software has detected a match for the Barracuda in pit three near the dollar slots."

Nate smiled. Like a moth to a flame, Annie had walked right into his trap. He knew she couldn't pass up the chance to play at his poker tournament, even if it meant returning to the scene of the crime. As the owner and manager of the Desert Sapphire Hotel and Casino, it was easy to have Annie red-flagged by his security team. The moment she strolled back in to his casino he knew it.

"We have visual confirmation. She's on her way to the high-roller area." Gabriel Hansen, his chief of security, lifted his hand to his earpiece and listened intently for a moment before nodding in confirmation. "She's joined the Texas Hold'em game with Mr. Nakimori and Mr. Kline."

"Of course she has." Nate set aside his paperwork and made his way to the elevator. There was no time to waste. The Japanese businessman and the oil tycoon had credit lines in the millions, and they'd need every penny if he didn't get down there. They didn't call her the Barracuda for nothing.

"Do you need assistance with this, Mr. Reed?" Gabe was also his best friend, despite the formalities they used at work. Gabe knew what Annie's arrival meant. His offer to accompany him was less about work and more about helping his friend.

Nate sighed and straightened his navy silk tie. He suspected Gabe would relish handcuffing Annie and parading her through the casino so everyone would see. To be honest, he wouldn't mind that himself, but she'd never agree to his plan if he did. "No, I've got this handled."

A quick swipe of his identification card sent the elevator plummeting down the twenty-five floors from his suite to the main casino lobby. A soft chime announced his arrival, and the doors opened to the office corridors where casino operations took place.

The walk through the casino to the high-roller area wasn't long, but each step weighed more heavily on him than the last. Annie was here. In his casino. After three long years. He should be excited to finally confront her. To have his chance to exact his revenge and make her miserable. Or if not excited, perhaps smug. His plan was working just as he'd hoped it would. And yet he was none of those things.

His mouth was dry, his pulse racing in his throat. If he didn't know better, he might think he was nervous. Imagine that: Nathan Reed, millionaire casino owner, former most eligible bachelor in Las Vegas, nervous. It was a ridiculous idea. And yet Annie had always been his weakness.

Nate rounded the corner and spied the entrance to the high-roller lounge. Even across the casino floor, he could spot her. Her back was to him as she leaned over her cards, her legs crossed beneath the table. Her long raven hair spilled over the olive skin of her bare shoulders. Beside her Mr. Nakimori leaned back into his seat, throwing his cards down in disgust.

Nate stopped just behind Annie and placed a heavy hand on her shoulder. She didn't flinch. She'd been expecting him. Game on.

"Gentlemen," he said, flashing a confident smile at the other players at the table and extending a hand to each of them. "It's good to have you both back here at the Sapphire. Is everything going well for you this afternoon?"

Jackson Kline grinned wide and leaned back into his chair. "It was until this pretty little thing showed up. She's taken more of my money than my ex-wife."

Nate smiled and nodded. "Then I'm sure you gentlemen won't mind if I deprive you of her company."

"We're in the middle of a hand."

They were the first words she'd spoken to him since she disappeared. She didn't say "hello." Not even "I'm sorry" or "You're looking well." Just a complaint that he was interrupting her poker hand.

He leaned down and pressed his lips against the soft outer shell of her ear. The smell of her jasmine shampoo filled his lungs as he hovered near. The familiar scent was alluring and reminded him of the tangled sheets she left behind, but he wasn't going to fall prey to her this time. "We need to talk. Fold." The demand was simple and quiet, but powerful.

"Well, gentlemen—" Annie sighed "—I guess I'm done." She slid the cards across the table and reached up to gently extract Nate's hand from her shoulder. He complied, stepping back far enough to allow her to rise from her seat.

"Good afternoon," the men responded in their respective Southern and Japanese accents, although they both seemed visibly relieved to see her go.

Annie grasped her red leather handbag and strolled to the exit with Nate quick on her heels. He moved alongside her, scooping her elbow up with a firm hand and guiding her toward the elevator.

"Take your hands off me," she hissed through gritted teeth. She tugged against his grasp, but it was futile.

Nate couldn't contain a chuckle. "I will not. You and I both know what happened the last time I did that. If you'd prefer, I could have security escort you upstairs instead."

She came to a sudden stop, jerking Nate to turn back to her. Her azure-blue eyes were alight with anger. They penetrated him, a connection forming between them with a sudden snap of electricity. "You wouldn't dare," she said.

God, she was still beautiful. Nate felt the familiar pull in his gut, the heat flooding his groin. The sexual spark had always been there; it was what brought them together. It just couldn't keep them together. It pissed him off that he still reacted to her like this after everything she'd done.

"I wouldn't?" Nate retorted. Annie didn't know him at all. He leaned down, his face inches from hers. "You wanna call my bluff?" Nate didn't wait for an answer but quickly turned and tugged her behind him.

Annie silenced her protests and stopped resisting his pull. He didn't let go until they stepped off the elevator at his suite. She pulled away, turning left toward his office and dropping angrily onto the leather sofa.

"So?" she asked. "You've dragged me up here and cost me a five-thousand-dollar hand. What do you want?"

Nate avoided the couch, opting instead to lean against the large mahogany desk that had once been his grandfather's. He crossed his arms over his chest and took a deep breath. "I have a proposition for you, Barbara Ann."

Annie arched her eyebrow suspiciously at him, obviously not caring for his use of her given name. "You don't have anything I want, Nathan, or my lawyer would've asked for it already."

"That's not true. I can give you the one thing you've wanted for the last three years—a divorce."

Her blue gaze searched his face, probably looking for the catch. "You and your lawyer have been stonewalling the process for years. You've cost me a fortune in legal fees. And now you're just going to wrap it up in a bow and give it to me?"

"Not exactly." Nate smiled and turned to the bar to pour himself a scotch. He'd let her stew awhile and prolong the torture. She'd made him wait long enough. "Drink?" he offered with his glass held up, more out of politeness than a desire to be truly hospitable.

"You know I don't drink."

Nate stiffened. He'd forgotten. She hated the way alcohol made her feel out of control. It was amazing how the details could slip your mind when you were apart. What else had he forgotten? "A soda, then? Water?"

"No, I'm fine, thank you."

Nate dropped ice cubes into his own glass and nodded before pouring the golden liquid over it. "Very well." He took a sip, appreciating the warm sensation it lit in his stomach. It fueled his resolve and distracted him from the pangs of lust he was determined to ignore.

It was getting harder every minute he spent with her. There was something about Annie that made his blood sing. It was more than just her exotic beauty or her shrewd intelligence. He could still feel the silky slide of her ebony hair across his bare chest as she hovered over him. The musical sound of her laughter. All together it was an intoxicating combination. Just being around her again was enough to ignite the flames of his desire.

And then he would remember that she wanted a divorce. That she had left him in the night after less than two weeks of marriage without a word until he was served the papers.

He supposed he should be grateful that Annie had bothered to file for divorce. His mother hadn't gone to the trouble. She'd just disappeared and sent his father into a spiral of depression that nearly destroyed the Desert Sapphire and his grandfather's legacy with it. Nate was stronger than that. He'd rebuilt the hotel and helped transform the industry, even as she'd left him. He wasn't about to be broken by a woman.

Even one as breathtaking as Annie.

She watched him warily from her seat as he walked toward her and leisurely sipped his drink. "I know you haven't had a sudden change of heart. So what's going on?"

He certainly hadn't. Honestly, it pained him to finally give her what she wanted, but the tournament was more important. The organization that sponsored the most prestigious poker tournament in the industry had a long-standing agreement with another casino. To lure them to the Desert Sapphire, it had taken him three years and a few promises he needed Annie to help him keep.

"I am working on a side project of sorts during the tournament and you're just the right person for the job." He paused, sipping his scotch thoughtfully. "If I sign the papers and give you the divorce you want, you agree to help me."

"I don't understand. How could I possibly—"

Nate cut her protest short with a wave of his hand. "I'm sure you've heard about the cheating problem the poker circuit is having. The rumors are getting fairly loud and the tournament sponsor's reputation is suffering for it. Everyone is anticipating they'll hit the tournament."

Annie sighed. "There's always rumors of cheating, but nothing ever comes of it. The people they catch are usually small potatoes compared to the amount of money exchanged in one of these events. What's the big deal?"

"Hosting the tournament is a huge draw for my hotel. As you well know, it's been held at the Tangiers for the last twenty years. Talking the organizers into moving it here had taken more than some nice negotiating. They wanted concrete guarantees that anyone cheating during the tournament would be caught and prosecuted, to send a message to the community."

"And why are they so confident that your team can do a better job than the Tangiers?"

"Because I have one of the best security systems in the business, with some of the most qualified staff you can hire. We go well beyond the typical measures most casinos employ."

"Seems like overkill to me. I hardly think you can stop cheating."

"This hotel was on the verge of going under when I took over from my father. He wasn't well at the time and people took advantage of the situation. Our biggest issue was people gaming the house, especially our own employees. I wouldn't tolerate that on my watch and invested in cutting-edge technology to stop it. Over the last five years, our estimated losses from cheating are down by eighty percent."

"Then why do you need me?" Annie crossed her arms defensively, pressing her breasts tight against the low V-cut of her sleeveless red silk top.

Just a quick glance at the soft curves of her femininity sent a sharp spike of need down his spine and forced him to turn away. "Because," he said, "I suspect this is a more elaborate and well-organized operation than we're used to. More people are involved…new faces with clean records. But we have to succeed. If we manage to bust this ring, I've got a guaranteed ten-year contract for the tournament. That's something my grandfather wouldn't have even hoped for."

"And what?" she prompted. "You think I know who's involved?"

"I think you probably have your suspicions. You've been active in the community for several years and have to have heard your share of stories." He lifted his gaze to meet hers. "I also think you could flush them out with the right…*motivation*."

Annie leaped up from her seat, the nervous energy his proposal generated propelling her off the leather couch. "I'm not a snitch." There was no way she was going to ruin her reputation like that. Not for a divorce, not for the attentions of a charming, handsome man like Nate. Her honor was all she had in this business.

"If we do it right, no one will ever know that you are."

"And how's that? There are cameras everywhere. The odds are they have help on the inside, possibly even your own security guys and dealers. You don't think they'll notice us talking?"

"Nope. They won't."

He hadn't told her everything. Her game was poker, but Nate's game was chess. He was already three moves ahead of her. Annie hated being outmaneuvered. "Enlighten me."

His mouth curved up in a sly smile. "There are no cameras in here."

Annie looked around the office and down the dark corridor to his suite. She sincerely hoped not. They would've gotten an eyeful during their wedding night. "And no one will find it suspicious that I'm up in your suite? That I'm spending all my time with the casino boss?"

"Why shouldn't you spend time with *your husband?*"

Annie's blood turned to ice in her veins. If there was one thing she clung to, it was that no one knew about their mistake. Their marriage had been a secret she'd shared only with her sister, Tessa, and her mother. Yes, she and Nate would've told people eventually, but in the beginning they'd been far too wrapped up in one another to share the good news. Then it was over. "You don't think people will question that we're suddenly married? That we're together again after all this time apart?"

Nate shrugged. "We'll just tell the truth. We got married three years ago. It didn't work out. We separated. You came back for the tournament and we reconciled."

"That's not the truth."

"No, but the best lies have a good bit of truth in them. The paper trail will back up our story. And we won't give them any reason to doubt it." He smiled a wide, confident smile that started to melt her defenses away before she could think through his statement.

No reason to doubt they were married? "You…you don't honestly expect us to…?" The air in the room suddenly seemed cooler, her skin contracting with goose bumps. Annie crossed her arms protectively over her chest and ran her hands over the bumpy flesh of her bare upper arms.

"No—" he laughed "—of course not. It will just be for show. You'll need to stay here in the suite with me. We'll eat together in public, be affectionate. You might have to suffer through a few of my kisses so any time we spend alone will be chalked up to romantic interludes. No one will suspect what we're really doing together."

Annie felt the rush of blood rise to her cheeks and chase away the chill. When was the last time she'd blushed? Probably her first kiss in sixth grade. She learned to master her emotions not long after that. It made her an excellent poker player. It also made her a really crappy girlfriend. Or wife, as the case was here. Somehow Nate was the only one able to put a dent in her armor.

Suffering wasn't exactly the response she had to his kisses. They always made her head swim. Made her thoughts turn to mush and her body into a bundle of raw nerves. His kisses had been enough to convince her that getting married after only a few days together was a good idea. If Annie was going to kiss him, she'd have to be very careful. The phrase *one thing leads to another* had never been truer than with Nate.

This was a bad idea all around. Spying on her fellow players? Acting the happy couple with Nate? That was like playing with fire. No. This was a ridiculous suggestion. She wouldn't be a party to Nate's games. "What if I say no?"

Annie watched her estranged husband take a large sip of his scotch and cross his arms over his chest. His expensive gray suit coat strained against his broad shoulders as he leaned casually against his desk. He didn't seem at all affected by their conversation or the thought of kissing her. Apparently Annie was the only one still afflicted with that weakness. He was only interested in using her to make his precious hotel even more successful.

Despite everything, she remembered why she'd fallen for Nate. He was all that she was supposed to want in a man: tall, handsome, strong, intelligent, caring and exceedingly wealthy. What she didn't know was how to breathe when someone held her so tightly. She wasn't used to someone else having a say in what she could or couldn't do. Nate's expectations of his wife had been more than she could handle.

The women in her family weren't known for keeping men around. Her marriage, as short-lived as it might've been, was the first in several generations. Magdala Baracas had taught her daughters early on that men could be amusing, but in the end, they were more trouble than they were worth. And looking at her "husband" now just reinforced her mother's wisdom. Nate was infuriating. She'd filed for divorce and he'd contested, refusing to finalize the agreement just to punish her. Now he dangled her freedom as a carrot, but the price was too high.

Nate pinned her with his dark gaze. "No cooperation, no divorce. Simple as that."

Uncomfortable, she shifted her glance away, tracing the angles of his smooth jaw to the dark blond curls that hung just at the edge of his shirt collar. His hair was longer than she remembered. She liked it better this way. Not that it mattered anymore what she thought. Despite what the law said, Nate wasn't hers and hadn't been for a very long time.

Annie sighed in frustration but refused to just bite at whatever he dangled in front of her. "Come on, Nathan, be honest. This isn't about poker cheats. This is about bending me to your will and punishing me for leaving you. You couldn't possibly want to be married to me after everything that's happened."

Annie couldn't tell if her rambling was helping or hurting her cause, but she couldn't stop the words from gushing out of her after three years of silence. "I regret that we confused lust and love and got into this mess. But I want to close this chapter of my life and move on. I don't want to play these games anymore. Please."

At that, Nate took a step away, a Cheshire-cat grin crossing his face. The sudden shift in his mood was unnerving. The dimple in his cheek she'd kissed a hundred times was barely visible from where she was standing. "Did you really think it would be that easy? That you could just look at me with those big blue eyes and I would change my mind?"

Annie stiffened. No, but she wanted this over. Done. She didn't need a single reason to have to be in the same room with Nate again. It was too dangerous. She was too weak. The farther they were apart, the firmer her resolve.

"What's your lawyer charge by the hour, Annie? If you turn down my offer, we can see who runs out of money first."

That was certainly a losing game for her, even after a few fabulously lucrative years. Annie flopped back against the couch, unable to continue fighting with him. "Please, Nate." She wanted out of the marriage, but she knew she couldn't win this hand. She gazed down into her lap. "I can't change what happened between us in the past. But don't force me to jeopardize my future. If someone finds out I'm spying for you, my career will be ruined. I will be the most hated woman in poker."

Annie didn't look up but caught Nate's movement out of the corner of her eye as he settled into a nearby chair. She couldn't say anything else. She'd laid all her cards on the table, but the dispassionate look in Nate's dark eyes told her it wouldn't matter. Whether in court or in the casino, Nate would ruin her and have his revenge. After three years, he had her right where he wanted her.

"These are my terms," he said, his voice cold. "Do you want a divorce or not?"

Of course she did. But… She shook her head. "This is blackmail."

Nate smiled widely, his pleasure at watching her squirm plainly evident. "*Blackmail* is such a dirty word. I prefer to look at it as a mutually beneficial arrangement. I catch my cheaters and secure the tournament for a decade. You get your divorce without going bankrupt first. Simple as that."

That was a vast understatement. It couldn't be more complicated. "Why me?"

Nate watched her, his lips pursing in thought before he spoke. "I need an insider. You're an excellent player. You have a good read of your competitors. The odds of you making it to the final table are in our favor. And I have the leverage to incentivize you. It's perfect."

Not entirely perfect. She took a deep breath and squeezed her eyes tightly shut for a moment before she spoke. She wanted to walk away from the Desert Sapphire when the tournament was done and never have a reason to see Nathan Reed again. And yet the price was high. Spying for him. Publicly adoring him. Privately conspiring under the guise of their so-called marriage. It was dangerous territory. But the tournament was only a week long. If all went well, she could play poker as planned, throw Nate a couple leads to chase and hopefully walk away from the Sapphire a free woman.

"And I can trust you to keep your word if I keep up my end of the bargain?"

Nate arched an eyebrow. "Annie, *my* trustworthiness has never been in question. But yes. If you agree to see this through, I'll call my lawyer and have him withdraw the protest. If we get things started soon, the divorce should be finalized in a few weeks' time."

He'd left her no other choice. She met his gaze across the coffee table. "All right, Nate. You've got a deal."

Two

Annie regretted the words the minute they passed her lips, but she couldn't take it back now.

Nate glared at her in disbelief. It was obvious he'd been prepared for a battle. He thought she'd fight harder. There was a flicker of disappointment across his face as he straightened up in his chair and mentally regrouped.

Annie hated that she was so aware of his body. Every twitch of every muscle beneath the tight fabric of his suit registered in her mind. She could tell herself that she was just good at reading body language after years of poker, but it wasn't true. She knew him better than she cared to admit. Her own body remembered every inch of the hard physique hidden under those expensive suits. It wasn't something she could easily forget.

"Well, good," Nate finally managed to say. "I'm glad you could be reasonable about this." He set his glass onto the table and nodded. "Have you checked in to the hotel?"

She hadn't bothered. She'd figured Nate would have his security goons come after her before she could reach her room. She'd arrived a day early to get that unpleasantness out of the way so she could focus on her game. "No. Not yet. I wanted to play a little first."

"Okay, I'll radio to have your bags brought upstairs. I assume you left them with the bellhop?"

Annie opened her mouth to argue, but he was already barking orders into a push-to-talk cell phone at his hip. He'd told her she would stay with him as part of the cover. Somehow she hadn't let her mind process that part of the deal yet.

Her mind raced, thinking of the private suite that sat dark and quiet down the corridor. Nate owned a home in Henderson, but she knew he usually stayed at the Sapphire when he was working, which was all the time. As she could recall, there was a full kitchen, living and dining rooms…but only one bed.

She frowned, kicking herself for not getting all the details before agreeing to this. Now she had no negotiating power at all. "Where will I sleep?"

"The bedroom." Nate said the words as though it were the most obvious answer in the world.

Nate's gaze had been cool and detached since the moment they got upstairs. He was obviously more interested in power and revenge than seduction, but even then she wasn't comfortable with the idea. "And what about you?" she pressed. There. That should be clear enough.

Nate's lips twisted in a faint grin. "I don't sleep, remember?"

That was almost true. He did have the ability to make it on only three or four hours of sleep a night, but he *did* sleep. "You sleep enough."

This time he grinned wide, his perfectly aligned smile blazing white against his tanned skin. "We'll worry about that when the time comes."

The smile was not enough to charm her. He was being deliberately evasive. She glanced down at her watch. It was after seven. She was a night owl, but even then the time was coming sooner rather than later. "I'm going along with your plan because you've given me no choice, but I am *not* sleeping with you, Nathan Reed."

His heavy brows rose in response to her declaration. "I hadn't planned on seducing you." Nate stood up and rounded the coffee table. He leaned over her, trapping her between the long lengths of his arms.

Annie eased back into the couch, but there wasn't anywhere else to go. She could only breathe in his cologne and remember that same scent on her pillows as she slept in this very suite. Back then, Nate had the ability to play her body like a musical instrument he'd studied his whole life. She'd never been with another man who could bring her pleasure like he had. What they had was explosive. Mind-blowing.

The closer he came to her, the more she wondered if that connection had severed during their time apart. It didn't feel like it.

His gaze raked over her body. "But if I did...what's so wrong with that? It's not a crime to sleep with your own husband, Annie."

She felt a surge of electricity run through her body when he spoke her name. He'd said it the way he had in the past, with the low, soft tones she remembered him whispering into her ear as they made love. Whatever it was between them was still there. For her, at least. She couldn't even respond with him so close.

"Besides," he continued, "I don't seem to recall you complaining much about it before."

Her mouth suddenly felt dry. Annie ran her tongue quickly across her bottom lip. Even after all this time, she still wanted him. There was no question of it. "That was a long time ago," she said, her voice a little too breathy to ring true even to her own ears.

"We'll see about that." Nate stood up, pulling away from her and breaking the spell. Annie felt him take all the oxygen in the room with him as he stepped back and scooped his drink off the table. He took a sip, the ice clinking in the mostly empty glass, and turned his back to her. He was as calm and unaffected as he would be conducting a business deal.

Then she understood. She was right; this wasn't just about busting cheaters in his casino. There were other ways to go about catching them that didn't require them to pose as the married couple they were. Methods that didn't make him touching her necessary for their cover.

No, Nate wanted to make her pay. To get the small sense of justice he'd been lacking for the past three years. She couldn't exactly call it torture, but he would be using every weapon in his arsenal—from seduction to indifference—to ensure she was uneasy and off her game. She would get her divorce, but the next week would be anything but simple. The odds were she could kiss this tournament win goodbye. Her focus was already shattered and it hadn't even begun.

The chime of the elevator startled her. Annie looked over to see Gabe, the head of security, enter the foyer with her luggage. He was one of the only people with the card to access Nate's private suite.

Annie stood and rounded the coffee table to approach him, but his gaze stopped her cold. Gabe had always had a smile and a laugh for her, but not today. His hazel eyes were like knives, shooting sharp accusations at her from across the room. His jaw was tight, the muscles in his thick neck tense. There was more anger in Gabe than she'd seen in Nate. Perhaps Nate was simply better at controlling it.

Gabe turned toward the darkened suite without speaking and dropped her luggage carelessly beside the dining room table. "Call me if you need me, sir." He said the words while looking at Annie, the threat inherent. A moment later, the elevator doors reopened and he disappeared.

With him gone the heavy weight of his anger suddenly lifted from her chest. Annie had never realized how protective Gabe was of Nate. She bet if given the chance, he'd shoot her with his Taser just to watch her twitch.

Annie chewed her bottom lip thoughtfully. Of course he was angry. He'd been there every day of the past three years. He was probably the one who'd gotten Nate drunk and hauled him to a strip club to get over her. As a friend and as a security officer, he obviously disapproved of Nate's plan to use Annie in the sting operation. Especially the part about them living together. Gabe could see the potential problems a mile away.

To tell the truth, Annie wasn't entirely thrilled with that part of the plan, either. She wanted to follow him downstairs, to tell him she had no intention of getting involved with Nate again, but knew it wouldn't help. Annie turned around, stopping short when she found Nate smiling. It was the first sincere grin he'd cracked since she arrived and of course, it was at her discomfort.

"He's not your biggest fan."

"I gathered that much. I'd hoped you hadn't told anyone about us. Does anyone else know? Should I watch for flying daggers from housekeeping?"

Nate laughed and shook his head. "No, just Gabe. I wasn't even going to tell him, but he found your wedding ring."

The ring. Annie had forgotten. She'd left her platinum wedding band on the bedside stand. She hadn't felt good about taking it. Leaving had been the right thing to do, but taking the ring so soon after receiving it felt like stealing.

She watched, stunned, as Nate twisted a tiny band from his pinky finger and held it out to her. "You'll need this back. For the cover," he added.

Annie took the tiny silver loop from his hand and examined it like a lost artifact. It was a dull, brushed-platinum band with shiny accents around the edge. They'd picked the rings out in such a hurry. At that moment, all she'd wanted was to be Mrs. Nathan Reed. *What the hell had she been thinking?*

"Why are you wearing it?" she asked.

"I wear it as a reminder."

Annie got the distinct impression that he didn't mean it in a sentimental way. More a daily reminder of how much she'd suffer if he got his hands on her again. "Where's *your* ring?"

"Put away. I couldn't very well wear mine and tarnish my reputation as Vegas's most eligible bachelor." He said the last word with audible distaste before he walked around his desk, fished in the top drawer and pulled out a small black velvet box.

"I can see how being married might interfere with your social agenda."

Nate looked up, studying her face for a moment before opening the box and slipping the matching ring onto his left hand. He stretched his fingers out, testing the feel of the long-forgotten jewelry before making a fist. A slight frown pulled down the corners of his mouth when he spoke. "I have no social agenda, Annie. I thought that was one of the reasons you decided to leave me."

"No, I…" Annie's voice trailed off midprotest. She didn't really want to talk about why she left. Not now. It wouldn't change anything. What was done was done and their agreement would close the door on the past for good. Her gaze dropped down to the ring in her hand before her fingers closed over it.

Nate's brow furrowed, his eyes focused on her tightly clenched fist. "Put on the ring," he demanded softly.

Her heart skipped a beat in her chest. She'd sooner slip a noose over her head. That's how it felt, at least. Even back then. When she'd woken up the morning after the wedding with the platinum manacle clamped onto her, she'd popped a Xanax to stop the impending panic attack. She'd convinced herself that it would be okay, it was just the nerves of a new bride, but it hadn't taken long to realize she'd made a mistake.

Annie scrambled to find a reason not to put the ring on. She couldn't afford to start hyperventilating and give Nate the upper hand in any of this. "I thought I might wait until I had a chance to clean it. Give it a good polish."

It was stupid and she knew it. Why did putting on a ring symbolic of nothing but a legally binding slip of paper bother her so much? The smothering sensation was growing more oppressive, like a steamy, wet blanket draped over her face on a smolderingly hot Miami day. It was just how she'd felt back then. Why she'd had to run.

Nate frowned. He moved across the room with the stealthy grace of a panther, stopping just in front of her. Without speaking, he reached out and gripped her fist. One by one, he pried her fingers back and took the band from her.

She was no match for his firm grasp, especially when the surprising tingle of awareness traveled up her arm at his touch. He held her left hand immobile, her heart pounding rapidly in her chest as the ring moved closer and closer.

"May I, Mrs. Reed?"

Her heart stopped altogether at the mention of her married name. Annie's breath caught in her throat as he pushed the band over her knuckle and nestled it snugly in place, as he had at their wedding. His hot touch was in vast contrast to the icy-cold metal against her skin. Although it fit perfectly, the ring seemed too tight. So did her shoes. On second thought, everything felt too tight. The room was too small. The air was too thin.

Annie's brain started swirling in the fog overtaking her mind. She started to tell Nate she needed to sit down, but it was too late.

Nate was enjoying watching Annie squirm up until the moment her eyes rolled into her head. He moved on reflex, catching her slumping body in his arms. He quickly repositioned his hold and lifted her up, carrying her down the hall to the bedroom. He settled her onto the navy comforter covering his king-size bed and sat down on the edge beside her.

Annie had lingered on his mind since the day she left. Bringing her to her knees before giving her the divorce she wanted was a surefire way to put her out of his thoughts for good. Catching a couple cheaters and guaranteeing the success of his hotel for years to come was a great way to make her earn her freedom. And she made it too easy, really. He knew all the right buttons to push. He was pleasantly surprised at how gratifying it had been so far.

At least until she passed out.

Nate leaned over her. Annie's breathing had returned to normal. Her ruby lips parted, and her anxious expression faded as her body relaxed into the plush mattress.

Nate couldn't help reaching out and running a finger along the blush of her cheek. Her skin was as soft as he remembered, like silk. She sighed as the back of his hand slid down her face and along her jaw.

The Annie the public saw was always so cool, so put together. He'd watched her on televised tournaments over the years and seen her in interviews. She was unshakable. Unflappable. Nothing like the wildly passionate woman who had shared his bed. Or the one who passed out cold at the idea of wearing her wedding ring.

She stirred so many emotions in him. Anger, jealousy, arousal, resentment, anxiety… Being around her now was like riding the roller coaster across the street. He was an even-keeled guy. A levelheaded businessman. That made it even more irritating knowing she could impact him the way no other woman had. He just hoped he could keep it all inside.

When she'd first left, he was confused and furious. His worst fears had been realized. It was as though his mother had abandoned him all over again. He had watched his father crumble under the weight of his grief. The only thing Nate knew for certain was that he wouldn't let Annie break him. He'd funneled his anger into building the greatest damn casino in Las Vegas and finding the perfect way to exact his revenge.

Yes, they might have rushed to the altar. Yes, they might have had little more than fantastic sex in common. But their marriage would end on his terms, not hers. She'd forfeited her vote when she walked out. Now that he had her back here, bending to his will, he would finally be able to put her, and them, behind him.

Perhaps. As he looked down at the beautiful, exciting woman…his wife…he began to wonder if luring her back here with the tournament was a mistake. The vengeance surging through his veins had dulled, leaving only the desire to possess her once again.

Back then, his need for Annie had been all consuming. Nate hadn't wanted to let her out of his bed, much less his life. Marrying her had seemed like the best way to guarantee that Annie would be his forever. The irony was that it was the marriage itself that drove her away. Everything had been perfect before then.

Annie groaned softly, her eyes fluttering a moment before opening. She looked around the room in confusion before her sapphire gaze met his. "What happened?"

"You fainted. Apparently the mere thought of people knowing you were married to me was too much for you to take." He didn't bother to mask the irritation in his voice.

"What am I...?" She looked around again, the crease between her eyebrows deepening in thought. "Why am I lying in your bedroom?"

Nate smiled down at her. "*Our* bedroom, sweetheart. Like a gentleman, I carried you in here when you fainted. Anyway, I'm surprised you recognize the place. I'd have thought you blocked it from your memory with the rest of our marriage."

Annie frowned and pushed herself up onto her elbows. "Nate, the problems in our relationship had nothing to do with this room. The bedroom was the *only* place it worked."

She sat up and slowly inched off the foot of the bed. Pulling herself together, she quickly tugged down her fitted black skirt and smoothed her red top. Her expression hardened, her emotions unreadable. Within seconds, the Annie of the past was gone and *the Barracuda* had returned. He was glad. The cool, calm poker player was far easier for Nate to resist.

Annie left the room and returned with her two bags. "Where can I put my things?"

The large, red Louis Vuitton roller and toiletry bag

were just the right size for a woman on the move all the time. After she left, Nate had hired a private detective to find out more about his elusive bride. He'd told Nate that although Annie had a sparsely decorated condo in Miami, she was almost never there. She roamed from one tournament to the next, living in hotels out of these red bags.

As someone who had practically grown up in the same building he stood in right now, he couldn't understand her wanderlust. He'd known she traveled to the various tournaments to compete, but somehow he'd thought that marrying him would give her a reason to settle in one place. That her love of the game would give her an interest in helping him build up the Sapphire, working side by side as partners. He had been wrong.

Nate opened the door to the walk-in closet and moved some clothes to the opposite side. "You can hang up your things here. If you need any more space, just slide my stuff over."

Annie nodded stiffly and pushed past him to the closet. He took a few steps back to linger in the doorway and watch as she slowly unpacked. She was methodical as she unzipped the bag and carefully removed each piece. It was like a ritual she'd repeated a thousand times. How had he ever thought he could get her to unpack for good?

"If you have what you need, I'm going downstairs. I'll see you for dinner at Carolina's at eight-thirty. Be prepared for our first public outing as husband and wife."

At that, he turned on his heel and marched down the hallway to the elevator. He didn't wait for her response. He needed to get away from her for a while. To take a deep breath that wasn't warm with her scent. To clear his mind and replan his strategy. His stomach couldn't take the never-ending swing of the emotional pendulum being around her brought on. Wanting her and then despising her. Remembering every inch of her body and then realizing he didn't know a damn thing about her.

Once downstairs, he marched through the casino for his standing meeting with Gabe and Jerry Moore, his casino floor manager. They met in the Pit Three lounge, where they would catch him up on the hotel activities. Tonight, he would also get a drink. He normally wouldn't drink while working, but all bets were off the moment Annie walked into his casino. He needed something to dull his thoughts, to fend off the building arousal. Not to get drunk—he couldn't trust himself not to do something stupid—just enough to numb.

By the time he reached the lounge, Gabe and Jerry were already seated in the back corner booth. They went on easily with their normal routines from there. Gabe reported on any incidents worth mentioning, provided the latest security codes and gave him the access card for Annie. Jerry rattled on for a while about a couple high rollers and preparation for the tournament.

The tournament was not an easy event to arrange. Nate was happy to sip on his vodka tonic and give his mind over to the intricacies. A portion of the casino floor had already been roped off and tables rearranged. The kickoff cocktail party was under control. Patricia in the public relations office had been in contact with the event sponsors and working with ESPN for the past few weeks. Everything seemed to be going well.

His years of hard work really had paid off. Nate had fought hard to bring the hotel back after his father's negligent management. Now it was clear that his dedication and work ethic had rubbed off on his staff. The people he hired were inspired to make the Desert Sapphire the most successful hotel-casino in Las Vegas. His grandfather would be proud of what Nate had made of his life's work.

"So is everything in place in terms of the *arrangement* with Annie?" Gabe asked, drawing Nate back into the conversation he'd been having alone with Jerry.

Nate noted his tone. Gabe didn't like his plan at all and made no secret of it. "Yes. I think with her assistance we will have a very good shot of putting an end to this and securing the tournament contract."

Jerry nodded in approval. His casino manager had worked at the Sapphire for thirty years, helping Nate's grandfather start the place. After a heart attack and an unfulfilling decade of retirement, he'd come back to help his best friend's grandson. The whole Annie situation had happened during his hiatus.

"Remind me again of the story we're using?" Jerry ran his wrinkled hand over the balding dome of his head. "I want to make sure when people ask, I'm telling it right."

Nate repeated their cover for everyone's benefit. "Annie and I got married a couple years ago, but it didn't work out. She came back for the tournament and we've reconciled. I'd leave it at that. Too many details and we run the risk of messing up."

Jerry's radio squawked at his hip. He lifted it to his ear to listen to the message before responding and turning to Nate. "If we're done here, I need to get over to pit one."

Nate dismissed him with a wave of his hand and then watched the older man shuffle out of the lounge. He hoped he had half that much spunk when he was in his seventies.

Turning back, Nate could tell Gabe was biting his tongue. He wasn't happy, idly rotating a cardboard coaster on the table and glaring at the platinum band on Nate's ring finger. "Just say it, Gabe."

Gabe shook his head, his closely cropped goatee emphasizing his frown. "I just don't like this. I don't trust her. How do we know she isn't friends with one of the cheaters? She could tip them off or send us on a wild goose chase. We have no idea where her loyalty lies. Hell, she could be in on it herself."

Nate doubted that. Annie had too much pride in her skills. But Gabe was right about her loyalties. She'd been in the game a long time, knew everyone. If it wasn't for the divorce papers he was dangling, he couldn't be sure. "She wants a divorce. Her loyalty to herself will trump everything else."

"I know why this is important for the hotel, but why her?"

"Why not use Annie? She owes me after all this time. If I can make her miserable and teach her a lesson this week, all the better. Once the tournament is over, I'll let her walk away and never give her a second thought."

"For someone who says he doesn't care about a woman," Gabe commented dryly, "you're sure putting a lot of time and effort into this."

"I deserve my chance to get back at her, don't I?"

"Sure. She deserves everything you'll dish out and then some. I just worry this isn't going to end well."

Nate appreciated Gabe's concern but wished his friend had more faith in him. "It will all go as planned. We will bust those dirty crooks, Annie will pay for her irresponsible and thoughtless actions, and I'll finally have some peace."

"I've seen the way you look at her, Nate. Even today. It's still there. It may not be love, but whatever it is was strong enough for you two to lose your minds and elope after a few days together." Gabe paused, leaning across the table toward him. "If she's your sexual kryptonite, what do you think will happen living in such close proximity for over a week?"

Nate could handle Annie. "Nothing is going to happen. I've learned my lesson, I assure you."

Three

After Nate left, Annie finished unpacking and found herself at a loss for what to do. Her day had taken a radical turn since Nate interrupted her game, and she had far too much nervous energy running through her veins. The situation was nerve-racking, but Nate made it even worse. As usual, he'd managed to stir her suppressed arousal and send her libido into overdrive.

She had an hour before dinner, so she opted for a hot shower and some fresh clothes. It had been a long flight from Miami.

By the time she rounded the corner to the entrance of Carolina's Restaurant, it was eight-thirty on the nose. The dark, romantic steak house was the jewel of the hotel's restaurants. There was always an extensive waiting list for those wanting to propose or celebrate an anniversary. Nate and Annie had eaten there only once. It was here, among the candlelight and low, sultry music, that the idea of eloping had been conceived.

Nate, ever punctual, was standing there waiting for her. He was preoccupied with his smartphone, typing something with his right thumb while his left hand anxiously jingled the keys and change in his pocket.

Annie lingered, taking a moment to watch him while he was distracted. He typed for a few seconds and then laughed, scrolling with his thumb and shaking his head. This Nate was more like the man she remembered. His cocky, businessman veneer had been in place when he spoke to her earlier today. He'd constructed pretty high walls since she left. Annie didn't blame him—she'd given him the bricks to build it—but she did miss the thoughtful, charming man she'd fallen for.

She'd never tell him the truth, but she had been completely consumed by her attraction to Nate. Part of her still cared about him. It just didn't change her decision. It had all been too much, too fast.

Maybe it was her roaming Gypsy blood that kept her from settling down. Maybe it was her fiercely independent streak that wouldn't stand for a man trying to control her. Annie didn't know. But the first time Nate had scoffed at the idea of her traveling to a tournament, she could feel the constrictive hold choking her.

Nate slipped the phone into his pocket and looked down at his watch impatiently. She couldn't run this time if she ever wanted her freedom back. It was time to be man and wife for the crowds. Annie took a deep breath and prepared to begin her performance.

"Hey, there, sexy." Annie spoke loudly enough for those around them to hear as she strode quickly to him. Before he could react, she snaked a hand around his neck and tugged him down into a hello kiss.

She had every intention of making it a quick peck for show, but once their lips touched, something stronger than she was held her there. Annie remembered the feeling… The sensation from her past that had nearly ruined her. She could feel the live current running through her body, every nerve awakened after years of dormancy.

When the initial shock of her assault wore off, Nate did his part, wrapping his arms around her and pulling her against him. His mouth molded to her lips, just as her every curve did to his hard, angular body. They matched perfectly. It was such a natural feeling. It was how she imagined coming home would feel if she had one.

It was only this thought that propelled her to pull away and push gently against the lapels of his dark gray Armani suit. This wasn't home. This was a ruse. Nothing more.

Nate released her lips but kept her body still and close. "Well, hello," he whispered low, one eyebrow curiously raised at her.

"Hello," Annie responded, her voice weak with her own shallow, rapid breathing. She didn't want him to know she still responded to him like this. Quickly, she searched for the words to convince them both it was only a part of the cover. "Was that convincing enough?"

Nate's dark eyes searched her face for a moment before he frowned slightly and released his grip on her waist. "Yes, quite. I see you've dedicated yourself to your new role." His voice had returned to the polite and formal.

Annie smiled sweetly and took his arm as he offered it. "I'm absolutely starving," she said, effectively changing the subject.

"I hope so. I've had Leo reserve a very romantic and very—" he leaned in to add the last part quietly "—*public* table for us." They bypassed the crowd waiting to be seated and Nate gave a quick wave to Leo, the maître d'.

"Good evening, Mr. Reed. Your table is ready for you and Mrs. Reed." The tall, thin Asian man grabbed two menus and led them through the restaurant to a candlelit table for two in the center of the room. Leo pulled out Annie's chair and seated her, placing both their napkins and providing the menu with the night's selections. "Enjoy your meal and congratulations to you both."

When Leo disappeared, Annie felt the sudden weight of being alone with Nate in such a romantic setting. The first time they'd eaten there, he'd reserved a cozy table in a dark corner so they wouldn't be disturbed. Now, although the table was still quite nice, it was out in the open where everyone would see them together. And apparently, the word was out about their marriage. Leo knew. It wouldn't take long to spread.

Nate reached across the table and took Annie's hand. She had to remember not to jerk away and instead leaned into him.

"You know, you did a very good job just now. Fooled even me for a moment," he began, his voice soft as velvet. "Makes me feel better for falling for it last time. Sometimes I forget you're a professional liar."

Annie tried to tug away from him, but his iron grasp held her tight. He glanced down at her hand, ignoring her quiet groans of protest. "You really need a manicure." He murmured the casual insult like a lover's words in her ear and released her.

She forced a smile, gently untangling her fingers to take a sip of her water. "Well, it's hard to keep up with the little things when you're like me, always on the run."

"Indeed." His dark eyes pierced her as sharply as his words, although the rest of his face and body language oozed nothing but adoration. She wasn't the only one that excelled in deception. "I'll send Julia up to the suite tonight. She works in the hotel salon."

"That won't be necessary. I'll make a point of going to see her instead. The less time I spend in that suite, the better."

Nate smiled wide. "You'll have to sleep in that bed eventually, Annie."

"Not while you're in it," she snapped.

Their server interrupted at that exact moment, introducing herself as Renee and ending their argument. She had a basket of warm, crusty bread and herb butter. "Good evening, Mr. Reed. Mrs. Reed," she said with a grin. Everyone seemed exceedingly pleased about their boss's big news. It was quite the little family here at the Sapphire.

Renee continued on about the fresh catch of the day, but Annie didn't pay very much attention. She was focused entirely on Nate. He was still glaring at her under his blond lashes, despite appearing to look down at the menu with interest. In the past, his glance could send shivers of anticipation up her spine. At the moment, it made her skin crawl. He was surveying her the way she would another player at the poker table. Reading weaknesses. Judging their reactions.

She didn't like it one bit.

"Champagne, I think. We're celebrating tonight."

The single word snapped Annie out of her thoughts. *Champagne?* She watched Renee disappear around the corner. "You know I don't drink."

Nate took a deep breath, fighting to maintain the look of adoration on his face. "Smile, sweetheart. You do tonight. We have to celebrate our reconciliation. Normal people would order champagne."

"I didn't drink champagne when we married. Why would I do it now?"

"Because you want a divorce." He spoke softly, leaning in. "Don't you?"

"More than anything." Annie smiled.

Renee returned with a bottle of champagne and two

crystal flutes. She filled the glasses, leaving the bottle chilling in a bucket beside the table.

Nate raised his glass, holding it out until Annie reluctantly did the same. "To our marriage," he said, clinking the crystal against hers.

"And its timely dissolution," Annie mumbled, quickly bringing the glass to her lips. The golden, bubbly liquid filled her mouth, the flavor surprisingly pleasant and sweet on her tongue. It splashed into her empty stomach, creating a warming sensation that started spreading throughout her body. "Mmm…" She sighed, taking another sip.

Nate watched her suspiciously with his full flute held in midair as she drained half her glass and set it down. "Do you like it?"

"I do." Annie smiled again, the expression coming much easier than it had before. She had been wound so tightly today, but in an instant she was starting to feel languid, like a house cat stretched out in a sunbeam.

Renee returned just then, ready to take their orders. Annie was suddenly ravenously hungry, ordering more than she would normally. Nate actually smirked through a sip of champagne as she ordered the bacon-wrapped filet and shrimp with the garlic mashed potatoes. He didn't even know she intended to have dessert, as well. The crème brûlée at Carolina's was not to be missed.

Renee finished writing and took their menus before she offered to refill her empty glass. Annie accepted gratefully. "What kind of champagne is this? It tastes better than I expected it to."

"French. And expensive." Nate frowned, as though he were pinching pennies. More likely he was irritated that his power play hadn't turned out as he'd hoped.

"Good." She nearly giggled as she sipped the golden

bubbles. The champagne had immediately gone to Annie's head. She'd told Nate once that she didn't drink because she didn't like losing control. That was true, but not entirely. The other reason was that she was a lightweight. Add in that she hadn't eaten since her layover in Dallas, and you had a recipe for disaster.

She considered tearing off a hunk of the warm bread to soak up some of the alcohol, but resisted. For one thing, she didn't need the extra carbs. Two, she wanted to be drunk. If he insisted she drink, he was going to find out how big a mistake that truly was.

They sat silently for a few minutes after that. Annie ate her salad ferociously, stopping only long enough to drain her second glass of champagne and pour a third.

Annie knew she should stop, but she just didn't want to. She didn't want to sit here, pretending to be in love with him. She couldn't play nice while her heart was aching every time he looked at her. It was too painful. She wasn't happy about the way things had ended between them, but she couldn't change it. There was a good reason she'd run and stayed gone for so many years.

And yet she had a responsibility to fulfill, so she slipped off her heel and let her bare foot roam up under the cuff of his pant leg.

Nate jumped in his seat, his knees whacking the bottom of the table and jingling the glassware. Several people turned to look in their direction, but he quickly recovered with a nervous straightening of his tie.

Annie ignored his pointed gaze, tipping a sip of champagne into her mouth. "You said we had to be convincing, darling." She set the flute back onto the table with a sweet smile and stroked the firm muscles of his calves with her toes. "Besides, we both know I lose all my good sense when I'm around you."

* * *

Nate looked at the woman who had occupied his thoughts for the past three years. The giggling mess across the table was not exactly as he remembered her. She'd managed to eat every morsel laid in front of her and drink at least four flutes of champagne.

At the moment she was licking the spoon after her last bite of crème brûlée as though she might never eat again.

He had to give her credit, though. She'd kept up her end of the bargain. Through the meal, she'd looked at him adoringly, fed him bites of her food and leaned in to kiss him on more than one occasion. Anyone watching their exchange would think they were blissfully in love.

The truth was that she was blissfully drunk. A quick glance under the table revealed his biggest fear—four-inch stilettos. Did the woman not own any sensible shoes? There was no way she would be able to walk out of this restaurant with any dignity at all.

Nate quickly surveyed the room. Their dinner had run quite late and most people had cleared out for the evening. It was a Thursday, a big night at some places in Vegas for senior bingo, but that wasn't the crowd he drew at the Sapphire. If she was determined to embarrass him, she'd chosen the wrong day.

He quickly scribbled his information onto the restaurant tab, tipping Renee heavily. Then he turned back to Annie with a heavy sigh. "Are you finished?"

She reluctantly put her spoon back into the empty ramekin. "I guess so. That is, if I can manage to stand up."

Nate moved quickly, coming around to help her. She stood, probably too fast, and wobbled for a second before gripping his outstretched arm for dear life.

"Why don't you—?"

"No," she insisted, her brow drawn in drunken concentration. "I can *do* this." She took a few unsteady steps beside him and then seemed to recover nicely. Just as they approached the entrance to the restaurant, her heel turned beneath her and she threw herself onto the maître d' stand.

"Whoa there," she said with an uncertain laugh. In one quick motion, she righted herself and plucked off her shoes. "Much better," she said, wiggling her toes into the plush and wildly colored casino carpeting.

"What are you doing? You can't just walk through here barefoot." Nate frowned.

Annie laughed, walking on and answering casually over her shoulder. "I know the owner. He won't mind."

Nate was quick to follow. "I mean it isn't safe. You could step on something. Drunks break glasses in here all the time. We try to get it all up, but you never know. Besides, the floor could be filthy."

"You are an old ninny, Nathan." Annie turned to him and planted her hands on her hips. Her heels dangled helplessly at her side as she wrinkled her nose and actually stuck out her tongue at him.

He could barely trust his eyes. No one on the poker circuit would believe this story if he told it later. *The Barracuda,* drunk and acting like a fool, albeit a beautiful one. It was unheard of. Unprecedented. And hysterical.

The bubble of laughter rose up in his throat. He couldn't contain it. The pent-up frustration and disappointment and confusion of the last three years all pooled together at once and exploded out of him in a roar of laughter. His whole body shook with the power of it. Nate actually bowed over, his hands braced on his knees as he chuckled until tears started gathering in the corners of his eyes.

He looked up to see the laughter had doubled Annie's

irritation. Her expression only made it harder for him to breathe. Nate stood up, attempting to calm himself and wiping his face with the back of his hand. It was incredibly therapeutic—more so than the glasses of scotch or hours angrily lifting weights in the hotel gym.

"That's it, I'm leaving!" she announced, turning and marching away from the restricted area, shoes in hand.

"Annie, come back here." Nate jogged after her, reaching out to grasp her wrist and jerk her to a stop.

"Let go of me," she whined, her anger doused by the champagne and reducing her to childish behavior.

Nate tightened his grip. "I will not. You're going the wrong way. The elevator upstairs is over there." He pointed.

Annie looked around her, confused, and then recognized her mistake. She started walking in the correct direction but was once again tugged to a stop by Nate. "Would you *please* let go of me?" she asked, exasperated.

Nate shook his head. "Not until you put your shoes back on."

"Are you going to make me?" Annie taunted, tugging away again.

That was the wrong thing to say. Nate couldn't take any more of this. If she wanted to make a scene in his casino, so be it, but he wouldn't be the one everyone whispered about tomorrow. In one quick motion, he bent and scooped Annie up, tossing her over his shoulder like a kicking, screaming sack of potatoes.

"What the…?" she cried in surprise, but it was already too late.

Nate marched through the casino, his arms tightly gripping her legs to his chest to keep her from kicking him. Her free fists were already pounding at his back, but that was easy to ignore.

"Put me down, Nathan Reed! Put me down this instant," Annie wailed.

Nate chuckled and disregarded her, walking through the casino as though it were his dry cleaning over his shoulder instead of his wife. Eyes were glued to him from every side, but he didn't care. He nodded politely to the staff as he passed, just as he did every day.

"Nathan!" she howled.

"You're only drawing more attention to yourself by yelling, Annie."

The squirming mass on his shoulder quieted at once, although she still attempted a kick every few feet for good measure. Nate looked up at one of the domed ceiling cameras. He had no doubt that Gabe was watching them and laughing hysterically in the security office. He'd have to remember to save this tape for posterity. Or future blackmail.

Nate swiped his badge and ducked through the doorway to the restricted area. Once safely enclosed, Annie began kicking and screaming anew.

"Put me down!"

"Nope." Nate called his private elevator and ignored the stiletto heels being pummeled against him. Instead, he held her legs more tightly. He enjoyed the feel of her in his arms, even in the less than ideal circumstance. The warm scent of her perfume was instantly familiar, stirring a heat in his veins. He couldn't resist letting his fingertips softly stroke the smooth skin of her legs. Her skirt was long enough to protect her virtue as he'd walked through the casino, but it still provided him an excellent view of the firm thighs he'd missed all these years.

When the doors opened, he stepped inside the elevator. Now that they were out of the public view, he could put her down, even though he didn't want to. Nate wrapped one arm behind her legs and another across the small of her back, slowly easing her to the floor. She clung to him, their bodies in full contact as she slid, inch by inch, to the ground. The simple motion caused a delicious friction as he felt her every curve press into him.

When her feet finally touched the ground, Annie looked up at him, her eyes blazing with blue fire. But not from desire. The impact of the powerful moment was overshadowed by his stunt. Either that or it just made her angrier that she reacted to him.

"You jackass," she screeched as she swung her purse to strike him. Nate reached out and grabbed hold of her wrist before she could make contact. It only fueled her irritation. "How dare you manhandle me like that? I…I am not one of your employees you can shuffle around at will! I—"

Nate interrupted her tirade by capturing her mouth with his. He wasn't about to let her poisonous words ruin this moment. Annie fought it for only a moment before succumbing to her desires and wrapping her arms around his neck to tug him closer. The kiss was hard and almost desperate as they came together for their first real kiss in three years.

He backed her up until she was pinned against the brass doors of the elevator. With the heavy thud of their bodies against the cold metal, it was as though the floodgates had opened. Nate could feel the intensity of their touches start to build, their hands feverishly dancing over their bodies as their mouths threatened to devour each other. He'd waited three long years to touch her body again and at last, he could.

His palm cupped her breast through the silky fabric of her shirt. She moaned, her body arching to press against him. "Oh, Nate," she whispered.

The elevator came to a stop. Nate pulled her to him as the doors slid open behind her. He knew that he should let her go. This was not part of his plan, but he just couldn't make himself do it. It felt right to have Annie in his arms again, even if she'd done nothing but aggravate him all evening.

He let his thumb gently trace the line of her jaw and relished the feel of her soft skin. Her eyes closed and lips parted slightly with a soft intake of breath. Her whole body relaxed into him, her anger a distant memory.

Annie opened her eyes and looked up at him. There was an obvious invitation in her blue gaze. Despite her earlier protests, too much champagne and not enough kissing had changed her mind. It had changed his, too. No matter what happened after they married, the times they'd spent in one another's arms had always been fantastic. Every nerve in his body urged him to indulge it. If he stepped off this elevator with her, he would have her naked and in his bed in minutes. Exactly what he'd told Gabe he wouldn't do.

So what the hell was he doing?

Nate straightened up and gently grasped Annie's shoulders. "Good night, Annie."

She frowned for a moment before he gave her a firm but gentle push. The movement was enough to send her stumbling backward out of the elevator and into the foyer of his suite. He quickly hit the button, closing the doors and sending him back to the casino, leaving them both aroused and alone.

Four

Annie was awakened the next morning by the sound of the shower running. She pushed herself up in bed, eyeing the pristine blankets on Nate's side. He must have slept on the couch.

She hoped he had a crick in his neck from it. After he'd wound her up then dropped her like a rock last night, he deserved it. When he'd kissed her so fiercely, she'd thought that perhaps he was as attracted to her as she still was to him. But when she stumbled back onto the landing and watched the cold, impassive expression on his face as the elevator doors closed, she'd known she was wrong.

Nate hated her. Anything and everything he could do to make her miserable—including turning her on and leaving her unsatisfied—was on the table for the next week. He'd lured her back to Las Vegas with this poker tournament just so he could slowly torture her. It was a devious plot, and a part of her knew she deserved it for leaving the way she had, but that didn't mean she was just going to sit back and take it.

If Nate thought he could use their physical connection to manipulate her, he had another think coming. Two could play at that game. He'd desired her once; she could make him want her again. Silently seducing and manipulating men was at least half of her poker strategy. That's why her sweaters were so low cut and her skirts were so tight. Poker required concentration, and she'd learned early on that being attractive was one of her biggest advantages in a game dominated by men.

The water turned off and Annie heard the glass door of the shower stall open and close. She quickly smoothed her hands over her hair and wished she was wearing pajamas with more seductive appeal. Her thin cotton shorts didn't quite fit the bill, so she tugged up the sheets so only her skimpy matching tank top would show.

The door opened a moment later to reveal a wet and steamy Nate. He had a dark blue towel wrapped low on his hips that drew the eye down his hard belly to the line of darkening hair that disappeared beneath the terry cloth. His golden curls were damp, his face freshly shaved. Annie tried to focus on looking alluring, but it was hard when she was face-to-face with a body like his. Every inch was hard-carved muscle.

Nate paused in the doorway. His glance flicked briefly to the snug fit of her top over her breasts and returned to her eyes. "Good, you're up. You need to get ready. Gabe will be here in about an hour to brief you on our strategy."

Annie abandoned her attempt at alluring Nate and frowned. "Strategy?"

"For you snitching, as you've called it."

Annie had been so distracted by last night's events that she'd forgotten about the deal she'd made. She wasn't just posing as his happy bride in public and feuding with him in private. She was supposed to be spying. Cracking the ring. Earning her freedom. The tournament officially started tomorrow, but everyone would be arriving today for the kickoff, registration and the cocktail party.

"Okay." She sighed. "As long as you promise to keep Gabe on his leash. Putting up with his crap was not part of the agreement."

Nate nodded and disappeared into the closet. "I'll do my best." He came back out with a blue pin-striped shirt and a navy suit. He laid them across his side of the bed and went back toward the bathroom. The towel fell away as he tugged on it, giving her a glimpse of his tight, bare rear end as he disappeared out of sight.

Annie immediately averted her eyes and took a deep breath, wishing away the warm stirring of desire in her belly. Her attraction to Nate was counterproductive. She needed to get her body and brain on the same page, and fast. She flung back the sheets and slipped quietly from the bedroom. If he was going to parade around naked while he got ready, it was probably a good idea for her to go get some coffee in the kitchen.

She was sitting at the granite-topped breakfast bar, taking her first tentative sips of the hot drink, when Nate strode into the kitchen, fully dressed and handsome as ever. He poured his own mug and turned to face her.

"What do you have on your agenda today?"

Annie frowned. She didn't like having to report her every move. She didn't have any firm plans, but she didn't care for him knowing each step of her day, either. He'd been that way after they got married. He didn't have the ability to be with her every moment while he ran the casino, but he checked in with her enough to make her thankful she had an unlimited texting plan. "I don't know yet. Is there something we have to do?"

"I don't think so. After we meet with Gabe, you'll probably have most of the afternoon free until the cocktail party. Do you have a dress for tonight?"

Annie arched her eyebrow at him over her mug. Yes,

she had a dress. She had two, in fact. She'd been planning to wear the more elegant and tasteful of the two dresses, but as punishment for his behavior last night, she was going to wear the sexier, more scandalous one. If she was successful, tonight *he* would be the one tossing and turning with unfulfilled fantasies. "Yes," was all she replied.

"Good. Most of the players start arriving today and will be registering. Perhaps this afternoon you can make some headway in your investigation by socializing with them."

Annie hated the idea of turning her social time with friends into a manhunt. "My sister comes in today. I'll probably have dinner with her and meet you at the party."

"I forgot you have a sister. What's her name again?"

"Tessa. She's playing in the tournament, too."

"Good. I'll be happy to finally meet her."

Annie swallowed a large gulp of coffee and tried not to choke on it. "Yeah, I'm going to have to talk to her before we play happy family and do formal introductions."

"You're not telling her what we're really doing, are you?"

Annie shook her head. "No, but the cover story will raise enough questions. Commitmentphobia runs in our bloodline, and she's even more firmly entrenched in our family traditions than I am."

"She disapproves of us?"

"Tessa certainly did the first time, especially after I left and she got to rub it in my face. I have no doubt she'll give me hell for getting mixed up with you twice."

"What did your mother think about us?"

"I come from a long line of independent, distrustful women," she explained.

"Ahh..." Nate said. "Our marriage was not their favorite dinnertime subject."

"I don't suppose so. We're really not that close. I haven't seen my mother in several years. She's in Brazil at the moment. She was in Portugal before that." Annie at least tried to travel with a purpose and had found a career to soothe the itch to move. She had a condo in Miami as her home base between tournaments. Her mother just wandered to wherever the wind blew her. Annie had seen her four times in the ten years since she'd moved out on her own. "Are you close with your family?"

"Define close." He laughed. "It depends. I've always been pretty close with my father and my grandfather before he died. Dad got a wild haircut and bought a ranch in Texas a few years ago, but until then, almost my whole family lived here in Vegas. The Reeds have been here since 1964, when my grandfather decided to relocate from Los Angeles and open a hotel."

Annie knew her mother couldn't even tell her where she *was* in 1964, much less every place she'd been since then. "A family legacy, then."

"Yes." He straightened up, a smile of pride curling his lips. "I was happy to be able to make the Sapphire everything it could be. I pretty much grew up running the halls and doing my homework in my father's office. When the hotel was passed on to me, I knew it was important to keep my grandfather's dream alive."

"What about your mother?"

The light of pride in Nate's eyes dimmed, his smile fading just slightly enough for her to notice. "I haven't seen my mother since I was twelve." His words were cold and matter-of-fact. "She got tired of the casino life and took off one night."

Annie felt a sharp pang of guilt stab her in the gut like a knife. He spoke impassively on the topic, but she could tell it was a sore subject, having happened to him so young. No wonder he seemed to be so focused on punishing Annie for abandoning their marriage. She'd not only left him, but she'd jabbed him in his most tender spot. Hit his Achilles without aiming.

She swallowed hard and shifted her guilty gaze down into her coffee cup. "I didn't know that." Would it have kept her from leaving? Probably not. But she might have handled it differently if she'd known about his mother. That was just one more reason why marrying a stranger was so treacherous. You had no idea how badly you could really hurt someone and not even know it.

"How could you know? I don't talk about it."

"I know, but…" she began, but couldn't think of what else to say other than the most overdue words of all. "I'm sorry I left like she did. It was cowardly of me not to talk to you about the anxiety I was having. If I had known about your mother, I—"

"Don't," Nate interrupted, his jaw tight. "Don't handle me with kid gloves like I'm damaged somehow, because I'm not. You didn't hurt me, Annie. I wouldn't let you."

He turned his back to her and put his empty mug in the sink. Glancing quickly at his watch, he said, "Go get dressed. Gabe will be here soon."

Nate was already in a bad mood, brought on by an uncomfortable night's rest and the miserable and near-constant ache in his groin from being so near to Annie. Talking about his mother had been the damned cherry on his day so far. But even then, he couldn't help but be amused by the animosity between Gabe and Annie. They were glaring at each other across the table as though *they* were the feuding couple. They'd been silent and still for the past few minutes as Nate gathered paperwork from his desk and brought it over to the conference table.

"We're on the same team," he reminded them.

His words did little to unwind the tension in Gabe's shoulders. He was suspicious of Annie, and nothing Nate said or did was going to change it. Gabe was good at reading people. Nate tried not to ask him too much about the things he'd done when serving in the military, but he knew Gabe's instincts were always spot-on. He hoped his friend's suspicion of Annie was just residual distrust from years ago, but there was no way to know for certain. Annie was a stranger. His wife…his past lover… but still a stranger.

Gabe opened his portfolio and focused on the task at hand. "I've done quite a bit of recon. Talked to a few of my sources. Here's a short list of our most likely candidates." He slid the paper with ten or twelve names on it across the table to Annie. "These might be your best bets to start with."

Nate watched Annie review the names, her face betraying none of her opinions. She had one of the best poker faces in the game. "If I had to put my money on one of them," he said, "I'd bet on Eddie Walker. He reeks of it, but he's slippery."

Annie nodded but again didn't offer any information she might have on him. Nate was certain she'd heard something about Walker over the years. He was practically notorious for never getting caught red-handed. It had always confused Nate because, to be honest, he didn't seem that bright. But apparently he had a mind for dirty dealing. Or he had a silent partner who was the real brains behind the operation.

"You can go ahead and cross off Mike Stewart," she said, her face still blank, as though they were perched in front of playing cards instead of paperwork. "And Bob Cooke."

"How can you be so sure?" Gabe challenged.

Annie shot a lethal gaze at his head of security. "You brought me into this because I have inside knowledge of these people," she said sharply. "If you contradict everything I tell you, this whole ruse is pointless. I'm telling you they're not cheats."

"*I* didn't bring you into this, Nate did. Personally, I don't think we can trust you. You say they're on the level, but we've got no way of knowing you aren't just protecting your friends. Or cohorts," he added with an accusatory tone.

Annie sighed and shook her head. "Neither are friends. Or cohorts, *thankyouverymuch.* Here's some honest inside information for you. Mike is actually a pervert who cheats on his wife. He comes on to me at every tournament, even when she's with him. But he's not a poker cheat. And neither is Bob. Bob is bipolar. His playing fluctuates wildly depending on whether or not he's taken his medication. Recheck your sources," she said, shoving the paper back at Gabe.

"What about Jason Devries?"

"Jason won the tournament two years ago and typically makes it to the final table."

"So?" Gabe challenged.

"So," Annie continued, "he doesn't need the help. You're looking for someone who improves suddenly or performs well inconsistently. If they're smart, the people behind this will rarely take the grand prize. It's too obvious. You're looking for a lower-level player. Someone who will slink away with their eighth-place prize money and never rouse suspicion. These people aren't stupid or someone would've caught them by now."

Nate's eyebrows went up at Annie's bold words. Perhaps she wouldn't hold back as much as they thought.

Gabe didn't appear as impressed. "I want you to wear a wire."

Even Nate was surprised at Gabe's sudden declaration. They'd never discussed that possibility before. If they had, he would've eased her into the idea instead of bulldozing her like that. His friend knew how to handle suspects and terrorists but not a woman like Annie.

"Absolutely not." Annie crossed her arms over her chest, her brow knitting together in a defiant frown. A bit of her facade crumbled at the challenge, and Nate noticed a very becoming blush rising to her cheeks. All the times they argued, he was too busy being upset to really appreciate how beautiful she was when she let emotion slip through. Annie was far more attractive than the Barracuda.

"I don't trust her," Gabe said, not caring that Annie was three feet away. Nate reluctantly returned to the conversation, taking in Gabe's rapid explanation. "You think this is the only way, but I disagree. If you insist on involving her, the only way we can be certain, that we can know for sure she's doing her part and not tipping anyone off, is if she wears a wire."

"I'm not doing it. This was not part of the agreement."

Nate held his hands up. "Let's just talk about this for a second, please. Annie, I know you don't like the idea of it, but wearing a wire may actually be a good idea. For reasons *other,*" he emphasized, "than the ones Gabe suggested. It would take the pressure off you to remember everything people tell you. Someone on the listening end could be taking notes and doing investigations on players while you're still sitting at the table. Gabe could start pulling security tapes and adding plainclothes guards to keep watch."

"Some of these people could be dangerous. Suspecting

me of spying is one thing, but catching me with a wire? You don't know what they're capable of."

"You would be surrounded by security at all times. There's no way you could be any safer. The audio recordings are the evidence we need to convict someone. With security cameras the way they are, it's very hard to capture someone cheating when they're a professional. The tapes could make all the difference." He urged her to consider it. He didn't want to start bullying her around and force her to do it by holding the divorce over her head again. She'd completely shut down and that wouldn't get them anywhere.

"I can guarantee your safety. I wouldn't let anyone hurt you, Annie. I promise you that."

Annie looked up, her concerned gaze meeting his serious one. He meant every word. Nate might want to punish his wife for what she'd done, but if anyone else touched a hair on her head, they'd regret it.

It seemed to calm her. After a moment she nodded softly and looked away. "Fine," she said, clearly defeated and unhappy about it. "But—" she pointed sharply at Gabe "—he doesn't get to tape it under my blouse."

"Fair enough," Nate said. "Gabe, why don't you go get the equipment and we'll do a test run this afternoon before the tournament starts. I want all the bugs worked out so it doesn't interfere with her game."

Gabe nodded and left the room.

"I'm surprised you're so interested in not impacting my card playing. You never seemed to care much for my career before."

Nate knew he hadn't been supportive enough of Annie. For some reason, he hadn't seen playing cards as a career. It was a game, not a job. Time had given him perspective on his mistake, but their disagreement on that point had likely been a deal breaker for her. He didn't push all the blame for their ruined marriage on Annie—just the fact that she'd run instead of talking through their issues like adults.

"I know it's important to you," he said. "But it's also important to us. We need you to play in the tournament as long as possible. If you get eliminated on the first day, we've lost our insider."

Annie glanced down at the table with a sigh. "I should've known you had an angle."

"You're kidding me, right?" Tessa Baracas glared at Annie across the bright turquoise table of the Desert Sapphire's Mexican cantina, Rosa's.

Annie didn't look at her. Instead, she focused her gaze on her uneaten dinner and the platinum wedding band searing her finger. She hadn't been looking forward to having this conversation, especially with a wire taping their every word. "No, I'm serious."

"Did you not learn your lesson the last time?" Tessa looked horrified. Her skin, so pale compared to Annie's olive tone, was even lighter with shock, if that was possible. Her red-gold hair was pulled back into a tight, sleek ponytail, her jewel-blue eyes wide with surprise and confusion.

The eyes were the sole feature Annie and Tessa seemed to share. The sparkling-blue color was the most noticeable trait they'd inherited from their mother. Sure, they had similar builds, with ample curves and heart-shaped faces, but that's where the similarities ended.

They had different fathers, ones that their mother had apparently hand selected for the sole purpose of creating beautiful babies. Tessa's father was a ghostly pale Irishman with hair like fire. Annie's father was Italian with jet-black hair, warm brown skin and a full sensual mouth—at least, that was what she'd been told. She'd never met him. Their mother had never stayed in one place long. Never kept a man longer than he was of use to her. Which was why Tessa looked as if Annie had just slapped her across the face when she mentioned reconciling with her husband.

Tessa shook her head and slumped back into her seat. "You need to be focused on the game. Not on men. You of all people should know that. It was the first thing you taught me when I started playing."

"Do you think I planned this? Because I didn't."

Tessa anxiously moved food across her plate with her fork. "You shouldn't have come back here. I just knew you weren't strong enough to resist Nate's magic penis."

A nervous laugh burst from Annie's lips before she could stop it. Her sister's irritated expression immediately silenced it. Tessa was being totally serious. "Did you really just say that?"

"Yes. And it's true."

"Well, first," Annie began, hoping Gabe wasn't listening in yet, "thank you for thinking so little of me that I could be easily manipulated by good sex. Second, a magic pe— *Hell,* I can't even say that, it's so ridiculous. There's no such thing, not even on Nate, as gifted as he might be."

"I just don't trust him. I don't like him."

Annie felt the unfamiliar urge to defend her husband. "You've never even met him," she argued, realizing as she spoke that she'd thought of Nate as her husband for the first time. "You're letting Mom's paranoia cloud your judgment."

"And you're letting the magic penis cloud yours."

Annie sighed. "Please stop calling it that."

"Then is it about the money? I mean, you eloped, so there wasn't a prenup, right?"

Annie's mouth fell open in silent shock for a moment before she could gather the words to respond. Money had never even been a consideration in their relationship. She made great money at poker. She didn't need Nate's fortune, or anyone else's, for that matter. "This doesn't have a thing to do with money, Tessa. How could you even ask me something like that?"

"Okay, if you say so."

Annie tried not to frown at her sister and diverted her angry gaze back at her food. Tessa was so bad at reading people. She was passable at hiding her own emotions but clueless when it came to figuring out her opponents. Until she had that down, she wouldn't go very far in poker.

"Are you finished eating?"

Annie looked down, completely disinterested in her food. "Yeah."

Tessa glanced at the expensive-looking new watch on her wrist. "It's still pretty early. I don't have any plans between now and the cocktail thing tonight. What do you say we hit the tables and play a few hands? I think that would be fun. I haven't gotten to actually play with you in almost forever."

Annie reached for her purse, nodding absently into it. She'd forgotten about the cocktail party, worrying about everything else. Tonight would prove interesting, she had no doubt. Every eye in the room would be on her and her royal-blue dress.

Including Nate's.

Five

"Her sister sucks."

Nate winced at Gabe's sudden observation as they watched Annie and Tessa play from the security room. He'd noticed that, too. He didn't know much about Tessa, but he'd thought the Barracuda's younger sister would be a better player. Had Annie taught her anything about poker, or was she just throwing away her tournament registration fees? Maybe she was having an off night. A very off night. She hadn't won a single hand yet. Another round and she'd be out of chips.

"On a good day, I think Annie could make the Captain look like a novice." Nate spoke the words with a touch of pride. He could appreciate the skill it took for Annie to get this far in her career. Few women did in a field dominated by men like the Captain.

He was famous around the poker circuit for his faded white officer's cap and tacky Hawaiian shirts. He wanted everyone to believe he was some retired Navy officer, but he'd once secretly admitted to Nate's grandfather that he'd bought the hat in a thrift store in 1979.

The Captain was eccentric and annoying as hell to play against, but very, very good. Over the past thirty years, he'd won four championship bracelets, almost always making it to the final table in the main events. He was known for talking his opponents to death. He rambled on with old tales about his so-called Navy days, making crude comments about where he docked his ship in a storm and pestering people with inane nautical trivia.

His plan worked like a charm. His fellow players' concentration crumbled when they went up against the Captain. It was just like when men found themselves face-to-face with *the Barracuda,* although for very different reasons. With Annie, a man's pulse quickened, his groin stirred and he came close to forgetting how to play poker at all.

Nate could understand that. She was a hard woman to resist. Honestly, he wasn't sure how he'd managed to go this long with nothing more than a kiss. This week might be torture for them both.

He swallowed the lump in his throat and shifted in his seat to disguise the uncomfortable development the mere thought of her had brought on. He wasn't sure how much more he could take of looking but not touching. His ability to feign indifference to Annie's allure was eroding away.

He wanted her. Badly. He didn't want to stay married to her or play house with her. He didn't want to have feelings for her. He just needed to touch her and soothe the raging beast inside of him. Perhaps a little indulgence wasn't as dangerous as Gabe seemed to think. It was just sex. The last time they were together the sex was incredible, tainted only by their marriage. Why couldn't they have that physical connection again before they went their separate ways? Certainly he could have sex with Annie and not completely lose his perspective.

Tonight was the tournament kickoff, with a cocktail

reception for the competitors. Nate wanted the Sapphire to put a little old-school Vegas class into it, the way his grandfather would've done it. Tonight there would be flowing drinks, low lighting and sultry music to set the tone for the week.

Of course, having Annie on his arm made it that much more interesting. The thought of her in some slinky dress that clung to each voluptuous curve…the music of her laughter as she sipped a drink… Maybe he would be able to slip an arm around her waist and take her for a spin around the dance floor. Then he could press himself against her stomach and dip down to leave a searing kiss on the soft curve of her neck.

Nate swallowed a groan, shifting in his chair and returning his attention to the monitors. That line of thought really wasn't helping at all.

He narrowed his eyes and shook his head. Tessa really was a horrible player. Her instincts were all off. He could tell that Annie knew it, too. She wasn't going in for the kill. Wasn't trying to lure her sister to bet more when she should.

"Annie looks really uncomfortable," he noted. She always seemed so at ease in her skin, but not tonight. The changes were subtle—she was a blank canvas while she played—but Nate could tell the difference. She fidgeted on her stool; her shoulders were curved over her cards, her muscles tensed. Her gaze darted back and forth around the table, watching the other players.

"Maybe she's nervous about spying for us. It might be too much pressure for her. What if—" A loud hiss of static interrupted Gabe. He frowned, looking down at the control panel and hitting a few buttons without improvement.

"What's wrong?"

"Something's wrong with the wire. We've lost the feed. It must have gotten disconnected."

Nate was glad they were doing this today and not in the middle of tournament play. "I'll go pull her aside and adjust it."

By the time he reached the poker table, Tessa was out. She hovered beside Annie, watching her play with intense study.

Nate had watched them on the black-and-white monitors but hadn't fully appreciated the differences between the sisters until he saw them in person.

They were like night and day. Annie was dark and exotic, Tessa, pale and delicate. They had the same lush curves and straight, shiny hair, but they obviously had different fathers.

Annie had never mentioned a stepfather. Come to think of it, she hadn't mentioned a father at all. Or any family aside from her sister and mother. Of course, this morning she'd practically had to drag information about his family out of him. He normally didn't talk about his mother. Some details of life were better left out of the conversation.

He took a few steps until he was almost touching Annie. Tessa turned briefly, looking him over with the same deep blue gaze as her sister, but didn't acknowledge him aside from the quick, appraising glance. Her disgust was poorly hidden as she turned back, disinterested, to watch Annie play.

It was unnerving to see such animosity coming from eyes so like Annie's. Nate hadn't really anticipated that kind of hostility from her family. What could she have told Tessa about him? He didn't bother to ask; instead, he leaned in to press his chest against the back of Annie's stool.

She stiffened at his touch for a moment before realizing who was behind her and why. "I was wondering where you'd gotten off to. Working, no doubt?" She didn't turn but leaned back ever so slightly against him.

The scent of her shampoo and spicy perfume mingled to tickle his nose. The heat of her body penetrated his suit and almost made him forget why he'd come down here. "Apparently, I'm the only thing around here that works," he hinted. "When you finish this hand, we need a private moment." He leaned in close to her ear so Tessa couldn't hear. "For adjustments."

Annie nodded softly and waited for her turn, tossing a few chips into the pot and causing an older gentleman across from her to shift nervously in his seat. He folded. Another man beside Annie groaned as the river card was laid out. He obviously hadn't mastered his bluff. Annie didn't react at all.

Tessa stood silently, watching, attempting to somehow absorb her sister's skill through sheer concentration. She still didn't look at Nate but for the occasional sideways glance.

He leaned in, pressing his warm lips to the sensitive hollow under Annie's ear. He left a soft kiss that sent a shudder through her body before whispering, "Are you going to introduce me to your sister?"

At that, he could feel Annie's muscles tense under his hands. She hesitated, trying to focus on the game for a few seconds more. The other player folded at last, allowing her to claim the pot and shift her attention. She turned on her stool to face them.

"Nate, this is my baby sister, Tessa. Tessa, this is…" She paused, struggling to form the words on her lips. "My husband, Nate."

He extended a hand and Tessa warily accepted it. “A pleasure to finally meet some of Annie’s family.”

Tessa nodded, her expression smug for some reason. “Well, don’t hold your breath to meet Mom anytime soon. I may be the only family you ever get to see before *this* is done.”

“Well,” Annie interjected, sliding from her bar stool, “I’ll see you at the party, Tessa. Nate and I have to tend to something.”

“Okay. I’d better get upstairs and get ready for tonight.”

Annie waved off her sister without a second glance. “Sorry,” she muttered once Tessa was gone. She gathered up her winnings slip to take to the cage. “She thought I lost my mind the first time. The idea of us getting back together now is pure insanity to her.”

“I’m not worried about what she thinks. But let’s go somewhere private.”

“Back to the room?”

“No, I need to do a couple things down here before I go upstairs and shower.” Nate took her hand and pulled her into an empty corridor that connected the pool area to an older section of the casino. This part of the hotel didn’t get as much foot traffic, especially when it was filled with poker players who were generally disinterested in the hotel amenities.

He backed Annie against the wall and stood close to block her from view. His hand went to her back, checking the battery pack. The red light was on, the cord connected. “It must be the microphone,” he said.

Annie’s eyes widened slightly. “That’s, um…between my breasts.”

“Maybe the underwire in your bra has pinched it.” He slipped his hand beneath her sweater, gliding his fingertips over her stomach and up the length of the wire to where it met with the rough lace of her bra. "I'm not sure what this thing is supposed to—"

Nate caught movement out of the corner of his eye. Someone was coming down the hallway. Without hesitating, he leaned in and kissed Annie. He moved his hand from the wire to the round curve of her breast beside it.

Annie gasped at the sudden change but followed along. She wrapped her arms around his neck and tugged him to her. It might be a kiss to cover their tracks, but this was nothing like their kiss outside of Carolina's. She'd caught him off guard last night, but he could still sense her holding back. Now there was only their very public location to restrain them.

Whoever was in the hallway was long gone, but it didn't matter. The kiss grew harder and more desperate the longer it went on. Her teeth nibbled at his bottom lip. His tongue thrust inside her mouth, tasting her. Annie's body molded against his.

Nate groaned. If he wasn't careful, he'd end up taking her on a nearby blackjack table. He forced himself back, breaking the electric connection that held them together.

"Sweet lord," he whispered against her mouth.

"Yeah," Annie agreed. "Do you think we're good now? With the reception?"

The radio at Nate's hip squawked out Gabe's reply. "We're good," he responded. "Not as good as you two are, though."

Annie pulled away, smoothing her green satin top and brushing at the edges of her smeared lipstick with her fingertips. "Since we're done, I'm going to go," she said, walking unsteadily toward the cashier.

Nate took a deep breath and turned to keep from watching her leave. He didn't think he could take the sight of her sauntering away from him in that tight skirt. He might sweep her over his shoulder and carry her through the casino again.

This time to ravish her.

The suite was silent as Annie stepped off the elevator. She'd expected Nate to be there getting ready, but there was no sign of him. It was just as well. She needed to dress, and the fewer…distractions…the better. She'd already killed too much time lingering downstairs.

She'd been afraid to come up too soon. Afraid to walk in on Nate, wet and naked from another shower. Their kiss in the casino had been to cover their activity in the hall, but once he touched her, the world around them could have vanished. It was unerringly clear—their resistance to one another was wearing away quickly. Their magnetic pull was stronger than her fears or his sense of injustice. None of that mattered when he touched her.

He would have her soon. And she would give herself freely. And enthusiastically. But she would draw the line there. She would indulge no thoughts about a future or a real reconciliation. That's where she went wrong the last time.

Annie stepped quickly down the hall to the bedroom. Nate's suit was thrown across a chair in the corner. The bathroom mirror was still foggy. He had been there. Just briefly.

She kicked off her heels and started absentmindedly undressing, pulling together the pieces of her outfit for the evening.

The heels that matched her royal-blue dress rubbed miserably if she didn't wear stockings. She selected a pair of lace-topped thigh highs from the drawer along with panties. She couldn't wear a bra with her dress, so the wire was out tonight. She peeled away the tape and switched off the battery pack before leaving it on the nightstand. From there, she slipped into the low-riding black lace boy shorts that wouldn't show panty lines. She followed them with the silky, sheer stockings.

Annie stood to retrieve her dress from the closet but stopped when she heard a soft groan from behind her.

"Damn."

She spun in her stocking feet to find Nate in the doorway. Annie was topless but didn't even bother covering herself. She wasn't the most modest person in the world. She had as many body issues as any woman, but she didn't waste the energy worrying about them. Besides, he'd already seen it all and touched a lot of it less than an hour ago.

Letting Nate see what she was wearing—or not wearing in this case—under the dress would make him just that much more miserable tonight.

Probably about as miserable as she would be. Nate looked fabulous. He'd upgraded his suit for a tuxedo. Instead of a tie, he wore a collarless ivory shirt with a shiny black button at his throat. He had a matching ivory handkerchief in his lapel pocket. The suit was custom, of that she was certain. He was not average by any means, and the fit was like a glove.

She wanted to press her bare breasts against the cotton of his shirt and knot her fingers into the curls at his neck. Her nipples tightened at the mere thought of scratching against his suit coat. That, however, would sidetrack the entire evening. Nate had to be at the party. He was throwing it.

Feigning disinterest to disguise her growing desire, she turned and walked into the closet. "Ever hear of knocking?" she asked.

"It's my place. I don't have to knock."

Annie knelt to pick up the heels, slipped the dress from the hanger and draped it over her arm. When she returned to the bedroom he was still there, his hands buried in his pockets, his dark gaze silently appreciative of everything he saw.

"Do you like it?" she asked, holding the dress out for him to see. The dress was short, jewel-blue and had a halter collar with tiny silver studs that wrapped around her throat. The reverse was wide open, draping below the small of her back. It was decadent and sexy, a completely unexpected detail, so she didn't share that with him. She'd let that be a surprise.

"Very much." His voice was slightly strained. "It matches your eyes."

Annie draped the dress over the bedspread. She'd thought the same thing when she bought it. "Are you going to watch me dress?"

Nate thought for a moment, his lips puckered in amusement, his eyes still drinking in every inch of her. He let his gaze dart to the curve of her backside peeking out beneath the lacy panties. "No…I just wanted to let you know I was going down to the reception to make sure everything is set up."

Annie nodded. "I'll meet you there in a bit."

Nate eyed his watch. "Shall I order you a drink?"

"A diet soda this time." Annie smiled. "Thank you." The last thing she needed was a repeat of the champagne incident.

Nate returned the smile, clearly following her thoughts. His gaze slowly traveled over her once more, then he turned and disappeared down the hall.

Annie had to take a moment to sit on the edge of the bed. He'd looked at her so intently she could almost feel it like a caress. The heat of it traveled over her body, making her breasts ache and her skin tighten. A deep throb of longing echoed in her core, acknowledging the connection between them that she denied. Perhaps tonight was the night.

A half hour later, she was downstairs and heading toward the Sapphire Lounge. The slinky bar was usually packed with tourists and locals alike for mingling and dancing to the sounds of the talented jazz singer and pianist who played there.

Tonight it was reserved for those registered in the tournament and the bigwigs from the sponsors. A quick look around the room confirmed that many of the players had brought their wives. That would cut down on how many of them would ask her to dance. She was relieved.

It was a male-dominated sport, and wives didn't always follow their men along from game to game. Nate had gone out of his way to schedule several events at this year's tournament to include them. Tonight was the reception, of course, but over the next week there was also a poker widows' luncheon and an excursion to Hoover Dam and the Grand Canyon. Nate was good with the details.

As Annie stepped into the lounge, she was greeted warmly by several friends. Benny the Shark hollered, "The Barracuda!" and before she knew it, the Captain was clasping her in a musty bear hug and Eli was trying to buy her a drink.

She declined, trying to disentangle herself, but got stuck chitchatting. They were boisterous and loud, going on and on as though they hadn't all seen each other in Atlantic City a month ago. The Captain was wearing his best Hawaiian shirt—it was a special occasion, after all—but most of the others had forgone their jeans and polo shirts for suits and ties. It was a nice change. She almost didn't recognize Rodney Chan, he cleaned up so well.

Of course, the first words out of his mouth were about her and Nate. It was apparently all over the tournament that someone had snagged the Barracuda. Most of her friends had already heard the whispers, and those that hadn't turned to her in surprise and pumped her for details. Annie wasn't very close with her family, so these were the people who knew her the best. They were also the people who would be the most surprised to see that ring on her finger.

Annie took the congratulatory drink forced on her by Eli and chatted for a while before she made excuses to leave and find Nate. She weaved through the crowd but couldn't see him anywhere. Normally he stood out, a head taller with a booming voice and contagious laughter, but the lounge was too full tonight to find anyone.

She was about to give up and find a stool at the bar when she caught the flame of red hair out of the corner of her eye.

Tessa was looking lovely in a Kelly-green satin cocktail dress. It was strapless, showcasing her creamy, flawless skin. Her hair was down now, falling over her bare shoulders like liquid fire. Annie had always been jealous of her younger sister's hair. It only got worse as Tessa got older and grew into a stunningly beautiful woman. She was only twenty-two and had a lot of growing up left to do, but she was off to a fine start.

A man with his back to Annie stood near to Tessa, slipping a hand around her waist. It was an intimate gesture, one Annie was not accustomed to when it involved her baby sister.

Then he turned to speak to someone and she saw his face. It was Eddie Walker. A touch of bile started rising in her throat, but she forced it back down. *Hell, no.* That dirty bastard was not touching her sister.

Before she could stop herself, Annie marched across the dance floor and grabbed her sister by the wrist.

"Hey!" Tessa protested as Annie tugged, but she stayed firmly in place with the assistance of Eddie's grip around her waist.

"Tessa, come with me *right now.*" Annie could hear her mother's scolding tone in her voice.

The demand obviously chafed her sister's pride and she clung with more determination to Eddie. "No."

"Don't get your panties in a twist, Annie. This is a party." The leech had the nerve to speak to her, a cocky grin spread across his face. "It might be better if you just stayed out of this."

"Don't you tell me what is or isn't my business when it comes to my sister and a sleaze like you. Tessa, come on." She tugged again, this time shooting eye daggers at Eddie until he released her. She pulled Tessa into a dark corner near the ladies' room, well out of anyone's earshot.

"What is *wrong* with you?" Tessa complained, yanking her hand away.

"Me? What's wrong with *you?* Eddie Walker? Are you kidding me?"

Tessa's face hardened, her jaw setting defiantly as she crossed her arms over her chest. "You're one to talk, *Mrs. Reed.*"

"That's not what I mean. Eddie is…" Annie struggled to find the right words.

"Wonderful?"

"No. He's a dirty, stinking, lying poker cheat."

Tessa's eyes widened for a moment, an expression of shock paralyzing her mouth in an open O. Apparently she thought Eddie's reputation hadn't spread that far. Had he convinced her that no one knew about his activities?

"Please don't get involved with him."

"It's too late, Annie. I've been seeing him for almost six months."

Six months? How had Annie missed this? She wasn't very social with Tessa, but she must've been trying fairly hard to avoid the subject this long. Why did she have to break her relationship streak of two months with a scumbag like Walker? "He's bad news, Tessa."

"Oh, please. You're just jealous."

"Why would I be jealous? He's not a great catch, Tess. You've known him six months. I've known him six *years*. Everyone knows that he plays a dirty game. They just haven't caught him yet."

Tessa's expression changed then. It almost beamed with subdued pride. Was she honestly proud that Eddie was too crafty to be caught? That would all change, and quickly, with Nate involved. He wouldn't tolerate it in his hotel and he was using Annie to ensure it.

"I know what I'm doing."

Annie sighed. There was no more sense in arguing. For one thing, Tessa was stubborn. Telling her she couldn't do something was like a challenge. Annie realized she'd already made that mistake when she saw the defiant look in her sister's eyes. Second, the harder Annie pushed, the more closed off Tessa would become. They weren't close, but the gap could easily widen. She couldn't afford that, especially now.

Her sister was playing with fire, thinking it was safe because she believed she was the one in control. How quickly would she get burned?

Annie knew this was her last chance to say her peace, to warn her sister before Gabe would start listening in on every conversation she had. "Just be careful. Don't get in too deep with him."

Tessa exhaled roughly, nodding slightly in relief that her sister backed off the uncomfortable subject. "I don't get in too deep with men." She smiled. "You should know that. You used to be the same way."

Six

By the time Nate looked down at his watch, the cocktail party had been going strong for over an hour. Certainly Annie was here somewhere. Fashionably late had passed quite a while ago. He'd kept an eye out while glad-handing all of his VIPs, but there'd been no sign of her. At least not from his side of the bar. He'd thought there was no way he'd miss that blue dress, but he'd underestimated how many people would be here tonight.

Then he saw her.

Annie came charging from the bathroom, leaving her befuddled sister in her wake.

Nate's breath caught in his chest at the sight of her. The dress was like a dream, the bright blue playing beautifully against her tan skin and jet-black hair. The high, firm breasts he'd seen earlier moved tantalizingly beneath the fabric as she walked, reminding him that they were free beneath it. The short cut of the dress highlighted the sculpted muscles of her calves and rhinestone-covered sandals.

In that instant, the last of his resistance was blown to pieces. He would have Annie in his bed tonight, consequences be damned. He could no longer convince himself otherwise.

She looked gorgeous…and agitated. Her skin was flushed, her brow furrowed, her delicate jaw tight. That was unusual for her. He didn't like it. Not one bit. It made him wish he could listen in on the sisters' conversation. It was a shame she wasn't wearing the wire tonight, but that dress left no place to hide it. It barely hid what it was supposed to.

Nate signaled for a refill on his vodka tonic and a Diet Coke from the bartender and carried the drinks to where she'd stopped. She was leaning against one of the high-top bar tables, her beautiful face buried in her hands.

"Here's your soda." He leaned over to her. "I can have Mike add a shot of rum if you need it."

Annie stood up with a start, her face quickly composing into her usual cool demeanor. "Oh! You startled me." Whatever was bothering her was rapidly compartmentalized and put away. She eyed the glass in his hand and accepted it with a forced smile. "Thank you. The rum won't be necessary."

Nate came to her side, leaning in to kiss her on the cheek and slip an arm around her waist. To his surprise, his hand came in contact with her bare, smooth skin instead of fabric. Thoughts of her earlier agitation vanished as he let his fingers travel across her skin, searching for where the dress began. He was forced to stop short of public fondling.

"You should've told me," he murmured into her ear over the buzz of the crowd.

A slight look of panic widened her eyes for a moment. "Told you what?"

He let his warm palm press into the small of her back, the heat of her skin almost burning him. "That you could only afford half a dress. I would've bought you a whole one if I'd known."

Annie sighed, wrinkling her nose and sipping her drink. "You don't like it?"

Nate chuckled. "Of course I *like* it. The problem is that so does every other man in this place."

"Ahh." She smiled. "You're jealous."

He had every damn right to be. Everyone knew the Barracuda used her looks to distract her opponents. She'd developed a long list of admirers over the years as a result. The mere thought of another man looking at Annie like that was enough to send his blood pressure skyrocketing. Even after all this time there was a primitive part of Nate that still considered her to be *his*.

"I am not jealous. Simply territorial." He picked up his glass and sipped.

"Are you going to piss on me?"

Nate nearly choked on his vodka tonic. Annie was unpredictable. He had to give her that. "I don't think that will be necessary." He coughed.

"Good. I don't think this fabric is washable." Annie smiled, taking another sip of her drink. The worries of just minutes ago were so far buried Nate wouldn't know they were even there if he hadn't seen her upset.

"Are you having a good time?"

Annie shrugged. "It's a very nice party."

"I think so. But you didn't answer my question."

She turned, her blue eyes penetrating him as she attempted to read what he was really after. "Yes, I am," she said slowly, watching his face for changes.

Nate nodded and took another sip of his drink. "A poker player should be a better liar. What happened with Tessa just now?"

"Nothing." Annie responded too quickly, breaking eye contact and gazing down into her glass.

Nate looked in the direction Annie had come from. Her sister had sat down at a table, but she wasn't alone. Now she was in the arms of a despicable man. If Tessa were his sister, he'd be pretty damn upset, too. "Hanging out with Eddie Walker isn't nothing."

Annie's head snapped up, her eyes narrowing at him. "She just told me they're dating and have been for several months. I had no idea."

Nate raised an eyebrow at her response. Weren't sisters supposed to share everything? "That's no revelation. I can see that much just by the way he touches her."

They both turned to watch Eddie and Tessa in the corner. They were talking to one another in the dark, rounded booth. Their body language screamed sex; their legs crossed together as they leaned in and gazed into one another's eyes. Eddie had one hand on her bare knee, the other rubbing strands of her red hair together between his fingertips.

Nate turned to watch Annie instead of the secluded lovebirds. Her nose was wrinkled, her brow furrowed again in concern. Whether or not she had prior knowledge, she obviously didn't care for this love match. Eddie had a rotten reputation, and he wasn't the kind of guy you'd pick for your sister.

Eddie had been his number-one candidate to watch from the beginning. Everyone knew he was cheating; they just couldn't catch him. Whether he was involved in the big operation the tournament sponsors were after, he wasn't certain.

That's why he'd asked Annie to help him. She could lure him out, get evidence to charge him. It required someone on the inside who really knew the game. Annie was perfect for the job. She wouldn't let anyone get in the way of her winning the grand prize, and he had no doubt she would do what she could to stop Eddie. And now that her sister was dating him, what better way to break them up than to send the creep to jail?

He would talk to Annie about that. But not tonight.

Tonight he had better things on his mind. Like getting Annie back in his bed. He'd fought with himself since the moment she'd arrived, but damned if he didn't still want her. Even after everything. Their three years apart had only amplified the hum of arousal that buzzed through his veins. He wouldn't love Annie. He wouldn't even let himself care about her. But he could get his fill of her before she walked away.

When Nate was a child, his grandfather had once given him a huge bag of cherry jelly beans. With his father busy and his mother off shopping, he'd sat in front of the television one afternoon and eaten the whole bag. Nate had never been so sick in his life. To this day, he couldn't abide cherry jelly beans. Or cherry anything, for that matter.

Perhaps the same would be true of Annie. Resisting was the wrong tactic. He needed to fully indulge himself in her soft body and silky skin. Overdose on her. Get her out of his system. And maybe by week's end, when the divorce paperwork was drawn up, he would be just as disinterested by the thought of her as he was by that noxious candy.

Nate eyed a tray of appetizers being passed by a server. "Are you hungry?"

Annie turned to look at him, then shook her head, waving away the waiter. "No, watching those two paw at each other made me lose my appetite."

The loud, upbeat music came to an end and a crowd of

people returned to their tables. The next song was slow, and he watched several couples step out onto the dance floor. "Well, then, would you care to dance? This would be a good opportunity for everyone at the tournament to see us together."

Annie eyed the people on the dance floor anxiously, then nodded with hesitation. "Okay. But you should know I'm a terrible dancer."

Nate laughed, reaching out a hand to her. "Somehow I find it hard to believe that you could be anything but graceful, Annie."

Her hand slipped into his, her soft velvet skin unusually cool as he clasped it. He squeezed it to warm her fingers as he led her gently into the center of the dance floor. With a turn, he wrapped an arm around her waist, his palm resting low on her bare back once again.

"That's it." He smiled down at her. "I'm buying you a new dress. Your hands are like ice."

Annie smiled with uncharacteristic nerves and shook her head. "It's not the dress," she admitted. "It's the dancing. I go cold when I'm nervous."

Nate couldn't help the look of surprise that spread across his face. His eyebrow arched high, his eyes narrowing at her. "The Barracuda, nervous? Never."

Annie was tough. She could take on every man in this room and beat them thoroughly. No doubt, she'd do it in stilettos and a skintight skirt. And yet the idea of dancing made her go cold in fear?

Annie wrinkled her nose and shifted in his arms, struggling to find a natural position. "Don't say that too loud." She leaned in. "It's one of my secret tells. All the players will come up with lame excuses to touch me if they think it will give away my bluff."

Nate chuckled, easing her into his arms, their bodies close but not quite touching. He wasn't sure he could take it if she pressed the full length of her against him.

Not here, at least.

He glanced around the room at the men watching them from the bar before meeting her unsure blue eyes. "Something tells me most of these men would need little excuse to touch you."

His firm hand guided them to the rhythm of the band playing. Annie was hesitant at first but fell easily into the motion. The song was slow with a slinky beat that the body couldn't help but respond to.

After a few moments, she leaned in and placed her head on his shoulder. Nate closed his eyes, hugging her closer and changing their motion to a subtle shifting of weight on his feet.

It felt so good to just hold her.

He leaned down to plant a kiss in the silky strands of her hair and breathed in deeply, letting the warm, seductive scent of her fill his senses. It was eerily familiar, like a distant memory he couldn't quite place and yet its name rested stubbornly on the tip of his tongue.

Annie was so soft in his arms. She fit there perfectly, as though her body had been made for him. It was the most comfortable feeling in the world, like slipping into a warm bath. He let himself submerge in the sensation.

Soon, the rest of the dancers, the musicians…even the room itself faded into nothingness. It was just Nate and Annie in each other's arms. Why did it feel as though he'd never held her like this before?

Perhaps because he hadn't. Yes, he'd made love to her. He'd explored every inch of her body. But never truly held her. Not like this. Annie was like a hummingbird, always flitting from one flower to the next. She was beautiful to look at, but you couldn't hold her. If you tried, she would vanish again. He'd learned that lesson the hard way.

Annie sighed, nestling deeper into his chest.

Nate's jaw tightened at the small cooing sound she made into his lapel. It was the same contented sound she made as she fell asleep. He remembered it in that instant. It had been so long since he'd heard it and at the same time, like yesterday that he'd made love to her.

The last night they were together she'd curled into a ball and had fallen asleep while he was in the shower. When he returned, he'd stood for a good half hour watching her sleep. He'd been mesmerized by her loveliness, her well-fortified facade wiped away by sleep. Her coal-black lashes had fluttered gently against her flushed cheeks, her kiss-swollen lips mouthing sleepy, confused words into her pillowcase.

His heart had nearly burst with pride when he realized she was his.

Nate had almost woken her up to make love to her again. If he'd known how quickly she would vanish from his life, he would've. He'd thought, foolishly, that he had all the time in the world to be with her and so had let her sleep.

Perhaps tonight he would make up for lost time and pick up where they'd left off.

He shouldn't have gone there. The instant heat flooded his groin, his body going from relaxed to uptight like the flick of a switch.

Annie noticed the sudden change as his body tensed, lifting her head to look at him with concern worrying her deep blue eyes. "What's wrong?"

The ballad came to an end, another upbeat song on its heels. People came and went on the dance floor, but Nate held them both in place. A slight shift of his body pressed the hard length of him against her stomach. "Nothing," Nate said with a wicked grin.

Annie's eyes grew wide before her lips twisted into a knowing smile. "I think we should go upstairs and do something about that."

Annie couldn't move fast enough. They said no goodbyes as they made their way through the crowd and slipped out of the lounge. As the private elevator doors enclosed them, she turned to him, expecting him to devour her the moment they were finally alone.

Instead, Nate stuffed his hands in his pockets, leaning casually against the opposite wall. Despite his relaxed stance, his entire body was tense, his jaw flexed. His gaze penetrated her as it raked from top to bottom, but he didn't make a move except for a hard swallow that traveled down his throat to the buttoned collar of his tuxedo.

She'd forgotten how controlled he was. His gratification had always come from taking his time and enjoying every delicious second. Annie could never understand it. She was burning up for wanting him. She could feel the warmth between her thighs, the painful hardening of her nipples as her breasts tightened with desire. Her every nerve ached for the touch he denied.

She glanced down at the control panel. They still had fifteen floors to go. She couldn't wait that long. In one quick motion, Annie smacked the emergency button, bringing the elevator to a shaky, abrupt stop. Nate adjusted his footing but didn't argue with her.

She looked him straight in the eye as she reached behind her neck and unfastened the halter of her dress. It was the only thing that held the dress on, so with a quick shimmy of her hips, the slinky blue fabric pooled to the floor. She stepped out of it, her eyes never leaving his dark gaze.

"Nate?" Gabe's voice barked at them from the two-way radio on Nate's belt.

Nate unclipped the radio, his gaze still fixed on Annie. "Yes?"

"We've got a report your elevator has stopped in between the tenth and eleventh floors."

His lips twisted in amusement as he pressed the button to respond. "That is correct."

There was a long silence before Gabe spoke again. "Okay, then. Radio if you need assistance."

"Will do." Nate turned the radio off and tossed it to the floor with a loud clank.

With the interruption behind them, Annie crossed the floor in two long strides and stopped just short of pressing her rock-hard nipples into his chest. He watched her, one hand still buried in his pocket, the other perched on his hip. She took a ragged breath and stared into the tensed muscles of his neck and jaw as they twitched beneath the skin. She ran her fingertip along the line of this throat, stopping at his collar.

Then she spoke. "Touch me, Nate. Don't make me wait any longer."

It was all that needed to be said. Nate's arms wrapped around her in an instant, pulling the full length of her body against him. His lips dipped down to brush against hers with a featherlight touch that sent a shiver of desire to the base of her spine.

"I want you," he whispered against her skin.

Annie answered with her lips, standing on her toes to reach up and capture his mouth. The kiss was tender at first, soothing the ache for a moment before the fire raged anew. Her fingers weaved into the blond curls at his neck, tugging him closer, but knowing he could never be close enough.

Nate's hands slid down her bare back, letting one dip lower to cup one lace-covered cheek. With a gentle squeeze, his hand continued down her silk-covered thigh to behind her knee, hitching her leg up to wrap around his waist.

Annie groaned as the new angle brought his erection into direct contact with her moist, aching sex. The sensation was overwhelming, and she knew it was just the beginning. Her mouth moved hard against his, her hands clawing at his tuxedo coat in a frenzy until he let it slip to the floor.

Her fingers were at his collar, undoing his shirt and thanking the heavens he wasn't wearing a tie for her to deal with. With his chest bare, she ran her hands over it, marveling at the hardened muscles she remembered. She let them dip lower and lower until the tips slid beneath the waist of his pants. She brushed the skin there, eliciting a groan and a sudden start as Nate grabbed her hand.

In one quick movement, he spun them around as though they were still on the dance floor. Now Annie was the one pinned against the wall, Nate pressing the length of his entire body against her. The brass was cold against her bare back, but she didn't care. It did little to soothe the fire that ran through her veins.

Nate's lips traveled from her jawline to her ear before moving slowly down her neck to the hollow of her throat. A tingle of anticipation coursed along her spine, her body shuddering at the searing caress of his mouth on her sensitive skin.

Annie tugged off his shirt and threw it to the floor. She wanted to keep her eyes open, to drink in the breathtaking sight of Nate, but she just couldn't. His mouth had traveled to the swell of her breasts. As he took one tight peach nipple into his mouth, her head flew back, her eyes closing on their own.

"Oh, Nate," she cried out, her fingers running through his golden curls, clutching his head and pulling him closer.

Oh, how she remembered this feeling. She'd suppressed the memory of it all these years, fearing she'd weaken and come back. Annie was addicted to him, addicted to how he could make her feel. As his hands and mouth slid over her skin, the craving burst to the surface once again.

Nate got down onto his knees, his lips nipping at her tensed stomach, his tongue circling her navel and dipping lower. Every muscle in her body tightened into knots when his hands brushed over the edge of her lace panties. She let go of his head to grip the railing and brace herself.

The panties came down inch by inch, the anticipation making her crazy until he eased up one leg, then the next, to cast them to the side. She was left wearing only her stockings and heels. Annie couldn't open her eyes. She was exposed, her trembling, aching body on display for him. If she looked at him, she might give herself away. She couldn't let him know just how badly she really wanted this. How long it had been…

His hands traveled from her ankles up the length of her silky stockings. Her legs trembled as he moved higher, his touch blazing a trail across her skin. She clutched the railing with all her might, her eyes squeezed shut, her bottom lip clamped between her teeth.

With gentle pressure, he eased her thighs apart, exposing her to the cool air before his warm breath tickled her skin. His fingers danced lazy circles up her thighs, teasing her hip bones. Annie swallowed hard, her breath caught in her chest as she waited.

Nate did not disappoint. He tasted her, drawing a strained cry from her throat with its sudden attack. It was followed by a second, then a more lingering caress that was nearly enough to undo her. He must've sensed it because he paused, giving her time to recover, then continued his erotic assault on her body.

Annie cried out again, her hips straining to reach for him. "Nathan, please," she panted. She wanted him. Needed him. After three long years without his touch she didn't want to wait another second to have him again.

"Please…*what*…Annie?" With each pause, his tongue flicked over her.

"I want you inside me, Nate. Now, please." Annie opened her eyes when the cold air tickled her skin.

He had moved to the other side of the elevator, undoing his belt and slipping out of his pants. He wasn't looking down at his hands, though. He was looking at her. Devouring her with his eyes. Annie could see him mentally planning, the chess player in him working on his next move.

She really didn't care what he did next as long as she was covered by his massive warmth. He was just so beautiful. His body was even better than she remembered, as though he'd spent the lonely nights since she'd left in the hotel gym. Every inch of his body looked chiseled from stone, the kind of male perfection that the great artists of the Renaissance struggled to capture.

In one last move, his pants and briefs slid to the floor. Instantly, he was as exposed as she was, his desire just as obvious as it thrust proudly at her. Annie's breath caught in her throat. Her lips were suddenly dry, forcing her to snake her tongue across them.

Nate stepped out of his clothes and slowly walked back to her. Without a word, he circled his arms around her waist and lifted her up. She wrapped her legs around him and held his shoulders to keep her steady as he slowly lowered her onto him. He groaned, low and loud, as he was buried deep inside her.

They stood there, nearly still for a moment as they savored the sensation. It had been so long. She couldn't explain the feeling, but somehow it was so much more than just the physical pleasure of sex. There was a connection there that had never been broken. It had never wavered.

Nate eased her back against the wall, his hands cupping the swell of her bottom. His fingertips dug into her ample flesh. Slowly, agonizingly so, he withdrew and thrust forward, beginning an easy rhythm.

Annie clung to him, her face buried in his neck as he moved. With every movement, he went deeper and thrust harder, driving her closer and closer to the edge. His breath was hot and ragged in her ear, mingling with soft whispers she couldn't quite understand over her own cries.

She was nearly there, aching to go over the precipice, yet hesitant to let all this go. Her teeth gritted tight, her nails digging into his flexing shoulder blades. "Not yet," she panted. Annie wasn't ready to stop. She hadn't had enough of him yet.

She couldn't resist Nate. The rush of her addiction pumped through her veins, and the fears from her past slipped into her mind. This was why she had stayed so far away. She knew she wasn't strong enough. She couldn't deny him her body when it was all she wanted to give him.

Nate was not deterred by her apparent refusal. He widened his stance, gripping her with almost crushing strength to thrust in short, quick movements that left her no choice in the matter. The pressure built up, washing over her like a tidal wave. She was swept up in it, overwhelmed by the sensations she had deprived herself of for so long.

"Yes," Nate hissed into her ear, coaxing her release as he held her thrashing body tight against him. When she stilled, softening in his arms from exhaustion, he moved quickly, shouting out her name with his last few thrusts.

Exhausted, he eased her back against the wall, resting her bottom on the railing. It was cold, but Annie didn't care. Her whole body was throbbing, her skin feverish and slick with sweat.

Nate propped his elbows on the wall beside her and leaned against it to breathe, his body still cradled between her trembling thighs. "That—" he spoke between rapid breaths "—was worth the wait, but let's not go another three years before we do it again." His dark eyes studied her face for a moment before he lifted her up off the railing. With her wrapped around him, he reached over to hit the button and let the elevator continue up to his suite.

Seven

Annie wasn't certain how the first day of the tournament would go. She was used to playing on her own terms. Free to indulge her superstitious rituals without personal distractions. This mess was the opposite of how she liked to work.

For one, she got almost no sleep. She and Nate had made love until her muscles gave out and she simply couldn't do anything but collapse onto the bed. When she finally did sleep, it was like a minicoma until Nate shook her shoulder and told her she had to get up.

It felt odd to wake up in Nate's bed with him beside her. Strangely comforting and familiar. She didn't remember this feeling from before. Then there had only been the panic of knowing she was married. Today she was still married, but that didn't seem to bother her as much.

It was an interesting and unsettling development. She'd sat up in bed and watched him disappear down the hall in nothing but pajama pants. Almost immediately her body was ready for more of him, but she knew now was the time to focus. She had a big day ahead of her.

Before she could go downstairs, she had to get briefed

by Gabe for the tenth time. She also had to get wired. That experience itself was uncomfortable enough, even with Nate's warm hands under her blouse to distract her. The head of security had said several important things after that, but all she knew was that the tape that secured the wires pulled at her skin and itched something fierce. She still hadn't adjusted to the idea of having Gabe listening in to her conversations all day. Same team or no, every word out of her mouth was subject to his scrutiny and she didn't like having to worry about it on top of everything else.

Add all that onto the pressure of scoping out her fellow players and she was completely unprepared to play poker. With the way she felt, she might just choke and get eliminated before she could fulfill her end of the bargain with Nate. What would his price be then?

Annie settled into her assigned seat and eyed Gordon Barker. He was three seats down. Gabe had arranged for her to share a table with him today because he was on their short list of suspects. She'd heard a rumor or two about him over the years, but they'd never been as loud as the ones about someone like Eddie Walker. If he was involved in some elaborate scheme, he was smart enough to keep it quiet.

Personally, Annie hadn't had a lot of experience playing with him, so she wasn't sure either way. As the tournament started, she decided to spend the first few hands focused on her game and building her chips. Once she had a healthy cushion above the other players, she would feel more comfortable breaking her focus to watch Gordon. She had to play well if she was going to be successful in any of this.

As the lunch break approached, Annie was pleased with how the day had gone. A few players had been eliminated. Gordon was still playing, but she'd seen nothing suspicious and she hadn't lost any hands to him. He was probably another name she could cross off the list, but she wasn't about to rule him out yet. If she was too good at her job, soon there wouldn't be anyone but Eddie on Nate's radar. Toppling him would not only be difficult, but destructive. Tessa would not be happy if she found out Annie had sent her boyfriend to jail.

When the tournament stopped for lunch, she grabbed her food and went to sit down beside the Captain. She figured he was probably her safest bet for company. He wasn't much for gossip. With any luck, she could attempt to make conversation and dig for information as required, but he wouldn't deliver anything but another one of his long-winded Navy stories. It was the perfect choice.

"Afternoon, *Mrs. Reed.* How's your game going today?"

Annie smiled and shrugged. "Too early to tell."

"Don't let yourself get distracted by thoughts of that handsome husband of yours. You two seem to be enjoying this second honeymoon of sorts, but it can mess with your game. It's no coincidence that every time I won the championship, I was between marriages."

She opened her bag of chips and let a smile curl her lips. The Captain always seemed to be between marriages. She'd lost count at six. Her one marriage was too much for her to handle. "I'll try. I'm worried about Gordon Barker, though. I've heard rumors he doesn't play a fair game. I'd hate to get bumped out because he's dirty."

The Captain shook his head and took a bite of his sandwich. "You don't need to worry about Gordon. He's been clean for years. Had a brush with the law that was a little too close for comfort a while back and he straightened right out."

"Oh," Annie said. Well, at least the conversation was

getting her somewhere and Gabe couldn't accuse her of not doing her job. She was hoping to string Gordon along as an option for a while longer, but now she could focus on the rest of her game instead of him. "That's a relief."

"You'll want to watch out for Eddie Walker, though."

Annie stopped, her bottle of water hovering in midair. She hadn't expected this at all, but she should've known the Captain would want to look out for her. He'd been the closest thing she'd had to a father over the years. "He's not at my table today."

"Well, the problem with Eddie is that he works with a circle of players and dealers. It's actually better if he's at your table because he always keeps his own game clean. He's a tricky bastard. I wish to God someone would catch him so we wouldn't have to deal with the scrutiny. It messes with my game to know how many security people are circling around and watching my every play."

She immediately felt guilty for talking with him while wearing a wire. "I'm surprised no one has caught him yet, given how many people know about it."

"He's careful. And smart. There's one main player they try to push through to the final table and a good ten or more in the tournament just to help them along. You never know who's in on it. I heard he's got a new partner working with him this year. I haven't seen her myself," he continued. "But I heard she's—"

She? Annie sucked a sip of her bottled water into her lungs accidentally, launching into a mad coughing fit. The Captain immediately stopped talking and patted her on the back, watching with concern as she wheezed and viciously hacked.

"Are you okay?" he asked when several minutes had passed and the bright red faded from her face.

"Yes, I'm sorry." She nodded. "If you'll excuse me, I think I'll run to the ladies' room."

"Of course."

At that, Annie dashed away to the safety of the restroom and hoped Gabe's security goons had the good sense to stop listening in.

With the way the tournament play fell, Annie was scheduled Saturday so she had Sunday off. They had a record number of registrations, so the breakup allowed everyone to participate. The numbers dwindled exponentially after that point, so the top players from Saturday and Sunday would then combine to continue on Monday.

In theory, Nate should've been down on the casino floor making sure everything was going as planned, but he just couldn't make himself do it. Saturday had been agony. He'd watched Annie play from a distance all afternoon, unable to touch her the way he ached to. His fists had been curled tight in his pockets for hours, a fake smile plastered onto his face.

When she finished for the day, victorious, he'd whisked Annie away to the suite. She'd barely been able to bask in the glory of her poker domination before she was naked and writhing under him again. They'd spent the entire evening holed up in the suite, ordering room service and making love on every piece of furniture he owned.

As the sunlight began pouring in the windows Sunday morning, Nate rolled onto his side and stared down at her. She looked as though he had thoroughly exhausted her. The long strands of her dark hair were messy and sprawled across the pillow, her eyes dancing under her lids with dreaming.

Throwing back the covers, he disappeared silently

down the hallway. By the time he reached his desk, he could hear the chattering music of his smartphone. It was Gabe's ringtone. He hadn't spoken to him since the end of tournament play yesterday. He was certain his head of security had been anticipating a daily debrief with Annie, but Nate hadn't felt like sharing her last night.

"Hey," he answered.

"Good morning, sunshine," Gabe said dryly. "We need to talk about something that happened yesterday."

Nate frowned and settled into his desk chair. "What?"

"I was down on the floor watching Eddie as you directed, but one of my guys, Stuart, was doing surveillance and listening to Annie's conversations."

He didn't really want to know what his friend would say next. It would ruin his sex buzz. "And?" he said reluctantly.

"She was talking to the Captain and having a fairly blunt conversation about Walker. He indicated that he'd heard Walker had recruited a new woman to work with him. Just when he was about to elaborate, Annie went into a mad coughing fit and immediately dismissed herself."

That wasn't good. Knowing the accomplice was a woman reduced the suspect list dramatically. Knowing Annie had abruptly ended the conversation, hadn't followed up and hadn't passed any information on to him or Gabe narrowed it to a party of one. Was it possible that Tessa was more than just Eddie's girlfriend? Could she be involved in the cheating, as well, or was the Captain just misinformed? He needed to get Annie away from the casino and all the intrusions.

"I think I'm going to take Annie to the house today. We both know Eddie is up to something, possibly Tessa, as well, but I'm not sure about what Annie knows. I was thinking I could get more information out of her if we're away from the casino."

"Make sure you don't get played. You don't know how involved she is with all this. For all we know, she's the ringleader and using her relationship with you as a diversion."

"I guess we'll find out." At that, Nate hit the button to disconnect the call. He didn't like thinking about Annie like that. He would do what was smart, but he hesitated to be instantly suspicious of her like Gabe.

Flipping through his address book, he punched in a name and within seconds had his housekeeper, Ella, on the phone. The older woman was in her late fifties and lived exclusively at Nate's house. She kept the place clean and organized. If he decided to do something at the house, Ella would make sure everything was taken care of.

He explained his plans and she was all too eager to prepare everything for their arrival. Honestly, he hadn't been back to the house in more than a month. The poor woman was probably bored to tears and suddenly all atwitter as she readied the house.

"Nate?" Annie's sleepy voice called to him from the bedroom.

Nate switched off his phone and headed back to her. "Good, you're up," he said and sat on the edge of the bed. "Get dressed."

"You mean you're going to keep your hands to yourself long enough for me to put clothes on?" Annie sat up in bed, the navy sheets clutched to her bare chest.

Nate eyed her for a moment—the sexy mess of her hair over her shoulders, the smooth length of her leg peeking out from beneath the covers, the full swell of her breasts pressed against her arms. That was a very good question. He was considering having her again before they left. The only thing stopping him was the opportunity to make love to her someplace new.

"Only if you hurry." He grinned and disappeared into the closet.

They did hurry, hopping into his convertible Mercedes as the valet pulled it around. Within minutes, they left the bustle of the Strip behind and settled into the sprawling suburbia that surrounded it. He'd told Annie to dress casually and bring a swimsuit. He expected her to ask questions, but she seemed content to watch the scenery go by.

It took about twenty minutes to get to his subdivision. The two-story Spanish-style house was typical for the area, with the sand-colored stucco walls and red clay tile roof. The yard was well landscaped but lacked any sort of personality. It could've been anyone's house. Were it not at the very end of the cul-de-sac, it might've been hard for even Nate to pick it out from the others.

Nate hit the button to open the garage and pulled in beside the empty spot where Ella's green Buick normally parked. He felt bad about the sudden plans, so he'd sweetened the deal with the offer of an afternoon of pampering at the Sapphire Spa. She deserved it. It also got her out from underfoot. Ella didn't know about his marriage to Annie and he wanted it to stay that way.

Nate sighed and opened the door. "I'd give you the tour, but I'm a little rusty on it myself."

Annie chuckled, scooping her purse off the floor and climbing out of the car. "You really need to focus on some work-life balance, Nate."

He held his arms out wide. "I'm here, aren't I?" He fished the keys out of his khaki shorts and unlocked the door. "Besides, I'm not taking any criticisms from a woman that lives out of her suitcase."

"Touché." She smiled, slipping past him into the dark, empty house.

As promised, the tour was short. They made a pit stop in the master suite to christen the king-size bed, then slipped into their swimsuits and took a dip in the cool turquoise pool in the backyard. Like children, they splashed each other and roughhoused in the water, then ambitiously napped in lounge chairs until the rumbling of their empty stomachs distracted them.

Without room service to call on, they wandered into the kitchen to see what Ella had left for them. An ivory note card on the counter informed them about the fixings for homemade pizza in the refrigerator.

"Do you think we can handle this?" Annie looked dubiously at the ball of dough on the counter.

"Oh, come on," Nate prodded, scooping an armful of food off the shelf. "Certainly we can manage a pizza. Ella's already done most of the work. It will be fun to try, at least. If it's a disaster, we can order something later. Here." He slid a few tomatoes and a pouch of fresh basil across the granite countertop. "You get the toppings for the pizza ready while I work on the dough."

Nate assembled the pizza, ladling Ella's homemade sauce and spreading fresh mozzarella slices on the crust. He watched Annie out of the corner of his eye as she worked busily, cutting tomatoes. She looked really beautiful today. Yes, she looked sexy almost all of the time, but most definitely beautiful now. The pool had washed away all traces of her makeup. Her long dark hair was still damp, the thick, corded strands running down her bare back. Her golden skin seemed even darker against the stark white of her bikini. She'd wrapped a colorful cotton fabric around her waist, tying it in a knot slung low at her hip bone. It hid the tiny white string bikini bottoms she'd pressed against him in the pool.

She caught him watching her and she smiled, giggling in a girlish way that made his chest ache unexpectedly. Annie away from the casino was like a new person. She didn't just look different, she acted different. In only a few hours' time, he'd gotten to see a more casual, easy-going version of her. He liked this Annie even more than his superconfident but guarded card shark.

But that wasn't all of it. There was something familiar and soothing about the banality of their actions. Making lunch together in his house away from the casino…it was more significant a moment than he'd expected.

Yes, making love to her again had been great, but this kind of experience seemed important in a different way. They'd never had any real domestic moments together. Suddenly that bothered him more than he wanted it to. They'd never had a real marriage. They'd just had some fantasy honeymoon that existed only within the walls of his hotel. His work quickly became her prison. Making lunch, watching television, even grocery shopping were things they'd never experienced together and it made him sad. Perhaps they would've had a shot if they'd done this three years ago.

This week was supposed to be about making Annie miserable and finally being able to put her out of his mind for good, but he wasn't getting over Annie as he'd planned. The more he had her, the more he wanted of her. He should've just signed the divorce papers instead of luring her back here.

"You have sauce on your cheek."

Nate looked up, his thoughts disturbed. "What?"

Annie reached out and wiped a dab of renegade marinara off his face. She licked it off her finger and smiled. "Ella makes wonderful tomato sauce."

"She does. It makes me want to stay at the house more often so she can cook for me all the time."

"Why don't you?"

Nate shrugged, scooping a few tomato slices off the counter and scattering them on the pizza. The answer was that there was really nothing to come home to. Work always needed him. This empty house, not so much. If he'd had a family, it would be a different story. "No real reason to be here, I suppose."

"Then why do you have a house?"

"I bought it when the market was low, so it's a good investment. Someplace to go when I need to get away from work. And…" He hesitated before completing the thought. "I'd hoped that I'd get married one day and have a family here." He looked up at Annie with a playful grin. "That hasn't quite panned out for me yet."

Annie uneasily matched his grin, quickly turning back to slicing the last of the tomato and starting on the basil. "So if you never come here, Nate, why exactly did we make this little field trip today?"

Nate stilled over the pizza. He'd been waiting for the right moment, enjoying his afternoon with Annie too much to ruin it. But she'd opened the door. It was time. "I wanted to bring you here to ask you something."

Annie frowned slightly. "Sounds ominous."

"I guess it depends on your answer." He shrugged. "I wanted to get you away from the casino, the tournament and the wires recording your every word in the hopes I could get an honest answer out of you."

Nate laid the last of the tomato slices onto the pizza. "I'm worried about the conversation you had with the Captain about Eddie. If Eddie really is working with a woman, the list of partners dwindles significantly. You can imagine what my concern is." He paused, watching her look down at the herbs to avoid his gaze. "Hit me with some basil."

Annie's expression was neutral as she sprinkled the leaves across the pizza and dusted her hands together to brush the remaining bits into the sink. "You think Tessa might be more than just his flavor of the month?"

"It's a scenario we have to consider. She is registered in the tournament."

"And you're worried I won't cooperate in convicting my own sister."

Leave it to Annie to cut to the chase. "I hope it doesn't come down to that, but yes. Gabe is concerned that you can't be trusted to bring us information if it might implicate her. Or even that you might try to use our relationship as a distraction to protect Tessa."

"And you? Are you suspicious of me, too?"

Nate turned and looked her directly in the eye. "Yes. It would be stupid not to at least consider it as a possibility." A flicker of emotion ran across Annie's face, but it was too quick for Nate to detect whether it was guilt, pain or irritation.

"Let me ease a couple of your concerns," she began. "First, *you* came to *me* with this arrangement, so you can hardly accuse me of manipulating the situation to protect or distract attention from Tessa. Two, my sister and I aren't very close. She doesn't confide in me, so if you think I have any inside knowledge into what she's doing, you're wrong. If I had any evidence of her or anyone else cheating, I'd turn it over so I could focus on my game and stop wearing that itchy damn wire.

"And finally," she said, reaching a hand up to cup his cheek and looking him directly in the eyes, "I'm sleeping with you because I want to. You're the sexiest man I've ever encountered and I can't help but want you."

Nate's chest tightened. He didn't know if it was her brutally honest answers or the way she looked at him when she said how badly she wanted him. Before he could reach out to her, she pulled away to scoop up the pizza stone and carry it to the oven. Annie slid the pizza stone inside and shut the heavy stainless-steel door. "How long does it bake for?"

Nate examined the card Ella had left for them. "She says about fifteen to twenty minutes but that we should watch for the crust to brown."

She set the digital clock for twenty minutes. "Okay, that's done, so I'm going to hop in the shower."

With that, she turned and sauntered out of the kitchen, the colorful wrap falling seductively from her hips to the tile floor.

Annie hadn't been surprised by Nate's questions. She'd been caught off guard by the Captain's words at lunch the day before, which was why she'd choked, but her fears about it being true were why she hadn't returned to follow up. She didn't want to turn in Tessa. And she would go to great lengths to avoid uncovering her sister's involvement. But at this moment, she had absolutely no evidence of anything but her sister's poor choices in men and no problem telling Nate as much.

Her answers seemed to satisfy him. For now.

When she got out of the shower, Nate had taken the pizza and a pitcher of iced tea out onto the covered patio. They dined, then moved to the poolside chairs. Annie lay out on her stomach and was very nearly asleep when she felt Nate's gaze on her. She opened one eye toward him, wincing at the sunlight despite her fashionably oversized sunglasses.

He was openly appraising her body, his jaw hard set in restraint as he took in the dark expanse of her skin. When he realized she was watching him, he smiled sheepishly. "Your body should be bare and sun-kissed more often. It belongs on the white sand beaches of the Caribbean. Not in a dark, smoke-filled casino."

Although Nate hadn't specifically said it, Annie's brain immediately went to being on that beach with him. Being here with Nate had been an eye-opening experience, to say the least. She'd been given a glimpse, however small, of what life with him could be like. Life away from the casino. Just him and her living their lives together the way they'd first envisioned.

Annie had expected their time together to be uncomfortable. Nate had made it perfectly clear that he'd wanted her to suffer. Adding sex to the mix had changed their dynamic, but she still anticipated the panic to come eventually. The urge to run. Now she was envisioning herself in a hammock swinging in the breeze on the beach *with him.* She didn't feel oppressed. She didn't feel tied down. She actually felt...great. Which was terrible.

"There isn't much money to be made on a beach." She rolled onto her back and smiled at him. "I follow the tournaments. If there's not a casino to host one, I probably won't go there."

Nate frowned at her. "So you never just take a vacation for the sake of vacation? No break from cards and casinos?"

Annie shrugged and closed her eyes. "Not really. I travel so much as it is that I don't exactly relish the idea of traveling just to spend money instead of making it."

"What about as a kid? Didn't your family ever go on trips to Florida or the Grand Canyon?"

"As a child, I saw almost every corner of this country, but not to vacation. We just moved all the time. My mother was on this constant journey, looking for something that she never found. To this day, I still don't know what it was."

"What about your father?"

Annie tried to shrug dismissively, but it wasn't convincing. "She left him behind. Apparently I wasn't important enough for him to chase after. And even if he'd wanted to, she would've vanished again."

"So that's where you get it?"

Annie frowned. She hated her childhood. Hated growing up never keeping friends or a real home. Being compared to her mother wasn't exactly the highest compliment in her eyes.

"I suppose so," she admitted. She knew what he meant. Through someone else's eyes, she supposed she looked flighty. And part of her was. When she was of age, her inner nomad had immediately taken over and she'd nearly become as bad as her mother. She fought it, maintaining a home in Miami and finding a line of work where she filled the urge by traveling a lot. But there was a difference. She was alone, doing what she pleased. She'd never subject a child to her lifestyle. Or a husband.

"Why did I have to marry a woman with a long family history of nomadic male abandonment?"

"You should never fall for a gypsy, Nate. It always ends badly."

"I'll take that under consideration, though I might suggest that in the future you throw that line out on the first date."

Annie rolled her eyes and lay back into the chair. "It

sounds like you're the one that needs a vacation. You've been killing yourself at that casino for years."

"I was thinking about it. My family owns a house on St. Thomas. I haven't been there since I was a kid, but it might be time. Where are you off to after this?"

"I have another tournament in a few weeks, so I'll be heading up to Vancouver, then Monte Carlo a month after that. Not quite a vacation, but it's my first chance to see Monaco."

Nate perked up in his chair. "Monte Carlo? I've always wanted to see the Formula One race. It's in early May, around when you're going, but I'm always too busy to get away."

He hadn't said he wanted to go with her, but Annie sensed an interest she didn't expect. She never imagined that Nate would follow her anywhere, especially for something as insignificant as a poker tournament. She'd always envisioned their marriage inside the sphere of the Sapphire, as though they were both trapped within a snow globe. That was the way he'd seemed to like it back then. He didn't want to leave and he certainly didn't want Annie leaving without him. It definitely changed her outlook on things to know he was branching out.

Annie sighed, shifting the uncomfortable subjects from her mind. It was easy to do. The warmth of the sun was so soothing, soaking into her bones. "I don't want to go back to the hotel. Can't we just stay here?"

Nate chuckled beside her, a low rumble on the breeze. "That does sound tempting, but it's hard to win a tournament that way. Even for someone as talented as you are."

Annie laughed and closed her eyes. "Ruin all my fun, why don't you?"

All this talk of vacations was just that…talk. Here, away from the troubles that surrounded them, it seemed possible. But once they returned to the Sapphire, she was certain it would fly out the window. If he was right and her sister was involved, their reunion was just a ticking time bomb. Annie was sure if she didn't leave first, Nate would be the one to push her away.

She wasn't certain she could stand mourning this relationship a second time.

Eight

Nate was tired of the tournament already and they still had three days to go. Hosting it was good business, but now that he had Annie in his bed, the tournament and the chaos that surrounded it could disappear for all he cared.

He eyed his watch impatiently. There were two hours left of play today. Annie was doing well. She'd already single-handedly eliminated three people at her table. Before long, she would move on to another.

He'd tried not to hover. There were dozens of tables to watch and VIPs to entertain, but he kept wandering back in her direction. She had a gravitational force that seemed to impact only him. No matter how hard he tried to pull away, she'd draw him back to her. If he'd been smart, he would've left a few hundred miles between them. Now he had no way to fight it.

And he no longer wanted to.

Nate needed to focus. His short list of potential cheaters required his attention. Annie was watching another player at her table today, but she'd muttered under her breath into the wire that it was another dead end. He wasn't about to give up, though. An entire team of security staff was watching the tables from overhead security cameras in addition to the people on the floor. A couple were plainclothes, but most were in the standard navy blazers with earpieces that gave them away. Gabe had been assigned to watch Eddie. A few of his best guys were assigned various other people, which now included Tessa.

As much as Annie insisted she would turn over her sister if necessary, he knew she wouldn't go out of her way to collect evidence against her, either. If she was more than just Eddie's girlfriend, his team would have to be the ones to uncover it.

Annie's laughter called to him over the chaos of the room. He turned, drawn back to her. She looked so lovely today. Her shiny dark hair hung loose around her face. Her vivid purple blouse was clingy and unbuttoned low enough to give all the players an ample view. She knew it, too, leaning forward innocently onto the table. If she wasn't careful, someone might see the tiny black microphone nestled between her breasts.

Nate's jaw tightened. He knew it was simply a part of her game strategy, but that didn't mean he had to like it. They might not have much of a marriage, but they were telling people they had reconciled. Seducing her opponents at the table didn't do much for their cover. If it was even a cover anymore. His pangs of jealousy felt real. The lines had become terribly blurred lately.

He took a deep breath and tried to focus on her game. The other player went all in. Nate watched, knowing Annie wouldn't give away a single thing. Her face was serenely calm, her lips parted in a smile that would confuse any man. She sat for a second, mentally calculating her hand and how best to play it. The cards on the table didn't give much away.

Annie's fingernails ran down a stack of chips, counting them out, and then she tossed them onto the pile in the center. Both players flipped their cards, but Nate didn't get to see them. It wasn't until he saw the man shake Annie's hand and walk from the table that he knew *the Barracuda* had claimed another victim. Nate tried not to smile, but he couldn't help it. He was beaming with pride. His wife was beautiful and talented, and everyone knew it.

His wife.

Nate stopped in his tracks when he realized what he'd just thought. His mouth went dry. Despite being legally married the past three years, Nate had never really thought of Annie as his wife. He'd barely adjusted to the idea of being married when she left. Then she'd simply become *"her."* But now…now that he knew she had one foot out the door of his life, never to return…now he decided to stake this mental claim to her?

He'd thought he had done well to compartmentalize this week and what it really meant—nothing but some great goodbye sex. Focusing on their physical connection was the smart choice. It was the piece that had always worked between them. But recently, it was not Annie's naked body or cries of passion that occupied his thoughts. He'd started thinking beyond the tournament and the potential for more.

He glanced across the tables to where Annie was sitting. He wanted to ask her to stay. To give them another shot at the relationship they never really tried. But what would she say if he asked? Nate had felt them growing closer, felt her letting down her guard, but would it be what drove her away?

This was definitely not what he'd had in mind when he hauled her to his suite and blackmailed her into helping him.

"Mr. Reed?" A voice chirped over his radio.

Nate unclipped it immediately and moved away from the crowd for privacy. "Yes?"

"Sir, we've detained someone in the security office. Gabe has requested your attendance."

Nate frowned and cast a quick glance over to where Tessa had been sitting. She was still there, her flame-red hair giving her away. Richard, one of the senior security agents, was still watching her, and another security agent had taken Gabe's place watching Eddie.

He breathed a sigh of relief. "I'll be right there," he answered. Hopefully they'd get a break that wouldn't involve his sister-in-law. That would make everything easier.

When he arrived in the security office, he found Gabe sitting at a table in the conference room with someone he didn't recognize. The guy was short, thick through the middle, with pudgy fingers, greasy gray hair and a bristly beard. He was older, in his late fifties, maybe.

His eyes widened when he caught a glimpse of Nate standing in the doorway. He'd opened his mouth to argue something with Gabe, but froze, clamping his mouth tightly shut.

"Mr. Hansen," Nate greeted Gabe officially. "Who do we have the pleasure of meeting with today?"

"Mr. Reed, this is Keith Frye. Mr. Frye was participating in the tournament downstairs. It seems our cards weren't good enough for him and he felt it necessary to bring a couple of his own."

"I just wanted to—"

"That's fine, Mr. Frye," Nate interrupted. "We understand. Some people prefer to use their own, especially when they're better than the ones the dealer provides." He turned to Gabe. "Do we have everything we need?"

"Yes, sir. The overhead camera has clear film of him slipping cards from his pocket into his hand. We'll notify the authorities as soon as we're done here."

"Excellent." Nate was pleased things were under control but slightly curious as to why he had been summoned up for something this trivial. Yes, he liked to know everything that went on in his casino, but Gabe normally handled things like this on his own.

"I'm not the only one!" Keith blurted out as Nate turned to walk out.

Now they were getting somewhere. Nate met Gabe's grin with interest and returned. "Continue."

"He said it might help me out." He flipped a thumb in Gabe's direction.

"Might," Nate emphasized. "Let's hear what you've got first."

Keith looked down at his hands, nervously picking at his fingernails. "There's this guy, Darrell. I don't know his last name. A couple nights ago I was hanging out in the bar, having a few drinks, when Darrell and some other guy I don't know sat down at a table near me."

There wasn't a Darrell on his list of suspects. "Do you know this Darrell guy?"

"No, but he had a blue dealer's vest folded up beside him, and the guy he met up with called him Darrell."

Nate clamped his teeth together to keep from yelling at the man in frustration. That was why. He was a dealer, not a player. He hated to think that one of his own employees was involved in something like this, but it was inevitable.

"So these guys start talking about the tournament and what they're planning to do. They were sorta speaking around what they really meant, but I could follow along well enough. I pretended I wasn't listening, but it was easy to hear with them sitting so close."

"And?" Nate was anxious to hear the rest of this convoluted tale.

"And they sounded like they were plotting something. Arranging who was going to do what. Sounded like this Darrell guy was messing with the cards. That's where I got the idea, you see? It sounded like there were several people in on it. Other dealers, other players. Even some chick."

Nate perked up. "Some chick?"

"Yeah, she came into the bar later. They'd been talking about her on and off, but then this redhead strolls in and the other guy left with her."

Nate's stomach sank. A redhead. Every word out of this guy's mouth seemed to put another nail into the coffin of his future with Annie. "What did the other guy look like? The one Darrell was talking to?"

"Kinda skinny. Dark hair. He was wearing a Dallas Cowboys windbreaker. The girl was hot. Pretty tall for a girl. Nice rack."

Nate swallowed the lump in his throat. There was no question he was talking about Eddie and Tessa. "Anything else?"

"No, that's about it. So, hey, was that good enough to cut me some slack with the cops?"

He thrust his fists into his pockets and nodded. "Yeah. You leave your personal information with security here, in case we have any questions, and you'll be free to go. I'm sure the money you lost paying to enter the tournament will be punishment enough. If I ever see you back in this casino again, I won't be as lenient, Mr. Frye."

Nate turned to Gabe. "Find me this Darrell guy's personnel file. And see if you can find footage from that night in the lounge. I'm heading up to my office."

Gabe gave him a curt nod and continued filling out the forms on the table.

Nate spun on his heel and disappeared from the conference room. He needed to get out of there. Get away from the guy who had given them their big break in the worst possible way. He blew down the hallway, his friendly demeanor gone. Employees dodged out of his way as he stomped to the elevator and up to his suite.

He was pounding mercilessly on his laptop when the elevator chimed. Nate looked up, anticipating Gabe with the file he'd requested, but it was Annie.

She came over to him, dropping her purse onto the sofa and sitting on the edge of his desk to face him. Her pink grin was wide, born of confidence. She'd no doubt slaughtered the competition today. Her sapphire eyes searched his scowling face for a moment before the light in her expression dimmed. "What's wrong?"

Nate swallowed and looked down at her knee. He let his hand roam over the bare skin, distracting himself with the silky touch of her. "Work stuff," he said. He would leave it at that until he was certain there was something more to say. He wanted solid, convictable evidence on Tessa first.

"Aww," she cooed, slipping off the desk and circling his black leather executive chair. She leaned over the back, her fingers kneading at the tense muscles of his shoulders.

Her touch was enough to chase away all his dark thoughts. Her hands worked on the knots and nerves like a skilled masseuse. It was unnerving how she knew just how to touch him, just what he needed. There was a comfort in her mere presence that made the stress of his day not seem as important anymore.

"You know what you need? A dip in the spa." Annie walked out of the room, various articles of her clothing left in her wake. Nate shrugged out of his coat and tie, following the crumbs Annie left to the balcony.

The secluded balcony was off the large glass wall of the living room and overlooked the hotels across the strip. It had an in-ground spa, a fully stocked bar, a luxurious outdoor living room set, a fire pit and even a putting green. It was the perfect place for a party or an interlude for two. At least that was the idea. He almost never came out here.

A chrome-and-glass overhang and a few well-placed trees in glazed clay pots provided ample privacy, with a latticed alcove around the sunken Whirlpool. It was a necessity with the child-friendly Excalibur Hotel so close. Anyone with binoculars and an inclination could see onto the patio from the right hotel room.

Nate slid through the glass door and turned the corner just in time to see Annie's round, firm behind slip into the swirling, hot water. She'd clipped her hair up into a messy bun on the top of her head, but a few strands still trailed over her shoulders. He unbuttoned his shirt slowly, his eyes glued to her bare back as it disappeared beneath the surface.

With the water up to her shoulder blades, Annie turned and sat facing him. The steam from the water had dampened the loose tendrils around her face and gave her cheeks a rosy glow. She smiled at him, the cheerful pink lipstick ready and waiting for him to remove it.

"Well, come on," she urged.

Nate complied, tugging off his shirt, throwing it to the patio floor and following it with the rest of his clothes. He could barely feel the scalding water as he stepped into it. He was focused only on Annie. Even with his suspicion of her sister lingering overhead, he needed to touch her. His body demanded it.

He didn't bother sitting. Instead, Nate crouched low into the water and moved across to kneel in front of her. His hands pried her thighs apart, giving him a place to nestle in against her.

She moved in, wrapping her legs around his waist and tugging him closer. With a quick spin, he lifted her with him until he was the one sitting and she was straddling his lap.

"Mmm..." She sighed, pressing against him. "So, would you like to talk about your bad day?"

Nate smiled, gliding the length of him back and forth across her most sensitive parts. "What bad day?"

Annie ground her hips against him, closing her eyes to allow herself to fully experience the sensations coursing through her body. It amazed her how quickly and easily he could bring her to the edge. It seemed to take almost no effort at all on his part, making her wonder once again if he'd been given the instruction manual to her body.

In her new position, her breasts were easily within reach of his mouth. He didn't hesitate to lean forward and run his tongue through the valley in between. Nate turned his cheek, planting a kiss on the side of her breast, then continuing down around the edge of it. His caresses moved lazily around her hardened nipple, coming close but not touching the place she ached for him the most.

Nate continued to lick and nibble at her sensitive flesh as his hands slid down her back and cupped her rear. He guided the motions of her hips, sliding the length of him along her sex in such a way that coaxed her nerve endings to tingle from her fingertips to her toes and yet denied her the contact she craved.

Annie bit her bottom lip, struggling to catch enough friction, but he was stronger than she was. He was going to drag this out as long as he could.

"It's just too much temptation for you," he murmured against her breast.

Before Annie could respond, he took one nipple into his mouth and sucked hard. She cried out, her answer forgotten as the pleasure stabbed sharp through her. Her hips bucked against him, seeking out what she needed and failing once again.

In one fluid motion Nate stood, lifting her up out of the water and sending a wave over the side of the spa that soaked the surrounding concrete. She clamored quickly to wrap her arms around his neck, but he immediately sat her on the opposite edge of the Whirlpool.

He knelt in front of her, his mouth still tightly clamped onto her aching breast. Annie arched her back, clutching his damp blond curls and pressing against the hardened muscles of his stomach.

Nate let go of her breast at last, giving the tip of her nipple a quick flick with his tongue, then moving back to kiss her sternum, grazing down her stomach. He leaned into her then, forcing her backward until her shoulders met with the cool stone of the patio. His body nearly covered hers, and she pulled her legs up to cradle his body. She smiled, thinking perhaps she would finally get what she was after.

Instead, he pulled away, leaving a trail of kisses down her stomach. The muscles of her belly quivered with need, his mouth tickling and torturing her as he moved lower. She didn't know if she could take much more of this. He would tease and taunt her with his hands and his mouth until she'd agree to nearly anything.

It was unfair. As many times as he'd had her since that first night, she'd hardly been given the opportunity to reciprocate. He was so intently focused on her and her pleasure, it was hard to complain. But he was the one who needed the attention today, not her.

"Nate?" Annie whimpered, her whole body trembling with wanting him. "Nate?" she said again with more force when he didn't answer.

He paused, his lips hovering just above her dark, cropped curls, his hooded eyes watching her over the hills and valleys of her exposed body. "Yes?"

Annie took advantage of his hesitation to sit up and make a futile attempt to push his shoulders back. "I want my turn." She gave him a sly grin and slid into the water. Her eyes stayed intently focused on him as her lips took their turn to run down his stomach, her hands gently caressing and kneading his tensed muscles.

Nate was so tall that when he was standing, his erection rose proudly above the waterline. It brushed against Annie's breasts as she sank into the water, eliciting a shudder from him.

She took advantage, letting one hardened nipple run over the tip, then drag down the length of him. Annie smiled when she saw Nate's fists curl tightly at his sides. This was the only way she knew of to get Nate to lose control. He was always so calculating, so in command of his world. Here, now, Annie was the one in charge.

Without giving him time to prepare, she dipped and took him into her mouth. Her tongue ran over every inch, her teeth grazing lightly. She moved faster, sensing the tension build through his entire body, and then slowed to an agonizing pace where every inch she moved prolonged the torture.

Apparently, it was too much for him. With a growl, Nate grabbed Annie by her forearms and tugged her up to stand with him. His gaze penetrated her, his jaw locked in a hopeless attempt to keep control.

When Annie gave him a smug grin, he erased it with his mouth, searing her lips in a desperate kiss.

She was almost unable to breathe for the force of it. After a moment, she pulled away to catch her breath and watched the passionate fire blaze in his dark eyes. He didn't just want her. He wanted to possess her, consume her. Even after everything that had happened between them.

The weight of his desire was like an anvil pushing against her chest. Turning quickly in his arms, she pressed her bare back against him. In that moment, she needed to escape his intensity. It was almost frightening how much he wanted her. But even more so was how badly she wanted him. How much she craved not only the release, but the comfort and protection of being in his arms.

She'd always felt confined when she was held. It was never a comforting feeling for her but one that made her struggle for air. Nate's embrace had become like no other before. It was a safe haven from the world. It was...*home.*

Annie expected the panic to start welling in her chest, but it didn't. Which was even more disconcerting. She took a deep breath and eased back to let his firm arousal nestle against her rear. A quick sway of her hips brought a low hiss to her ear and was an easy distraction from her thoughts.

Nate's arms wrapped around her waist, tugging her back to sit in his lap as he plunged down into the spa. The buoyancy of the water made it easy for Annie to rise up and take all of him in with one quick thrust.

He groaned against her shoulder, holding her tight and still against him. After a moment, his hands glided across her skin to encircle her rib cage. They drifted higher until he cupped one breast in each palm. Annie's nipples ached, tightening against his fingertips as they brushed across the hardened peaks.

Annie leaned back against his chest, straddling his muscled thighs. Nate rested his chin on her shoulder and moved slowly beneath her. It was an easy, rolling motion. Neither too quick nor too slow, but building.

He played her like an instrument. It wasn't long before every muscle in Annie's aching body was tensed and primed for release. But even as Annie raced to her climax with Nate quick on her heels, she could feel the last of her barriers coming down. The last thread that held her back snapped when she no longer had the desire to hold it tight.

Annie didn't just desire Nate. She didn't just care about him or find comfort in him. She was in love with him. And it scared the living daylights out of her.

Nine

Annie's game ended late the next afternoon when she broke her table and there wasn't enough time to bother regrouping. That done, she had some free time to kill. It was too early for dinner, too late to get involved in anything else. Nate was probably prowling around the tables, trying to keep his distance and not distract her. Gabe would want her to talk to some people and try to dig up some more information. For that very reason, she opted to do the opposite and watch a couple of games still in progress.

Annie was surprised to find Tessa playing at a table three down from her own. She honestly hadn't expected her to still be in the tournament. There were five players at the table, including her sister. A quick glance showed that two didn't have long left to play. Their chips were quite low, especially in comparison to Tessa and another player, Paul Stein.

The crowd applauded as Tessa won the hand. Annie bit her lip, watching her sister scoop the chips and restack them in front of her. She was doing extremely well, even against a former champion like Paul. That alone should've been her clue to turn and walk away. But she didn't.

A few hands went by without much fanfare. Tessa and Paul went back and forth taking the pot until one of the other players went out. Then Annie noticed something odd. Tessa was fidgeting.

One of the first things Annie had taught her sister was not to fidget at the poker table. But she watched as her sister looked at her cards and started twisting a ring on her finger. One of the other players across the table folded his hand despite having quite a bit of money in the pot. Paul and the other player were both oblivious and focused on their game.

Fidgeting was not uncommon at the poker table because they sat for so long. But even then, something about Tessa's movements seemed odd and deliberate. In the next hand, Tessa absentmindedly twirled a strand of hair around her finger. Only Annie would know it was something Tessa didn't usually do. The other man raised, driving up the pot, then lost moments later, giving her sister a big boost in chips.

Maybe it was more obvious because Annie knew her sister and her tics, but Tessa and the other player were working together. She hadn't spent much time with Tessa over the years, but childhood habits died hard. Every move she made felt deliberate or forced. Most people didn't worry about partners working together at a tournament because the table assignments were random. You'd have to have someone on the inside to ensure you were placed together, and that was nearly impossible to do.

Annie's throat started to close on her as surely as if she'd been stung by a bee. The flop went down and Tessa bet conservatively. The way you would if you were trying to lure other players into putting more money into the pot. At the moment, Paul was contemplating his bet. Every eye in the room was on him, even those of the security guard who was supposed to be watching Tessa play.

All except for Annie's. Her gaze stayed glued on her sister as Tessa watched the other players and once again started curling a red strand of hair around her finger. It played out just as before, with her partner betting high. Tessa casually looked up and caught Annie watching her with a sad, disappointed expression.

Tessa froze for a moment in panic before smiling uneasily. She knew Annie had caught her but was confident her protective older sister was no threat to her scheme. She silently pleaded for Annie's silence, mouthing the word *please* before turning back to her hand.

Suddenly the last gap in her throat closed and Annie couldn't breathe.

From the moment she'd seen Tessa and Eddie together, this had been her secret fear. She'd been telling Nate the truth when she said she didn't know anything. Worrying about her sister's judgment and knowing for certain of her guilt were two very different things. Everything had just changed. She needed to get out of there. Now.

Without staying to see how the hand ended, Annie turned on her heel and began pushing her way through the crowd. She had no idea who was around her or who she knocked into on her way. All she knew was the panic and struggle for air. Her chest felt heavy, as though bricks were threatening to crush her rib cage.

She glanced at the entrance to the casino, but that wasn't enough. She needed clean air. Air without taxicab smog, tourists and the deafening bustle of the Vegas Strip.

Annie wanted to go to the roof.

Nate's private elevator didn't go all the way to the hotel roof, but she knew which one did. Her access card would take her almost to the top, and then she could scale the last few stairs.

"Annie?"

Someone called her name, but she couldn't stop to find out who it was. She darted down the hallway and into the secured area. The elevator was waiting when she arrived, and she slipped in her card to take her all the way to the top.

"Annie? Wait!"

It was Nate, she could tell now with the casino noises muffled by the doors. The voice was more urgent, his pounding footsteps echoing on the tile floor as he chased after her, but she ignored him. She needed to get away from everything, including Nate.

The doors closed and the car shot up from the ground floor at a dizzying speed. Annie closed her eyes. She was relieved to find the higher she climbed, the easier she could breathe. By the time she opened the door that led out to the roof, she felt infinitely better.

Annie took a deep breath and walked out onto the open expanse of the hotel roof. Her trembling hands gripped the railing as she stood, overlooking the twinkling lights of the Strip. The sun had already set, and the casino signs were growing more intense as the golden light faded from the sky.

She stood quietly listening to her surroundings, waiting for her heart to grow steadier in her chest. She strained to hear the deep boom of what could only be the Treasure Island cannons as the pirates battled out front.

She'd failed Tessa. If she'd been the sister she should've been, Tessa wouldn't have fallen into this sort of situation, letting herself be manipulated by a man. And after all the grief her sister had given Annie over her marriage! Marrying Nate wouldn't land her in jail.

What could she do now? Nate desperately wanted to secure the tournament contract. She had no doubt he would have Tessa arrested once he had enough evidence, and she'd told him she would turn the information over if she found it. The key was that she wouldn't look for her sister's guilt, but she'd just been slapped in the face with it.

How could she choose between her sister and the man that she loved?

She never should've come back to the Desert Sapphire. The tournament wasn't worth it. Not even the divorce was worth it. Nothing justified the pain and drama that coming back had brought. In the end, everyone would get hurt, including Nate. She'd promised herself she wouldn't hurt him again.

Alone in the rapidly deepening darkness, Annie let the last of the barriers go. The tears rushed down her cheeks in earnest, the first real tears she'd cried in years. Salty streaks ran down her flushed cheeks like a faucet had been turned on. She could only hold on to the wall for support as her body was racked with her emotional outburst.

When the sobs subsided and her face was impossibly red and swollen from her tears, she had to admit she felt better. Nothing had changed, but letting off the steam did wonders for her general outlook.

"Annie?"

At least she *was* feeling better. Nate's voice called to her from across the roof, but she didn't turn. Couldn't turn. She didn't want him to see her like this.

Nate's warm hand rested on her shoulder. His firm fingertips pressed soft circles into her tensed muscles. "Are you okay?"

Annie nodded, afraid to speak out loud and give away her lie.

"Tell the truth, Annie. What's the matter?"

"It's nothing." She sniffed, wiping at her cheeks in a dismissive way before turning to him. "Really."

"You are a terrible liar, Mrs. Reed."

Annie's stomach sank with the way he said those words. His voice had so much concern and emotion in it that her chest tightened. She'd never had that with anyone else. Her mother didn't tolerate weakness, and she had never really been outwardly affectionate. She loved her daughters, but sometimes it was hard to know it. Annie had learned early to keep her emotions on the inside. When she got older, poker seemed like the perfect career choice. But after years of holding it in, she didn't know how to let it out and truly open up to Nate.

He slipped a hand under her chin and gently turned her face up to look at him. She couldn't avoid eye contact now. The dark brown depths of his eyes pulled her into the comfortable warmth they offered. Standing there, she was almost able to forget the horrible mess she'd gotten into. At least until his hand glided around to her back and flipped the switch, turning off the recording device. At least he'd remembered before she lost her senses and started confessing to him while Gabe listened to every word.

"Do you need to get out of the hotel for a while?"

Annie's gaze narrowed at his words. She expected him to sense her weakness and pounce on it, but he didn't. Instead, he offered her an out and she would gratefully accept it. She wasn't ready to admit she'd seen Tessa cheat with her own two eyes. Or to confess she was in love with him and scared to death that she would lose him in all this.

He accepted her silence as a yes and pulled her into his arms. Annie accepted his embrace, collapsing onto him. She buried her face in his chest, drying her tears and keeping her from saying the words on the tip of her tongue. That he was right to be suspicious of her and of Tessa. That she was torn between protecting her sister and losing the man she loved.

"I've booked dinner reservations for us at the Eiffel Tower restaurant tonight." Nate took her hand and pressed a soft kiss on her fingertip. The loving gesture sent a warm surge through her that she wasn't expecting. She was distraught, emotionally spent, and yet she still wanted him. She craved not only the sensations he coaxed, but the safety and comfort she found in his arms.

He planted a kiss to the palm of her hand, then her wrist, working his way up to tickle the inside of her elbow and nip the soft skin of her upper arm.

The effect was immediate and powerful. Annie pushed everything out of her mind and let her body take over. She leaned into him, arching her back to expose her neck as he moved higher. If she was about to lose everything, she was going to indulge in every minute she had with him and savor each touch as her last.

Nate curved an arm around her waist, tugging her tight against him as his lips danced across her skin.

"Nate?"

"Yes?" he breathed against her ear.

"What time are our dinner reservations?"

"Not for another two hours."

"Good. Take me to the suite."

Nate arranged for the hotel limo to pick them up and whisk them down the Strip for dinner reservations at the Paris Hotel. Their table at the Eiffel Tower restaurant had premium views of the Bellagio fountains across the street. It was a breathtakingly romantic setting, even more so than Carolina's, she dared say.

He'd preordered the eight-course tasting menu with all the chef's specialties, substituting the first course because he knew Annie didn't care for caviar. As always, she was taken aback by Nate's ability to remember the details and make someone feel special. It was a powerful aphrodisiac to have someone that focused on her needs and desires both in and out of the bedroom.

"You're such a charmer," she said, sipping sparkling water from a crystal flute. "Hard for a woman to resist when you're in full-on Nate mode."

"What is that, exactly?" He looked at her quizzically. Apparently no one had ever pointed it out to him before.

"When you focus on someone. You make sure every detail is perfect, that they have everything they could possibly desire. It's an intense feeling."

"Did the other men in your life not treat you like the jewel you are?"

Annie chuckled softly. "Most men don't, actually."

He seemed surprised. "Then they're fools."

"Tell me the truth," she said, leaning across their second-course plates. "Are you like this with all women?"

Nate's smile dimmed almost imperceptibly. "No. Just you."

Annie swallowed her bite of food with difficulty, taking a large sip of water to try to force it down. She'd always told herself that Nate's charm was part of a savvy business strategy, that he treated her just as well as he did any customer. Knowing that was not the case was exciting and unnerving.

Their situation was complicated, to say the least. They were sharing a bed, knowing they were days away from divorce if all went according to plan. And yet now, sitting in this beautiful restaurant and feeling her heart swell every time he smiled, she knew things had changed. The thought of walking away from Nate in just a few days' time was almost painful.

But regardless of how she felt, divorce was still the smart choice. They wanted different things. That didn't mean her heart understood. It only knew what it wanted, and that was Nate. She'd been denying her feelings for so long it had become second nature. But she didn't want to suppress it anymore. She wanted to tell him that she loved him.

A shudder ran down her spine that she covered by slipping back into her sweater under the pretense of being cold. Just thinking the word *love* had given her chills. Saying it out loud seemed impossible. Especially with how things stood with Tessa. As much as her heart wanted to be free, it also needed to be protected. She couldn't trust Nate with it yet. Could she?

The dinner continued with relaxed, casual conversation. They enjoyed every bite of their food, paying their bill in time to walk downstairs and experience the fountains in person.

They stood at the railing along the dark pool, Nate's arm wrapped around her waist to hold her tight against him and keep her warm in the cooling desert air. "You'll love this," he whispered into her ear, planting a warm, affectionate kiss on her cheek. She'd told him she'd never seen the show, so he insisted they watch it here instead of from the restaurant.

She still fought the urge to tell him. There, with the swell of the music and the water dancing so elegantly among the colored lights, it seemed like the most natural thing in the world to say she loved him. That she always had. She needed to confess why she'd run and that she'd regretted it every day of the past three years. It was the right moment.

The music thundered the finale and, at last, the lights dimmed and the water went still. The crowds of people around them dispersed, but they stayed at the railing.

"Did you like it?" he asked.

"Yes, it was wonderful." And it was. But not nearly as wonderful as it was to watch it with him. How many other things in her life would be better because he was a part of it? If she didn't speak up now, she might never know. She wished she hadn't seen Tessa play today. Perhaps then she would have the confidence to speak her heart's desires without the fear of her sister's deception ruining it all. And it still might. But maybe if she told him how she really felt before any of it came to light, he would know she meant it. And they might survive it.

Annie turned to look at Nate. His dark eyes watched her face, a finger reaching out to gently move a strand of hair back behind her ear. It was those little things, those intimate gestures that convinced her he cared, even if he hadn't said it. It gave her confidence to finally speak.

"Nate?" she said, her voice nearly a whisper.

"Yes?" he said.

She'd spoken before her brain could talk her out of it, but now she wasn't certain what she should say. "I…I want to stay." She stumbled through her words.

"Stay? At the fountains?"

"No," she said, taking a deep breath. "I want to stay with you…beyond the tournament."

Nate's eyes widened with surprise, but he remained silent, almost as though he wasn't quite sure he could trust his ears.

"These last few days have been wonderful. I'm not

ready to give that up yet. If you're willing, I'd like to give us another try. A real try. Because…" Her heart stopped in her chest, the confession of love still lingering on the tip of her tongue. "I think I've fallen in love with you."

Nate swallowed, the lines of his throat working hard as he struggled with a response. She could see the conflict in his dark eyes. The hurt from before was still on his mind, and there was no way she could erase that from his memory. She could only replace it with new, better memories.

She turned away, looking down at the dark, swirling water. His silence pressured her to speak and fill the void. Somehow it was easier to confess in the dark when she didn't have to look at him. "If you aren't interested, I understand. I mean, I know this isn't what this week was supposed to be about. I know that you have no reason to forgive me for what I did to you. But I've always loved you. Even then. It just scared the hell out of me. It was such an intense feeling I couldn't take it. But being away from you was worse. I'd learned to live with the pain, but coming back here made it impossible. I don't want to leave again."

"Then don't," was his quiet reply. His fingertips pressed into her, pulling her closer. "Stay with me."

Annie closed her eyes and leaned into him. Her head rested against his shoulder. It wasn't a declaration of love, but it wasn't a rejection.

There was still hope that, in time, there would be more.

Ten

Nate couldn't sleep. He woke up just before dawn and found his brain whirring a hundred miles an hour. Something was bothering him, but he couldn't quite put his finger on what it was. He should be happy. Annie wanted to stay with him. She'd confessed she was in love with him. And yet…he hadn't quite let himself fully believe her words. She had said those things before and she'd left. What would make it different this time?

He rolled over in bed and looked at Annie in the dim light. She was curled into a ball beside him, her soft breathing the only sound in their room. Watching her sleep was always one of his favorite things. But he was too wound up to just sit there.

He quietly flung back the sheets, tugged on some lounging pants and made his way down the hallway to his office. He switched on the small lamp. It illuminated his corner of the room and revealed the blue personnel file sitting on his desk.

Darrell Thomas.

Nate had too many employees to know the names of every single one, but it frustrated him that he couldn't immediately put his finger on who this guy was. He reached out and flipped open the file. A color print of his badge photo and a copy of his sheriff's card were attached to the front.

He didn't recognize him. Darrell was fairly nondescript. He was slightly heavyset with short dark hair and a closely cropped beard. None of his features were particularly noteworthy. He was the kind of person you saw and immediately forgot. It probably suited him well, given his line of work.

Darrell had a clean record. You couldn't get a sheriff's card without one. They usually did a thorough screening before they hired someone, but if he was good enough not to get caught, there was nothing to stop them. He found several positive performance reviews. Good, solid work references. He had ten years of experience as a dealer in Vegas, with the past two at the Sapphire. He'd also worked at a couple downtown casinos and the Tangiers before coming here.

Nate's jaw clenched as it occurred to him how many opportunities this man had had to cheat not only him, but also other players, over the years. People like him had nearly destroyed this hotel when Nate was a teenager. His father had sat back, powerless to stop the vultures that pecked at the broken carcass of his life. Nate was not vulnerable like his father. Tournament contract or not, he wouldn't tolerate this in his hotel.

He glanced at his desk clock. Gabe was as poor a sleeper as he was. They both worked ridiculous hours and drank far too much coffee. Nate grabbed his radio and put out a call to his head of security. "You around, Gabe?"

"Yep. I've actually been here all night, running through those videos from yesterday afternoon. You may want to come down here. It's some interesting tape."

Nate frowned. He'd made a quick call to Gabe before

dinner while Annie was in the shower. He'd asked him to find video of Annie in the casino yesterday afternoon. He'd never seen her that upset. She wasn't the kind of woman who was easily rattled and wasn't really forthcoming with her feelings. Finding her on the roof, hysterical and sobbing, had him worried. Something had gotten to her. Something she didn't want to tell him.

Nate needed to see what had set her off and hoped that there would be a video clip of it. Nearly every square inch of the casino was monitored with surveillance cameras, so he was certain it was on film. It was just a matter of locating Annie in thousands of hours of digital recordings.

"I'll be right down." Nate dressed quickly and headed downstairs to the security offices. He found Gabe facing a panel of surveillance screens, cuing up a clip of tape date-stamped the day before. "What did you get?" he asked, leaning over Gabe's shoulder.

"Well, it took me a while, but as you know, I have no life. I was able to narrow down the tapes based on where you saw her last and the time. Although I do have to warn you, I ended up finding more than you probably bargained for."

A sinking feeling settled in Nate's stomach as the gray screen unscrambled and began to play.

"You said you saw her take off around this time, so I'm cuing up the video a couple minutes before." Gabe tapped a finger against a woman's image on the screen. "You can see her here, walking through the casino."

Nate watched as Annie moved through the crowd, stopping to watch another table still in play. She looked interested, nodding and clapping appropriately as hands were won. "What table is she watching there?"

"Five."

Nate flipped open his file and started looking at yesterday's play statistics. The winner of table five had been Tessa Baracas. She'd outplayed quite a few big names. "Tessa beat Paul Stein?"

"I know. It would take a miracle for her to beat out a former champion. Or maybe just a little help. Check out the name of the dealer."

Nate's gaze ran over the sheet, and what he saw forced a muffled curse. "Darrell Thomas. I know we let him keep dealing so we could catch him in the act and not tip off the others, but please tell me you got him for something."

"Darrell hasn't taken a leak without a security shadow since we caught wind of his involvement, but even then we've got almost no evidence to charge him. I keep letting him deal in the hopes we'll have a break. Whatever they're doing, they're good. Watch this."

Nate looked up to watch the video again as Annie's passive expression changed. Her face stiffened, her eyes visibly widening despite the poor video quality. Her head shook subtly from side to side as she looked at someone off camera. Then she started to hyperventilate. Her hand flew to her chest as she spun and disappeared from the frame.

"Wow." Whatever she'd seen at that moment had not only been bad, but unexpected. And yet she hadn't run to him with the news, either.

"That's what I said. She didn't like what she saw. Made me curious, so I kept digging." Gabe fiddled with the digital files, bringing up a clip from another camera. "This one was from the overhead camera on table five." His finger brushed over the tops of the remaining players' heads. "We've got Paul here, Tessa here and then Darrell Thomas dealing, of course."

They watched in silence, trying to detect what happened, but it was hard to see. Darrell dealt her cards. She looked at them, pulling them toward her, and then sat fidgeting with her hair. That had to be when it happened, but if they'd cheated in that moment, it would be hard to prove in court with a video like this.

"Run it back again." The recording ran a second time, but there was still nothing to see. Nate's frustration was mounting. There had to be something. A slight detail he was missing. Something, anything, to nail them with.

"Wait, watch this next part," Gabe encouraged.

Nate narrowed his eyes at the screen as Tessa looked up from her cards and gazed into the crowd. From the angle, they couldn't see her face, but after a moment, she turned back to her cards and continued to play.

"I think Annie saw it happen. Whatever they did." Gabe cued up the tapes to the exact same time on two adjacent screens and paused them. "It's hard to tell, but Tessa is looking in the direction where Annie is standing. Right after that, Annie shakes her head. Perhaps they had some sort of private exchange that panicked Annie and sent her running."

"Damn." Nate flopped back into a chair and clapped his hands to his thighs. He felt as if he'd been punched in the gut. "No wonder she was upset. She knows she has the proof we need."

This was exactly what Nate had been worrying about. Why he'd kept his feelings for Annie to himself even as she looked at him and silently pleaded for him to respond in kind to her declaration of love. There was something about it that hadn't rung true.

He wanted to trust Annie. He wanted to believe her when she said she didn't have any knowledge of Tessa's involvement. He wanted her confession of love and offer to stay beyond the tournament to be more than just a ploy to protect her sister.

But he was a cynical, practical businessman and knew better. If a person felt the noose tightening on them, they would say or do anything to save themselves. Or someone they loved. The truth of the matter was that Annie had come to Vegas to play poker and get a divorce, not for a reconciliation. Her offer might be nothing more than a bargaining attempt.

Or perhaps she really did mean it and was conflicted about her knowledge.

Either way, when the tournament was over, Nate was fairly certain he would lose Annie no matter what was said or done.

Hell, he wasn't certain if he'd ever had her back in the first place. He had no real way of knowing if Annie cared about him or anything but her tournament. But, damn it, *he* cared. He didn't want to choose his life's work over Annie. How dare she put him in a position where he had to choose between doing the right thing and losing out on their chance at happiness together?

Gabe's voice startled him out of his thoughts. "It gets worse. Look at your schedule for today."

He flipped open the file, grabbing the page. It was easy to find Annie's name among the rapidly dwindling roster. She was playing on table six today. His finger ran over the list, pausing at the other names there. So was Tessa. "How the hell did they end up at the same table? That's against tournament regulations. Patricia wouldn't do that. She knows better."

"Yes, like you said, someone is tampering with the schedule. Normally someone would complain, but they've both been doing so well, the other players might be happy to see one knocked out. This could be a positive development," Gabe reasoned. "At this point, we don't have enough evidence to get Tessa or Darrell, and even Keith Frye's testimony won't get us much unless we can use it to pressure one of them to confess. We need more time, and only one person in that group is going to make it through to the final table tomorrow. If you could get Annie to let Tessa win, we c—"

"Impossible," Nate interrupted. There was no sense in letting Gabe go on. "She'd never go along with that. This tournament is everything to her."

Gabe sighed. "Okay, well, how about getting her to help us expose them somehow? If she saw what happened yesterday, she knows how they work. She tells us, we watch closer. Maybe we can catch them in the act. Or if she sees them do it again, she can tip us off. Give us some sort of signal."

"That's a lot of *if*s, Gabe."

The security manager frowned. "You don't think she'd do it? She wants to win, doesn't she? If Tessa is cheating, it's possible that Annie might not make it to the next round. I don't know about you, but that would irritate me, even if it was my sister."

Nate nodded. He was right. If given the choice, Annie would choose the tournament.

Gabe said something else, but Nate didn't hear him. His mind was deeply entrenched in the best way to approach Annie. It was a delicate subject. No one liked cheaters, but it was even worse in their culture to be a snitch. They'd gone to a hell of a lot of trouble to keep her spying a secret, not that he'd minded, but now that it involved Tessa, he had no leverage.

If she wouldn't help him voluntarily, he'd have to set aside their personal relationship and play this game as he would with anyone else.

* * *

Annie made it to the tournament area that morning without seeing Nate or Tessa. To tell the truth, she was relieved. She needed to focus on her game, and seeing either of them would just remind her of the rock and hard place she was wedged between.

She checked in and was assigned to table six. Only a few tables were left, with the top nine players advancing to the final table. If she won today, Annie would have made it further than she had in any tournament. She'd be guaranteed a handsome payout even if she went out on the first hand.

Even with everything going on, she couldn't help but grin with excitement as her game chips were reissued and she made her way across the loudly colored casino carpeting to begin the game. It was enough to make a girl's heart flutter with nerves, like kissing her first crush.

Only two other players were sitting at her table when she arrived. She recognized them both by face but couldn't remember their names. They were good to have made it this far, but their streak would end. Annie would see to it.

She found her assigned chair at the table and settled in. There were still a few minutes before game time, so she closed her eyes and tried to gather her focus.

"Annie, may I speak with you privately for a minute?" Nate's voice came over her shoulder, but it was unusually stiff and formal. She told herself it was because of the tournament. They were publicly a couple, but he was always professional.

Still, she frowned, getting up slowly from the table. "What's the matter?" she asked. Was her wire malfunctioning again?

Nate caught her elbow and led her a good distance

from the tournament area. "There's a problem," he said once out of earshot. His face was gravely serious, without the slightest hint of the man she'd made love to beneath it. "It's about Tessa."

Annie froze, her desire to return to the game table dwindling rapidly. He knew. She hadn't told him, but somehow he'd found out. She looked into his dark eyes, searching for a hint of how much information he really had. Her face tightened, her defenses rising to prevent her from giving away anything he could use against Tessa. "What about her?"

"I've seen the surveillance tapes from yesterday. I know you saw her."

Her eyes widened with panic. "Nate, I—"

He held up his hand to stop her. "Don't bother explaining. It isn't important."

"Okay," she said slowly. This was not the reaction she was expecting. She would actually be less disconcerted if he was angry and yelling. That, she expected. "So what do you want?"

"I wanted to warn you that Tessa is going to be playing at your table today."

Annie groaned before she could stop herself. It was bad enough playing against her sister, given how badly they both wanted to win. Knowing Tessa was cheating and could possibly bump Annie out of the tournament was even worse. "How could that happen?"

"Someone is manipulating the roster. But this is our chance to nail them. Tell me how they're doing it. We need to know if we're going to catch them at it."

Her throat went bone-dry in an instant. "No."

"Annie," Nate pressed, his voice calm and cold. "It's already too late to save her."

Her eyes widened as she frantically searched his face

for a sign he was bluffing in the hopes she would reveal the critical information he lacked. His jaw was firmly set, his dark eyes hurt that she hadn't been honest with him. But there were no signs of a bluff. He meant every word.

What choice did he leave her with? Either betray her sister or destroy her career. She tried not to let the disappointment creep into her voice. It ended up coming out in a hushed whisper. "I didn't know anything until yesterday."

"What did you see?" he pressed.

Tessa had dug a hole deep enough to bury them both. Annie might as well jump in. "I saw her signaling to another player. Watch her every gesture. Each move is deliberate. Whoever her partner is today will drive up the pot to help her win."

He nodded, his grip tightening on her elbow. "We're going to need your help to catch them."

At this, Annie closed her eyes. "Don't ask that of me, Nate. I can't do it. Even if it means putting Eddie in jail where he belongs."

"Annie, please." Nate's voice softened as he tried a new persuasive angle. "We need more evidence to build a solid case against Eddie."

And was she supposed to provide the evidence they needed? Not when it would do nothing but incriminate her sister and let Eddie walk away as he always did. Annie crossed her arms defensively over her chest, trying to rebuild some of the barricade that she'd let down between the two of them. She loved Nate, but she had to protect herself. "No. I told you what I saw. Your security people will have to do the dirty work."

At that, she reached under her sweater and ripped the wire from her skin without a thought about the pain. She shoved it into Nate's hands. "I have to go." She spun on her heels and rushed back to the table before she changed her mind and did something she would regret.

She came to a halt several yards from the tournament area to gather her composure. She closed her eyes and took a deep breath. Her hands smoothed over her hair and sweater, tugging at her skirt. By the time she took her third deep breath and opened her eyes, her furious heartbeat had slowed in her chest and she felt fairly in control.

Annie settled in her seat just as the announcement was made that the tournament was beginning. Tessa was sitting two seats to her right, but she didn't look at her sister. She didn't greet the other players or chat with the dealer. She also didn't look around for Nate or the navy-clad security officers who swarmed around the tables like sharks. Whether or not she'd wanted to cooperate, her role in Nate's plot was over and at last she only had to focus on the cards.

Make that the cards and the sharp ache in her chest. Her fit just now might have cost her the second chance with Nate she'd wanted, and in the end, it probably wouldn't change anything. Her sister was going to jail. The only thing she could do was focus on the tournament.

They were over an hour and a half into playing before Annie finally started to feel at ease. She was doing well. She'd won several key hands and at least one player was on the verge of going out. Tessa was playing a solid game, winning a few hands, but nothing suspicious. Today, her sister's earrings seemed to be secure and she wasn't fidgeting much. Not that she was looking.

After successfully winning a big pot, Annie drove the first player from the table. She stood to shake his hand and caught a glimpse of Nate over his shoulder. He was watching her, as he had all week, but this time he was not beaming with pride. He was scrutinizing her every move, his arms crossed over his chest, threatening to rip the shoulders out of his expensive black suit.

She didn't keep his gaze, sitting quickly and returning to the next hand. Annie needed to hold her game together. She couldn't let thoughts of Nate throw her off. She flipped up the corners of her new cards and frowned. The cards were good, she had no reason to frown, but she just couldn't shake the sensation of his eyes on her. How was she supposed to play with—

"Mrs. Reed?"

Her head snapped up at the sound of the dealer's voice. All the players were looking at her, including Tessa. "I'm sorry," she said, tossing a few chips out.

Focus, woman.

And she did. The next hour flew by in a blur of cards. The afternoon break came just as she began getting mentally weary. Annie stretched her legs, pacing around and avoiding anyone who looked as though they might want to talk to her.

The question plaguing her was what she would do next. Tessa was doing okay—not fabulous, but she wasn't the closest to going out, either. Annie hadn't specifically targeted her to knock out of the tournament, but maybe she should. The less time Tessa played, the less time Nate and his gorillas would have to gather incriminating information.

The call went out to summon the players to the tables so the next portion of the game could begin. With a sigh, Annie chucked her plate into the trash and made her way back. A quick scan around the crowd made her instantly suspicious. Nate and Gabe were gone.

Annie leaned back in her chair and eyed the black dome on the ceiling above them. No doubt they were watching from the office. At least now she couldn't spy

Nate scowling at her from across the room. Some of the pressure was gone, even if the gravity of her situation still sat heavily on her shoulders.

As the game resumed, Annie glanced quickly at the stack of chips in front of her sister. It would take a couple hands to wipe her out, but it could be done. Especially if Tessa was certain she had a sure thing.

Which she very well might have. Annie eyed the dealer. She hadn't played at any of his tables before. There was also a man playing at her table who she didn't know. He could be helping Tessa, but she wasn't sure.

Several hands went by without much progress. Annie would win, then Tessa would win, scissoring back and forth. Before long, there were just four of them left. If Annie was going to take out Tessa, she needed to do it, and soon.

The dealer began the hand and Annie had a queen and a jack of hearts in the hole. She bet accordingly. The flop went down containing the ten of hearts, the nine of clubs and the king of hearts.

Annie had a straight and she was one card away from a *very* good hand. The nine or ace of hearts would give her a straight flush or a royal flush. But it was nearly impossible to get and too soon to get excited.

Tessa bet a fairly large amount. It was too early for that, but Annie didn't react. She probably had a pocket pair to go with the flop. The bet was still too large just for three of a kind. If Annie raised her, Tessa would have to go all in. She considered her options and chose to raise. The other player folded.

Tessa didn't hesitate, pushing all her chips out and going all in. Annie felt her jaw tightening. She kept forgetting that her sister was cheating. If she was going all in, she knew something Annie didn't. Perhaps she anticipated more. Maybe four of a kind.

If Tessa had four of a kind, the only hands that would beat her would be the straight flush or royal flush. Annie was one impossible card away from an unbeatable hand. She had enough money to match Tessa's bet without going all in. She could take the risk and still be safe. If she folded, Tessa would win, anyway.

Annie took a deep breath and called, pushing her chips out. They both turned over their cards. She'd been right. Tessa had a pair of tens. Her sister looked at her, the smug satisfaction paling slightly when she saw Annie's hand. She'd thought she had a sure thing. Now, she wasn't certain. She could read Tessa's face like a book.

As she anticipated, the turn was a ten of spades. Annie sighed to herself, staring off into the crowd as she mentally calculated the odds of the river card being the nine or ace of hearts. It was astronomical. Having one in the same hand as someone with a four of a kind made it damn near impossible. Well, at least when one of the parties wasn't cheating.

The murmur of speculation ran through the crowd as everyone saw the cards and came to the same realization. Everyone knew the hand would be determined by the river card. An almost unbeatable hand was about to be tested in a glorious fashion. The kind of moment that video montages of poker tournaments would play for years to come.

Annie closed her eyes and held her breath. That was all she could do.

"What the hell is she doing?" Nate cursed and pushed his rolling chair back from the panel of screens. "She's deliberately trying to take Tessa out of the game."

He shouldn't be surprised. She was doing what she had to do to protect her sister and her own stakes in the game. He'd given her no choice. Tessa might not like it, but if she had any idea what Annie had just done for her, she wouldn't complain.

"Whoa." Gabe shook his head. "That's a helluva hand they've both got. Might backfire on her."

Nate leaned in. If the last card was the nine or ace of hearts, Annie would win and Tessa would be out. He was a casino owner. The odds were miserably against her. And yet she was determined to take Tessa down. He stood and took a few paces away from the screen. He couldn't watch.

"Well, I'll be damned! The ace of hearts, man. Tessa is out."

"Damn!" He slammed his hand onto the console, making the screens flicker just slightly.

"We didn't get anything on her."

Nate sighed and shook his head. "Have security quietly escort Tessa upstairs. We didn't get anything conclusive, but she doesn't know that. She's young and inexperienced. With a little pressure, her mouth will start running like an old faucet."

Eleven

Annie knew better than to go up to the suite after the tournament was done for the day. There was a fight waiting for her there, she just knew it. Instead, she started wandering aimlessly through the casino. She wanted to get as far away from the poker tables and the cameras as she could. She turned down a narrow corridor, relishing the quiet and solitude. A placard on the wall indicated she would follow the route to get to the hotel gym and day spa.

Perhaps now was a good time for that manicure.

She turned to continue down the hall, then stopped when she found Jerry, the Sapphire's floor manager, standing in her path.

"Mrs. Reed," he said with a smile.

"Afternoon, Jerry," she said. "I'm off to get my nails done as a reward for another successful day of the tournament."

"Well, I'm sorry to interrupt your plans, Mrs. Reed, but I'm going to have to escort you upstairs."

Annie's blood froze instantly in her veins. Nate must be furious with her if he'd sent his casino manager to collect her. Her gaze dropped from Jerry's apologetic smile to the gun held close to his side. In an instant, she knew she no longer had the advantage in this hand.

"Jerry, I…" she started, taking a step back toward the chaos of the casino.

Jerry surged toward her, reaching out to grip her upper arm with his free hand. "It will be best for everyone involved if you come with me without making a scene."

Annie ignored the cruel fingers digging into her upper arm and nodded softly. He tugged her forward and she fell into step beside him. At first, she'd thought perhaps she was getting an inside view at the rougher side of casino security. But the farther they moved away from the part of the hotel where the surveillance and interviews took place, the more concerned she became. Casino managers didn't carry guns. And security would've taken her upstairs if she'd been implicated. Things had just gone unexpectedly awry.

Now it was too late. They walked the quiet, abandoned hallways, moving deeper into the bowels of the casino, away from the possibility that someone could help her or spot her on the security monitors that Nate was always watching. If she'd only kept that wire on instead of throwing it in his face…

They took one of the staircases up a few floors and into a hallway of guest rooms in one of the older segments of the hotel. Annie had never been into this part of the property. This portion was original to the casino Nate's grandfather had built. The shiny blue tower of fancy suites had been one of her husband's additions. These rooms here were nice, but you could feel the age, still smell the faint cigarette smoke from back before it was banned in most of the facilities.

Jerry didn't look at her as they walked, stopping only at the end of the hallway to open the door to one of the rooms. There was no room number, just a sign that designated the space as private.

He shoved her inside and to her surprise, it was less of a hotel room and more of an office space like Nate's quarters. There was a seating area with a television, a conference table with leather chairs and a desk piled high with paperwork.

"Where are we?" she asked.

"This used to be the suite where George Reed ran his casino. Any decisions were made in this very room. Nate, of course, wanted something a little flashier with his makeover, so he allowed me to use the space when I came back here to work for him."

"And why are we here?"

Before he could answer, Eddie Walker appeared through the doorway that led to living quarters of some kind. She was right. This had nothing to do with Nate. But everything to do with Tessa. It had never occurred to her that Nate wouldn't be the only one angry with her stunt today.

"Sit down, Annie." Eddie pointed to one of the seats surrounding a glass coffee table. When she hesitated, she felt the hard prod of the gun in her rib cage and it urged her forward.

She flopped into the chair, able at last to look at Jerry. She'd met him once over the past week but had never really given the man much notice. Nate had spoken of him a few times, grateful that a man with his experience was there to help him keep operations on track. She knew he'd worked with Nate's grandfather for years, then came back to work with Nate after an unfulfilling retirement, but that was it. No reason to suspect or ever consider Jerry had any reason to hold a gun on her.

"You played well today," he said, lowering himself

calmly into the opposite chair. "As always, I enjoy watching you. You're so much better than Tessa. Sometimes it's all we can do to keep her from putting herself out of the game, much less win."

Annie didn't know where they were going with this, but Jerry had the gun, so he could talk as long as he liked. He eyed her, the pistol now resting in his lap. She didn't doubt for a moment that the older man would spring to action with the gun if she even shifted in her seat.

"That, of course, is why I put you two at the same table today. With Nate and Gabe watching her every move, I knew you wouldn't let Tessa hang herself. Or interfere with you winning." He leaned back in his seat and chuckled. "That was quite a stunt you pulled off today. You're lucky my dealer was feeding you the cards you needed to beat her."

Annie let a ragged breath slip through her lips. The dealer helped her win? Suddenly, she realized her mistake. She'd thought she was doing the right thing, but she had played right into his plans. *She* was the one they were really after. They had just used Tessa to get to her.

"Tomorrow, the Barracuda is going to sweep the tournament," Jerry announced.

"Nate has probably arrested your dealer by now," she argued. "It won't work. They're watching everyone so closely."

"We have more dealers and another player heading to the final table tomorrow. They'll help us ensure that you'll win it all. After Tessa and Darrell are arrested, they'll relax their surveillance. No one will suspect you because they'll believe you were instrumental in catching the real cheaters. You'll be able to waltz out the door with your winnings."

Annie's heart started pounding frantically in her chest.

She had worked for years to win, but she wasn't a cheater. She couldn't. Wouldn't. "I don't want to win that way."

"You have no choice, Annie. Tessa going to jail could be the least of your worries. She was involved with some really dangerous people. Something might happen to her before her court date."

Annie swallowed hard and closed her eyes. She wouldn't let them hurt her sister. "My marriage will be ruined." She could barely imagine the expression on Nate's face if he found out she really was involved.

"From what I hear, your marriage was ruined the day you said your vows." He tapped the radio at his hip and sighed. "What's left of it will be destroyed tonight. You can't go back to the suite. I don't trust you not to tip Nate off."

"I won't, I—" she started, but he cut her off with a curt shake of his head.

"You're going to go to Nate and tell him it's over. That you've fulfilled your part of the bargain and now you want your own hotel room. After your stunt today, I doubt it will be a surprise. He'll be so distraught that tomorrow's outcome won't matter."

Annie's fists tightened in her lap, the anger coursing through her veins. Since she was old enough to make decisions, every facet of her life had been decided by her. Right or wrong, she was in charge of her fate. She'd left Nate before he could start telling her what to do. She certainly didn't want the likes of Eddie and Jerry calling the shots.

"What about him?" She jerked a thumb in the direction of Walker.

"He's leaving. They suspect him, so his disappearance will confirm they've caught the right people. It's all managed, Annie. I assure you that this is a well-organized plan. You'll walk away with the glory, a third of your winnings and most importantly, a guarantee of your sister's safety."

Somehow, winning the tournament paled in comparison to what it would cost her. She hadn't intended it to happen, but she had fallen in love with Nate. They had both grown up a lot since the last time they were together. They could have a future—one she'd never realized she wanted until she had Nate back in her life—but Jerry would force her to throw it all away.

And for what?

Even if she did everything she was told to do, there was no guarantee she could walk away from this. She would just be giving them more evidence to blackmail her into playing again. "And that's it?"

"Until such time that we see fit to call on your services again."

There it was. She was not just taking Tessa's place tomorrow; she was filling her shoes until Annie came under suspicion and they had to replace her. In the end, her career and her marriage would be ruined.

Despite his assurances, she would never be free of any of this. Tessa would never be safe. And Nate would never, ever forgive her.

Nate was having one of the longest days of his life. He'd kept telling himself that catching criminals and protecting his casino was the most important thing. After seeing Annie's reaction, he wasn't so sure. He hadn't had much time to think about it, though. Since Tessa was eliminated, he'd spent most of his evening in the security offices interviewing her and Darrell.

Hours of interrogation and working with the police had taken a lot of energy out of him. He wanted nothing more than to curl up in bed with Annie and sleep. Honest-to-God sleep, for more than four hours. Twelve would just about do it.

But he knew he was likely to get none of those things. He'd seen the look in Annie's eyes when he'd threatened her. He'd recognized the pain hidden there when he asked her to betray her sister and had forced her to choose. What choice did he have? He couldn't just let Tessa walk because she was his sister-in-law.

When the elevator chimed and the doors opened to his suite, he was surprised to find Annie sitting on the leather sofa in his office. The lights of the Strip shining through the picture window were the only thing illuminating her as she sat in the darkness waiting for him. She looked up when he came in, but there was barely a flicker of recognition in her eyes, much less a warm greeting.

Nate walked over into the mostly dark office, flipping on the lamp on his desk. The light was enough to highlight the tracks of tears that had dried on Annie's cheeks. His stomach immediately sank.

"How's my sister?" Annie spoke the words without looking at him. Her gaze was fixed firmly on her hands, folded in her lap.

"She's fine. A smart girl mixed up in something stupid. Hopefully they won't go too hard on her. She's working out a plea bargain with the D.A. for information to convict Darrell and Eddie."

"Just Darrell and Eddie?"

Nate frowned. Did she think he was going to have her charged, too? She should know better. Or should she? Hell, if she had been involved, Nate probably would've hauled her in, even if he regretted it later. "Yes. We don't have evidence of anyone else being involved at this point.

I think that's quite enough, to be honest. Tessa should be released on bail tomorrow morning."

"Good." Annie stood suddenly, scooping up her purse and grasping the handle of her rolling suitcase.

He didn't know why he was surprised. "Where are you going?"

She continued to hide beneath her dark lashes. Nate couldn't understand why she was hiding from him. What did she think he was going to see in her eyes?

"I'm going to check into my own hotel room. I think given the current situation it's the best idea."

"So you're leaving." It was more of a statement than a question, but Nate wanted to hear her say the words. When she left the last time, he hadn't been there. She'd written a note and slipped out in the night. If she was going to leave him again, he wasn't going to make it easy on her. It certainly wasn't easy on him.

"Yes, I'm leaving. I've fulfilled my end of the agreement. You've caught your bad guys. I don't see any need for us to continue with the charade."

Charade. It sure as hell hadn't felt like a charade. It had felt like she gave a damn. She'd confessed her love for him not twenty-four hours ago. Apparently it had all been smoke and mirrors to protect her sister. He couldn't keep the steely anger from his voice when he responded. "So I assume you're wanting me to keep my end of the deal and give you your precious divorce."

Annie took a deep breath, not answering right away. There was something in her hesitation that urged him to act. He was about to call her on it when her chin snapped up and her blue eyes fixed on him with unmatched intensity. "Yes. I still want the divorce."

Stupid. Nate was stupid. Even now, when faced with the truth about their relationship, he kept looking for reasons to believe in her. He'd started out this journey in the hopes of getting over Annie once and for all, but it had backfired. He'd ended up falling for her again. Gabe had been right about this whole thing being a bad idea. That fact pissed him off more than anything.

"So you're just going to run away again?" He stuffed his curled fists into his pockets to contain his anger.

"I am not running away!" A red flush rose to her cheeks and she crossed her arms tightly under her breasts. "I came here to play in the tournament and get a divorce. Just because you tried to twist this arrangement into something it wasn't doesn't mean I'm running away. I'm simply putting an end to this relationship once and for all."

Nate reached out to touch her arm and found her skin ice-cold. Her tell was giving her away. "Please don't lie to me, Annie."

"I never lied to you." Annie spoke the words, but the eye contact dropped and she turned to the window.

The frustration was starting to well up inside of him. How could she throw all this away? Again? He let his arm drop to his side. "You're lying right now. Acting like this week hasn't meant anything to you. Damn it, I think our relationship is more important than this situation with your sister. We can work this out."

"No, we can't. There's nothing to work out."

"Then you've changed your mind? You don't love me after all?"

"Nate, it doesn't mat—"

"Say it!" he interrupted, his voice booming loudly and reverberating off the walls of the small office. He hadn't meant to yell, but if that was the only way to get through to her, so be it. "If this whole thing is just a charade you went along with to get your prized freedom and protect your sister, then say it. I want to hear the words before you walk out on me again."

He expected her to get angry, to start yelling back at him. He wanted emotion out of her—any emotion. Instead, the expression on her face shifted in a way he almost couldn't see. She was struggling with something. Her feelings? Her loyalty to her family? Annie almost looked defeated, and he'd never seen that in her before. She was first and foremost a fighter.

Her eyes became glassy. She opened her mouth to speak two or three times before she finally found the words. "I...don't love you. I just said that because I thought I could talk you out of chasing Tessa."

Her statement rang with about as much truth as a politician's campaign speech. "I don't believe you." Nate stretched out a hand to her again, but she jerked back out of his reach.

She shook her head, blinking away tears she was too stubborn to shed. "It doesn't matter if you believe me. It doesn't matter if you love me. It's over, Nate. Goodbye."

Jerry better lock his bedroom door, or Annie would smother the old bastard in his sleep.

There were no words to describe how horrible it was to look into Nate's eyes and destroy their chance at happiness. Annie had managed to hold her tears back until the doors of the elevator closed, but she sobbed with abandon until she reached the casino floor.

Five seconds.

That's all it would've taken to tell him the truth, consequences be damned. To out Jerry for the rat he was. Instead, she'd done what she had to do to save her sister's life. At first, she hadn't been sure she could do it. When she said she didn't love him, he didn't believe her.

He saw through her bluff and wanted her, anyway. The redemption and love she'd found with him were everything she'd never known she needed. And she'd been forced to throw it all away.

Now she had nothing. Yes, she might walk away with the championship tomorrow, but there was no glory when she didn't earn it.

Defeated, she flopped down in front of a slot machine and stared blankly at the flashing lights of the screen that beckoned her to play. She wasn't interested. She preferred games of skill over games of chance. She liked having some control over her fate.

Her finger ran softly over the blinking buttons as she chuckled bitterly. Maybe she should give up poker for slots. She'd relinquished control in all the other areas of her life. Why not this, too?

"Ms. Baracas?"

Annie turned, surprised at being addressed by her maiden name for the first time in a week. Everyone in the hotel had been calling her Mrs. Reed. Apparently bad news traveled faster than the good.

It was a bellhop, dressed in the navy-and-gold uniform of the hotel. His name tag said his name was Ryan. "Mr. Reed requested that I bring you this." He held out one of the disposable room key cards. "Your new room is suite eleven fifty-three, up the west elevators near the keno lounge." With a quick, polite nod, he turned and vanished into the crowd.

Annie frowned and rotated the plastic key in her fingers. She should've known that Nate would think of everything. He always did. Even as upset as he'd appeared to be, he had managed to take care of all the loose ends. Her pride stung a bit for it. A part of her was hoping he'd be too distraught by her leaving, but what did she expect?

He'd managed to build a great hotel after she left the first time. Why would this be any different?

She was angry at him, although she had no right to be. She'd been the one to walk away. But it still hurt.

Annie stood up and headed toward her new room. She moved quickly, not wanting to run into anyone she knew right now. As it was, it felt as if every employee in blue was eyeballing her with contempt. Maybe it was just the guilt making her paranoid. She doubted a company-wide memo had been distributed in the last fifteen minutes.

As she reached the elevators, she was dismayed to find Jerry there, waiting for her. "I don't want to speak to you right now." Turning from him, she forcefully pressed the up button and crossed her arms over her chest.

He ignored her irritation and patted her on the shoulder in a paternal way that was completely alien to her. It was probably meant to be soothing and encouraging, but it wasn't. A real father wouldn't force her to do the things she'd done today.

"You're a good girl," he said before disappearing into the keno lounge.

Twelve

This was it.

Annie should be proud. This was the first time she'd ever made it to the final table of a main event. Unfortunately, what would've been a feather in her cap was tainted by what she was about to do today.

She sat down at the table, taking her assigned chair. As the others gathered, she pulled her compact from her purse and did a quick once-over of her makeup. The cameras and lights would be on her all day.

"You look like hell, kiddo." The Captain took his seat at the table, decked out in his favorite Hawaiian shirt. He always wore the blue one with the pink hyacinths at the final table. "Trouble in paradise?"

Annie tried to smile and dismiss his concerns, although she had to agree. The concealer did its best to cover the dark circles, but there was no hiding the drooping of her eyelids or the sleep-deprived fog that clouded her blue gaze. "I didn't sleep well last night. Just nervous about today, I think."

"Just focus on your game, Annie. Deal with the rest later."

They were wise words. She wished that she could,

but "the rest" had literally made its way into her game. She looked up at the Captain, a man who was probably as close to a father figure as she'd ever have. His blue-gray eyes saw straight through her in a way few people could. There was no way he could know what was really going on, but he had no trouble reading the strain etched into every inch of her body.

It probably wasn't hard, if she looked as bad as she felt. The granola bar and coffee she'd scarfed down were turning somersaults in her stomach. Her hands were shaking. She felt a sheen of nervous perspiration forming at her hairline and the nape of her neck. The needling sensation of anxiety was running up and down her spine. She was going to look like a nervous, sweaty, female version of Richard Nixon on national television, and that was the least of her problems.

"Thanks. Good luck, Captain."

He winked at her and Annie turned back to staring at her hands. For once, she wished she was one of the players who hid behind sunglasses and hats. Then maybe her vulnerabilities wouldn't show. Instead, she was on full display with her low-cut blouse and short skirt. She'd considered wearing jeans and a T-shirt today but felt the sudden change would alert the other players, and Jerry, to the fact that she was not at the top of her game this morning.

The Barracuda never showed weakness.

Annie closed her eyes to take a deep breath and center herself before the tournament started. When she did, Nate's face, pained with her betrayal, appeared in her mind just as it had last night every time she'd tried to sleep. Her eyes had popped open to avoid the disappointed expression of the man she loved, only to find the same look on his face across the room.

Nate was watching everything from a far corner. Not

her, per se, but overseeing the tournament. She'd expected he would watch from the security booth, but Jerry had been right. The bad guys were caught, the contract was secured and now the focus was on managing the VIPs and finishing up a successful tournament. What did they know?

His dark eyes ran across the room, stopping on her for just a fraction of a second. When their gazes met, there was a moment, an instant of connection. In that second, Annie saw the pain and confusion he was hiding behind his businessman facade. Then it was gone. He turned away to talk to one of his employees and Annie was once again alone in a room full of people.

The tournament started a few minutes later. The man seated to her far right was there to help her drive up the pots and win hands. Eddie had gone over all the signals with her. She didn't know his name, but she recognized him. Like her, he'd been specially "selected" to reach the final table without drawing suspicion. He smiled at her briefly before game play began. That would be the only recognition she'd get. The room was absolutely crawling with ESPN cameras. They had to be very careful.

Being stealthy was a whole new level of stress Annie wasn't used to when she was playing. She had to make subtle signals to the dealer and the other player so they knew what to do, all the while also focusing on winning.

The first few hours went well and without much help from the others. Two players were eliminated. She was so close to achieving her goal.

Then she spied Jerry and Nate talking to one another. Their discussion paused for a moment and both turned to watch her. Both gazes—that of the man she'd pushed away and the man who'd forced her to do it—were boring into her. The sensation was unnerving. It was as though her skin had been peeled back and she was thoroughly exposed. As though if he looked hard enough, Nate would see her for the poker cheat she'd always despised.

"Ms. Baracas?"

Annie's focus snapped back to the dealer. She wasn't paying attention at all. Making a quick assessment of what she'd missed, she tossed a few chips out and tried to regain her grip on the game. It didn't work. Despite the fidgeting and jewelry twirling, she lost a big hand. Then another.

It wasn't even lunchtime, but Annie could feel the tournament slipping away. It didn't matter what cards she was given or what else was going on at the table. She started losing. Not on purpose. She knew Jerry wouldn't stand for that and neither would her pride. And yet she watched her stack of chips dwindle away.

The remaining players could smell the blood in the water. She was short stacked and outnumbered. She folded her current hand to give herself time to think while the others played.

Annie was two big hands from being out of the tournament. Yes, she could still manage a dramatic comeback, but the odds were poor, even with help. The others would team up on her and drive her out of the game.

Easing back in her chair, Annie sighed. She was just prolonging her own demise and she knew it. So did Jerry.

She turned and caught his heated gaze from the left side of the table. He was alone, fuming and red faced as he watched. Apparently she was supposed to be doing better. Apparently she was going to be his big jackpot and meal ticket.

To hell with Jerry. To hell with him and this game, if dealing with the devil was her price for playing. He could hang his hopes on the other guy. It looked as though he would outplay her at this rate.

Annie scooted back up to the table with newfound enthusiasm. She was certain Jerry thought she'd been properly chastised for her performance and was ready to pick up her game. Hardly.

She took her cards. For a woman supposedly cheating, she had absolutely nothing. Not even a pair of threes or a face card. Running her fingers down the stack of her chips, she counted and raised, betting conservatively, as she would if she had a solid hand. She signaled to her partner that she had an excellent hand. He tossed in his chips while another folded. The pot grew, the flop went down. Annie still had nothing. She could see her friend and fellow player Eli out of the corner of her eye. He kept jiggling his sunglasses. That was his tell when he had good cards. Normally, she'd sit this hand out, especially with the crap she'd been dealt. Instead, she bet again. If this was the last hand of poker she ever played, she was going down in a blaze of glory.

The turn went down and as she hoped, she had the worst hand ever. She went all in. The remaining players folded. Eli called, they both revealed their hands and the river card was turned.

It was time to put an end to this.

Nate gave up watching the tournament early. Annie wasn't playing well, and his angry glare wasn't helping. Despite everything that had happened between them, he wanted her to succeed. So he'd gone to his office for a few hours.

On his desk, he found the courier's package from her lawyer that he'd fished out earlier. The first time it had arrived, he'd laughed and phoned his attorney to throw a monkey wrench into her plans. Now, he held it with a sense of somberness and finality.

There had been a fleeting moment this week when he'd thought he might not need this paperwork any longer. That night at the fountains when Annie had confessed to him, he'd had a glimmer of hope. Despite everything else going on, he'd started to believe that what really mattered—the two of them and how they felt about each other—might survive the rest. He'd held that tiny flame of possibility tight against his chest even as she told him she didn't love him and was just protecting Tessa.

But maybe he was just like a child who refused to believe the truth about Santa when he was faced with the cold, hard facts. He clung to the fantasy because he was certain Annie was lying. But why? There was no logic to her actions that he could find.

It might have just come down to being unable to stay with the man convicting her sister, no matter how much she cared. No matter how much he cared, although he'd never voiced his feelings to her the way he should've.

Nate flipped the cover page over to view the divorce paperwork. The settlement was simple—no assets to divide, no custody battles. They were each walking away with what they'd come into the marriage with, despite having no prenuptial agreement in place. Annie was technically entitled to half of what he had. She could take half of the hotel, force him to sell his home and raid his savings and retirement funds. It could be a huge hit to his finances. And yet, despite his stalling and aggravating her, all she'd wanted was her freedom.

So he'd give it to her.

Nate slipped the paperwork from the envelope and read over the divorce decree. It was amazing to him how one little slip of paper could dissolve not only a marriage, but all the promise and potential it had. Although he'd told her he'd refused to sign to force her here and make her suffer, he knew now that he hadn't been ready to give up on them yet. And he didn't want to give up now. He loved Annie. He always had—he was just too stubborn to admit it to himself before now.

But Nate knew it was time to let it go. Annie had made it perfectly clear that she was done. If he'd fallen for her again, that was his problem, not hers.

Pulling a pen from his coat pocket, Nate smoothed out the paperwork on the desk and signed his name on the dotted line. That done, he slipped the platinum wedding band from his finger and took a deep breath. It was as if a burden was taken off his shoulders. He'd carried this marriage on his own for far too long.

He slipped the papers back into the envelope and radioed someone to take it to Annie's suite. He didn't want the papers sitting near him any longer than they needed to be. He might be tempted to tear them up or run them through his shredder.

For a moment, Nate considered calling Gabe and seeing if he was up for a night on the town when the tournament was done. He couldn't remember the last time he'd gone out. His own hotel had a club frequented by the Hollywood elite where he could commandeer the VIP suite, gather a crowd of people and lose himself in the hedonism of the town he'd lived in his entire life. A couple drinks and a couple willing ladies might be just what he needed to put this mess behind him.

He eyed his cell phone and then with a sigh, Nate let reality creep back in. That was the last thing he needed. Instead, he pulled out some business papers and returned to the work of running his casino.

* * *

It was over. Finally.

She hadn't won, but that was fine with her because she didn't want to give Jerry the satisfaction of taking the tournament. Until today, she'd done well enough without his help, although now he was going to walk away with two-thirds of her winnings. It was a small price to pay if Tessa was safe. Perhaps he wouldn't bother either of them again if he thought Annie didn't have the chops to make it to the final table in another tournament.

She'd completed a couple interviews and gone through the motions of wrapping up her tournament. It was the typical process, but this time she couldn't bear it. The lights and the cameras and the questions were just too much for her to take. One reporter had even had the audacity to ask her about her marriage to Nate and if it had contributed to her choking today. It took everything she had to maintain composure and not take out her aggravation on the blonde.

She just wanted to get back to Miami. She had no idea what she would do once she got there, but anywhere was better than here.

She wasn't a fool, though. As badly as she wanted away, Annie asked casino security to escort her to her room and waited for someone to be available. She'd made that mistake once, but even Jerry wasn't dumb enough to pull a stunt with one of Gabe's guys with her. The guard saw her safely inside and waited until she'd securely bolted the lock and thanked him through the door.

Once inside, Annie headed straight to her bedroom to pack. If she was quick, she could catch a late-afternoon flight and get out of town before Nate or Jerry could come looking for her. Right now, she couldn't deal with either of them. Her only hope was that Tessa was smart enough to do the same once she made bail.

Annie grabbed her bag from the closet and swung it up onto the bed. It wasn't until then that she noticed the tan envelope lying on the comforter. Her name was written on it in Nate's neat penmanship.

She held the envelope in her hand for a moment before she could work up the nerve to open it. When her nail slipped under the flap, it popped open to reveal the familiar papers stapled to the blue binding of legal documents. Her gaze ran over the first few words of the page, her heart sinking deeper into her chest with each letter.

Decree of Divorce.

She jumped to the bottom of the page, where she found Nate's signature awaiting her own.

She'd expected to feel happy or at least relieved. This was what she'd wanted. What she'd practically sold her soul for. And yet tears immediately began welling in her eyes at the sight of his scrawled name.

Annie flopped onto the bed and let the papers slip from her fingers to the floor. This was what she'd thought she'd wanted for the past three years, but for once, achieving her goals didn't give her the adrenaline high she lived for. She felt awful. Her stomach ached with dread, her chest was tight with a pain she hadn't felt since…since she'd made herself walk away three years ago.

Then, she'd lied to herself and said she didn't really love him. Convinced herself that marriage was the terrible institution her mother had always ranted against. It had been enough then to propel her fast and far away from the temptation of Nathan Reed.

It took months, but eventually she'd believed it and the pain faded. At least until she lay in her cold, lonely bed and the truth crept in.

But Annie didn't want to lie anymore. Not to herself and not to Nate. She wanted to be with him. If that meant being married, she would be married. Their relationship was wonderful and special and she didn't want to throw it away again because of that bastard casino manager or her own irrational fears of commitment.

A knock sounded and she heard Nate call her name. Annie's heart soared as she raced to the door. This was her chance. She wanted to tell him everything. To confess her every sin and beg him to forgive her.

Flipping the locks as quickly as she could, Annie flung open the door. Nate was nowhere to be found. Instead, Eddie was there with a digital voice recorder in his hand. He hit the stop button with a smile.

She needed to run. To slam the door shut and call security. Her second of hesitation cost her the opportunity. She only had long enough to register the sharp pain to her head and the sudden blackness that followed.

Thirteen

Nate knocked twice without a response before he used his master key to open the door to Annie's suite. He shouldn't abuse his powers this way, but he frankly didn't care anymore. He needed to talk to her. He'd come back downstairs after she was eliminated, but she was nowhere to be found. She hadn't checked out of the hotel yet, so he'd come here.

He was discouraged to find the room mostly dark except for a light in the bedroom. There were no signs of life in the suite. "Annie?" he called out before approaching the bedroom door, easing it open with his hand. There was no answer.

The room was empty, the bed made. There was no luggage in the closet, no makeup on the bathroom counter. Annie was already gone.

Frustrated, he turned and headed back through the room, pausing only when he saw the tip of something white sticking out from under the bedspread. Kneeling down, Nate pulled out the pack of papers, recognizing them immediately.

It was the same divorce papers he'd signed and left for her. It had broken a part of him to write his name on the line, but he'd done it because it was what she wanted. Perhaps she'd left the papers for him, knowing he'd come here looking for her. Nice parting gift.

His gaze traveled over the page, his brain not registering a key piece of information for a few moments. When he saw it, his heart leaped into his throat with excitement.

Annie's signature line was blank.

Despite what she'd said, there was hope. She did love him or she wouldn't have left the papers she'd fought so hard for behind.

Crumpling the pages in his hand, Nate turned and marched out of the room. He didn't know where Annie had gone, but this time he wouldn't let her get away. He'd track her to the ends of the earth if he had to.

He blazed through the casino, noticing no one and nothing but the path to the restricted area. His heart felt lighter with every step, the situation less grim as the elevator ascended to his suite.

When the elevator doors opened, Nate came to a sudden stop on the landing. He was surprised to find Gabe restraining a visibly pissed-off Tessa in his office. He knew she'd been released on bail that morning, but he certainly hadn't expected her to return so quickly to the scene of the crime.

"Where is my sister?" Her pale skin was bright red with anger. It looked odd against the fiery auburn of her hair.

"I have no idea. Annie apparently left the hotel after she was eliminated from the tournament. She's probably flying over Mississippi by now."

"She didn't leave, and she isn't answering her phone. That's not like her." Her blue eyes, so much like Annie's it made Nate's chest ache, widened with newfound fear. She tugged at Gabe's grip but this time the head of security let her go. "Jerry. He told me he would do something to her if I mentioned his involvement to the police. I didn't say anything, though. I knew I couldn't trust him."

"Jerry who?" Nate knew Tessa couldn't possibly be talking about the only Jerry he knew. He was in his seventies with a heart condition. There was no way he'd hurt a hair on Annie's head, and if he tried, the stress would probably kill him. Annie never bent easily to anyone's will.

"*Casino manager* Jerry. He masterminded this whole thing. The bastard set me up so he could blackmail her into taking my place."

Nate had to take a moment to wrap his head around the idea of his grandfather's friend as a crook. "Take your place? Was she involved the whole time?"

"No, of course not. Don't you know Annie at all? She didn't get hauled into it until yesterday. It's all my fault."

The realization hit low to his gut. Yesterday. Everything had changed yesterday after Tessa was eliminated. If Annie had been forced into taking Tessa's place…that was why she'd left. Why she'd said it didn't matter how she felt about him because it didn't change anything. And he'd turned around and signed the divorce papers. He'd fallen for her bluff and now she was in danger.

"Would he hurt her?"

Tessa bit her lip and nodded. "Both Jerry and Eddie have guns. They never got physical with me, but the threat was always there. If they feel like their plan has fallen apart, they just might do anything."

The loud beep of Nate's cell phone chirped at his hip. He pressed the radio button and yelled, "Not now," into the receiver. It didn't matter who it was or what was wrong at the casino. Right now, only Annie and her safety mattered.

"Yes, now." It was Jerry's demanding voice that echoed in the room. "Turn your radio to channel five."

Channel five was almost never used, and when it was, it was for private conversations. Nate clicked over. "I'm here."

"You and your wife have ruined all my plans and owe me a lot of money to make up for what I've lost. But I'm giving you a chance to fix it. You're going to come to my hotel suite with a duffel bag filled with ten million dollars. You're going to come alone and you're not going to involve the police or hotel security."

Nate looked quickly to Gabe, who nodded in encouragement, staying silent. "And why, exactly, would I do that, Jerry?"

The old man chuckled over the static of the walkie-talkie connection. "There's an envelope on your desk. Open it."

Nate crossed the room to his desk and found the unmarked envelope setting on his blotter. It hadn't been there earlier. Inside, he found Annie's wedding ring. "If you hurt her…" he began, but didn't get to finish his threat.

"I don't intend to hurt her as long as you do what I say. I intend to get my money and set her free. You've got one hour. And remember, I'm monitoring the in-house communications system. If so much as a whisper about this comes up, Annie's dead."

The connection ended. Nate dropped the phone and the ring to the desk, bracing his hands on the wood to help him keep control of his anger.

"He didn't count on me being here," Gabe said. "We have the advantage."

"What do we do?" Tessa asked.

"We're going to do what he asked. I want you to stay

here," he said to Tessa, then turned to Gabe. "We'll have one of your guys sit with her up here. I want you to come with me."

"What do you need me to do?" Gabe was at his side in an instant, his years of strategic military experience finally being put to good use.

"I need you to give me your gun."

Annie had one hell of a headache.

She'd woken in a dark room, realizing fairly quickly that she was handcuffed to a hotel headboard. The metal cuffs were digging painfully into her wrists, and the movement made her stomach swim with nausea.

Turning her head, she could see the light coming under the doorway. Muffled voices were outside, but she couldn't tell who it was. She didn't need to be a detective to decide she was in Jerry's suite. The room had the same old smell of cigarettes and industrial cleaner, and she could hear children splashing and playing in the courtyard pool she'd noticed outside his window the day before.

She should've taken Jerry's threats more seriously. Somehow she'd believed that if she was out of the tournament and Tessa was safe in police custody, he'd no longer have control over her life. She'd been painfully mistaken.

Now she would pay. She didn't know how, but Jerry would punish her for her impudence. The idea was frightening, but a part of Annie had accepted this outcome the moment she'd chosen to throw the tournament. She'd retaken control of her life. If this was the price she paid, she only had one regret: that the last thing she ever said to Nate was a lie spoken in anger. He might never know the truth about how she felt.

The voices outside the door grew louder as they came

closer. Annie braced herself for their arrival, struggling to sit up and put her back against the headboard. She might not have the use of her hands, but she could move her legs and by God, she'd make sure none of them would ever breed.

When the door opened, Annie could see the outline of two men in the doorway. One was Jerry, she could tell by the bald dome of his head and the slouch of his aged posture. The second was Eddie. The light illuminated the stupid Cowboys jacket he always wore. She'd expected him to be in Atlantic City by now.

"Sleeping Beauty is awake," Jerry said, flipping on the light and temporarily blinding Annie.

"Now the fun begins." Eddie's mouth twisted into an evil grin as he crossed the room. He reached out to touch Annie's face but jerked away when the cold slime of her spit landed on his cheek.

"You don't touch me," she warned, but her bravado was short-lived. Eddie's hand flew at her face. The impact exploded across her cheek in a fierce wave of pain.

Eddie leaned in, his breath hot and rancid on her face. "Try that again and you and your sister will both regret it."

"I thought you'd be long gone by now, Eddie. You've always been too chicken to do the dirty work yourself." Annie prepared herself for another slap, but Jerry pulled Eddie back before his fist could fly again.

"We don't have time for that. Go in the other room," he demanded and watched Eddie slink out. "You are a hellcat, Annie. I never quite know what to expect from you. Makes me wish I was thirty years younger. You'd be a fun one to break." He sighed, returning to the doorway. "Instead, I'll just have to break Nate and let you watch. He should be here soon with the money he owes me."

"Money?"

"Ten million dollars in exchange for you. That's more than I would've made in the tournament, so I think it's a fair trade. Enough to get me out of this godforsaken town and afford me the lifestyle I deserve after nearly killing myself for this casino."

"I wouldn't be so sure he'll show up with the money," Annie said. A part of her prayed he would save her while another hoped her words were true. She didn't want to be the bait they used to trap him. Even if Nate brought the money, she didn't believe Jerry would just hand her over and stroll out of the hotel. "I did a pretty good job of pushing him away, thanks to you. We're getting a divorce. He may not care what you do with me."

"Oh, he cares, Annie." Jerry flipped off the light and pulled the door closed behind him. "I'd bet ten million on it."

The thirty minutes it had taken to get things in place had felt like hours. By the time Nate started down the hallway to Jerry's office, the adrenaline was pumping so furiously through his veins he was tempted to break down the door instead of using his master key.

But he was determined to stick to his plan. He shifted the duffel bag in his hands, checked on the gun in his suit coat pocket then slipped the key into the lock. The door swung open wide, his gaze sweeping the room until it locked in on his target. His hand slipped into his pocket, his fingers tightening around the grip of the gun.

Jerry was sitting at his desk, alone. As always, he was surrounded by paperwork, the space reminding Nate so much of how it looked when he was a kid visiting his grandfather. The betrayal of a family friend was still a bitter pill for him to swallow.

His target barely moved; his gaze focused intently on Nate without a hint of surprise. Jerry stood slowly, his hands held up to show Nate he was unarmed. “I’m glad you finally made it, Nate. We’ve been waiting for you.”

“Where is she?”

Jerry gave a condescending smile and came out from behind his desk. “Close by and feisty as ever, I assure you.”

Nate swallowed hard. He hoped it was true, but he wouldn’t take Jerry’s word for it. “I want to see her.”

“Or what? Are you going to use that gun in your pocket to shoot your grandfather’s oldest and dearest friend? The man who’s worked with you and helped you make this hotel a success? Come now, we both know that isn’t going to happen, so why don’t you just relax and have a seat.” Jerry took a step toward Nate, his hand held out to gesture toward the seating area.

Nate didn’t move from his spot. “What is this all about, Jerry? Money?”

“What’s wrong with it being about money? It makes the world go round. You of all people should know that.”

“Are you in some kind of trouble? Do you owe someone money?” Nate struggled to find a reason why Jerry would do something like this.

“That’s how it started, yes. I do have a fondness for the ponies but not much of an eye for picking a winner. I ran through all my retirement savings pretty quickly, which is why I came back to work. I got in with an interesting crowd when I couldn’t pay the bookies what I owed. Fixing poker tournaments started as a way to get them off my back, but I soon realized there were bigger payoffs and bigger thrills in this game.”

“Of all the people you could’ve chosen, why Tessa?

Why my Annie? Were you trying to get back at me for something I did?"

"Not really. We chose Tessa because she was young, stupid and could lead us to Annie. She was our real target in the end. If she met with great success, no one would ever suspect. It was a perfect plan. I didn't realize at the time that she was your wife. It was quite the pleasant surprise when I found out the two of you were coming together to catch the cheaters. I knew every move you made because you told Gabe and me everything."

"Did you really think Annie would be so pliable?"

Jerry laughed. "No, but everyone has a button you can push. Apply the right kind of pressure and you can make a woman madly in love betray her husband and sabotage her own career."

She did love him. It made Nate sick to think of how Annie had come to him at Jerry's demand. "How'd that work out for you?"

Jerry shrugged. "It worked great until Annie started crumbling under the pressure. She couldn't have won a game of Go Fish with the way she was mooning at you over her cards. She completely lost her focus. There wasn't a damn thing we could do to salvage her game. The two of you ruined all my plans. The polite thing to do—" he gestured toward the duffel bag with a smile "—is to make it up to me."

"Well, here it is," Nate said through angrily gritted teeth. He wanted to drop the bag and pistol-whip the old man, but he couldn't until he knew Annie was safe. "Where's Annie? I want to see her first."

Jerry sighed and shook his head. "You seem to be working under the impression that you're calling the shots. You're just like your grandfather, thinking you're in control of everything when it's people like me that make you successful. Give me the damn bag. And the gun."

"Not until I see her."

Before Jerry could answer, the bedroom door flew open and Eddie came in, dragging Annie with him. He held a gun to her head and had his arm wrapped around her neck in a chokehold. Seeing her like that made something primitive rise up inside Nate. It took everything he had not to pull out his gun and shoot Eddie on the spot. Unfortunately, he was not a marksman, and with Annie furiously struggling in Eddie's arms, Nate couldn't be certain not to hit her instead.

"So you've seen her. She's obviously still got some fight left in her. So put down the gun and the money and step away."

Nate ignored Jerry and took a few steps to the right toward Annie. Confused by his movement, Eddie dragged her back toward the window and away from Nate's approach.

"The money and the gun, Nate. Now."

Eddie nervously pulled back the hammer on the gun. Nate couldn't trust him not to shoot Annie, even if by accident.

"Okay, okay," he said, easing the gun down onto the floor and kicking it toward Jerry. "Please stop pointing the gun at her."

"After I get the money," Jerry said. The old man bent over to pick up the gun.

The rest happened in a blur. Nate yelled, "Now!" A loud bang rang out. Annie screamed. Nate swung the duffel bag filled with poker chips at Jerry, the heavy and unexpected blow knocking him to the ground. Nate quickly scooped up the gun. He held it on Jerry, his eyes darting back to the shattered window. Annie stood there alone, her entire body trembling in shock and fear as she tried to process what had happened.

The door burst open and a dozen men in navy security uniforms rushed into the room. Once they had Jerry in custody, Nate dropped his gun and ran to Annie's side. He crushed her against him, tugging her away from Eddie, who was howling in pain at her feet.

Gabe's sniper training had served them well today. With Nate's cell phone on in his pocket the entire time, Gabe had waited patiently across the hotel courtyard for Eddie to get into position and Nate to give the order to shoot. His bullet had crossed the distance and found its mark in Eddie's shoulder.

Nate pulled Annie from the suite, taking her far away from the scene of her captivity. She didn't speak, just cried against the lapel of his jacket until they reached the empty hotel room they'd set aside when they'd planned their attack. He sat Annie on the bed and wrapped her shoulders with a thick blanket.

"You're going to be okay," he whispered into her hair, gently stroking her back. "Gabe's calling the police, and the ambulance should be here soon. They'll take good care of you, okay?"

"I don't want a divorce."

Annie's voice was so small Nate wasn't quite sure he heard her correctly. "What did you say?"

Annie pulled away, gently brushing her tears from her cheek. She winced in pain as she moved, making Nate's chest ache. If Jerry rotted in jail ten years after he was dead, it wouldn't be long enough to make up for what he'd done.

"I said I don't want a divorce."

"We don't have to talk about that right now. You've been through a lot."

"No, we do. I've already waited too long and almost missed my chance to say it. I hate myself for what I said to you. Jerry made me do it, and it just broke my heart. I lied to you, Nate. I do love you. I always have, I was just too scared to say it. After today, I realize there are so many other things in life to fear than love. Tonight, all I could think about was that I might die without telling you how I really felt. That you might always think those horrible things I said to you were true."

"Annie, I—"

"Let me finish," she interrupted. "I don't know how to be a wife, and I can't always promise I'll be a good one, but I want to spend the rest of my life with you trying to figure it out. If you still want me, I'd love to plant roots here in Vegas and travel with you by my side."

Nate couldn't help but smile. His heart was leaping in his chest. "If I still want you? Annie, I've never stopped wanting you from the moment I first laid eyes on you. I love you. More than anything." Nate hugged her gently against him and pressed a soft kiss to her lips. "Don't ever believe otherwise."

They sat in silence for a few minutes, letting the truth of their words and the gravity of the situation they'd just experienced fully sink in. Nate could hear the police going up and down the hallway and Gabe's voice ordering the staff around. It wouldn't be long before their moment together would be disrupted by police interviews and EMT examinations.

"So you really think we can do this whole marriage thing?" Annie asked at last.

Nate sighed and leaned his head against hers. "I think we can have a great marriage. One you'll want to run to instead of run from."

Epilogue

St. Thomas

Annie could feel the Caribbean sun's rays sinking warmly into her bones. The combination of the heat and the rum was doing wonders for her state of mind. She needed this. After the shooting, she'd decided to take a break from the game. It seemed like a good idea to get away from the chaos and noise of the casino and the game that had ruled her life for so long.

Once the scandal with Jerry broke and hit the news, it became abundantly clear she wasn't going to get any peace in Las Vegas. On ESPN they were constantly showing pictures of her next to Tessa's, Eddie's and Jerry's mug shots.

Nate had decided they both needed to get away from the Sapphire and turned over the running of the hotel to his new casino manager. They'd spent some time at the house in Henderson, then visited his father in Texas. After that, Nate had suggested a few weeks on St. Thomas at the family beach house. They'd only been there a few days, but she had to say this whole vacation thing was pretty damn great. She'd have to make a point to schedule more of these in between tournaments and time in Vegas with Nate.

Annie took a sip of her drink and closed her eyes. This was the way to live. She was feeling so good nothing could ruin her buzz.

"I was thinking we should get remarried when Tessa gets out on parole."

Almost nothing. Annie rolled onto her side on the queen-size lounge chair. Nate was lying beside her, absentmindedly thumbing at the keypad of his smartphone. Getting him to take a vacation was a big step, although she was doing better at the actual vacationing part so far.

"Remarried? Did I miss the part where we divorced?"

"I mean like a vow renewal or something. Have a reception. Some cake. We could let our families and friends come this time."

Annie sighed and considered the idea of a real wedding. Their first had been such a blur. They'd rushed through it, so anxious to just be married that she hadn't relished the details the way a woman normally wanted to. She hadn't been raised dreaming about her wedding day like other little girls. And yet even there the tides had turned.

When she'd called her mother to tell her about Tessa's unfortunate incarceration, Magdala Baracas announced quite suddenly that she'd gotten married to her Portuguese businessman. The change of heart probably meant that not only would her mother and uh…*stepfather…* come to the wedding, they might even enjoy themselves. This was new territory for the Baracas women.

"Would we have it at the hotel?" The Desert Sapphire had a very nice wedding chapel. They'd made quick use of it the first time.

"No, I think we should do it here."

"St. Thomas?"

"Yeah. We could get married on the beach at sunset. I'll have some of the locals build us a gazebo. We could have a bonfire and eat seafood until we throw up."

"Sounds lovely," Annie said, her tone flat with sarcasm.

Nate put down his phone and rolled over to face her. "I'm being serious here. Barbara Ann Baracas Reed, would you do me the honor of marrying me again with our friends and family as witnesses?"

Annie opened her mouth to answer when Nate pulled a small velvet box from his shorts. "What is that?"

He frowned. "That is not the appropriate response." When he flipped open the box, Annie was nearly blinded by the large, heart-shaped diamond ring inside.

"You never got a diamond before. I thought you deserved one now." Nate pulled the ring from the box and slipped it onto Annie's finger next to her wedding band.

Annie couldn't tear her eyes from it. It was the most beautiful ring she'd ever seen. She didn't know what to say.

"Are you okay?"

She looked up to see Nate's dark eyes filled with concern. "I'm wonderful. Why?"

"The last time I did this you passed out on me."

Annie had to laugh. Her world had turned on its end since that day. In a month's time, things had changed so dramatically it surprised even her. As she looked down at her new ring, there were no nerves, no butterflies. No screams from generations past urging her to run away. Nate's love had slain the dragons. Such an achievement should be celebrated. A wedding on the beach with too much seafood was a good place to start.

"Yes, Nate." She smiled, leaning in to place a kiss on his full, piña-colada-flavored lips. "I will marry you again. And again. And again."

* * * * *

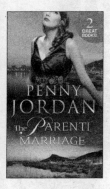

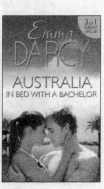